MR. WOLF'S CLASS

MYSTERY CLUB

ARON NELS STEINKE

graphix
AN IMPRINT OF
■SCHOLASTIC

For my students

Library of Congress Control Number: 2017962944

ISBN 978-1-338-04774-5 (hardcover)
ISBN 978-1-338-04773-8 (paperback)

10 9 8 7 6 5 4 3 2 1 19 20 21 22 23

Printed in China 62
First edition, March 2019

Edited by Cassandra Pelham Fulton
Book design by Phil Falco
Creative Director: David Saylor

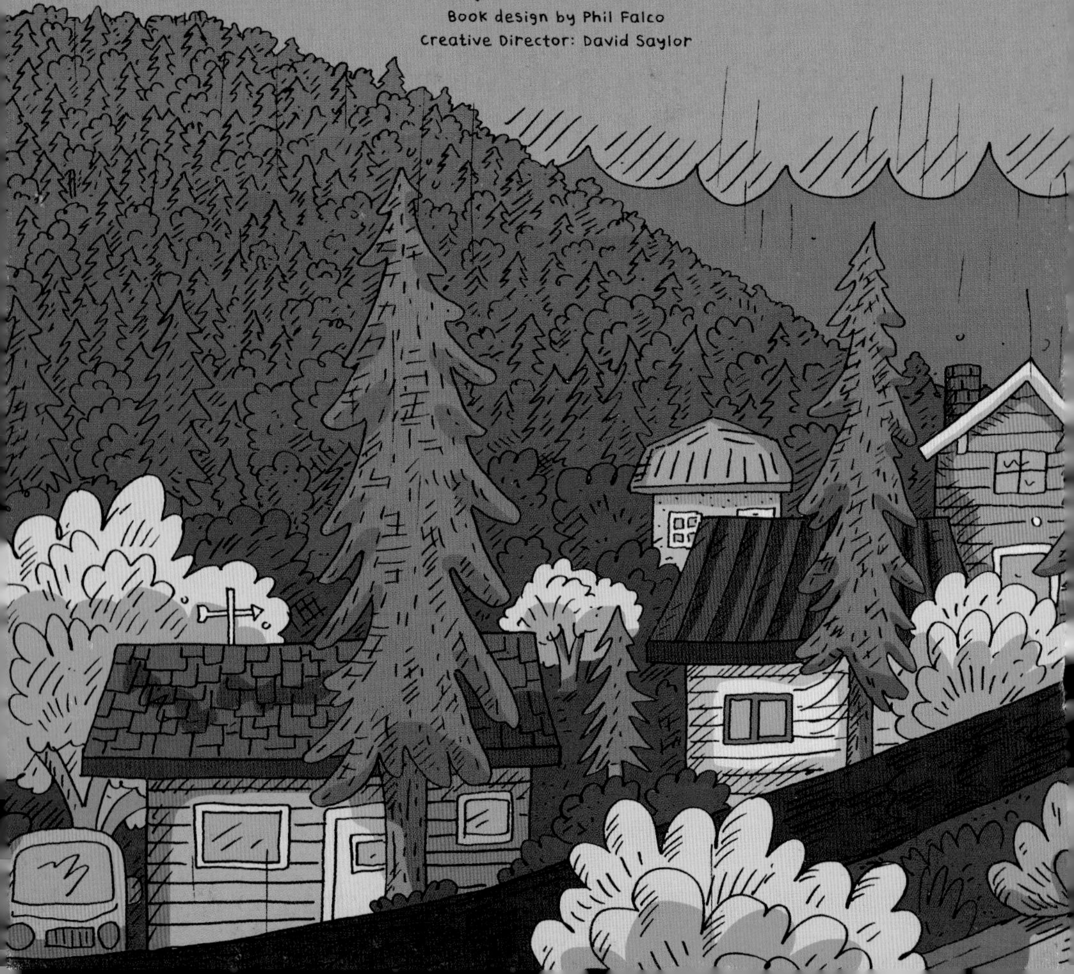

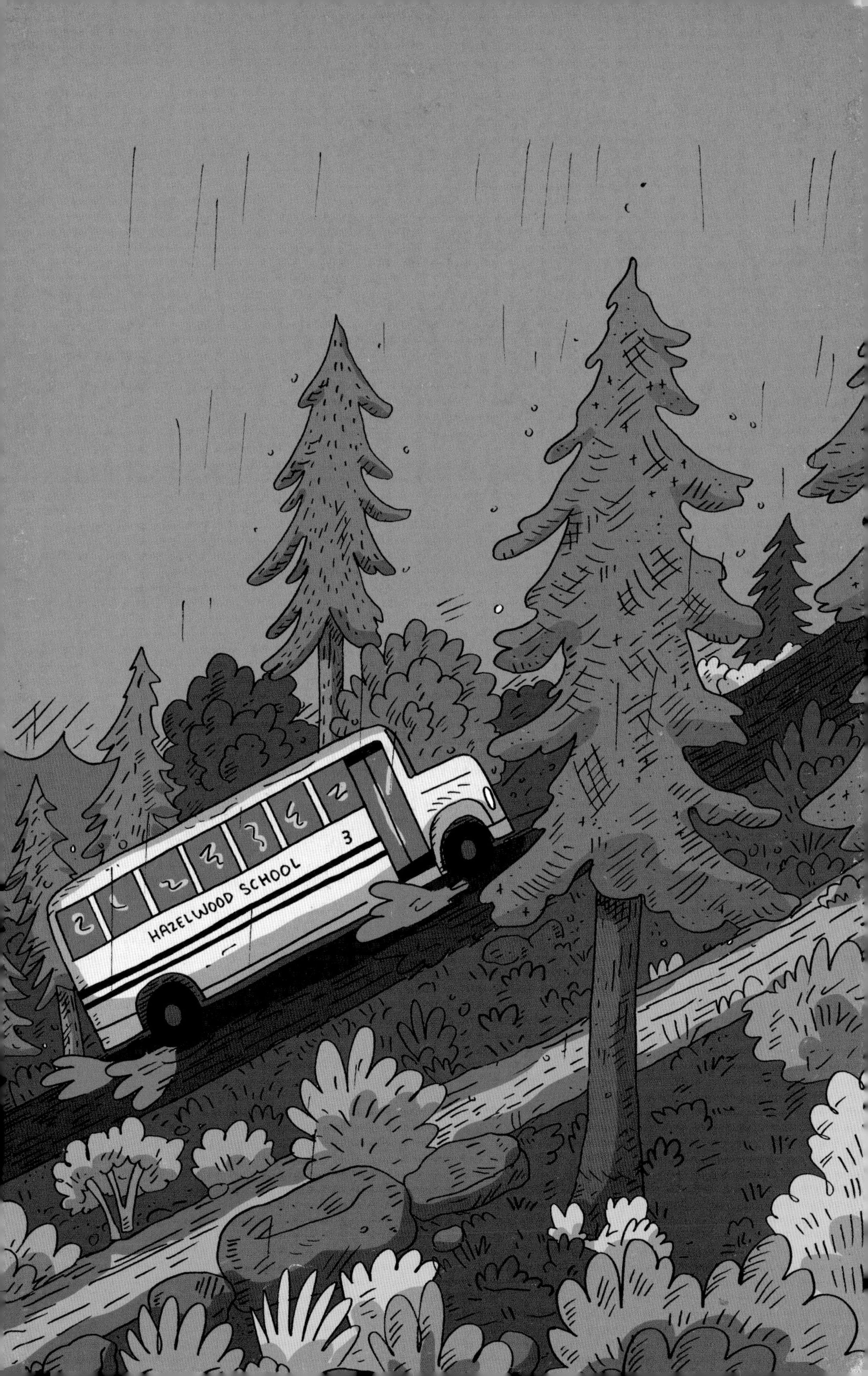
3
HAZELWOOD SCHOOL

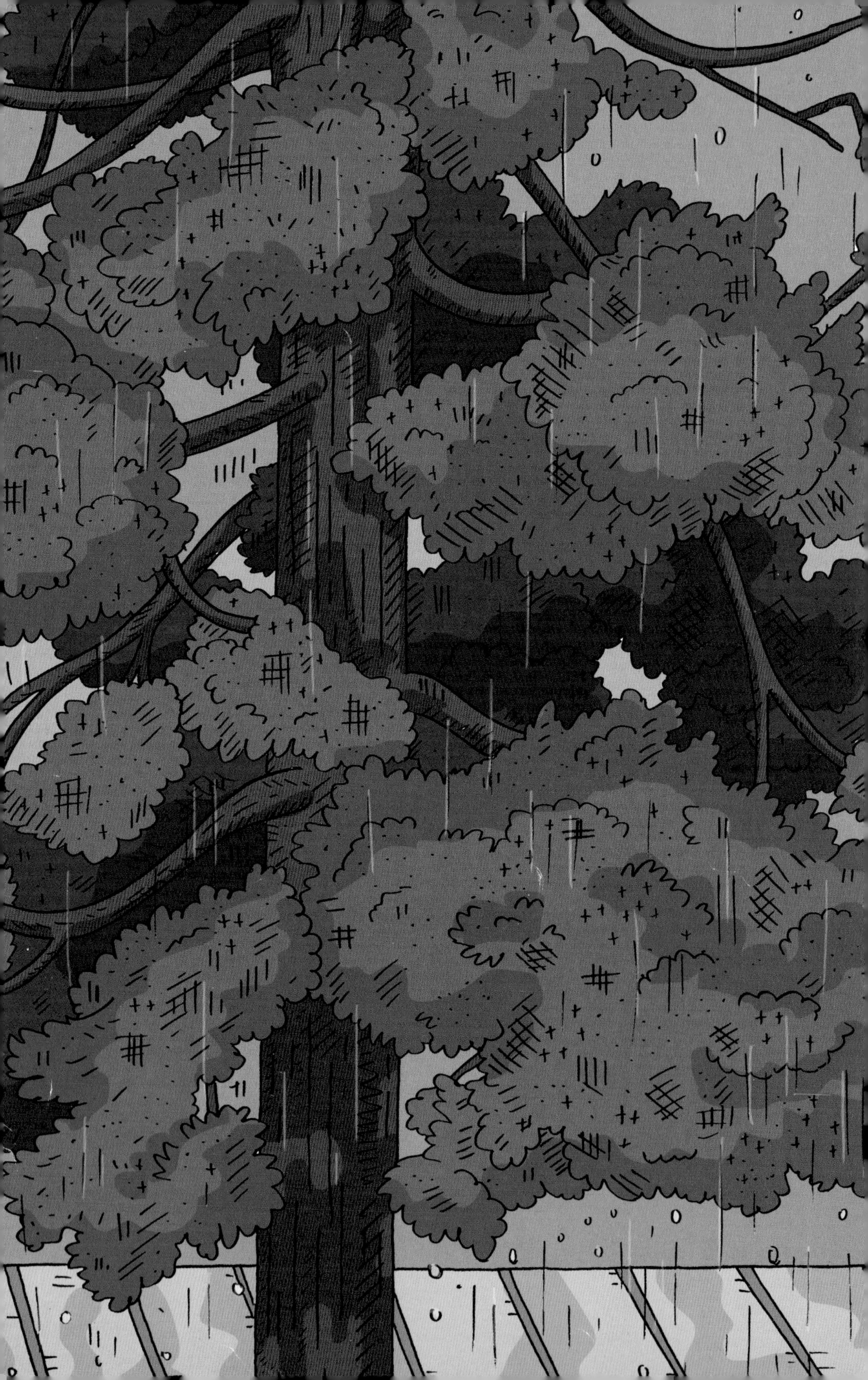

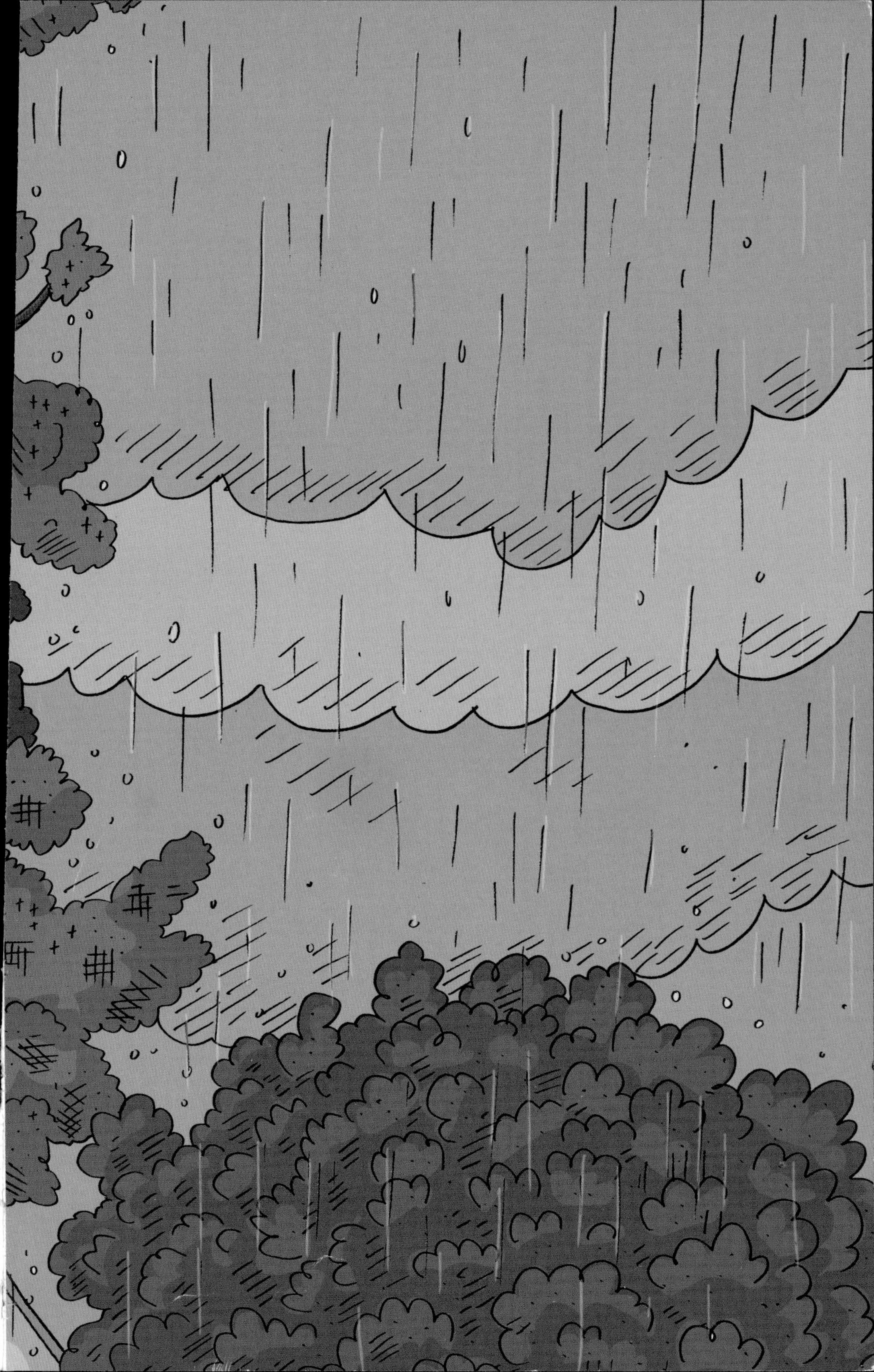

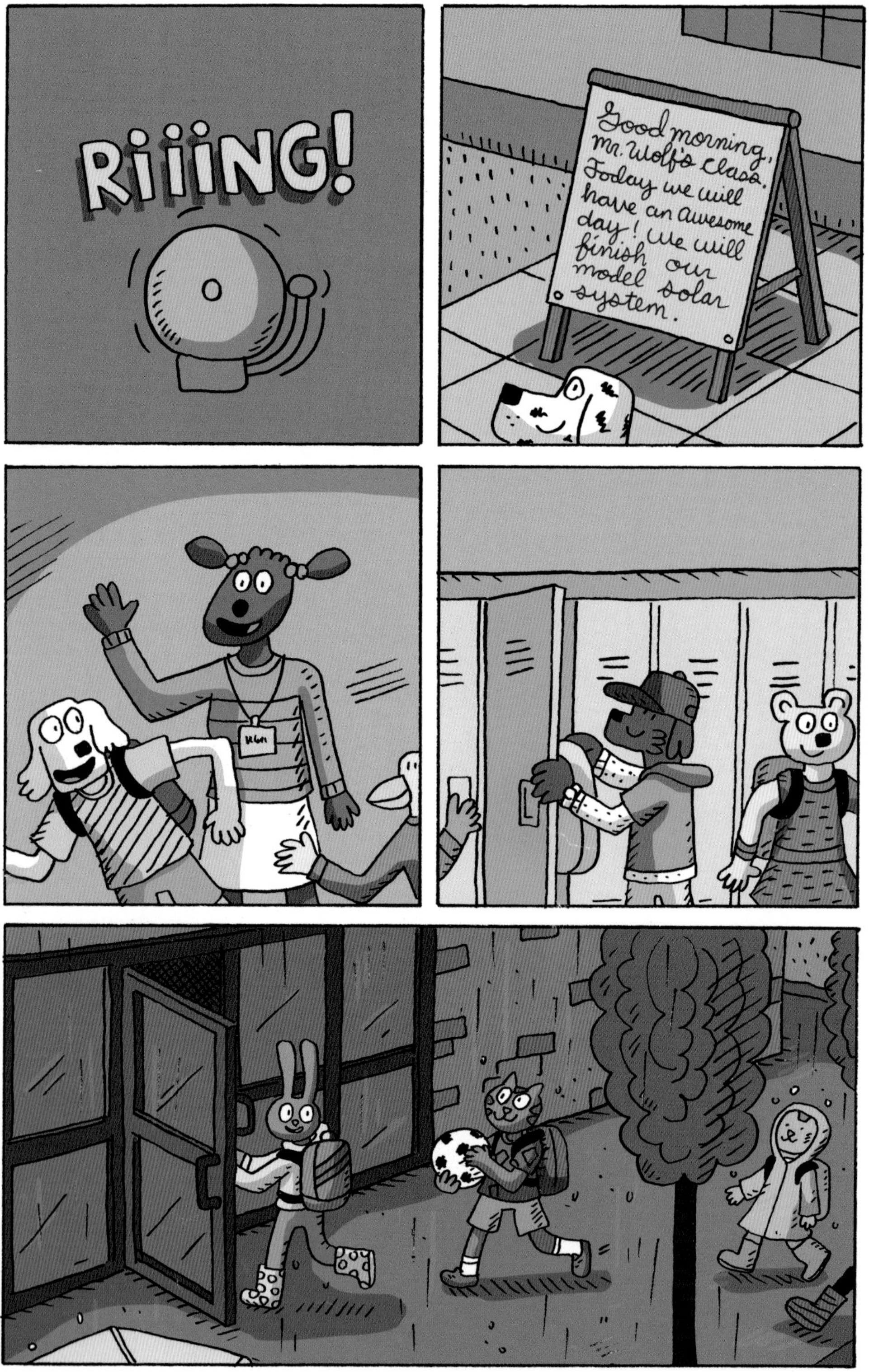
RiiiNG!
Good morning, Mr. Wolf's Class. Today we will have an awesome day! We will finish our model solar system.

CHAPTER ONE
You're All Invited

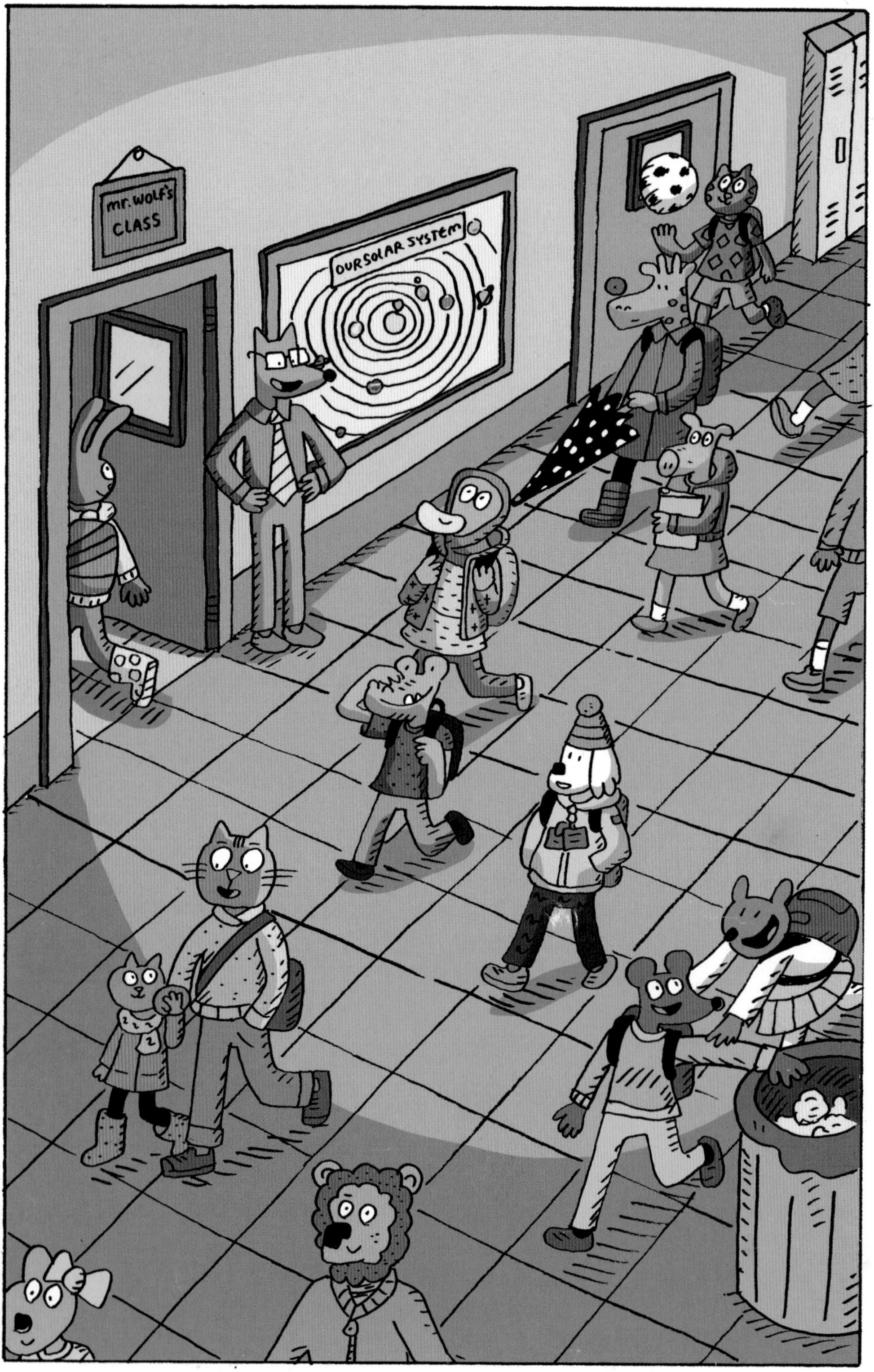
mr. WOLF's CLASS
OUR SOLAR SYSTEM

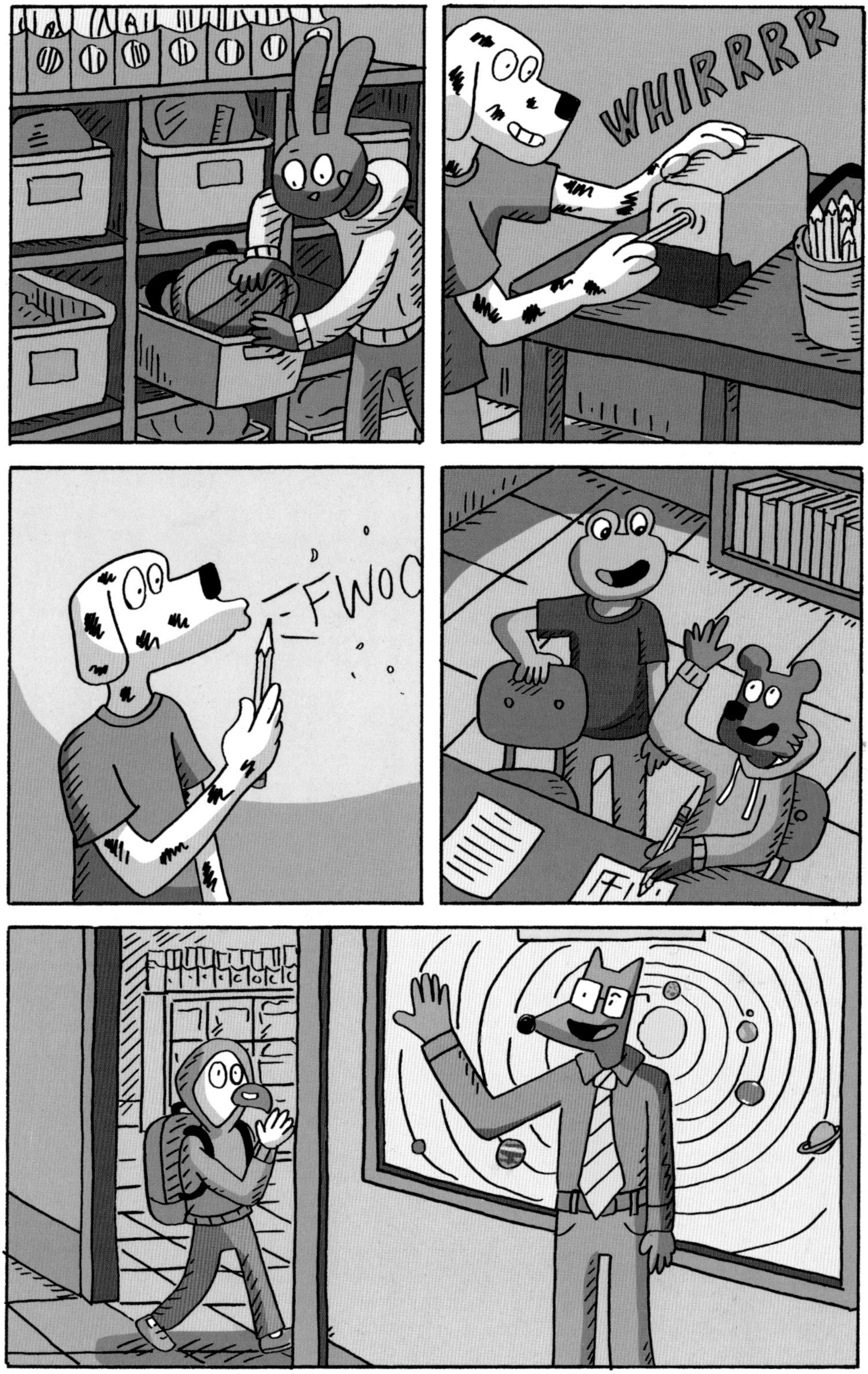
WHIRRRR
FWOO

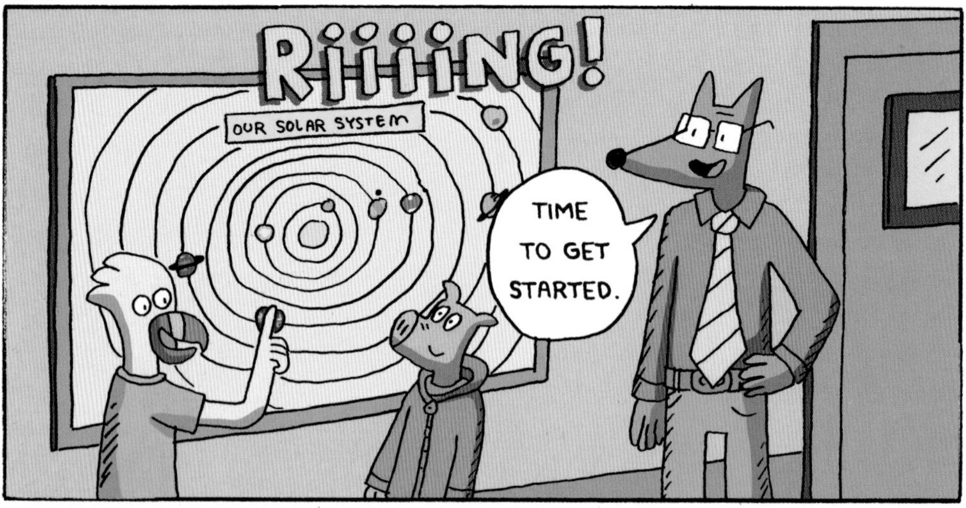
RiiiiNG!
OUR SOLAR SYSTEM
TIME TO GET STARTED.

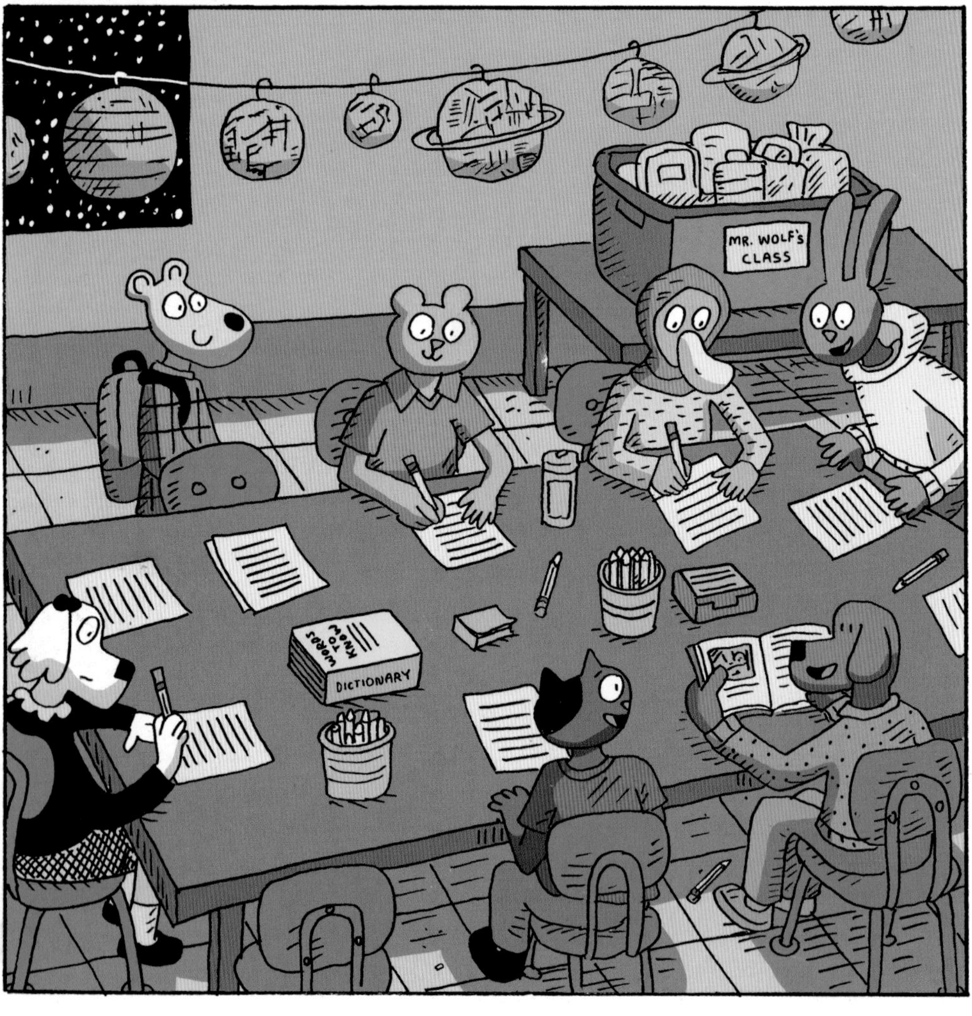
MR. WOLF'S CLASS
WORDS TO KNOW
DICTIONARY

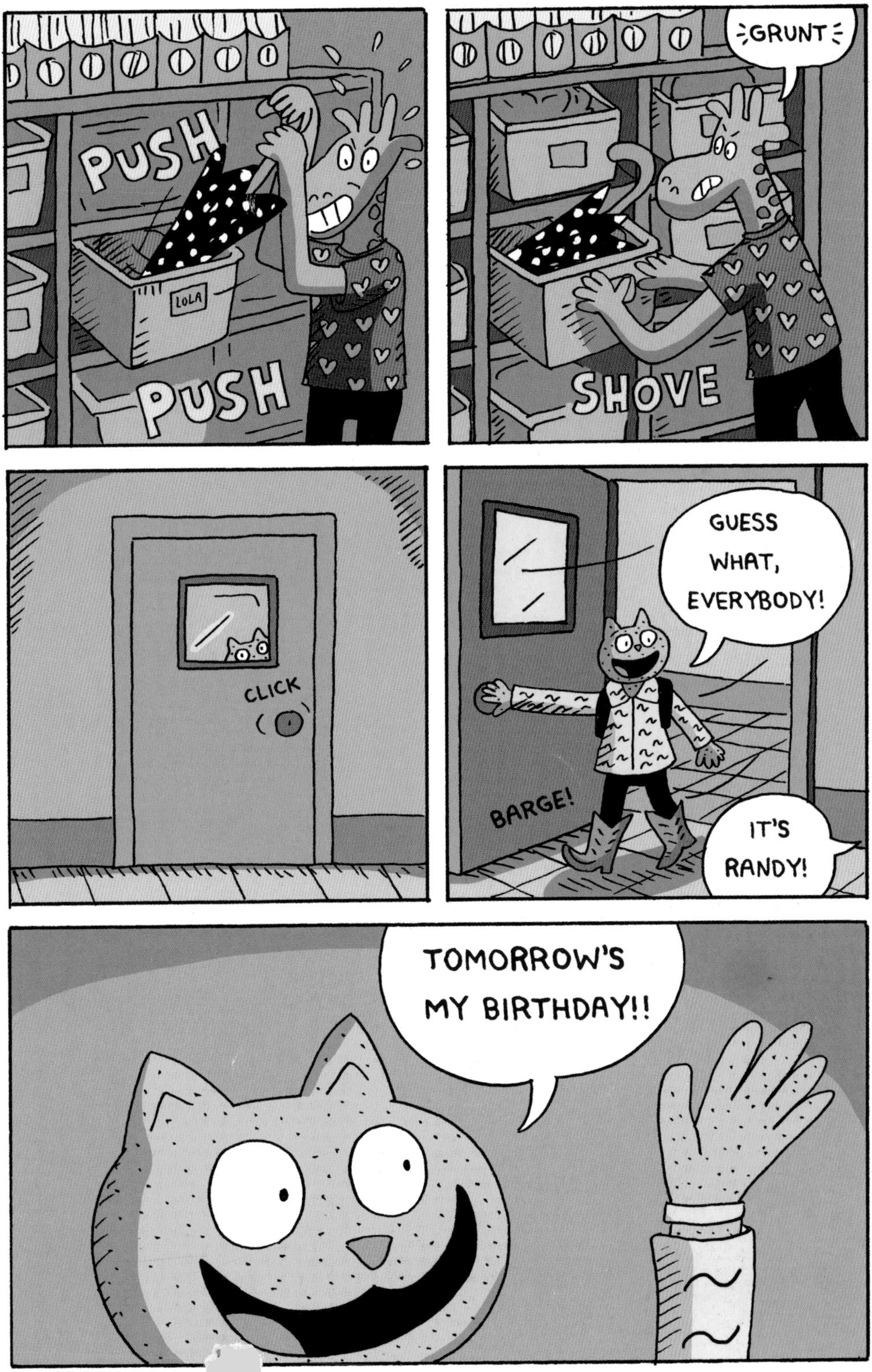
PUSH
LOLA
PUSH
GRUNT
SHOVE
CLICK
GUESS WHAT, EVERYBODY!
BARGE!
IT'S RANDY!
TOMORROW'S MY BIRTHDAY!!

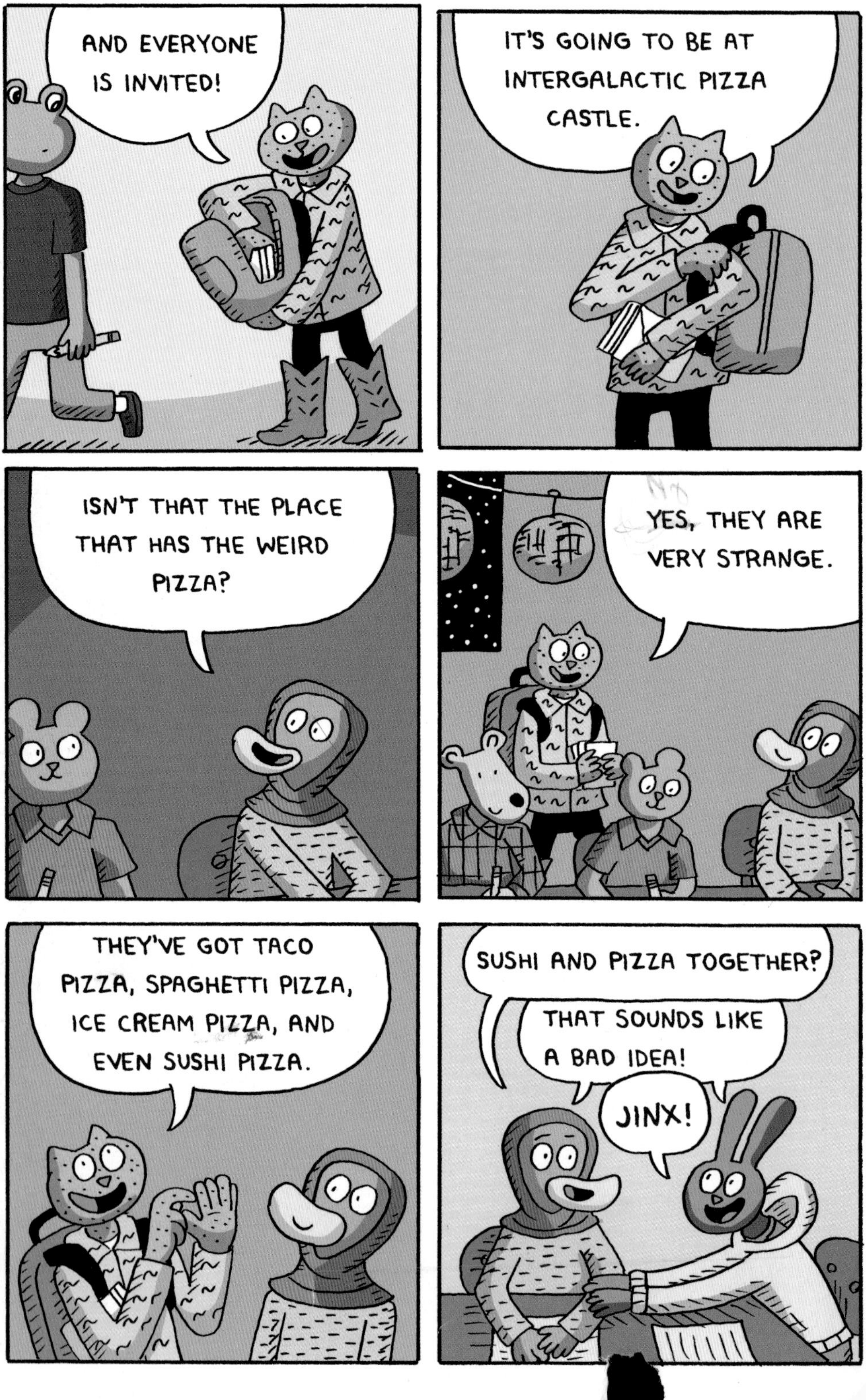
AND EVERYONE IS INVITED!
IT'S GOING TO BE AT INTERGALACTIC PIZZA CASTLE.
ISN'T THAT THE PLACE THAT HAS THE WEIRD PIZZA?
YES, THEY ARE VERY STRANGE.
THEY'VE GOT TACO PIZZA, SPAGHETTI PIZZA, ICE CREAM PIZZA, AND EVEN SUSHI PIZZA.
SUSHI AND PIZZA TOGETHER?
THAT SOUNDS LIKE A BAD IDEA!
JINX!

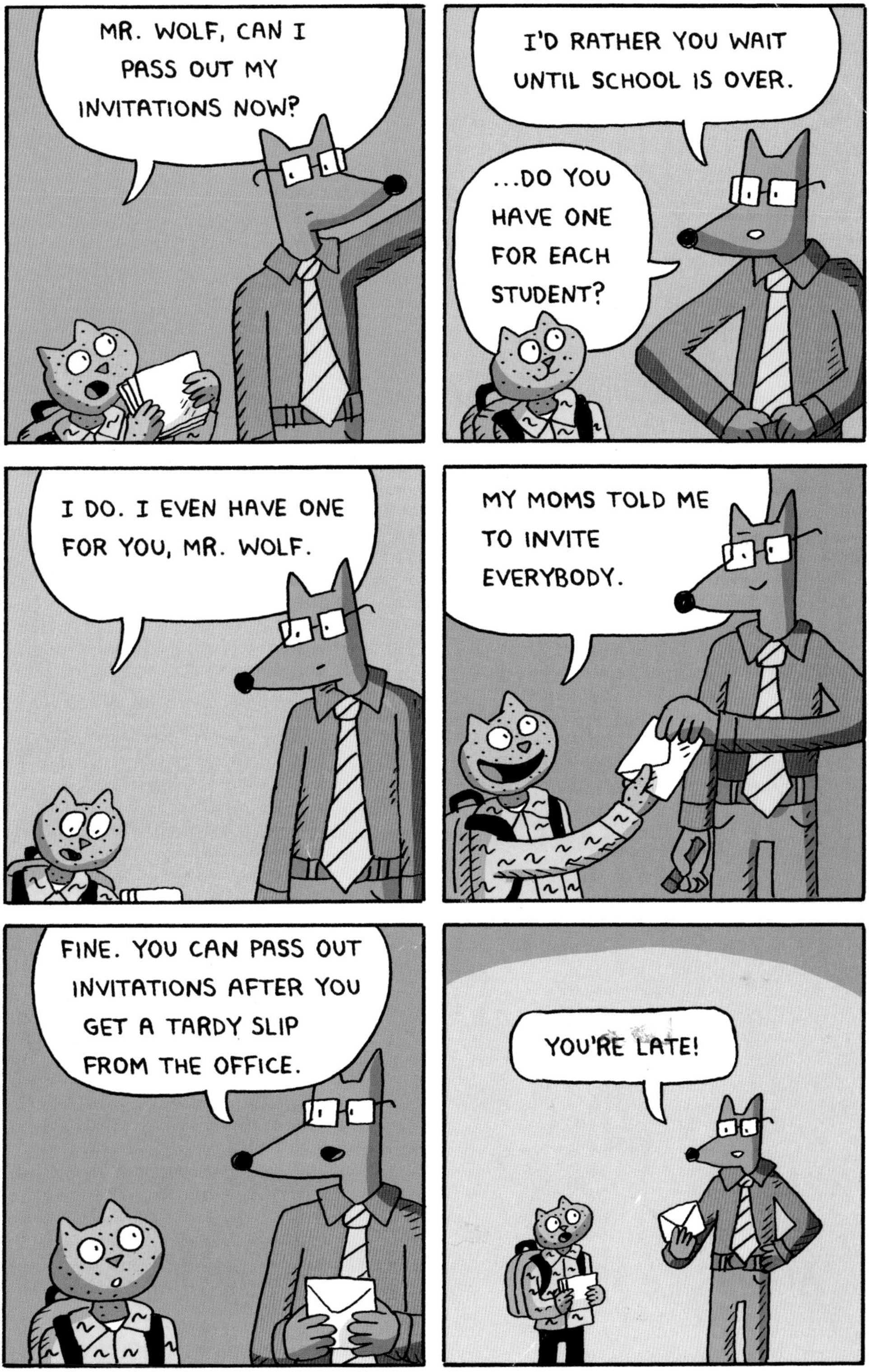
MR. WOLF, CAN I PASS OUT MY INVITATIONS NOW?
I'D RATHER YOU WAIT UNTIL SCHOOL IS OVER.
...DO YOU HAVE ONE FOR EACH STUDENT?
I DO. I EVEN HAVE ONE FOR YOU, MR. WOLF.
MY MOMS TOLD ME TO INVITE EVERYBODY.
FINE. YOU CAN PASS OUT INVITATIONS AFTER YOU GET A TARDY SLIP FROM THE OFFICE.
YOU'RE LATE!

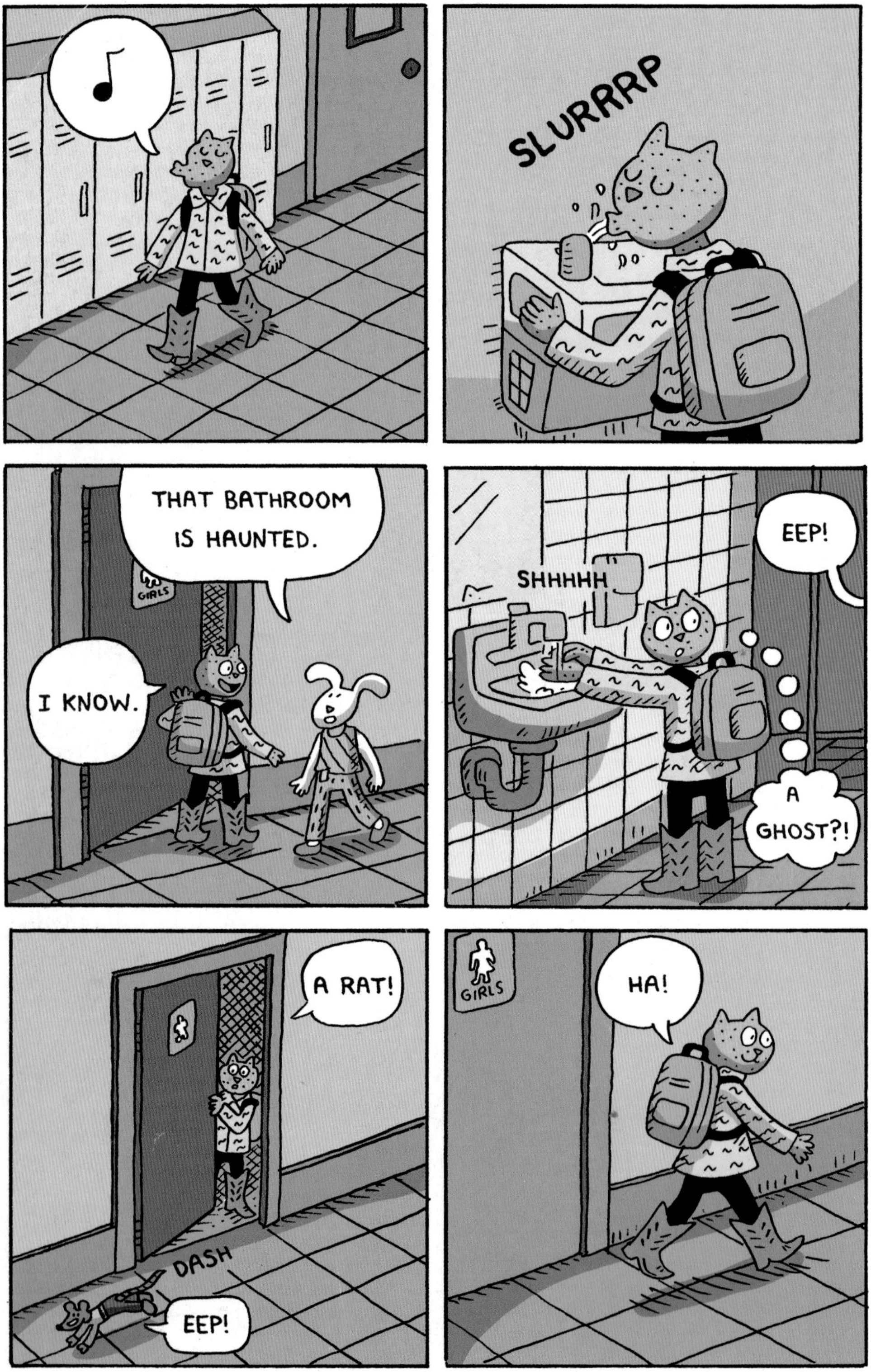
SLURRRP
THAT BATHROOM IS HAUNTED.
I KNOW.
SHHHHH
EEP!
A GHOST?!
A RAT!
DASH
EEP!
GIRLS
HA!

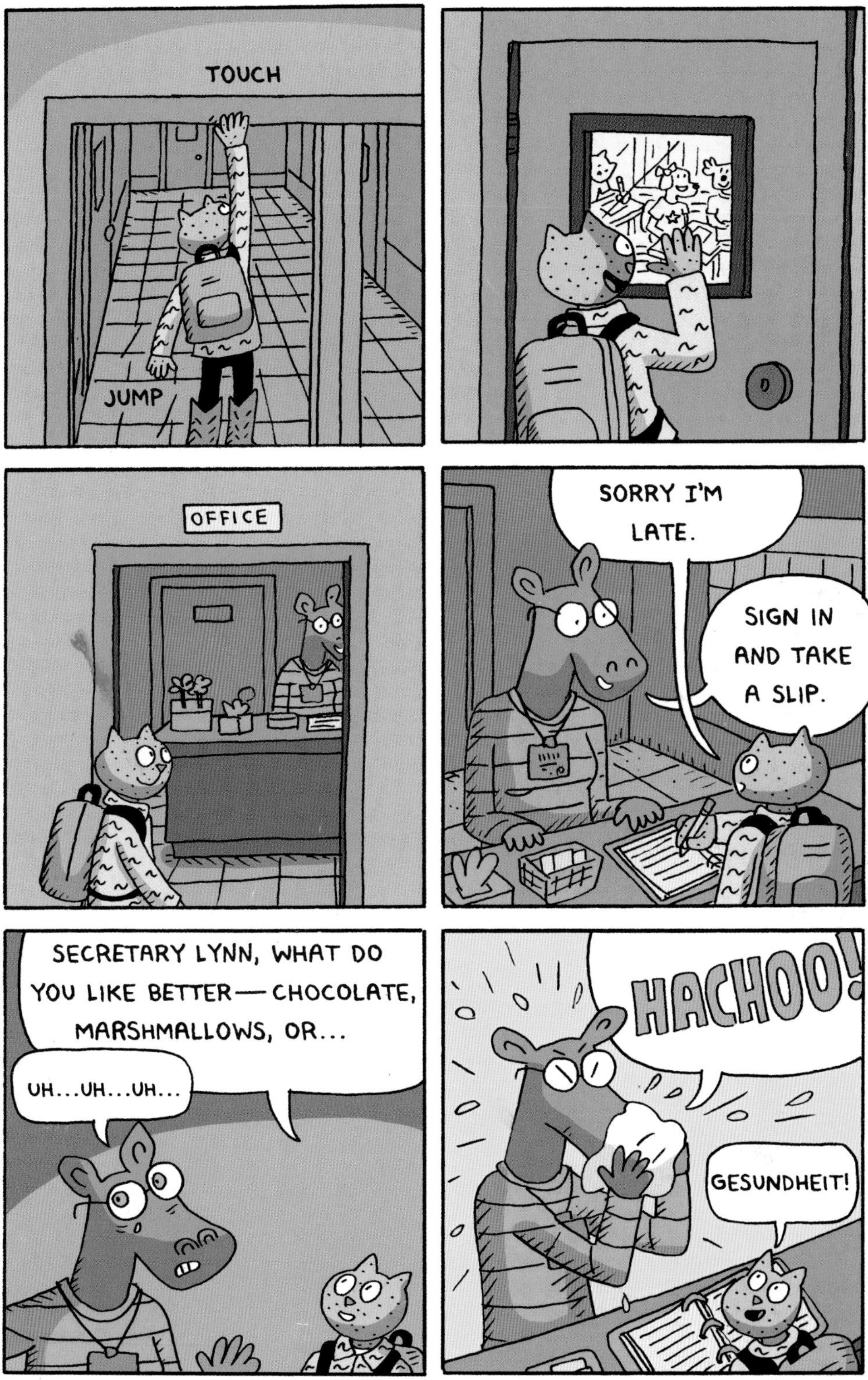
TOUCH
JUMP
OFFICE
SORRY I'M LATE.
SIGN IN AND TAKE A SLIP.
SECRETARY LYNN, WHAT DO YOU LIKE BETTER— CHOCOLATE, MARSHMALLOWS, OR...
UH...UH...UH...
HACHOO!
GESUNDHEIT!

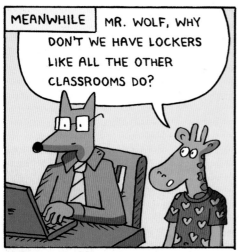

MEANWHILE MR. WOLF, WHY DON'T WE HAVE LOCKERS LIKE ALL THE OTHER CLASSROOMS DO?

WE HAD THEM LAST YEAR, IN MR. GREENS'S CLASS.

I DON'T KNOW... WE HAVE CUBBIES.

BUT MY BACKPACK BARELY FITS INSIDE MY CUBBY AND MY UMBRELLA DOESN'T FIT AT ALL.

IT **WOULD** FIT IN A LOCKER.

CLICK

POP

HEY!

WHOOPS!

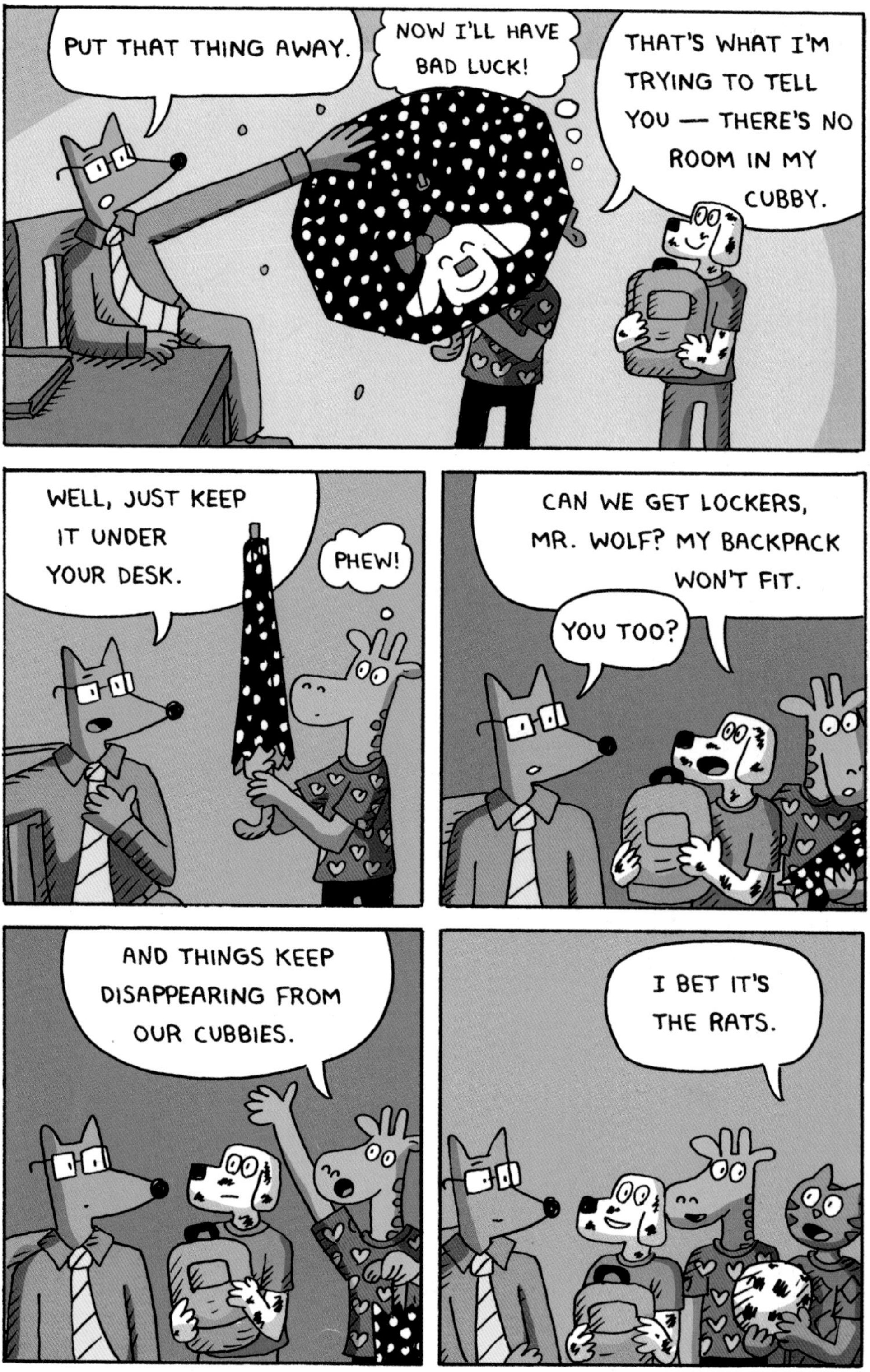
PUT THAT THING AWAY.
NOW I'LL HAVE BAD LUCK!
THAT'S WHAT I'M TRYING TO TELL YOU — THERE'S NO ROOM IN MY CUBBY.
WELL, JUST KEEP IT UNDER YOUR DESK.
PHEW!
CAN WE GET LOCKERS, MR. WOLF? MY BACKPACK WON'T FIT.
YOU TOO?
AND THINGS KEEP DISAPPEARING FROM OUR CUBBIES.
I BET IT'S THE RATS.

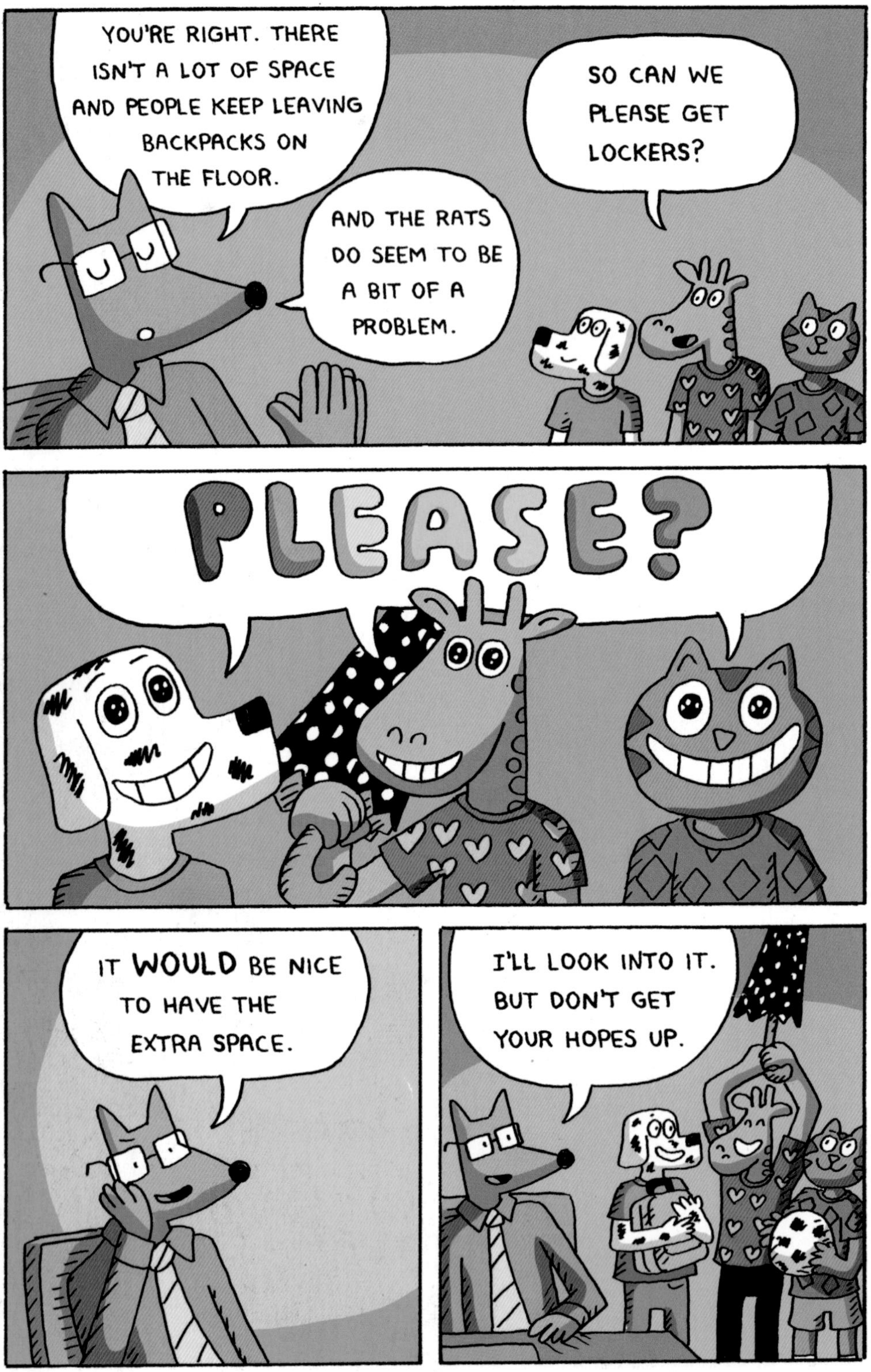
YOU'RE RIGHT. THERE ISN'T A LOT OF SPACE AND PEOPLE KEEP LEAVING BACKPACKS ON THE FLOOR.
AND THE RATS DO SEEM TO BE A BIT OF A PROBLEM.
SO CAN WE PLEASE GET LOCKERS?
PLEASE?
IT WOULD BE NICE TO HAVE THE EXTRA SPACE.
I'LL LOOK INTO IT. BUT DON'T GET YOUR HOPES UP.

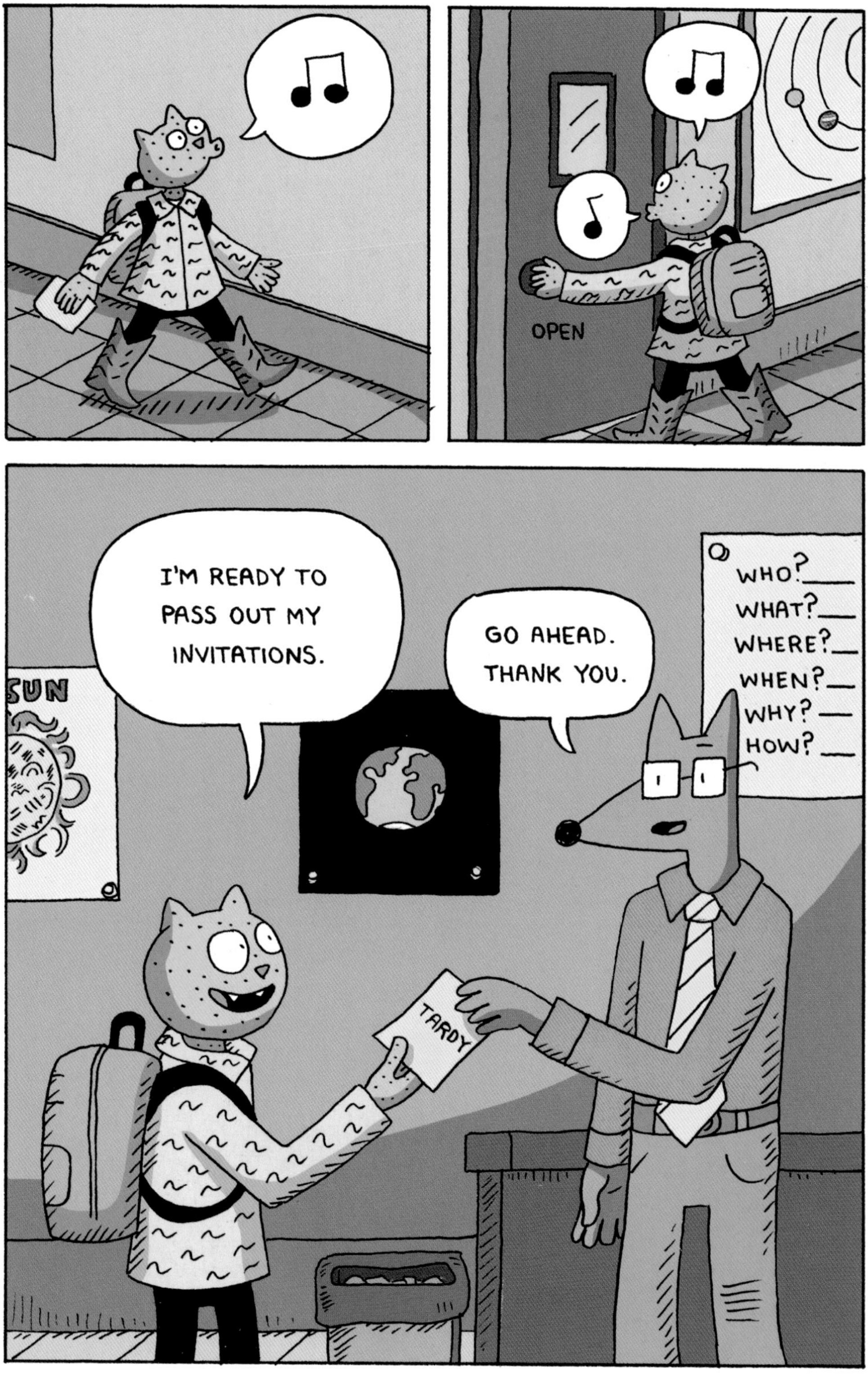
♫
♫
♪
OPEN
I'M READY TO PASS OUT MY INVITATIONS.
GO AHEAD. THANK YOU.
SUN
WHO?
WHAT?
WHERE?
WHEN?
WHY?
HOW?
TARDY

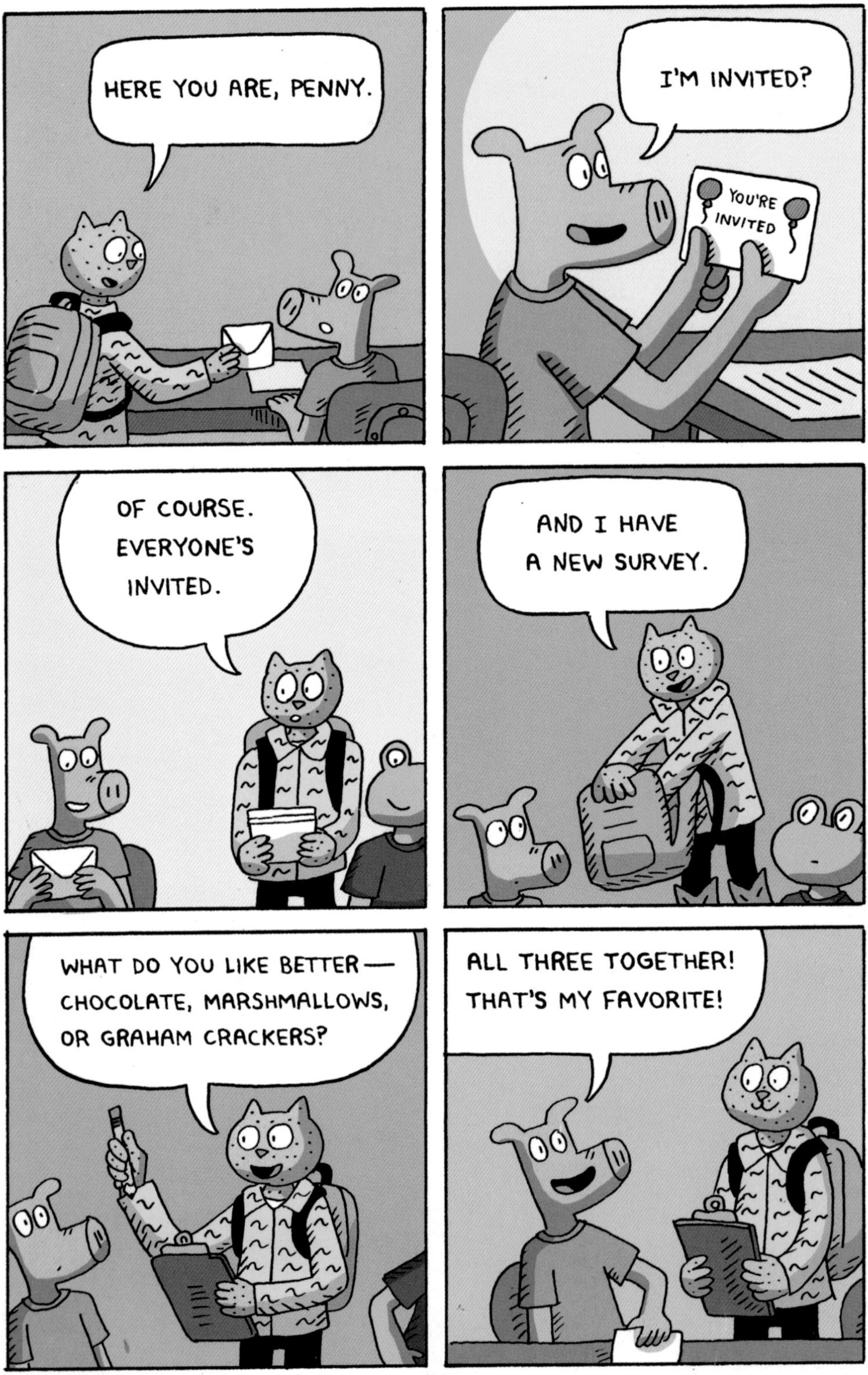
HERE YOU ARE, PENNY.
I'M INVITED?
YOU'RE INVITED
OF COURSE. EVERYONE'S INVITED.
AND I HAVE A NEW SURVEY.
WHAT DO YOU LIKE BETTER— CHOCOLATE, MARSHMALLOWS, OR GRAHAM CRACKERS?
ALL THREE TOGETHER! THAT'S MY FAVORITE!

IT'S CALLED S'MORES.

I KNOW THAT.

WRITE YOUR NAME IN THE MIDDLE OF THE VENN DIAGRAM, WHERE THE THREE CIRCLES OVERLAP.

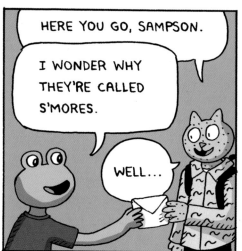

HERE YOU GO, SAMPSON.

I WONDER WHY THEY'RE CALLED S'MORES.

WELL...

IT'S BECAUSE WHEN YOU'RE DONE EATING, YOU ALWAYS WANT SOME MORE. GET IT? S'MORES.

THE INTERNET TOLD ME THAT.

OHHHHH!

THAT MAKES SENSE.

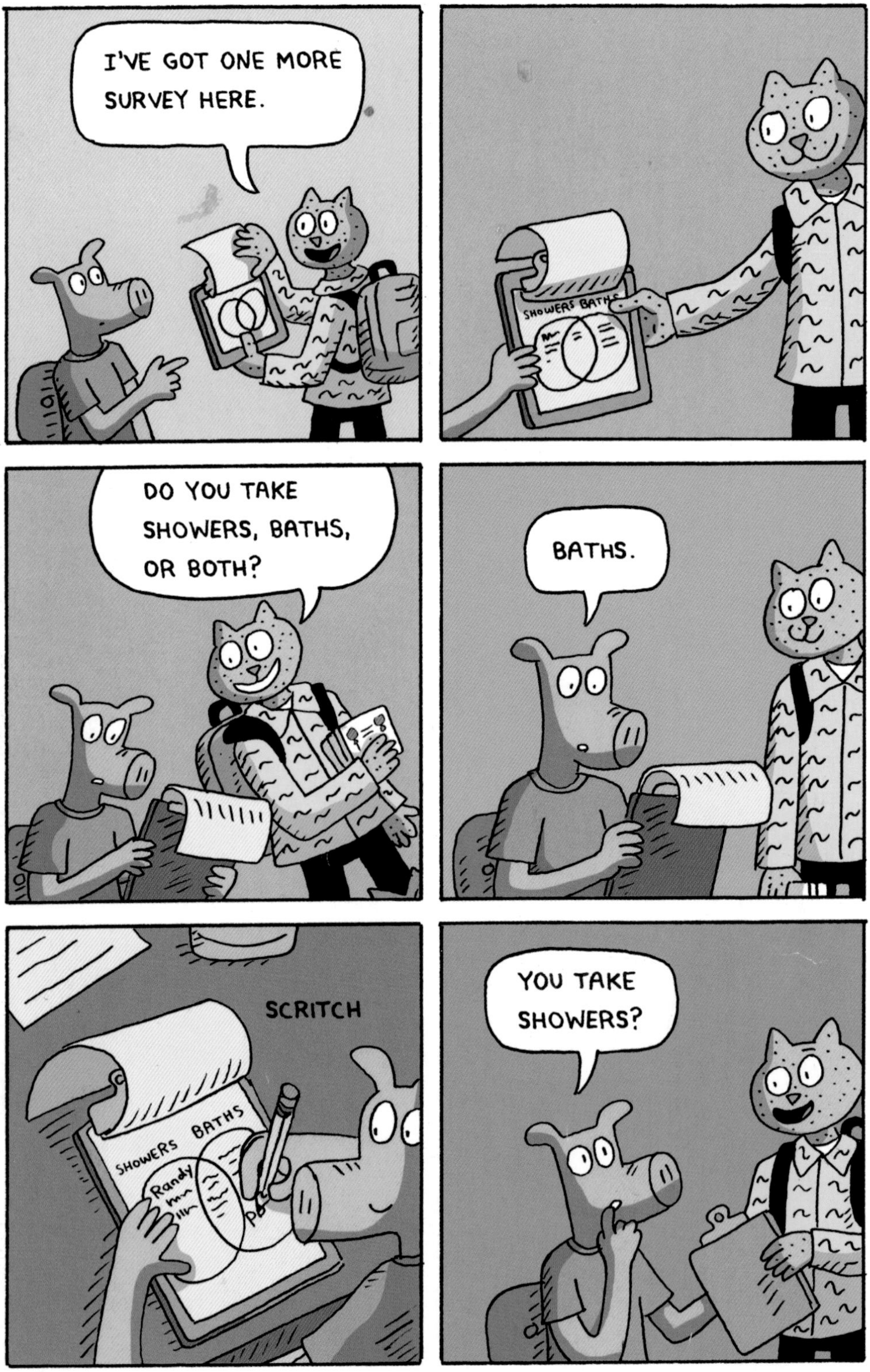
I'VE GOT ONE MORE SURVEY HERE.
SHOWERS BATHS
DO YOU TAKE SHOWERS, BATHS, OR BOTH?
BATHS.
SCRITCH
SHOWERS BATHS
Randy
YOU TAKE SHOWERS?

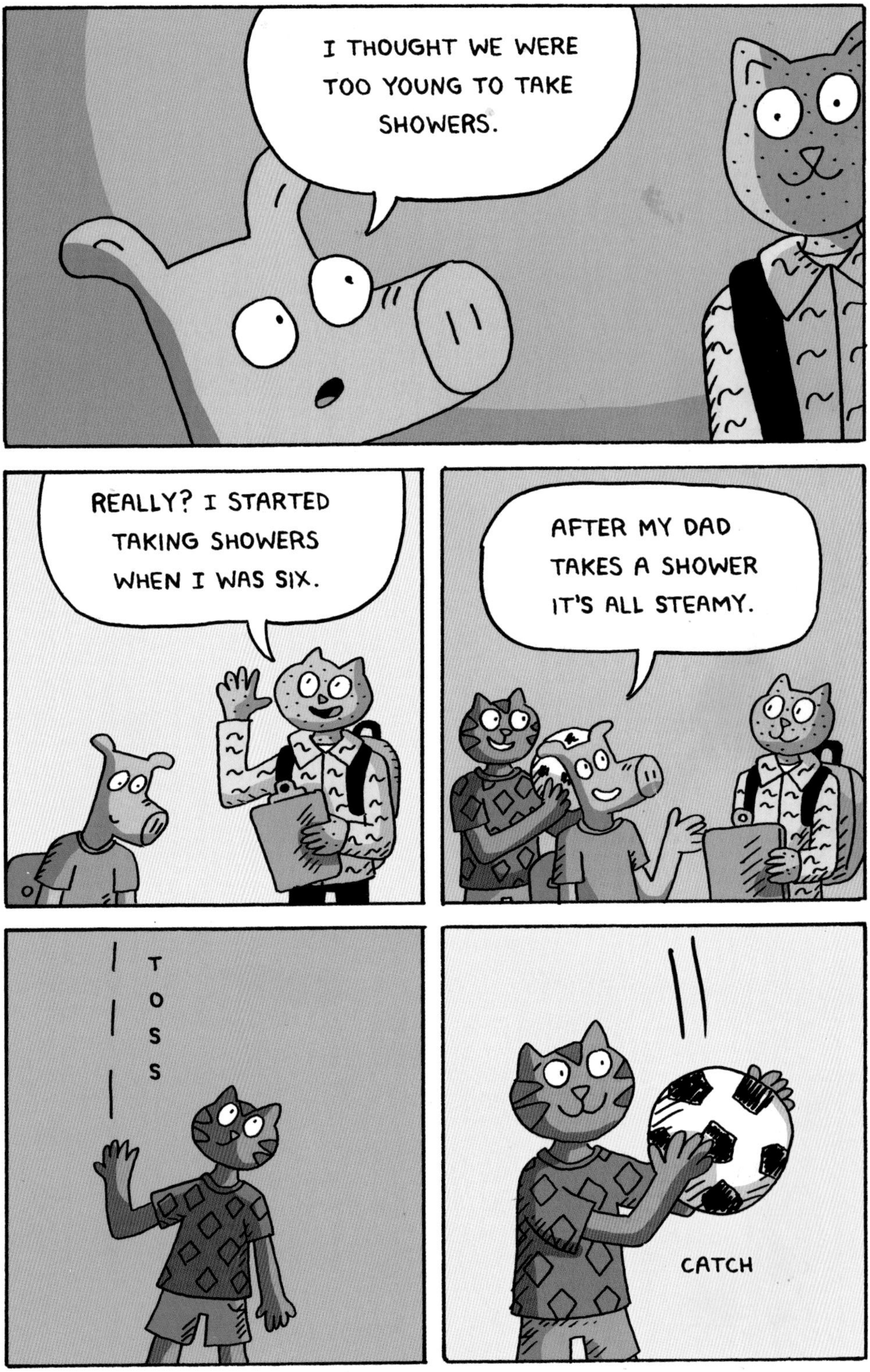
I THOUGHT WE WERE TOO YOUNG TO TAKE SHOWERS.
REALLY? I STARTED TAKING SHOWERS WHEN I WAS SIX.
AFTER MY DAD TAKES A SHOWER IT'S ALL STEAMY.
TOSS
CATCH

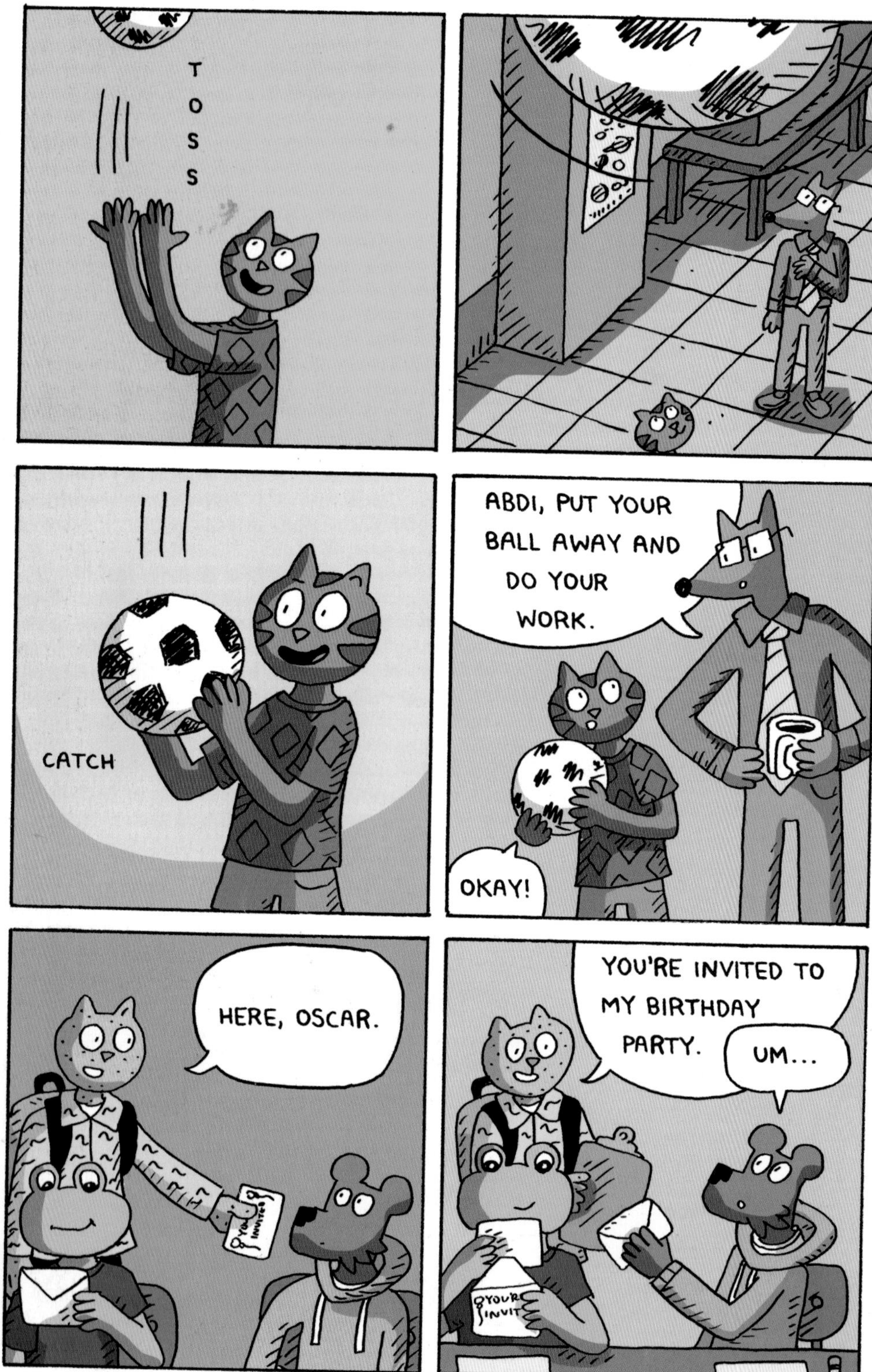
T O S S
CATCH
ABDI, PUT YOUR BALL AWAY AND DO YOUR WORK.
OKAY!
HERE, OSCAR.
YOU'RE INVITED
YOU'RE INVITED TO MY BIRTHDAY PARTY.
UM...

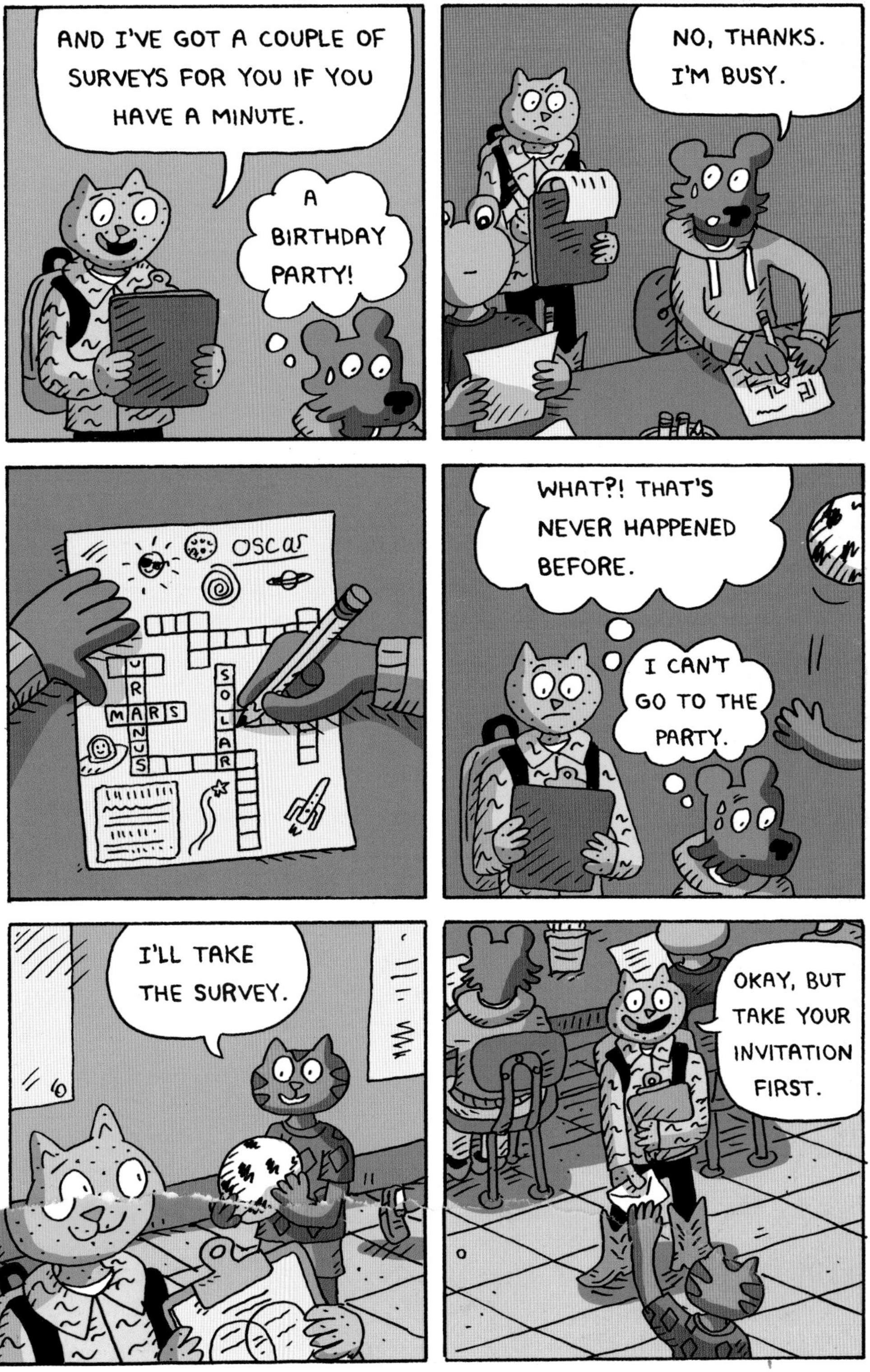
AND I'VE GOT A COUPLE OF SURVEYS FOR YOU IF YOU HAVE A MINUTE.
A BIRTHDAY PARTY!
NO, THANKS. I'M BUSY.
OSCAR
U R A N U S
MARS
S O L A R
WHAT?! THAT'S NEVER HAPPENED BEFORE.
I CAN'T GO TO THE PARTY.
I'LL TAKE THE SURVEY.
OKAY, BUT TAKE YOUR INVITATION FIRST.

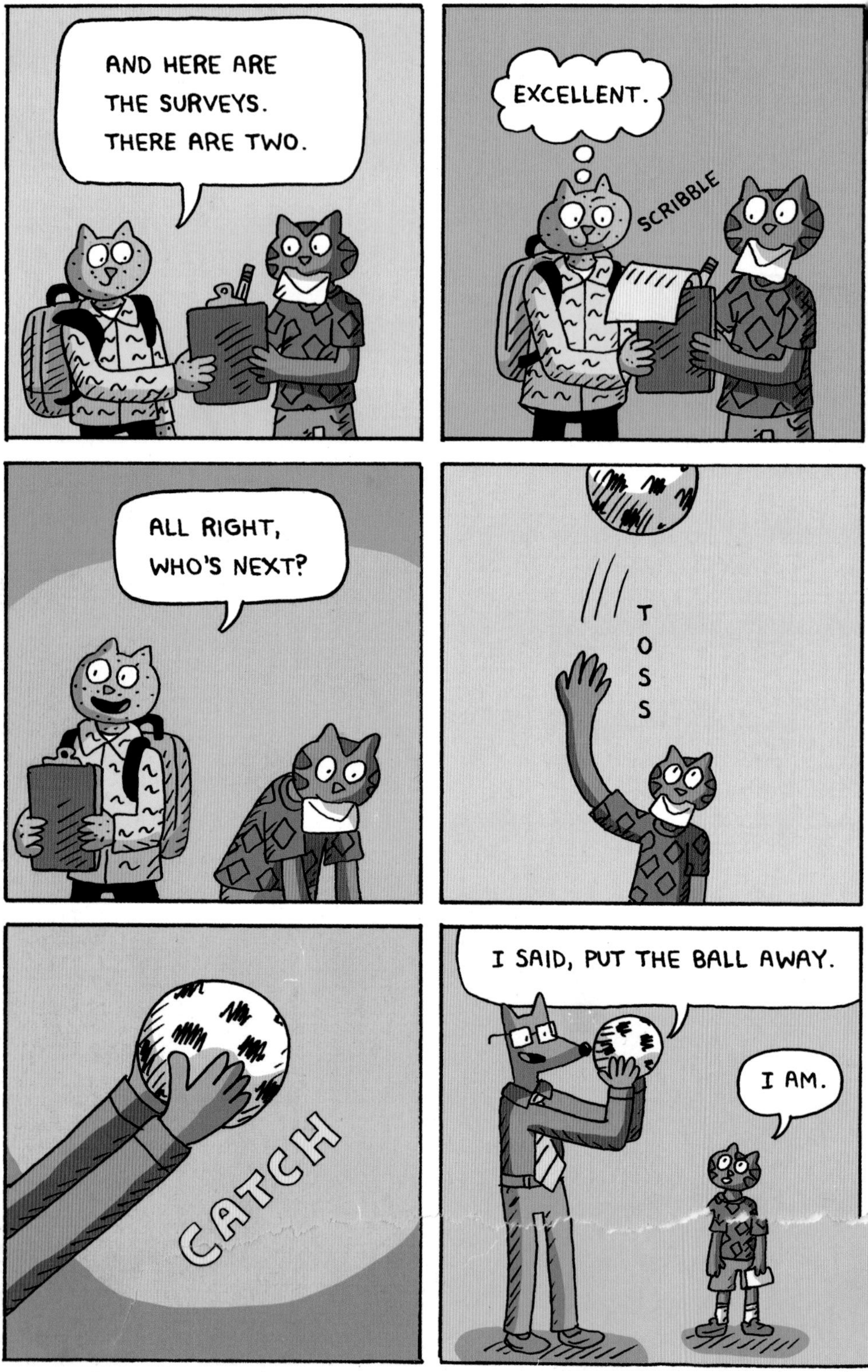
AND HERE ARE THE SURVEYS. THERE ARE TWO.
EXCELLENT.
SCRIBBLE
ALL RIGHT, WHO'S NEXT?
TOSS
CATCH
I SAID, PUT THE BALL AWAY.
I AM.

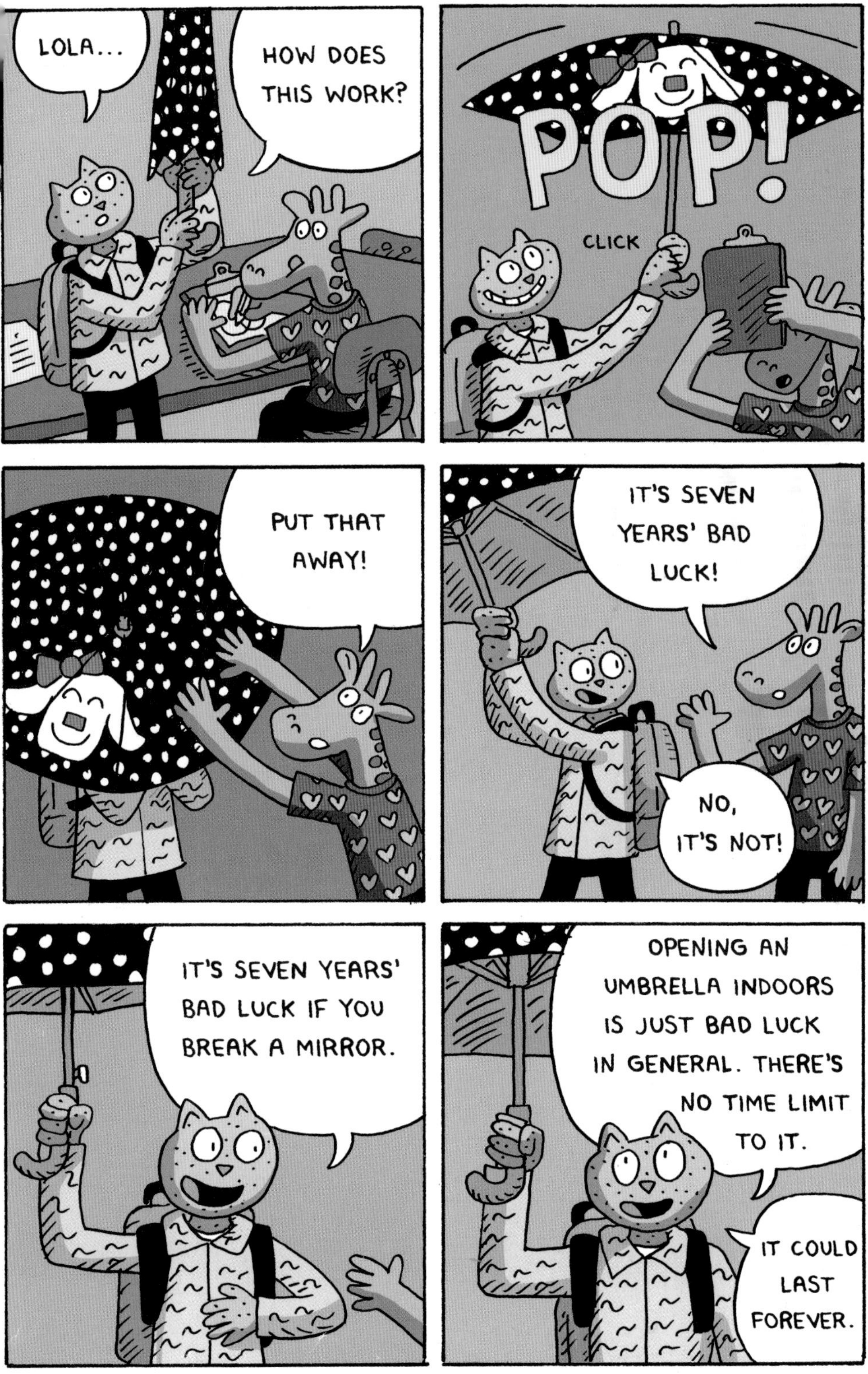
LOLA...
HOW DOES THIS WORK?
POP!
CLICK
PUT THAT AWAY!
IT'S SEVEN YEARS' BAD LUCK!
NO, IT'S NOT!
IT'S SEVEN YEARS' BAD LUCK IF YOU BREAK A MIRROR.
OPENING AN UMBRELLA INDOORS IS JUST BAD LUCK IN GENERAL. THERE'S NO TIME LIMIT TO IT.
IT COULD LAST FOREVER.

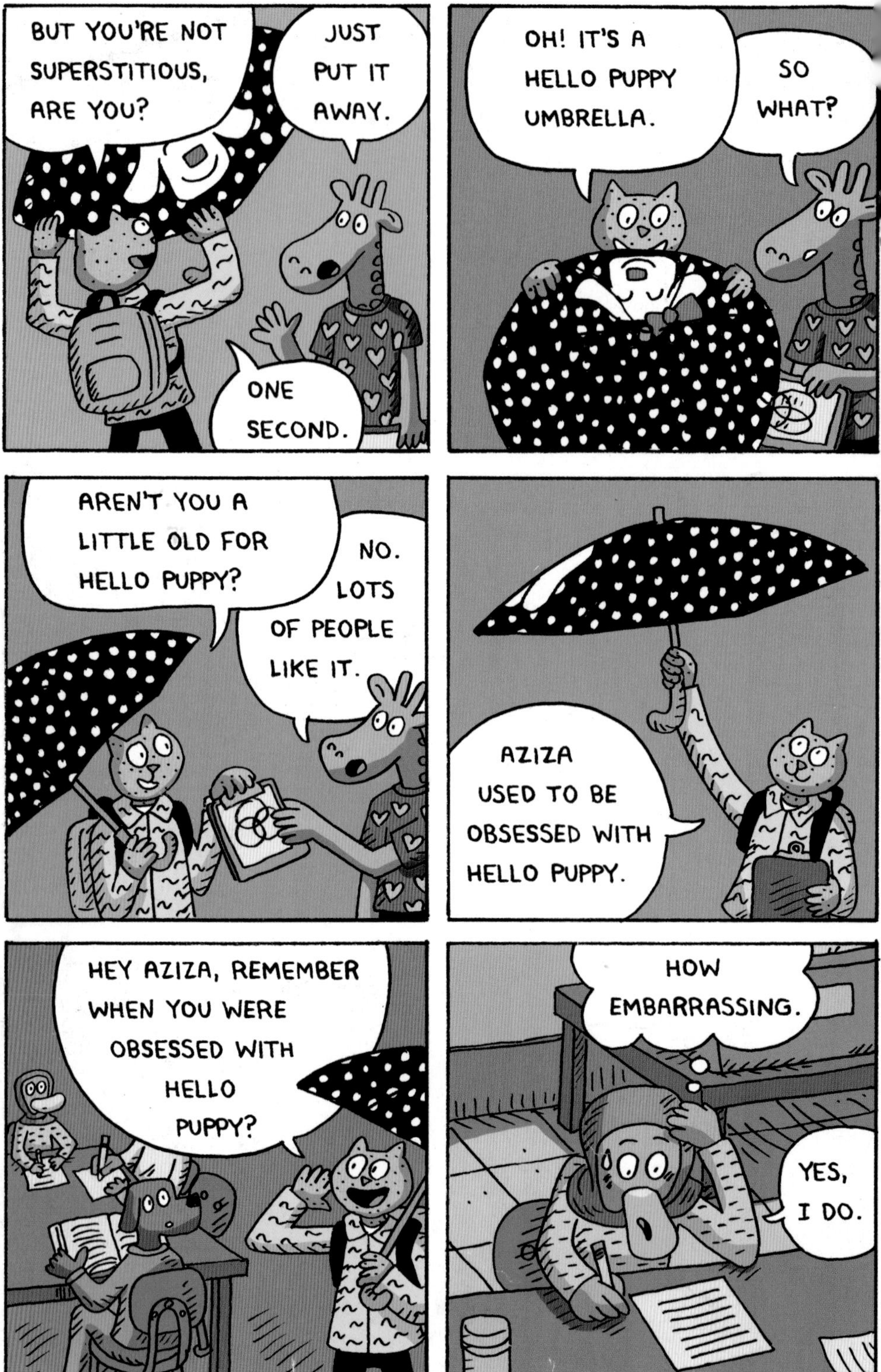
BUT YOU'RE NOT SUPERSTITIOUS, ARE YOU?
JUST PUT IT AWAY.
ONE SECOND.
OH! IT'S A HELLO PUPPY UMBRELLA.
SO WHAT?
AREN'T YOU A LITTLE OLD FOR HELLO PUPPY?
NO. LOTS OF PEOPLE LIKE IT.
AZIZA USED TO BE OBSESSED WITH HELLO PUPPY.
HEY AZIZA, REMEMBER WHEN YOU WERE OBSESSED WITH HELLO PUPPY?
HOW EMBARRASSING.
YES, I DO.

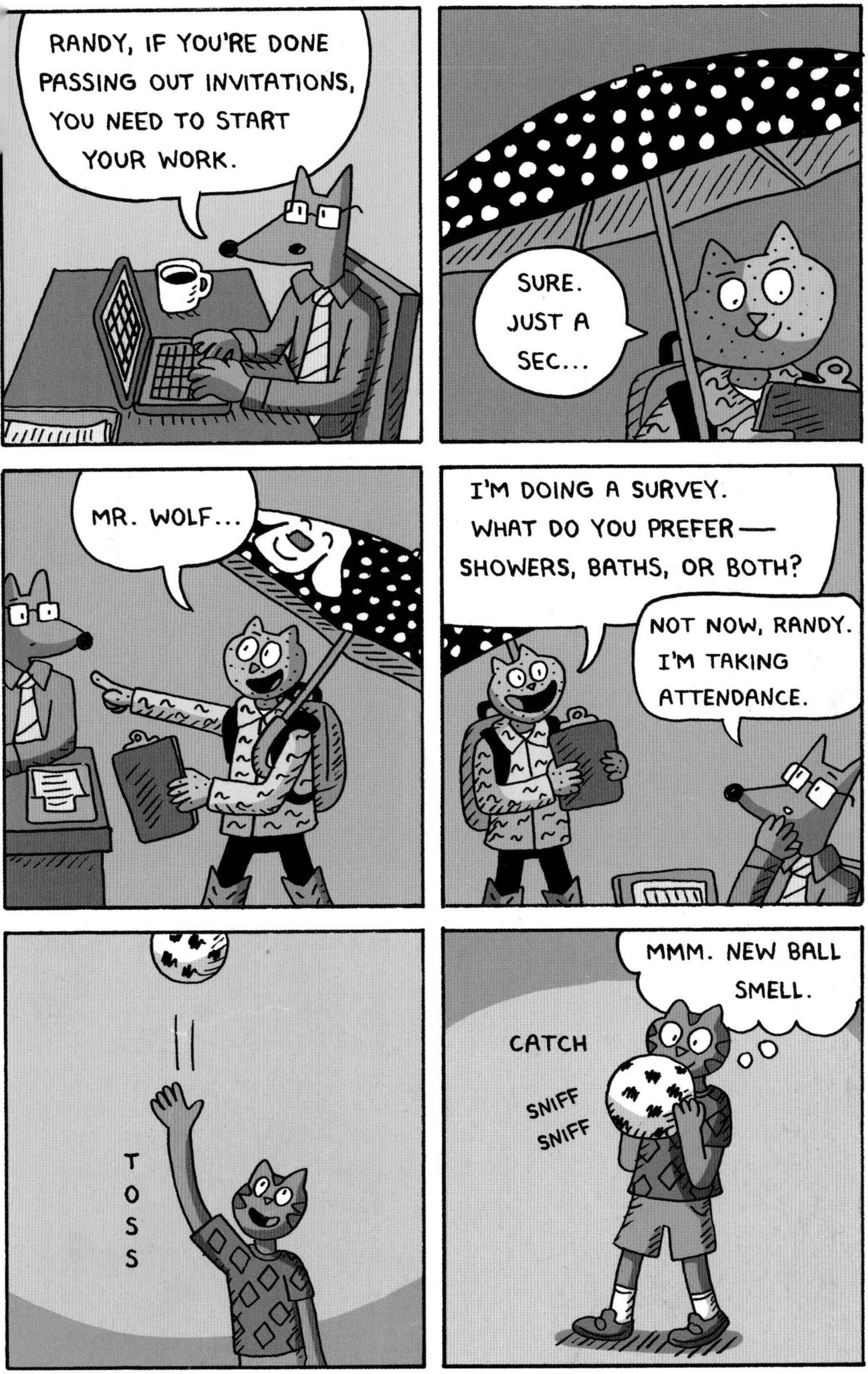
RANDY, IF YOU'RE DONE PASSING OUT INVITATIONS, YOU NEED TO START YOUR WORK.
SURE. JUST A SEC...
MR. WOLF...
I'M DOING A SURVEY. WHAT DO YOU PREFER— SHOWERS, BATHS, OR BOTH?
NOT NOW, RANDY. I'M TAKING ATTENDANCE.
TOSS
MMM. NEW BALL SMELL.
CATCH
SNIFF SNIFF

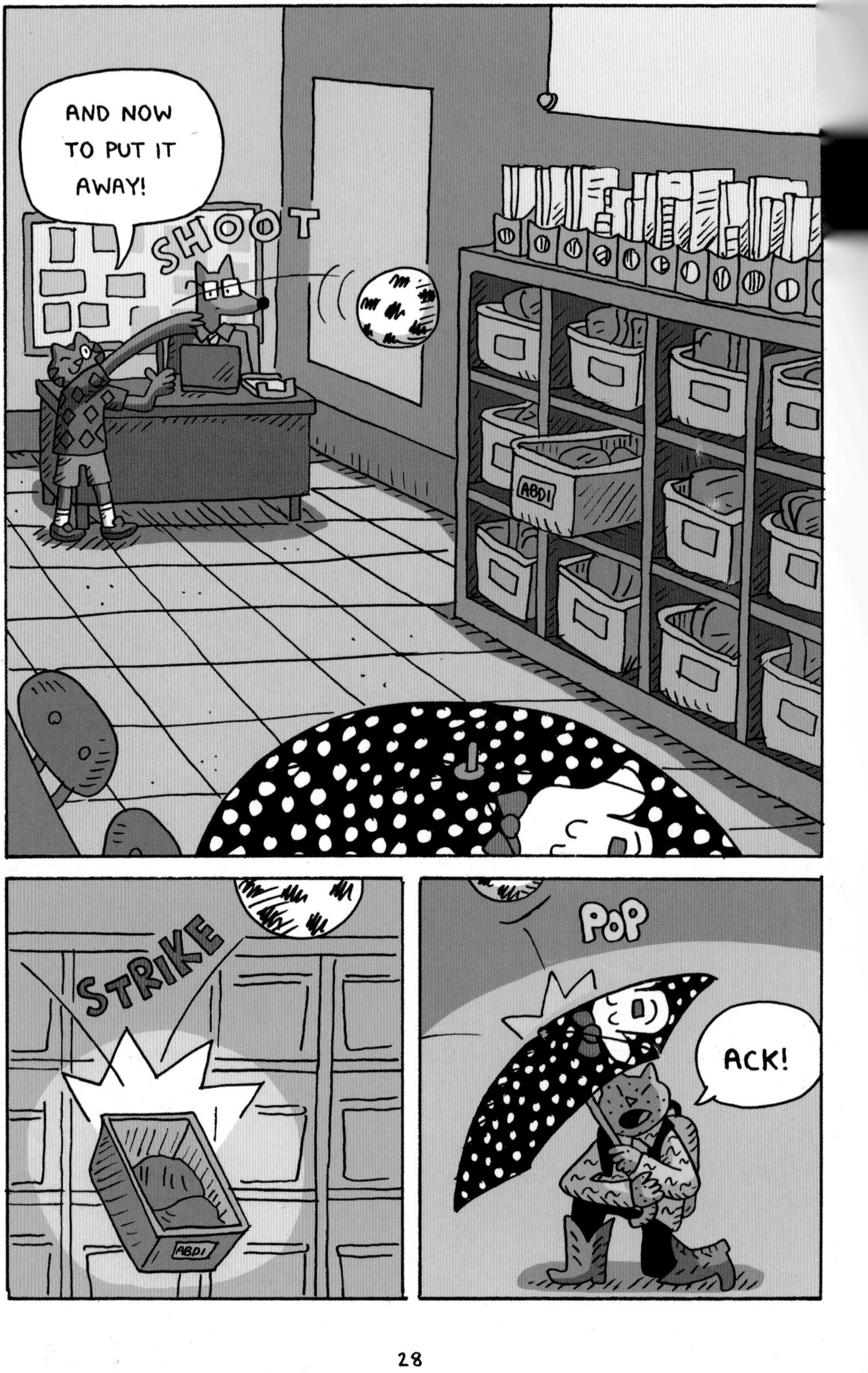
AND NOW TO PUT IT AWAY!
SHOOT
ABDI
STRIKE
ABDI
POP
ACK!

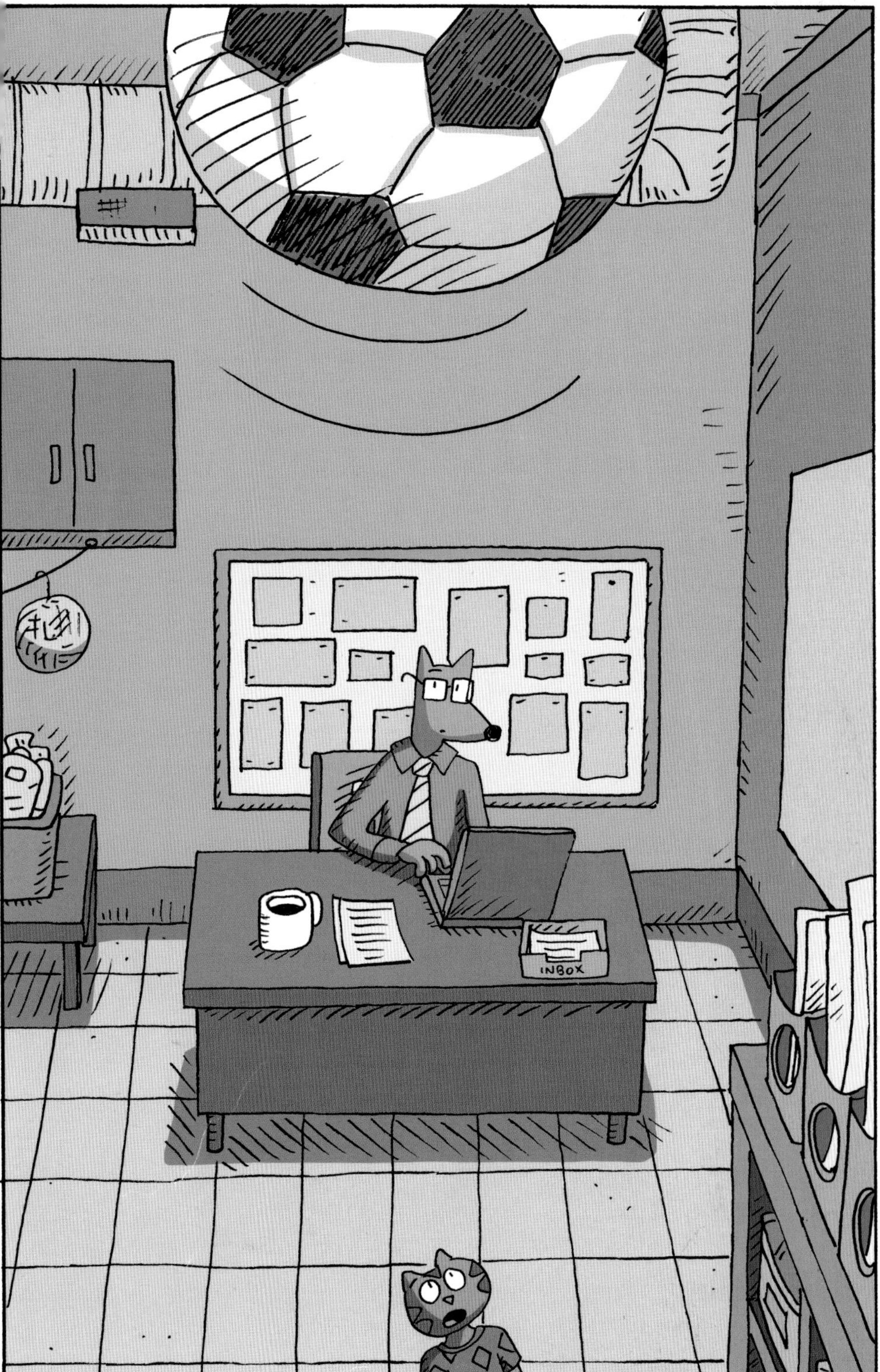
INBOX

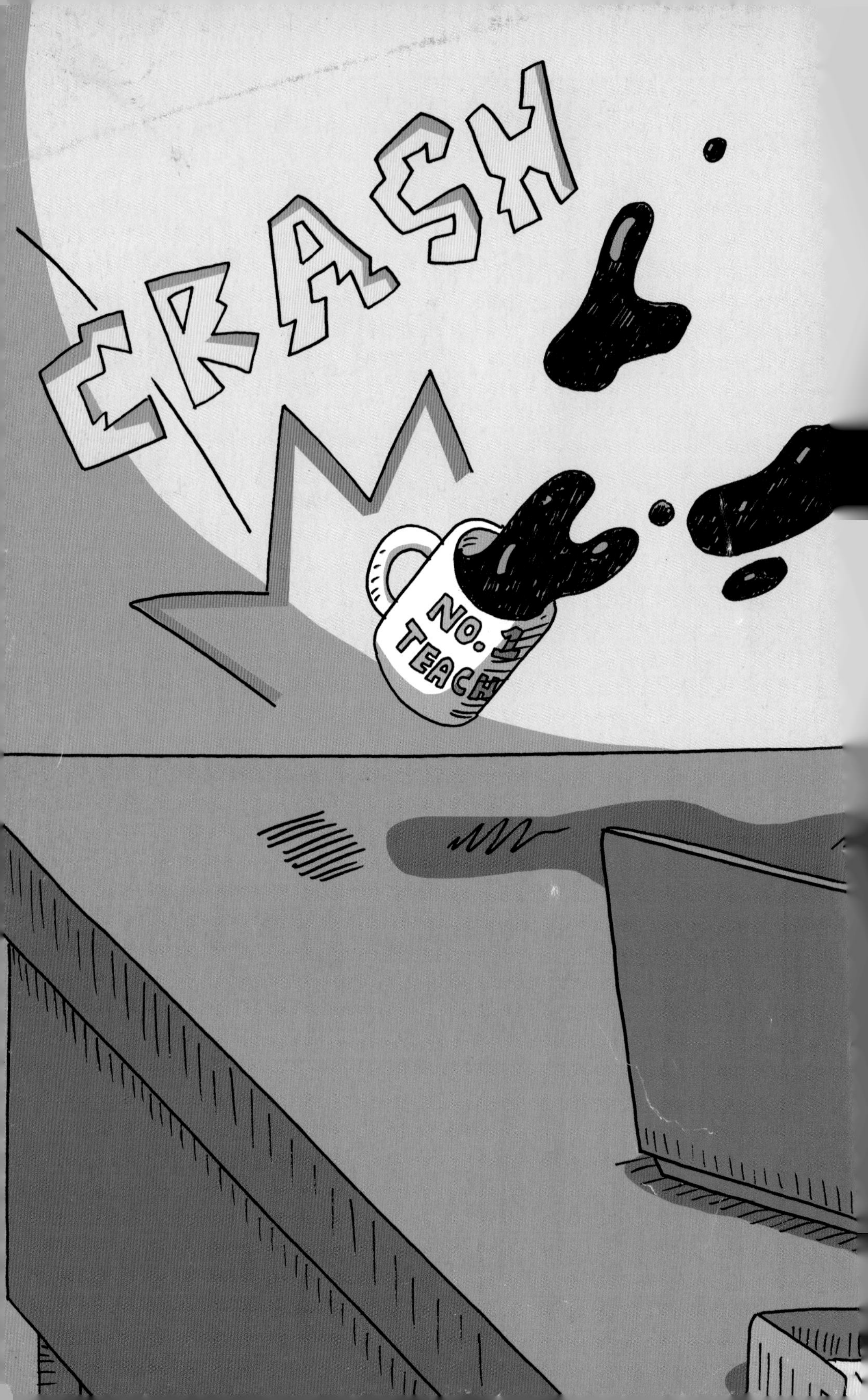
CRASH
NO. 1 TEACH

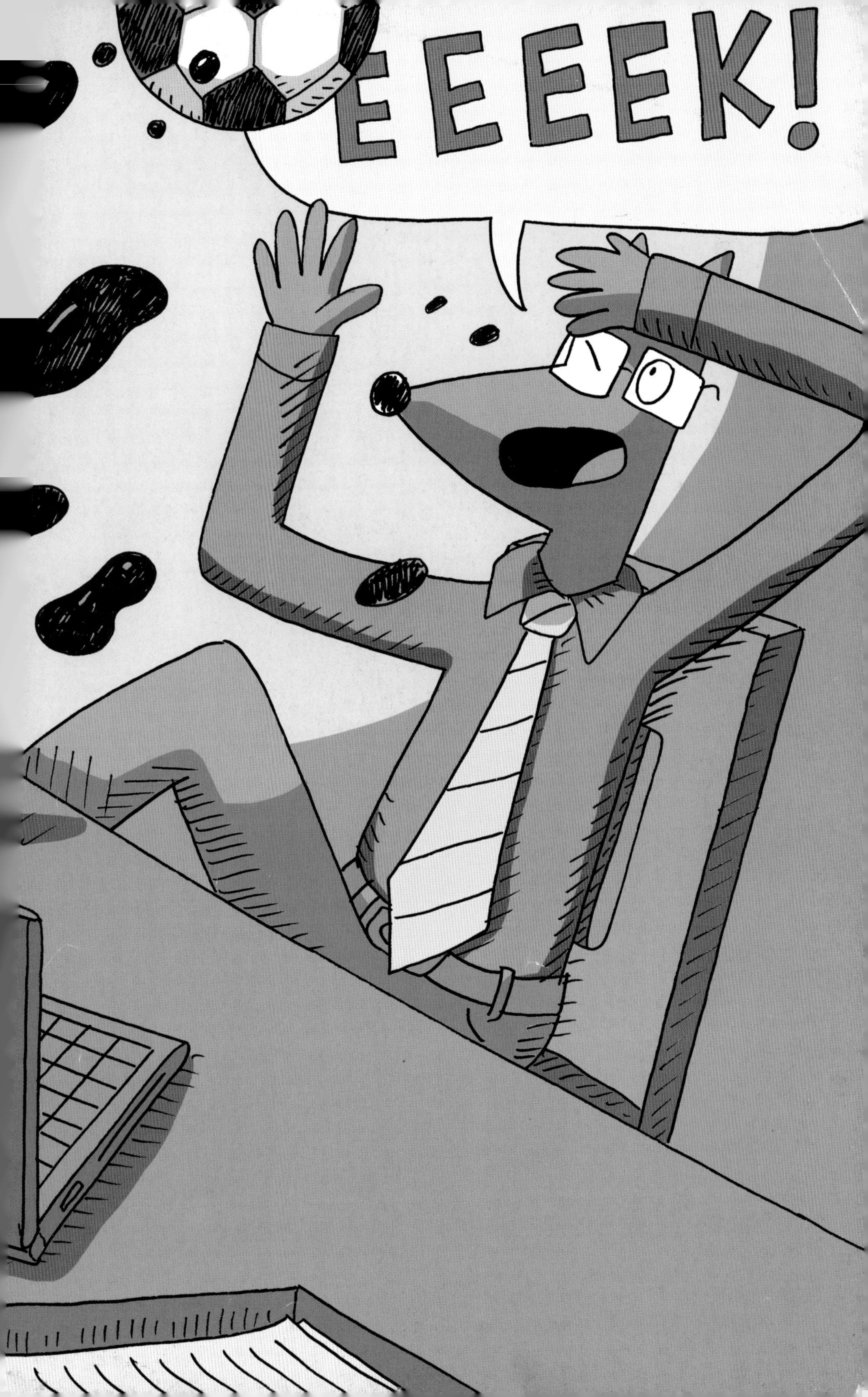
EEEEK!

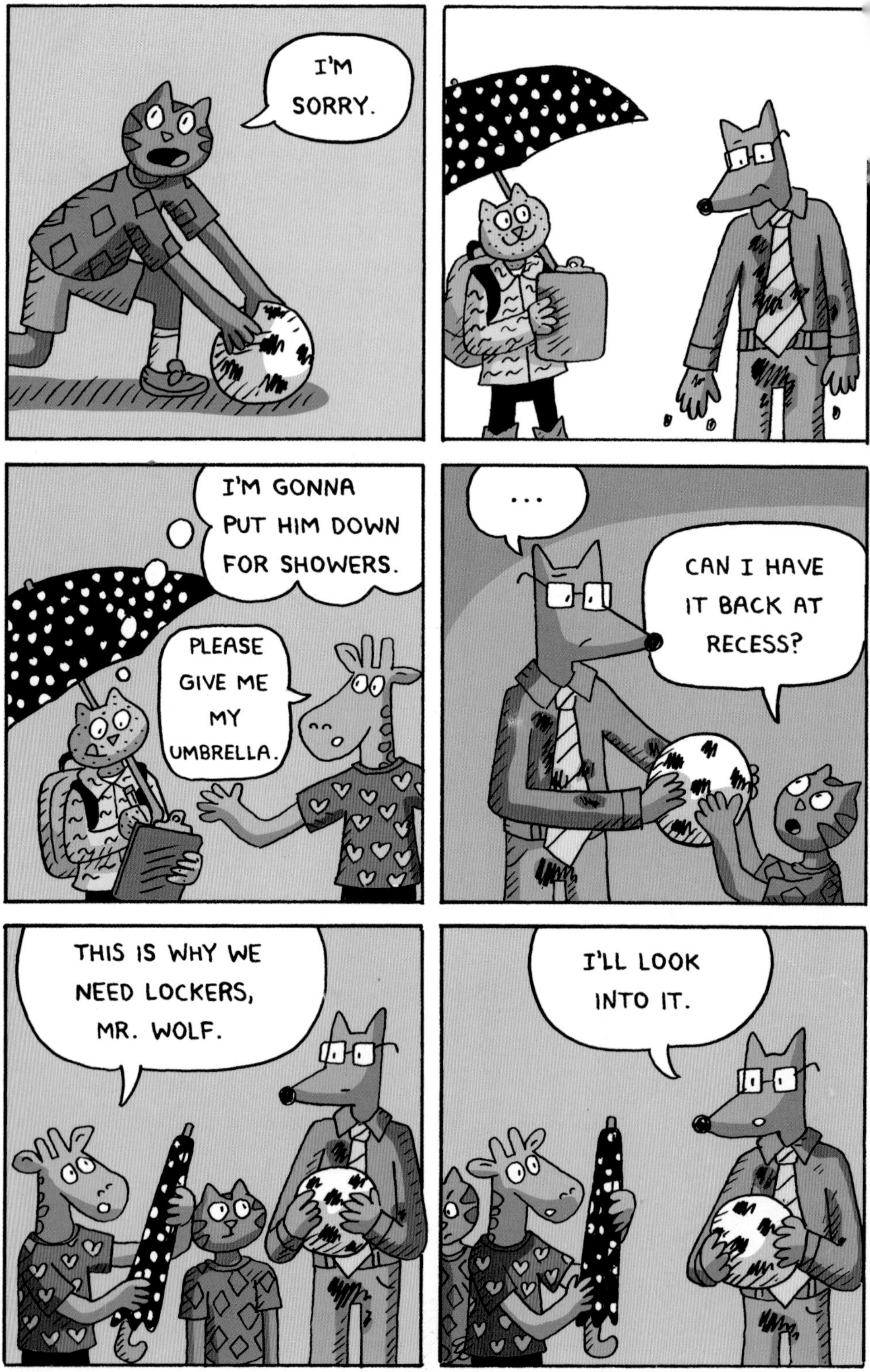
I'M SORRY.
I'M GONNA PUT HIM DOWN FOR SHOWERS.
PLEASE GIVE ME MY UMBRELLA.
...
CAN I HAVE IT BACK AT RECESS?
THIS IS WHY WE NEED LOCKERS, MR. WOLF.
I'LL LOOK INTO IT.

CHAPTER TWO
Mystery Club

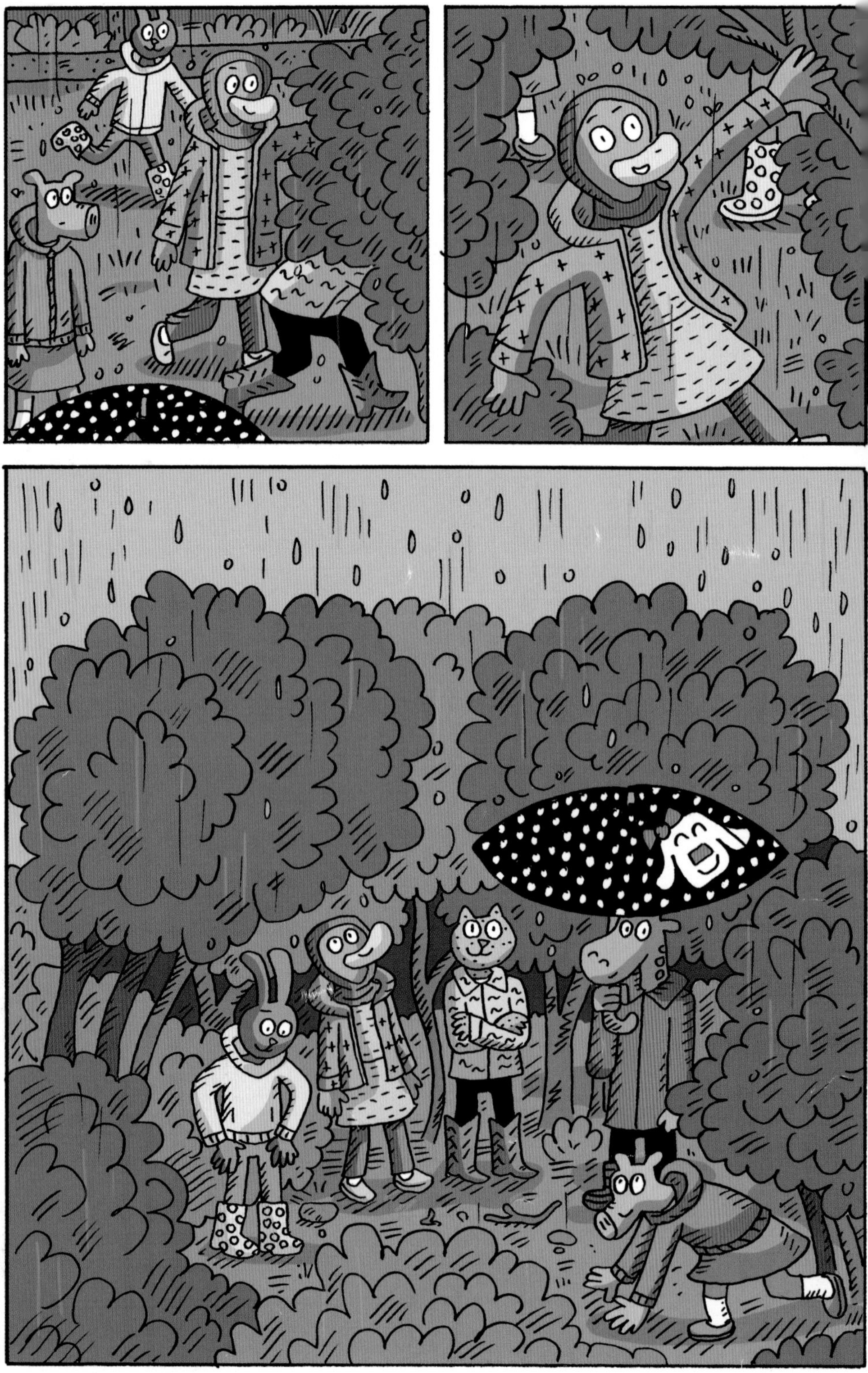

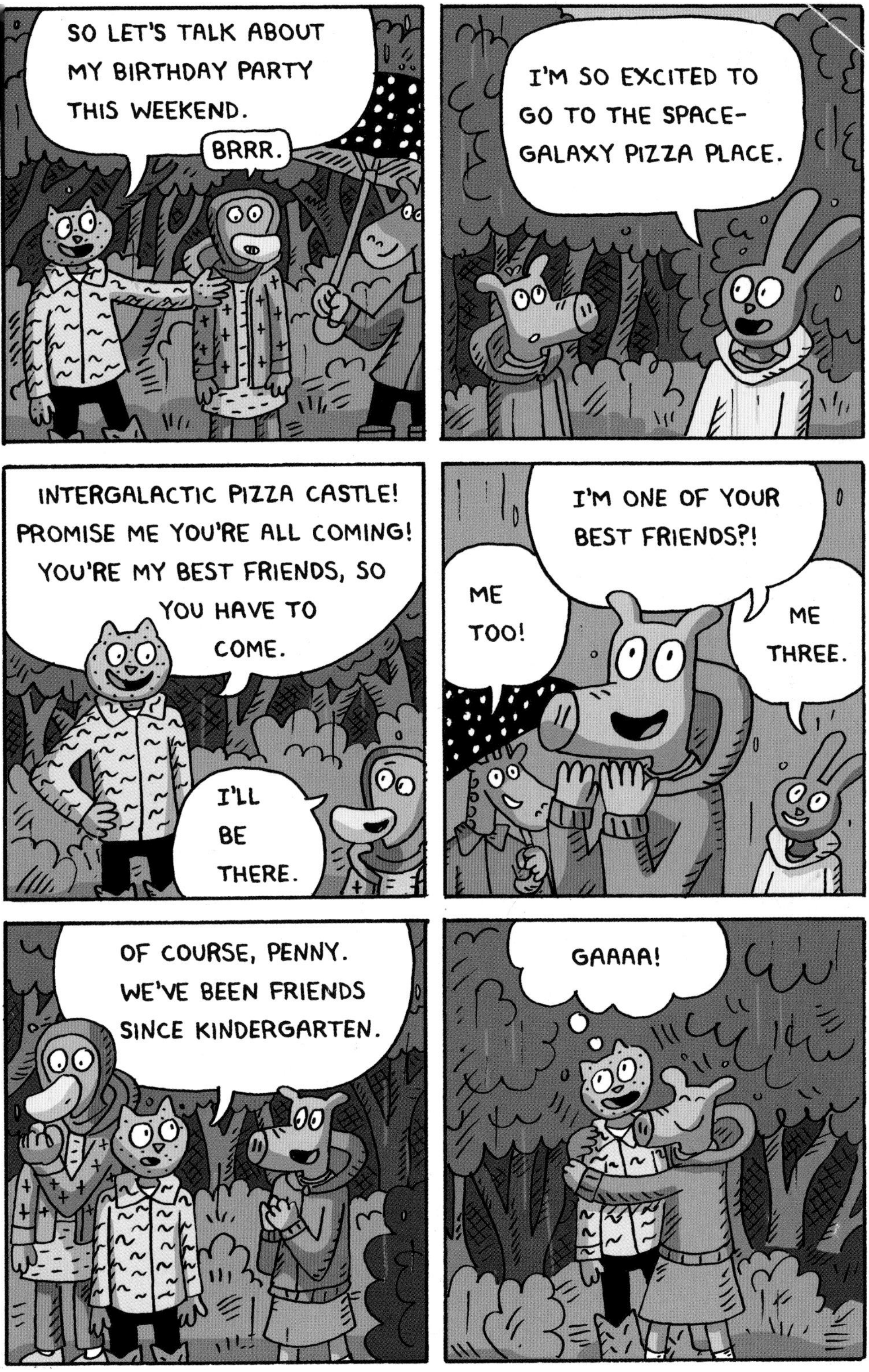
SO LET'S TALK ABOUT MY BIRTHDAY PARTY THIS WEEKEND.
BRRR.
I'M SO EXCITED TO GO TO THE SPACE-GALAXY PIZZA PLACE.
INTERGALACTIC PIZZA CASTLE! PROMISE ME YOU'RE ALL COMING! YOU'RE MY BEST FRIENDS, SO YOU HAVE TO COME.
I'LL BE THERE.
I'M ONE OF YOUR BEST FRIENDS?!
ME TOO!
ME THREE.
OF COURSE, PENNY. WE'VE BEEN FRIENDS SINCE KINDERGARTEN.
GAAAA!

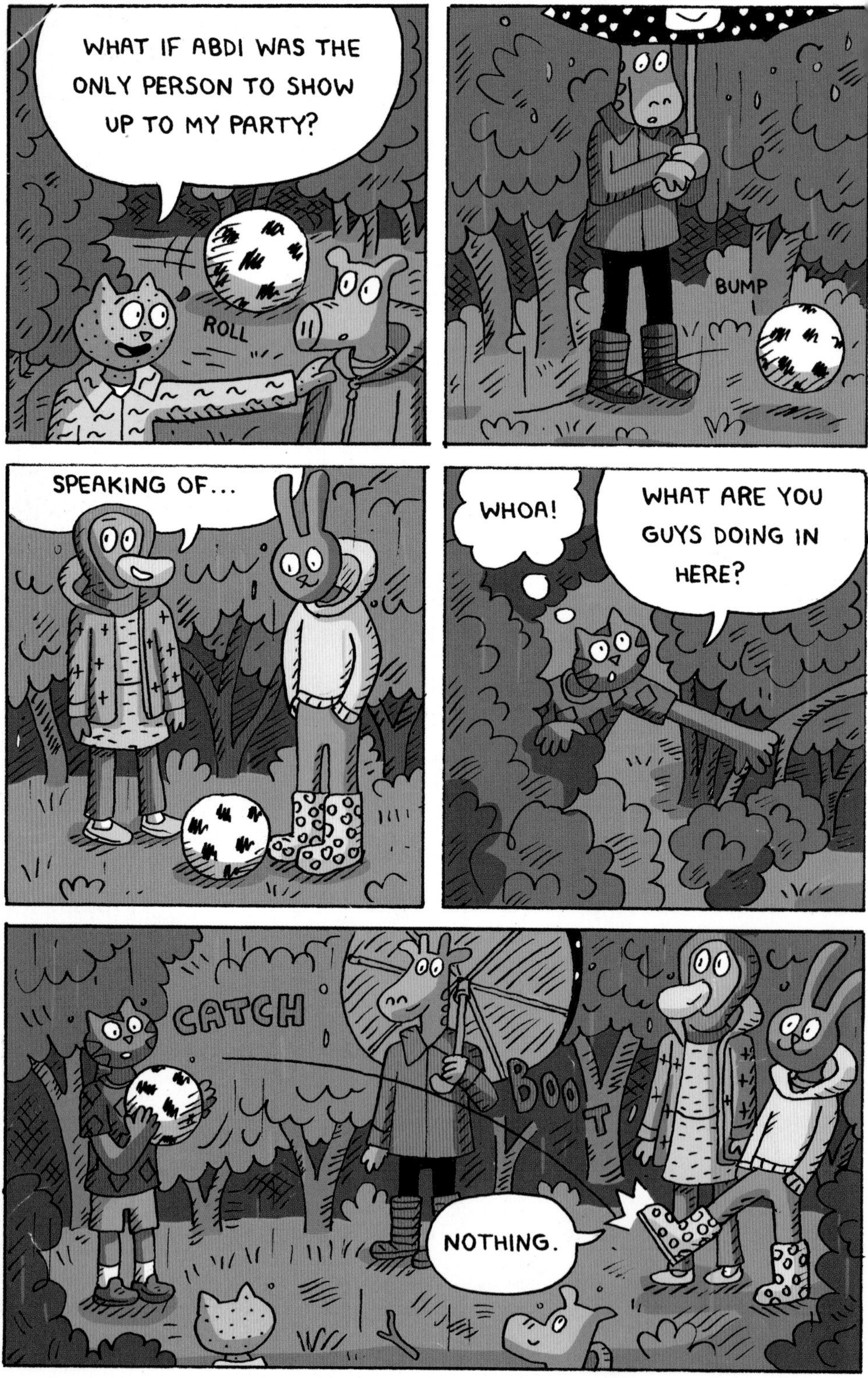
WHAT IF ABDI WAS THE ONLY PERSON TO SHOW UP TO MY PARTY?
ROLL
BUMP
SPEAKING OF...
WHOA!
WHAT ARE YOU GUYS DOING IN HERE?
CATCH
BOOT
NOTHING.

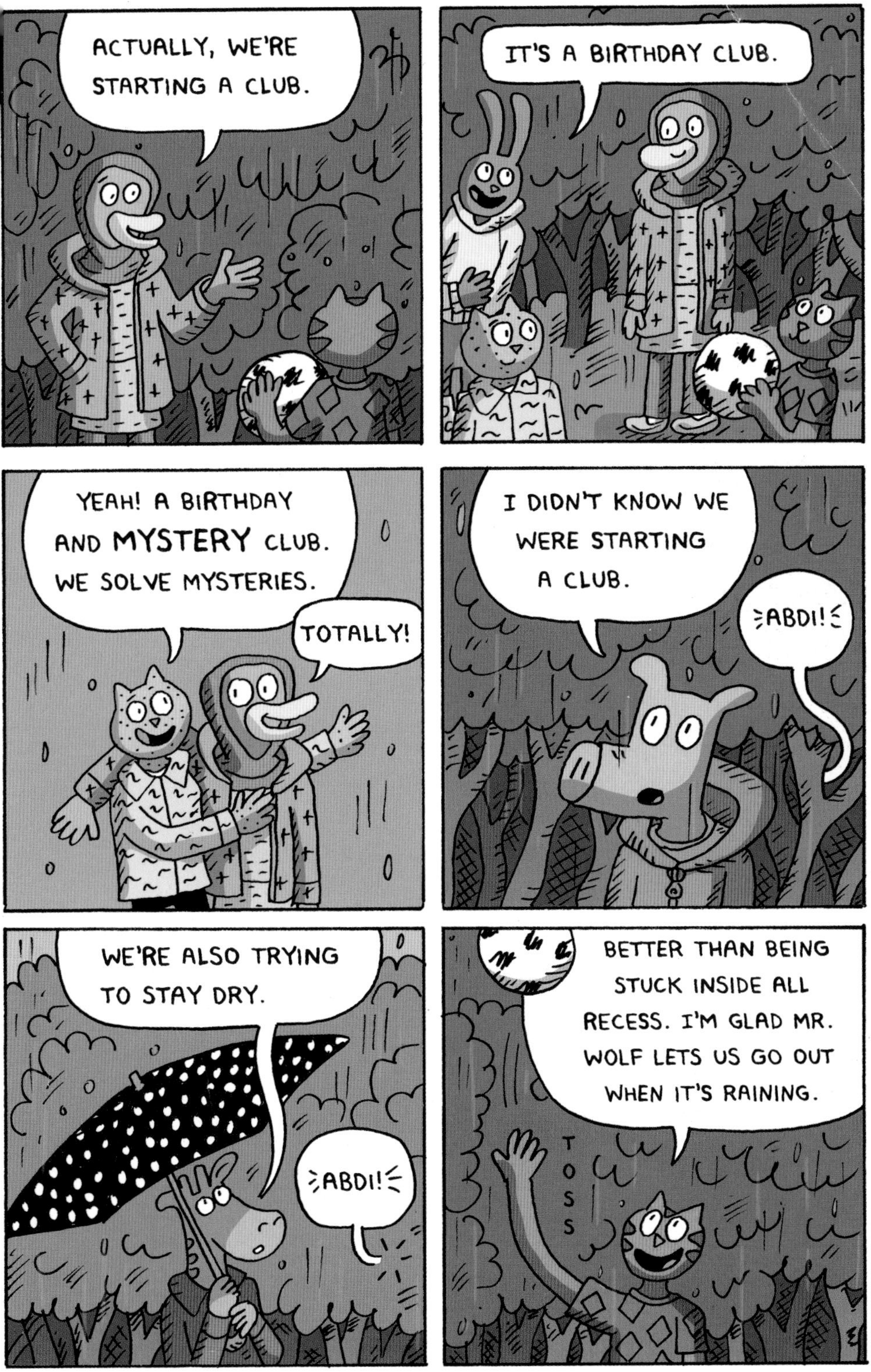

ACTUALLY, WE'RE STARTING A CLUB.
IT'S A BIRTHDAY CLUB.
YEAH! A BIRTHDAY AND MYSTERY CLUB. WE SOLVE MYSTERIES.
TOTALLY!
I DIDN'T KNOW WE WERE STARTING A CLUB.
ABDI!
WE'RE ALSO TRYING TO STAY DRY.
ABDI!
BETTER THAN BEING STUCK INSIDE ALL RECESS. I'M GLAD MR. WOLF LETS US GO OUT WHEN IT'S RAINING.
TOSS

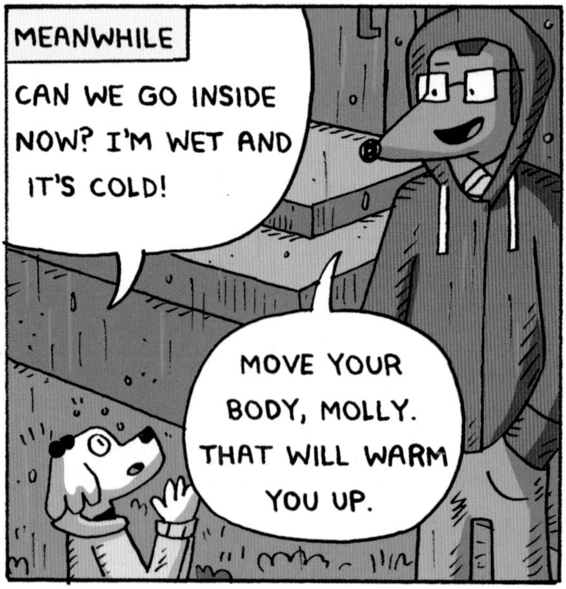
MEANWHILE
CAN WE GO INSIDE NOW? I'M WET AND IT'S COLD!
MOVE YOUR BODY, MOLLY. THAT WILL WARM YOU UP.

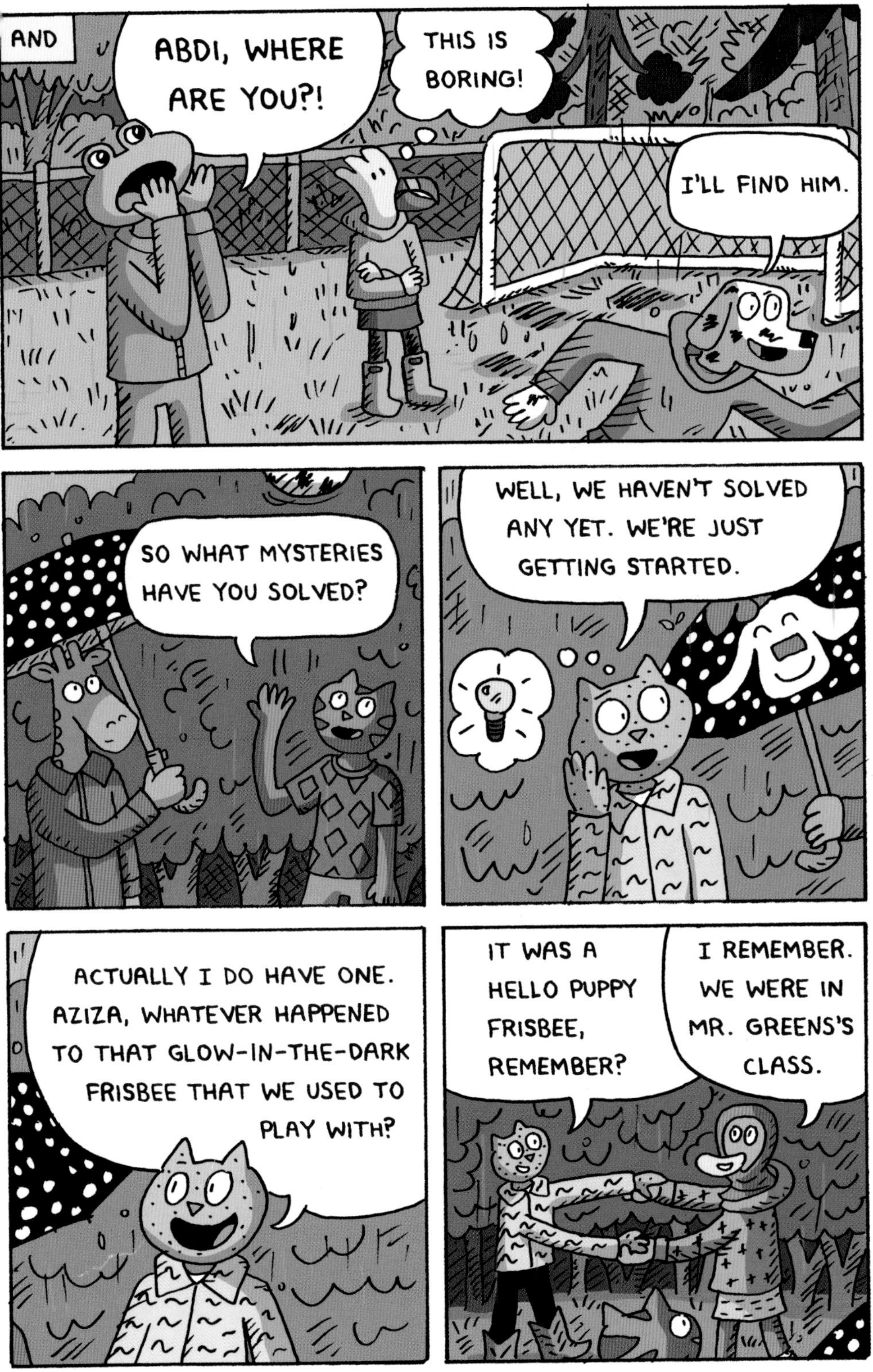
AND
ABDI, WHERE ARE YOU?!
THIS IS BORING!
I'LL FIND HIM.
SO WHAT MYSTERIES HAVE YOU SOLVED?
WELL, WE HAVEN'T SOLVED ANY YET. WE'RE JUST GETTING STARTED.
ACTUALLY I DO HAVE ONE. AZIZA, WHATEVER HAPPENED TO THAT GLOW-IN-THE-DARK FRISBEE THAT WE USED TO PLAY WITH?
IT WAS A HELLO PUPPY FRISBEE, REMEMBER?
I REMEMBER. WE WERE IN MR. GREENS'S CLASS.

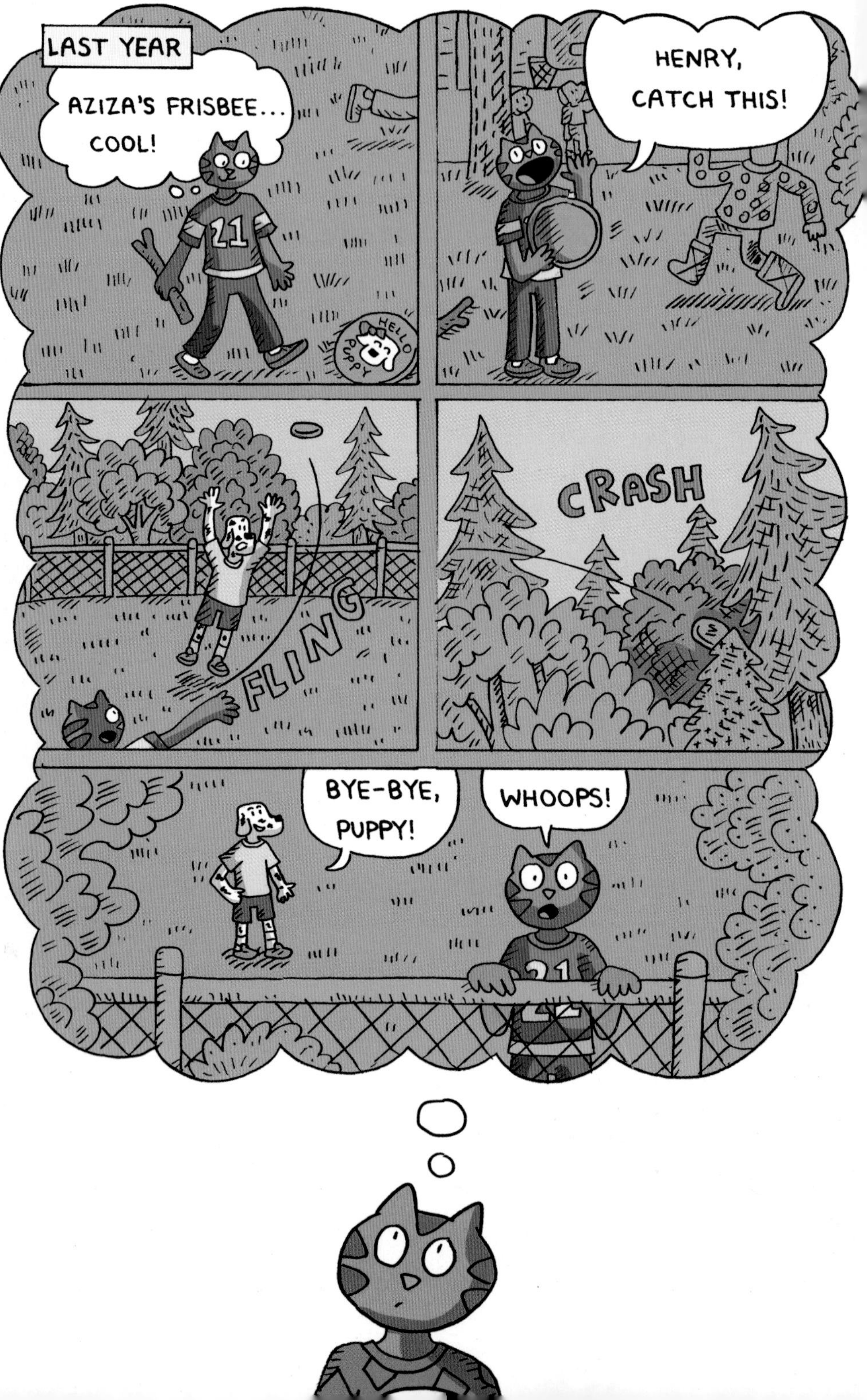
LAST YEAR
AZIZA'S FRISBEE... COOL!
HELLO PUPPY
HENRY, CATCH THIS!
FLING
CRASH
BYE-BYE, PUPPY!
WHOOPS!

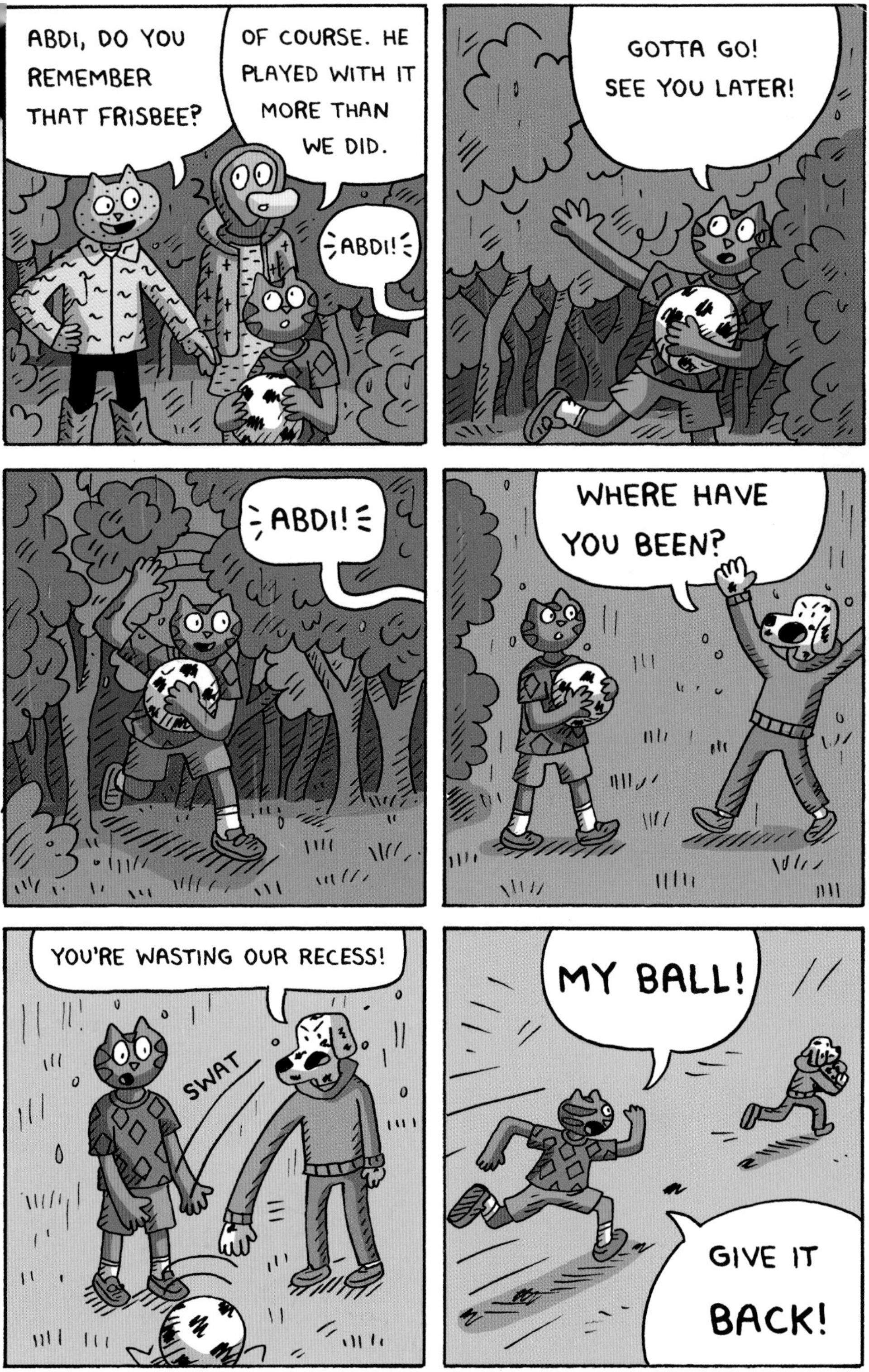
ABDI, DO YOU REMEMBER THAT FRISBEE?
OF COURSE. HE PLAYED WITH IT MORE THAN WE DID.
ABDI!
GOTTA GO! SEE YOU LATER!
ABDI!
WHERE HAVE YOU BEEN?
YOU'RE WASTING OUR RECESS!
SWAT
MY BALL!
GIVE IT BACK!

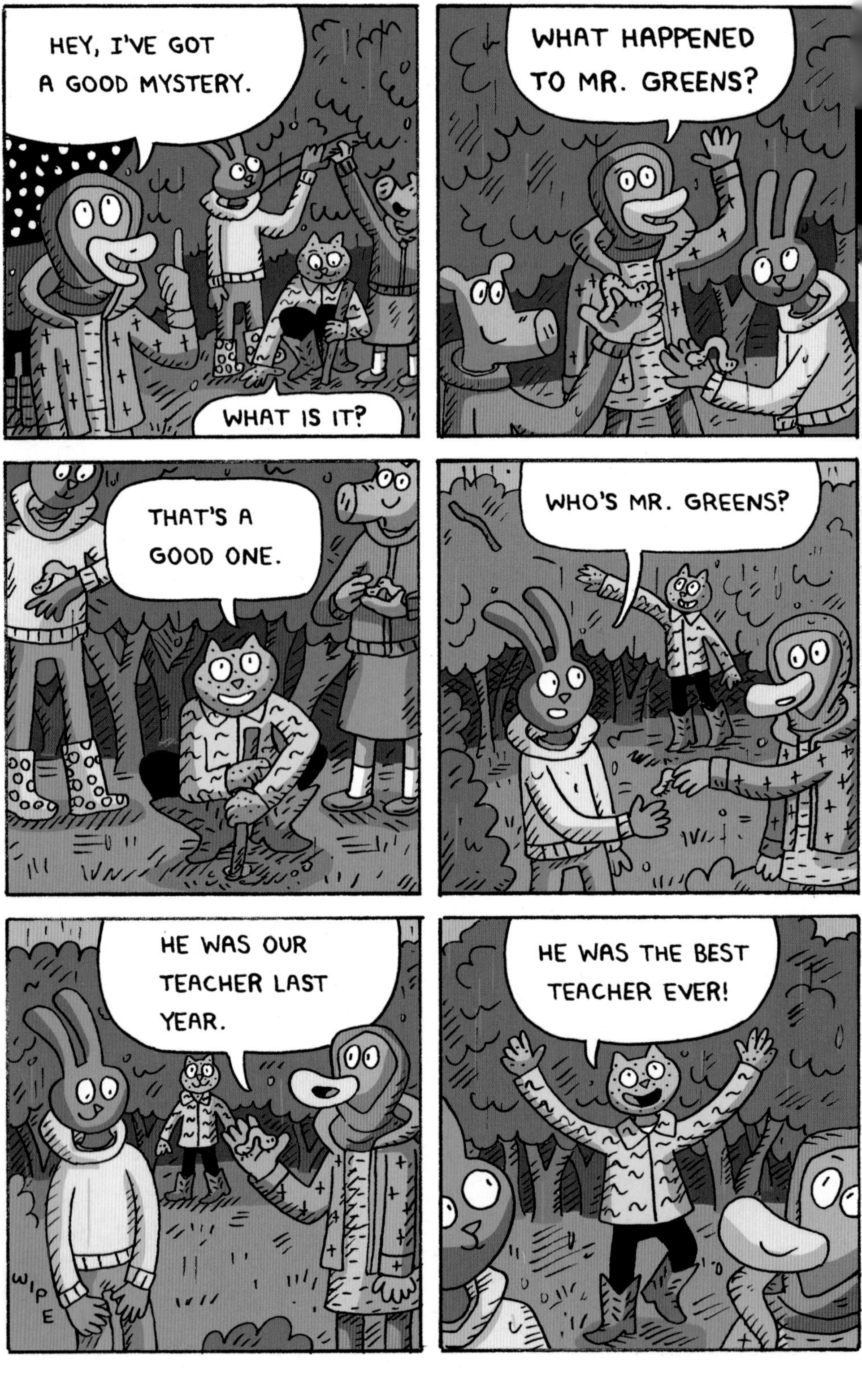
HEY, I'VE GOT A GOOD MYSTERY.
WHAT IS IT?
WHAT HAPPENED TO MR. GREENS?
THAT'S A GOOD ONE.
WHO'S MR. GREENS?
HE WAS OUR TEACHER LAST YEAR.
WIPE
HE WAS THE BEST TEACHER EVER!

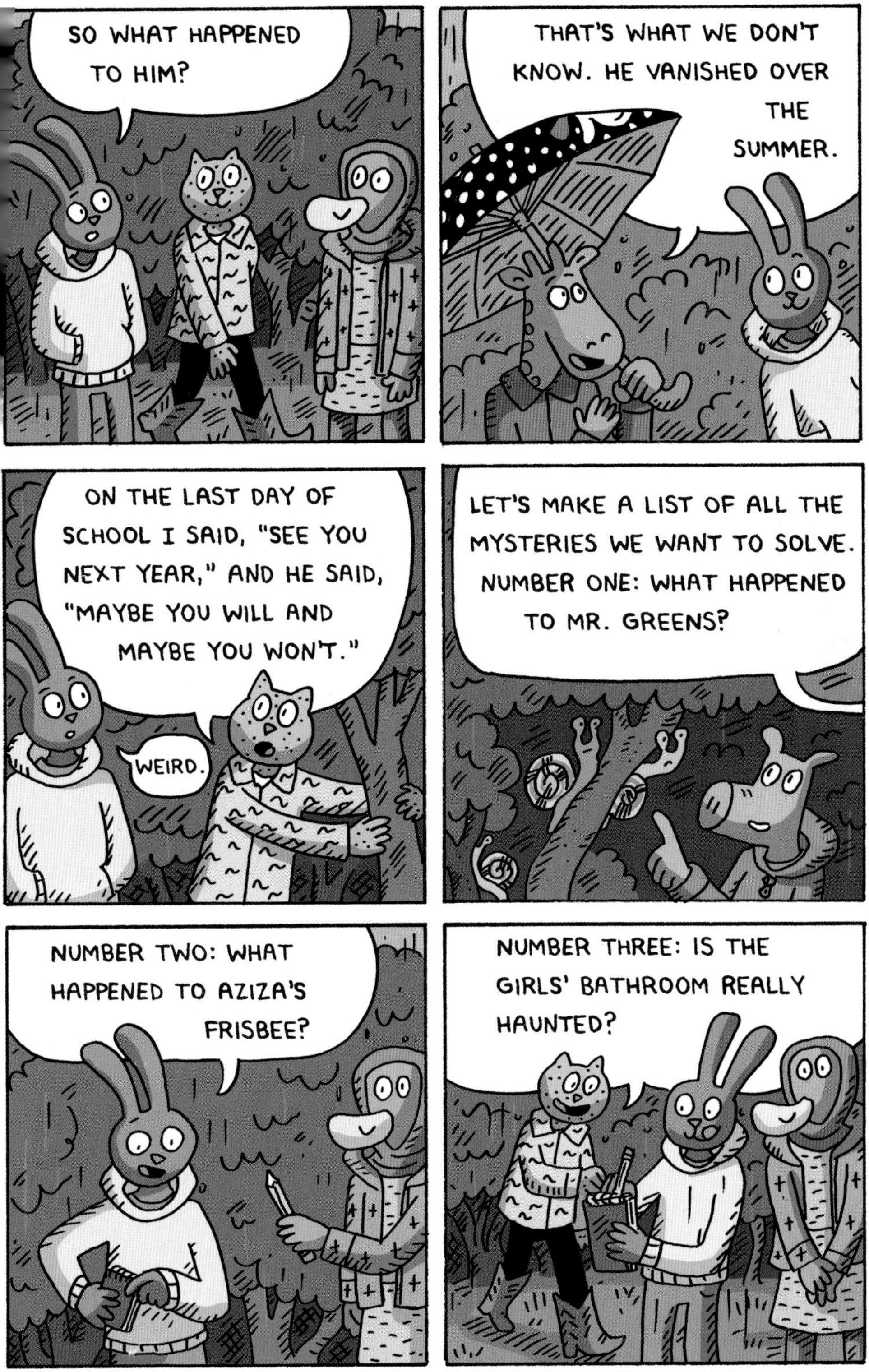
SO WHAT HAPPENED TO HIM?
THAT'S WHAT WE DON'T KNOW. HE VANISHED OVER THE SUMMER.
ON THE LAST DAY OF SCHOOL I SAID, "SEE YOU NEXT YEAR," AND HE SAID, "MAYBE YOU WILL AND MAYBE YOU WON'T."
WEIRD.
LET'S MAKE A LIST OF ALL THE MYSTERIES WE WANT TO SOLVE. NUMBER ONE: WHAT HAPPENED TO MR. GREENS?
NUMBER TWO: WHAT HAPPENED TO AZIZA'S FRISBEE?
NUMBER THREE: IS THE GIRLS' BATHROOM REALLY HAUNTED?

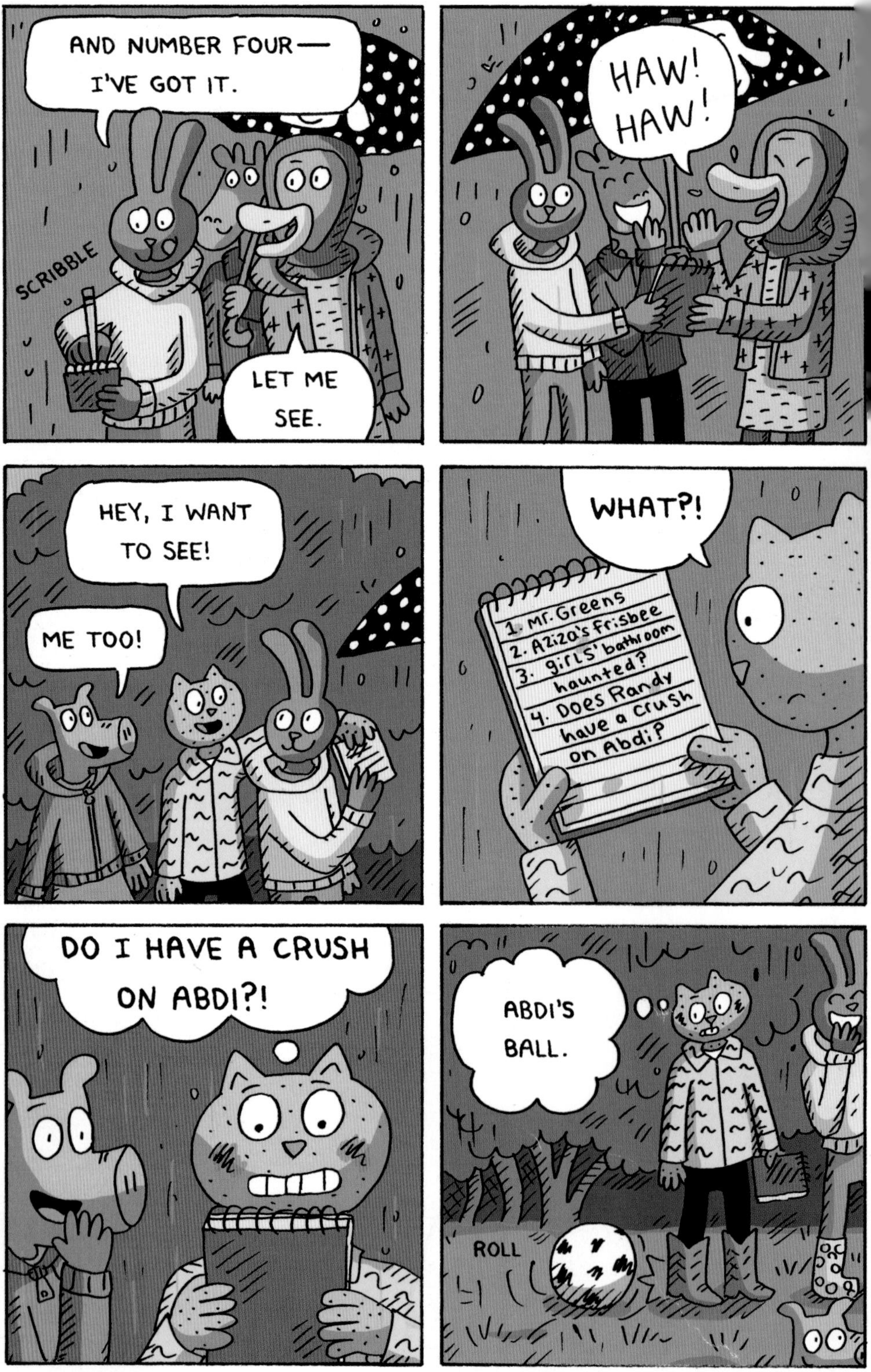
AND NUMBER FOUR— I'VE GOT IT.
SCRIBBLE
LET ME SEE.
HAW! HAW!
HEY, I WANT TO SEE!
ME TOO!
WHAT?!
1. Mr. Greens
2. Aziza's frisbee
3. girls' bathroom haunted?
4. Does Randy have a crush on Abdi?
DO I HAVE A CRUSH ON ABDI?!
ABDI'S BALL.
ROLL

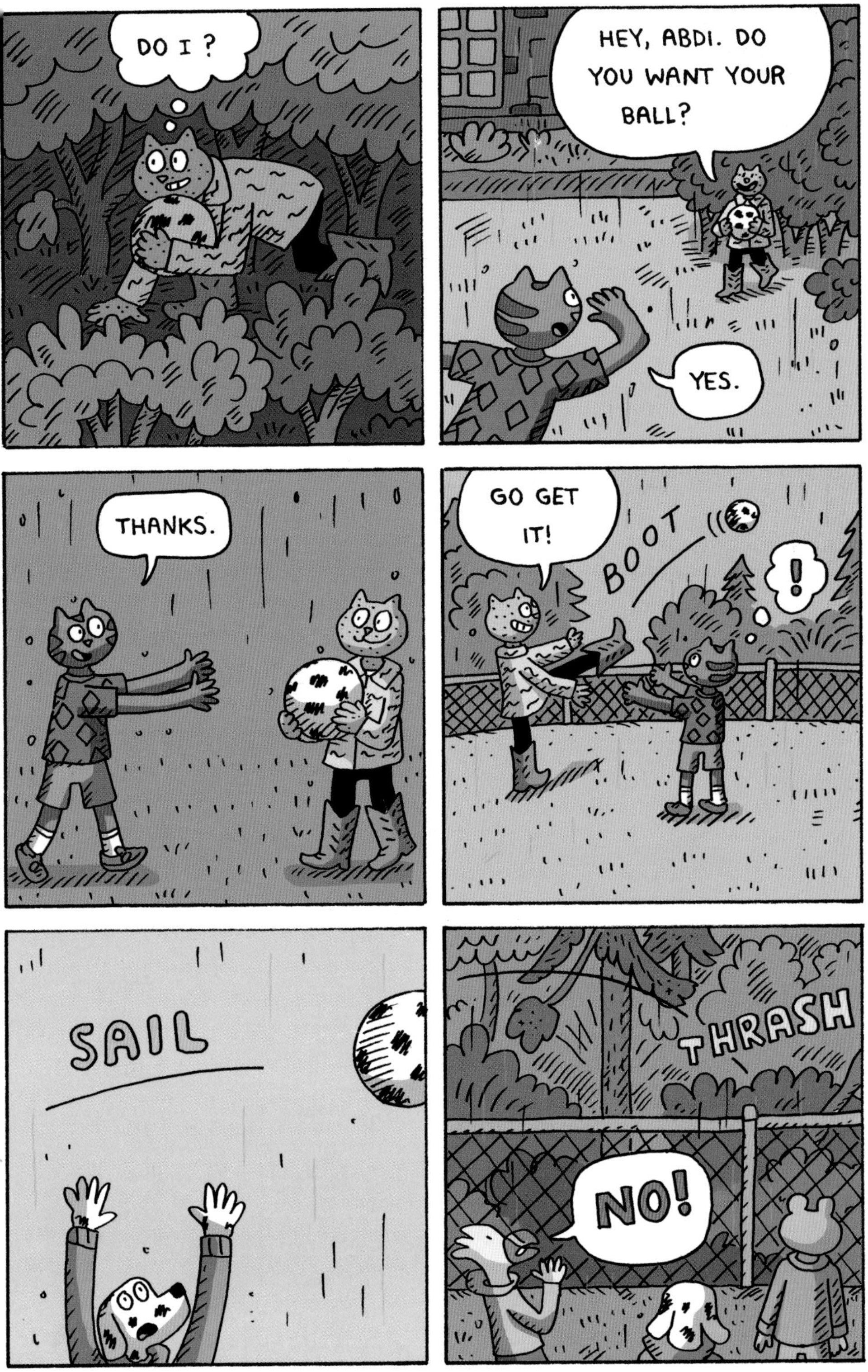

DO I ?
HEY, ABDI. DO YOU WANT YOUR BALL?
YES.
THANKS.
GO GET IT!
BOOT
!
SAIL
THRASH
NO!

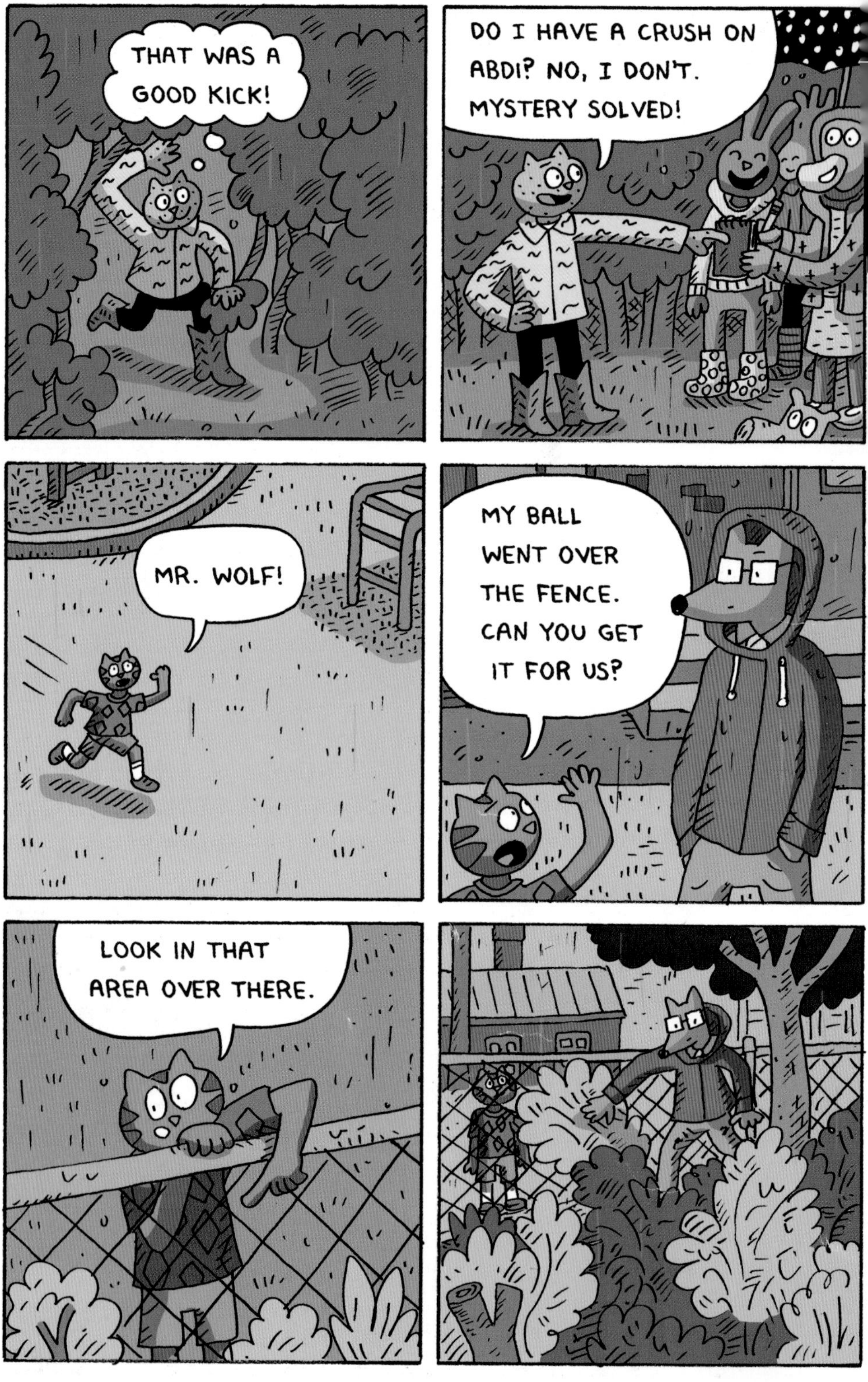
THAT WAS A GOOD KICK!
DO I HAVE A CRUSH ON ABDI? NO, I DON'T. MYSTERY SOLVED!
MR. WOLF!
MY BALL WENT OVER THE FENCE. CAN YOU GET IT FOR US?
LOOK IN THAT AREA OVER THERE.

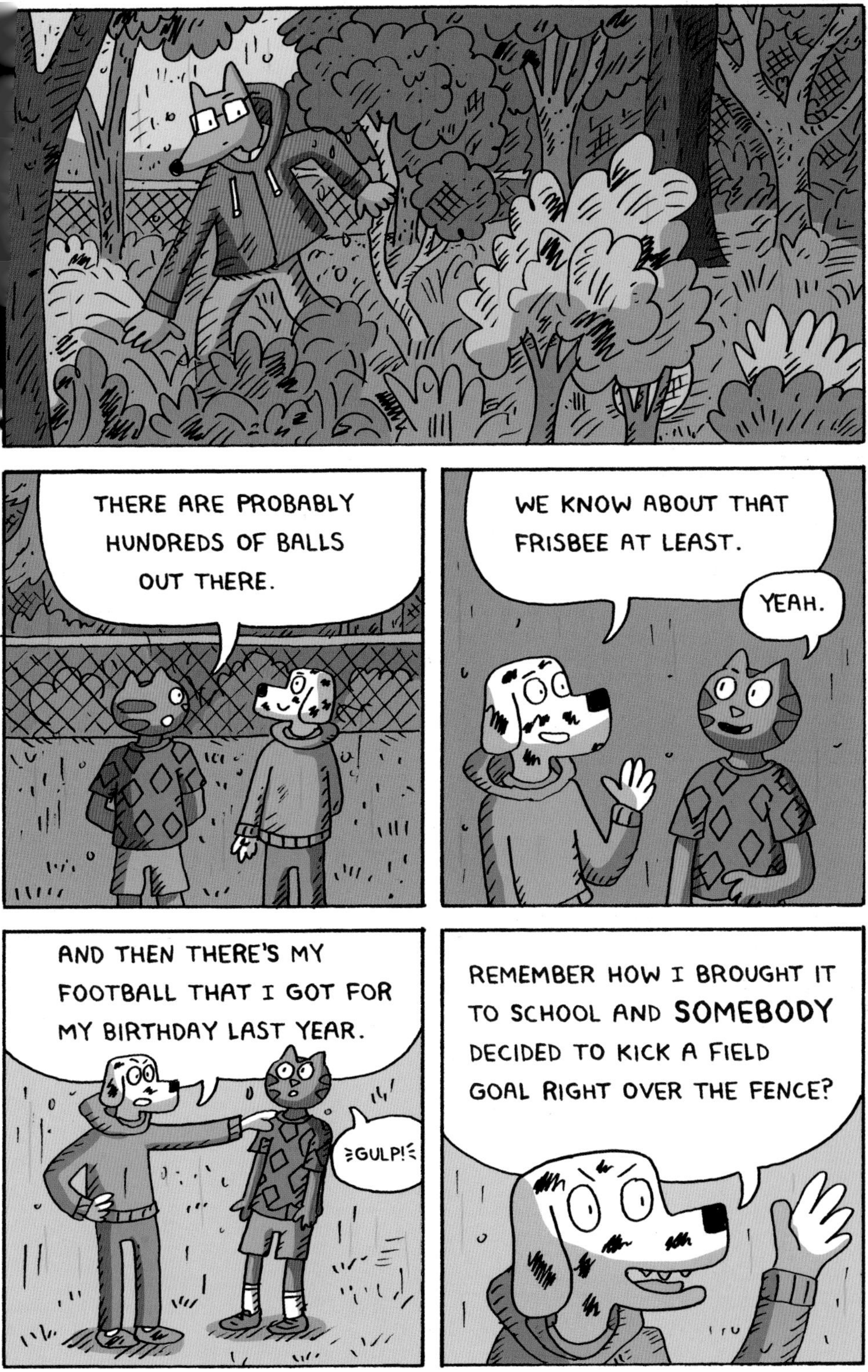
THERE ARE PROBABLY HUNDREDS OF BALLS OUT THERE.
WE KNOW ABOUT THAT FRISBEE AT LEAST.
YEAH.
AND THEN THERE'S MY FOOTBALL THAT I GOT FOR MY BIRTHDAY LAST YEAR.
GULP!
REMEMBER HOW I BROUGHT IT TO SCHOOL AND SOMEBODY DECIDED TO KICK A FIELD GOAL RIGHT OVER THE FENCE?

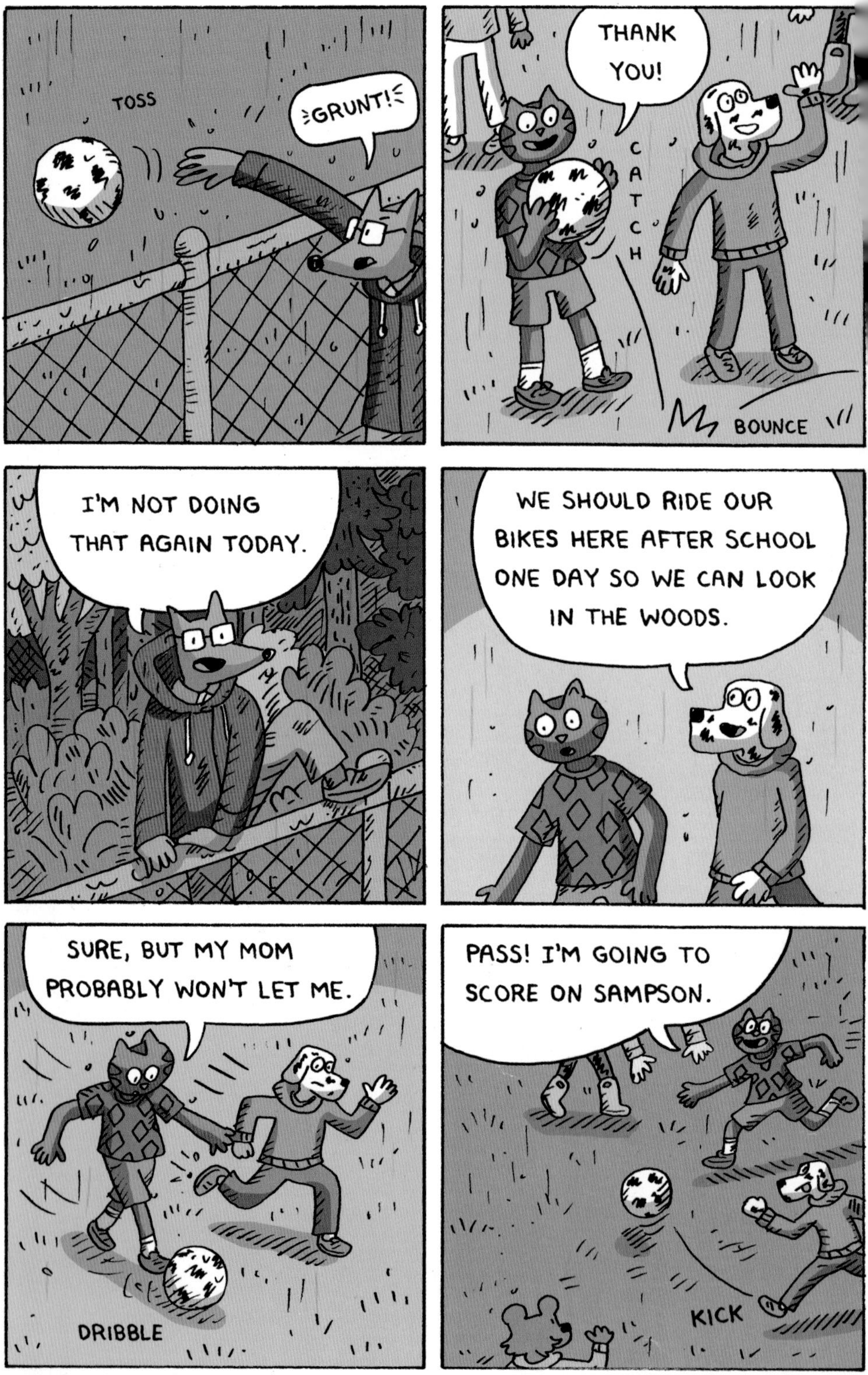
TOSS
GRUNT!
THANK YOU!
CATCH
BOUNCE
I'M NOT DOING THAT AGAIN TODAY.
WE SHOULD RIDE OUR BIKES HERE AFTER SCHOOL ONE DAY SO WE CAN LOOK IN THE WOODS.
SURE, BUT MY MOM PROBABLY WON'T LET ME.
DRIBBLE
PASS! I'M GOING TO SCORE ON SAMPSON.
KICK

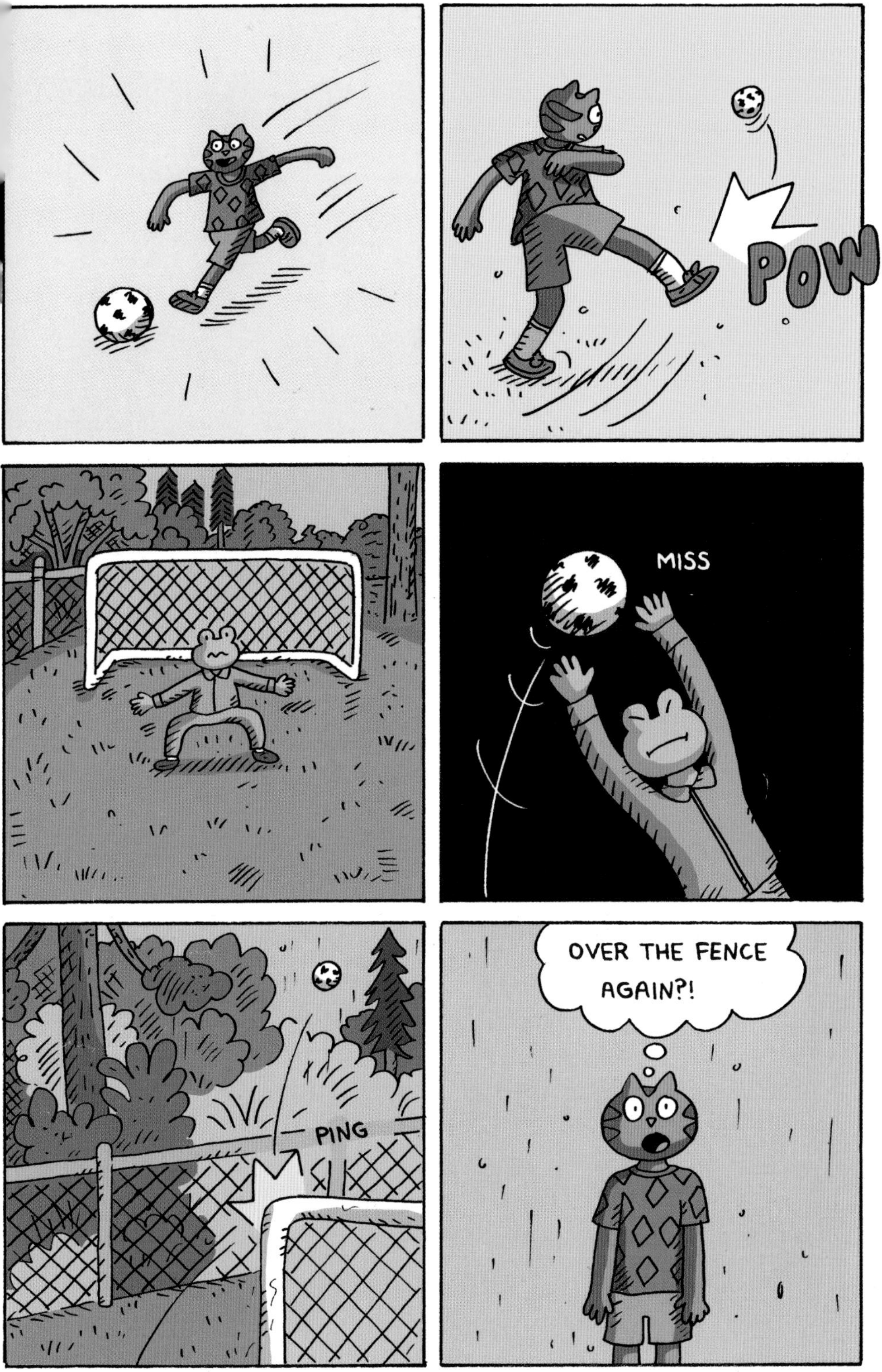
POW
MISS
PING
OVER THE FENCE AGAIN?!

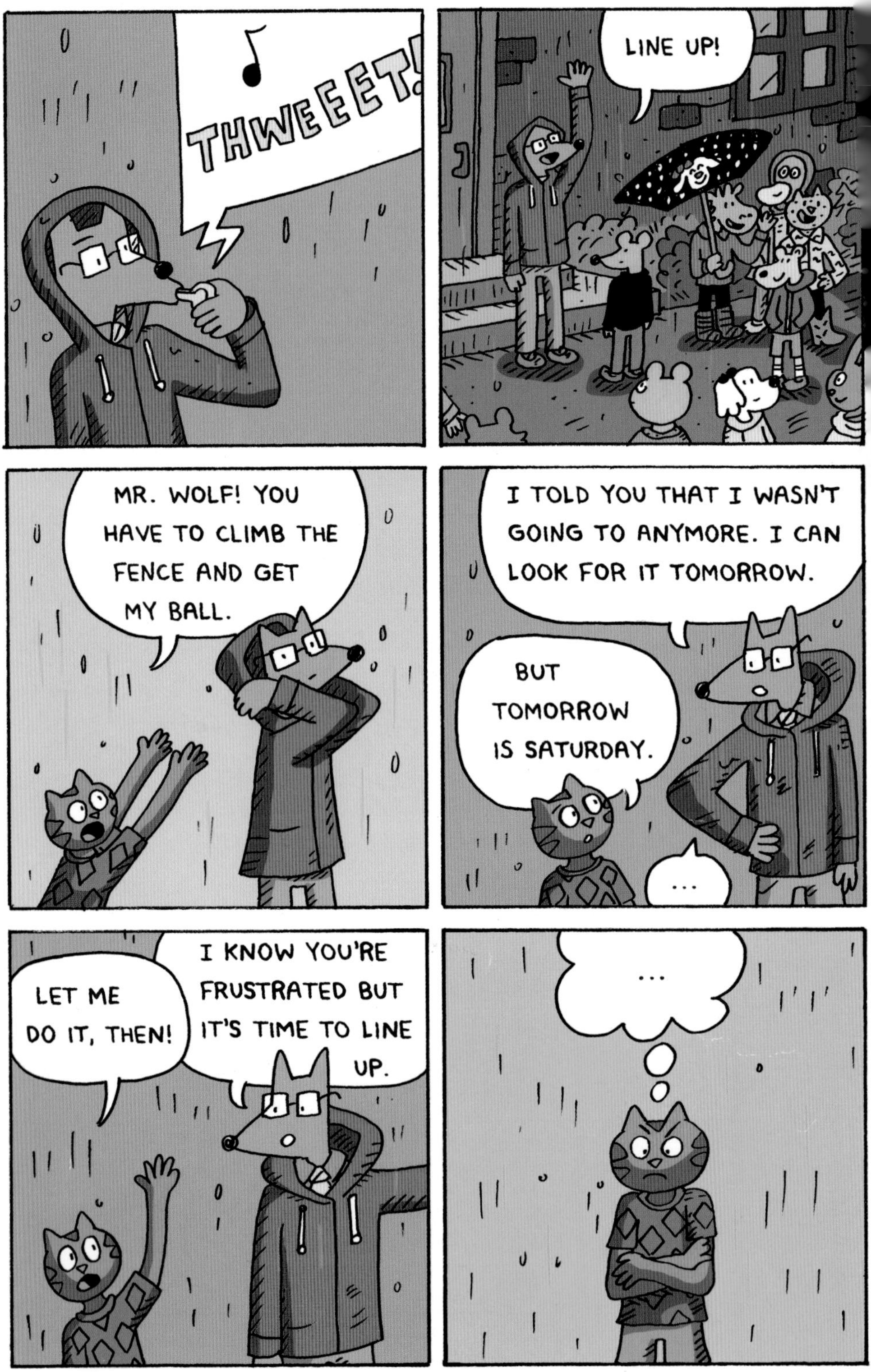
THWEEET!
LINE UP!
MR. WOLF! YOU HAVE TO CLIMB THE FENCE AND GET MY BALL.
I TOLD YOU THAT I WASN'T GOING TO ANYMORE. I CAN LOOK FOR IT TOMORROW.
BUT TOMORROW IS SATURDAY.
...
LET ME DO IT, THEN!
I KNOW YOU'RE FRUSTRATED BUT IT'S TIME TO LINE UP.
...

CHAPTER THREE

Anything Is Possible

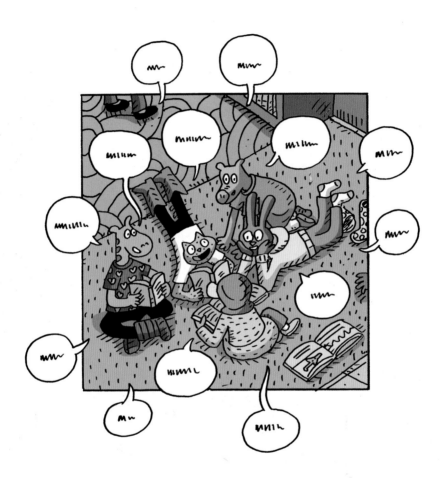

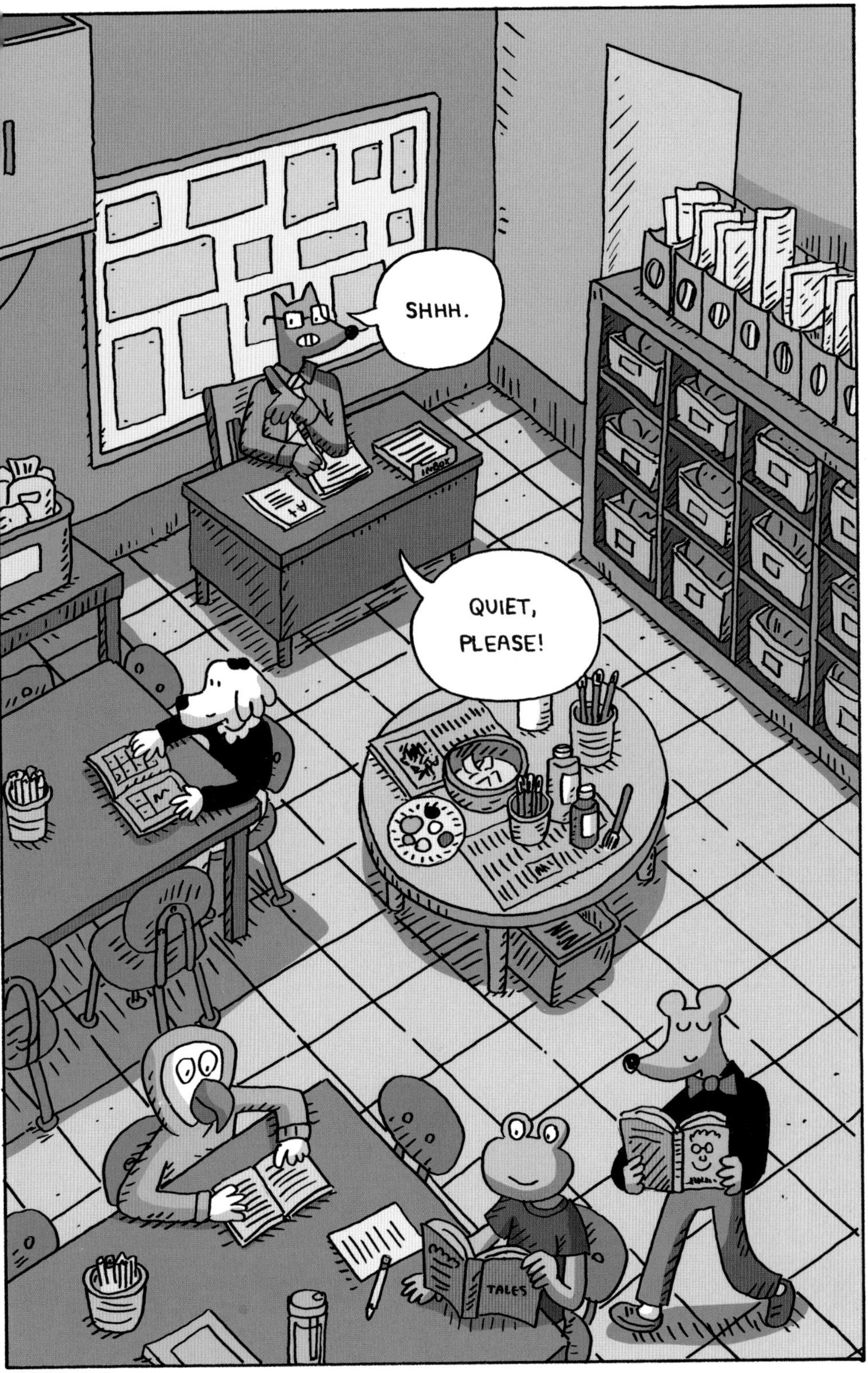
SHHH.
QUIET, PLEASE!
A+
INBOX
TALES

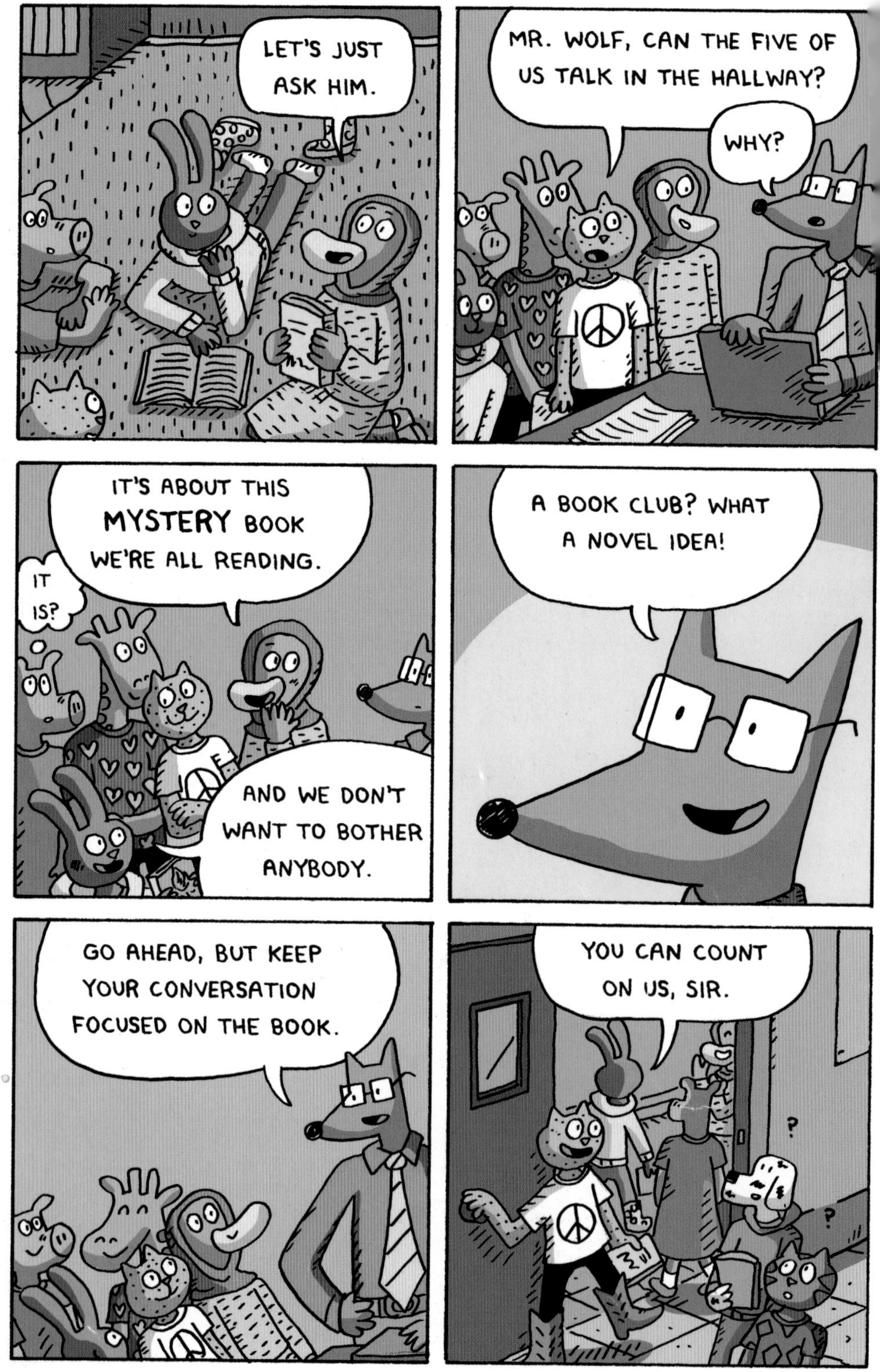

LET'S JUST ASK HIM.
MR. WOLF, CAN THE FIVE OF US TALK IN THE HALLWAY?
WHY?
IT'S ABOUT THIS MYSTERY BOOK WE'RE ALL READING.
IT IS?
AND WE DON'T WANT TO BOTHER ANYBODY.
A BOOK CLUB? WHAT A NOVEL IDEA!
GO AHEAD, BUT KEEP YOUR CONVERSATION FOCUSED ON THE BOOK.
YOU CAN COUNT ON US, SIR.
?
?

CAN WE GO IN THE HALLWAY, TOO?
PLEASE.
TO DO WHAT?
I DON'T KNOW.
SHRUG
TO READ, STUPID.
YOU CAN READ IN HERE. AND NO NAME-CALLING.
WHAT?!
BUT...
DON'T ARGUE WITH ME.
GET A BOOK.
SLAM
UNFAIR! UNFAIR!
QUIET, PLEASE!
POUND

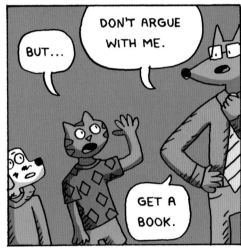

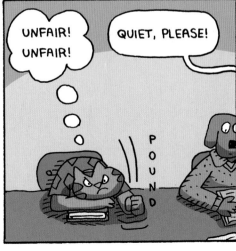

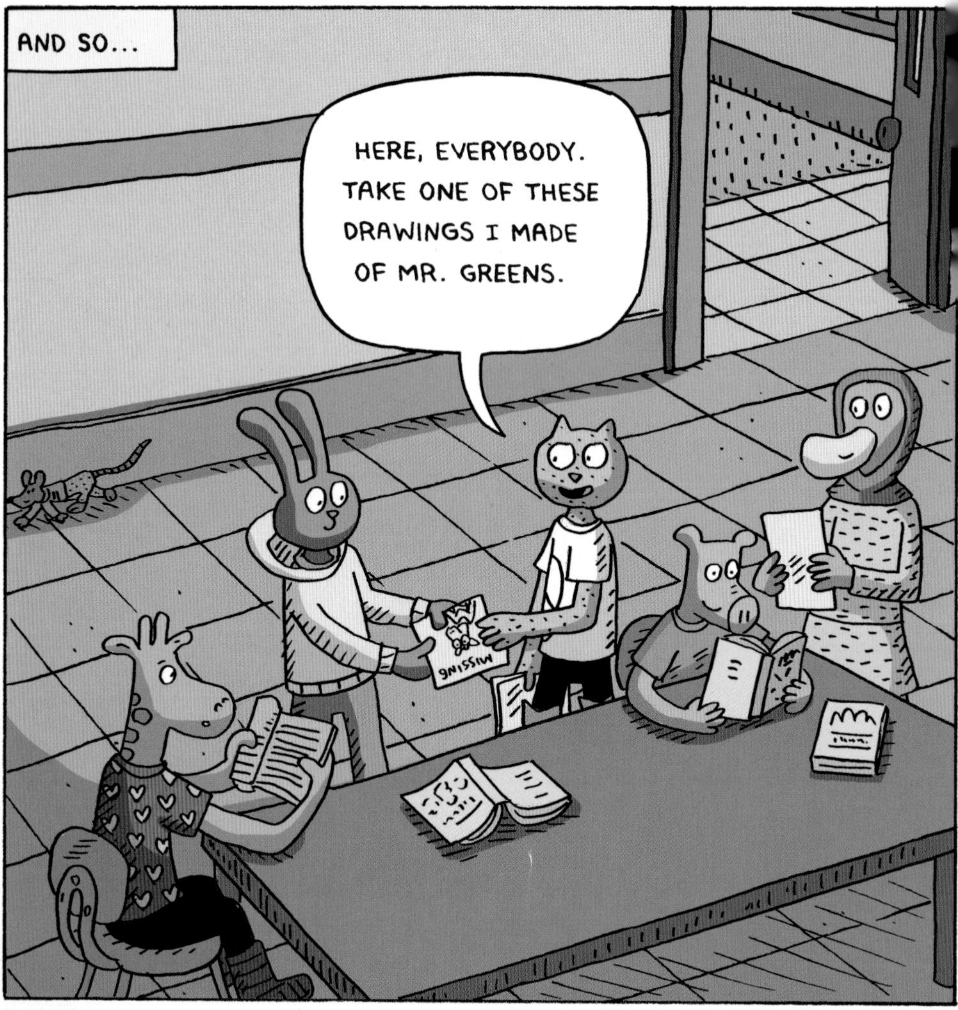
AND SO...
HERE, EVERYBODY. TAKE ONE OF THESE DRAWINGS I MADE OF MR. GREENS.
MISSING

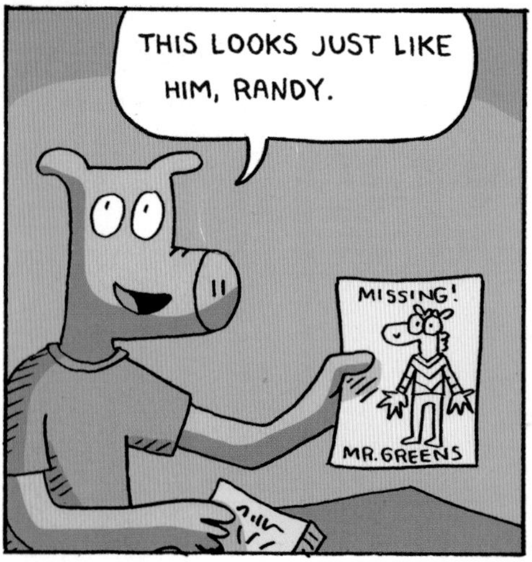
THIS LOOKS JUST LIKE HIM, RANDY.
MISSING!
MR. GREENS

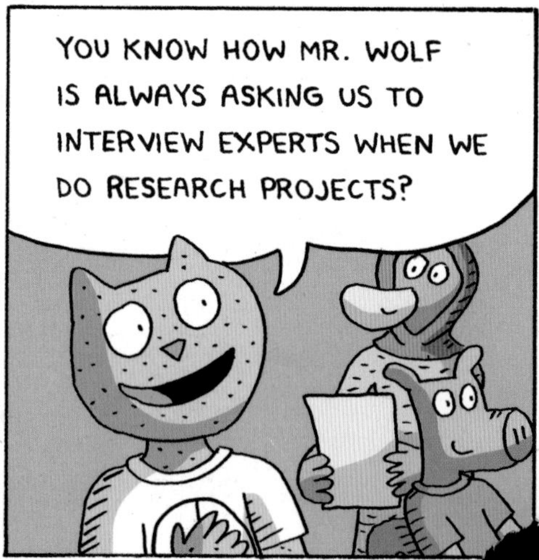
YOU KNOW HOW MR. WOLF IS ALWAYS ASKING US TO INTERVIEW EXPERTS WHEN WE DO RESEARCH PROJECTS?

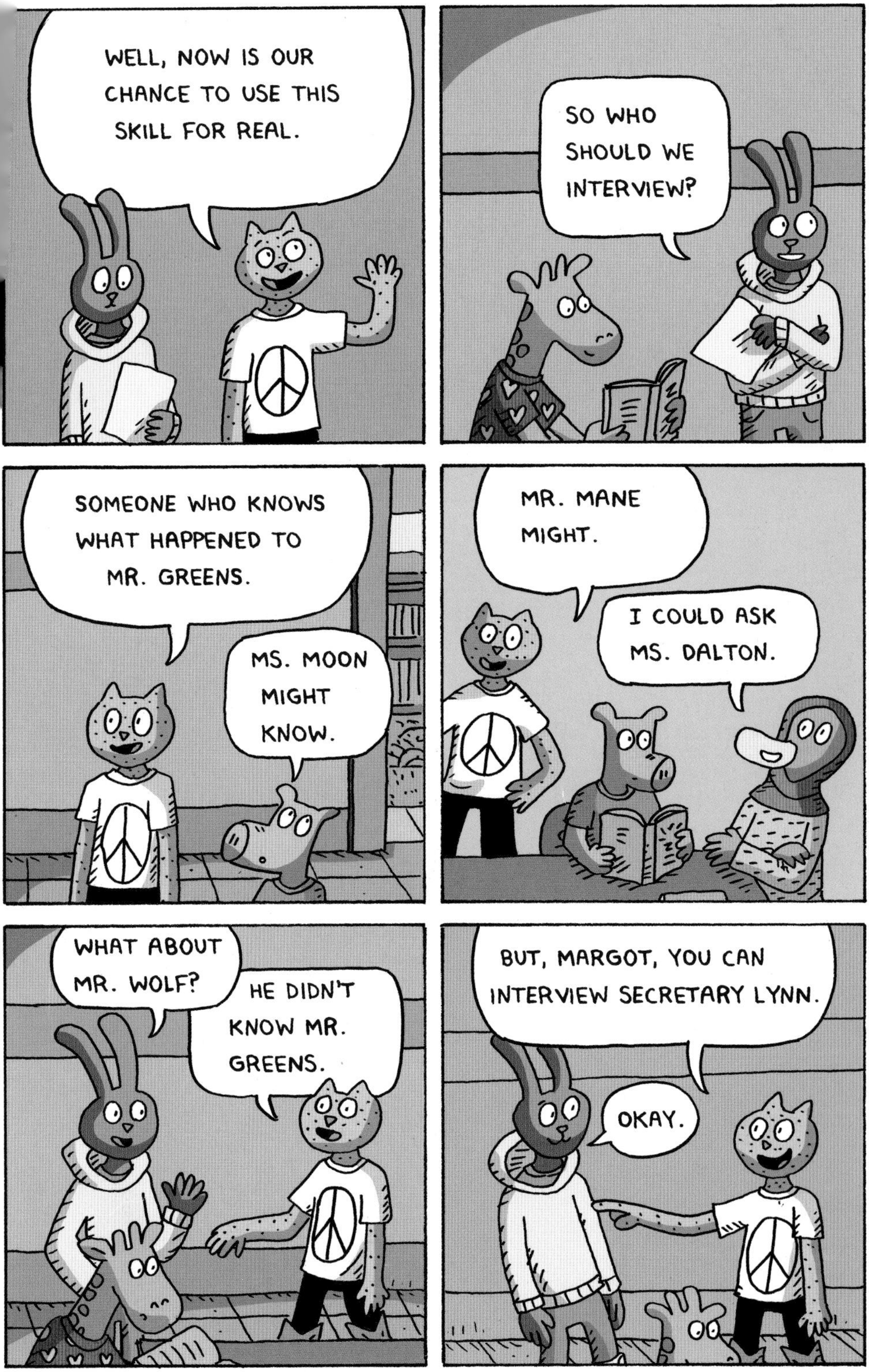
WELL, NOW IS OUR CHANCE TO USE THIS SKILL FOR REAL.
SO WHO SHOULD WE INTERVIEW?
SOMEONE WHO KNOWS WHAT HAPPENED TO MR. GREENS.
MS. MOON MIGHT KNOW.
MR. MANE MIGHT.
I COULD ASK MS. DALTON.
WHAT ABOUT MR. WOLF?
HE DIDN'T KNOW MR. GREENS.
BUT, MARGOT, YOU CAN INTERVIEW SECRETARY LYNN.
OKAY.

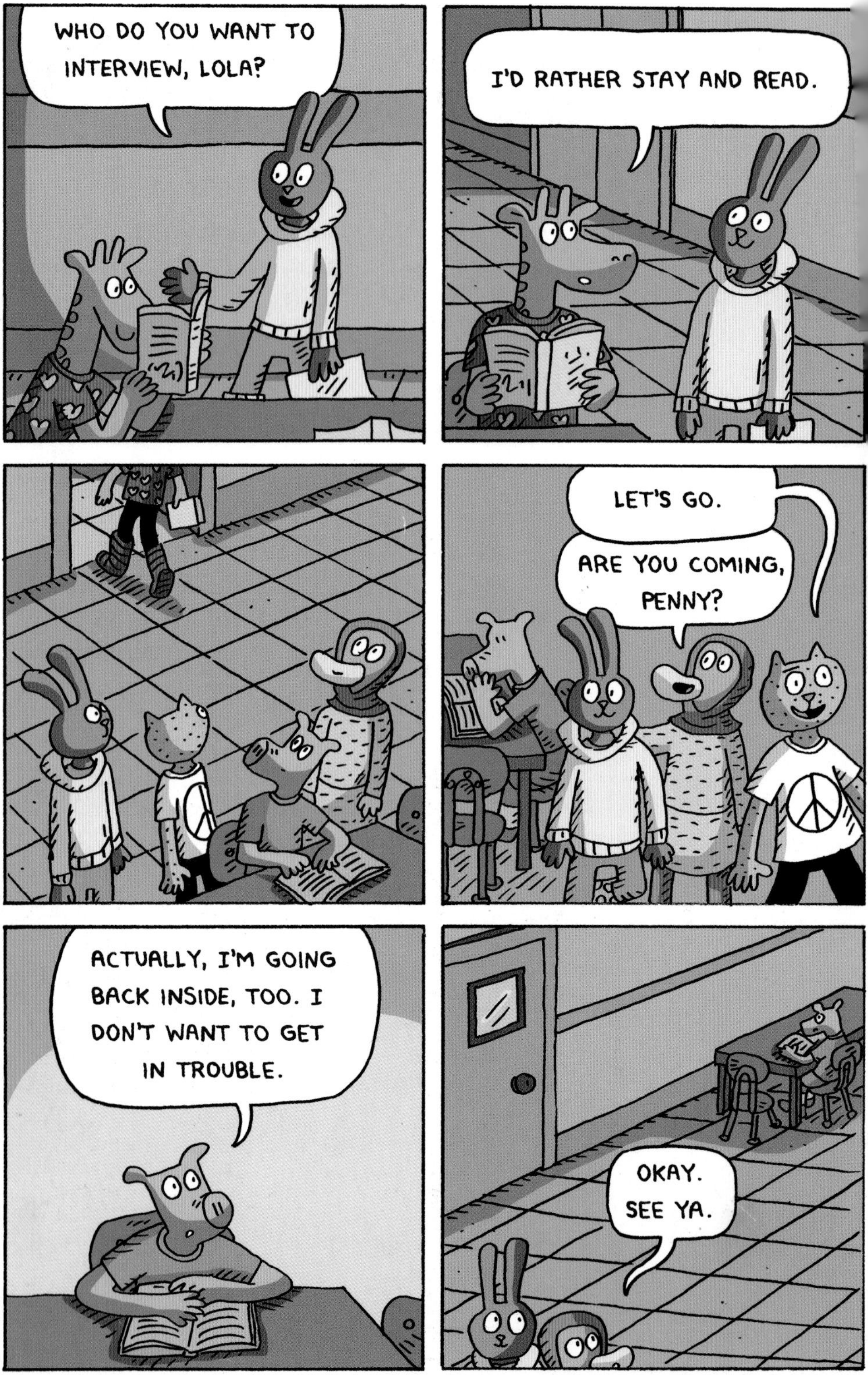
WHO DO YOU WANT TO INTERVIEW, LOLA?
I'D RATHER STAY AND READ.
LET'S GO.
ARE YOU COMING, PENNY?
ACTUALLY, I'M GOING BACK INSIDE, TOO. I DON'T WANT TO GET IN TROUBLE.
OKAY. SEE YA.

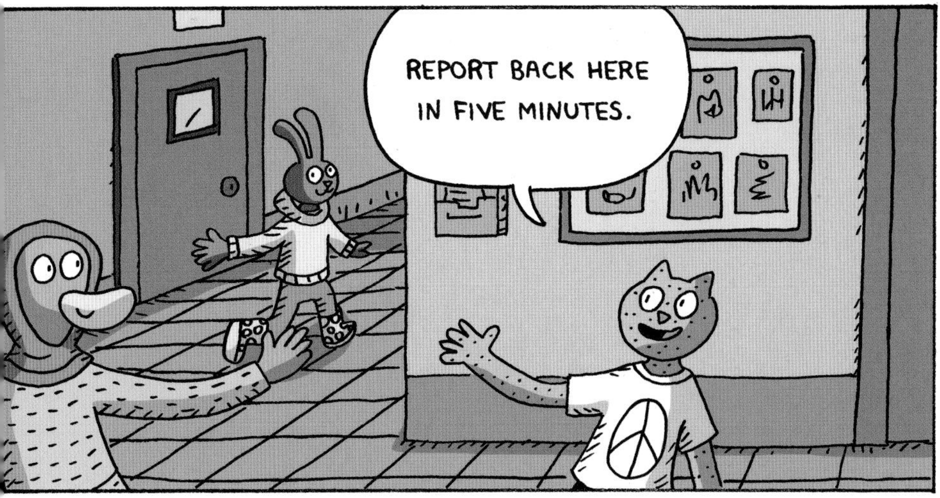
REPORT BACK HERE
IN FIVE MINUTES.

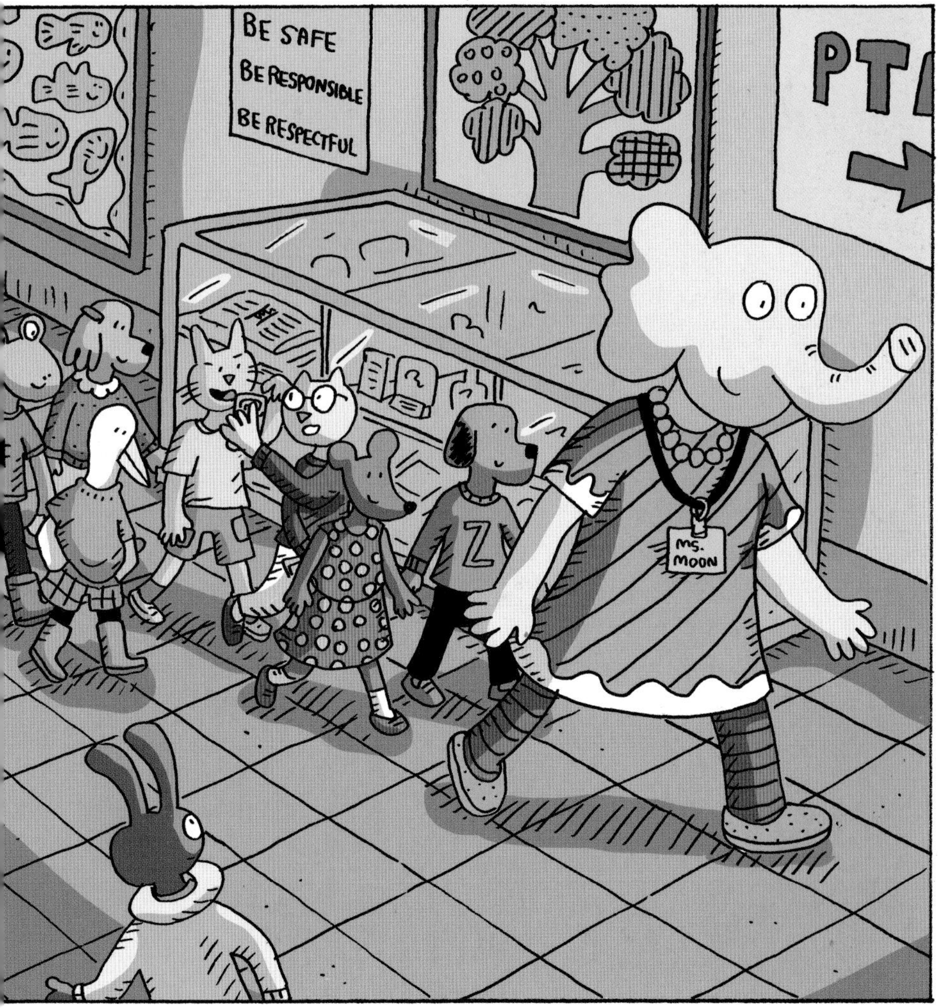
BE SAFE
BE RESPONSIBLE
BE RESPECTFUL
PT
Z
MS.
MOON

BOO-HOO.

≷SOB≷

≷SNIFF≷

mlm
uvm

UM, HELLO. SECRETARY LYNN?

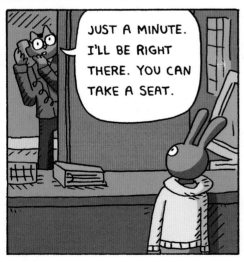

JUST A MINUTE. I'LL BE RIGHT THERE. YOU CAN TAKE A SEAT.

IS THAT THE PRINCIPAL?!

OKAY.

≷GULP≷

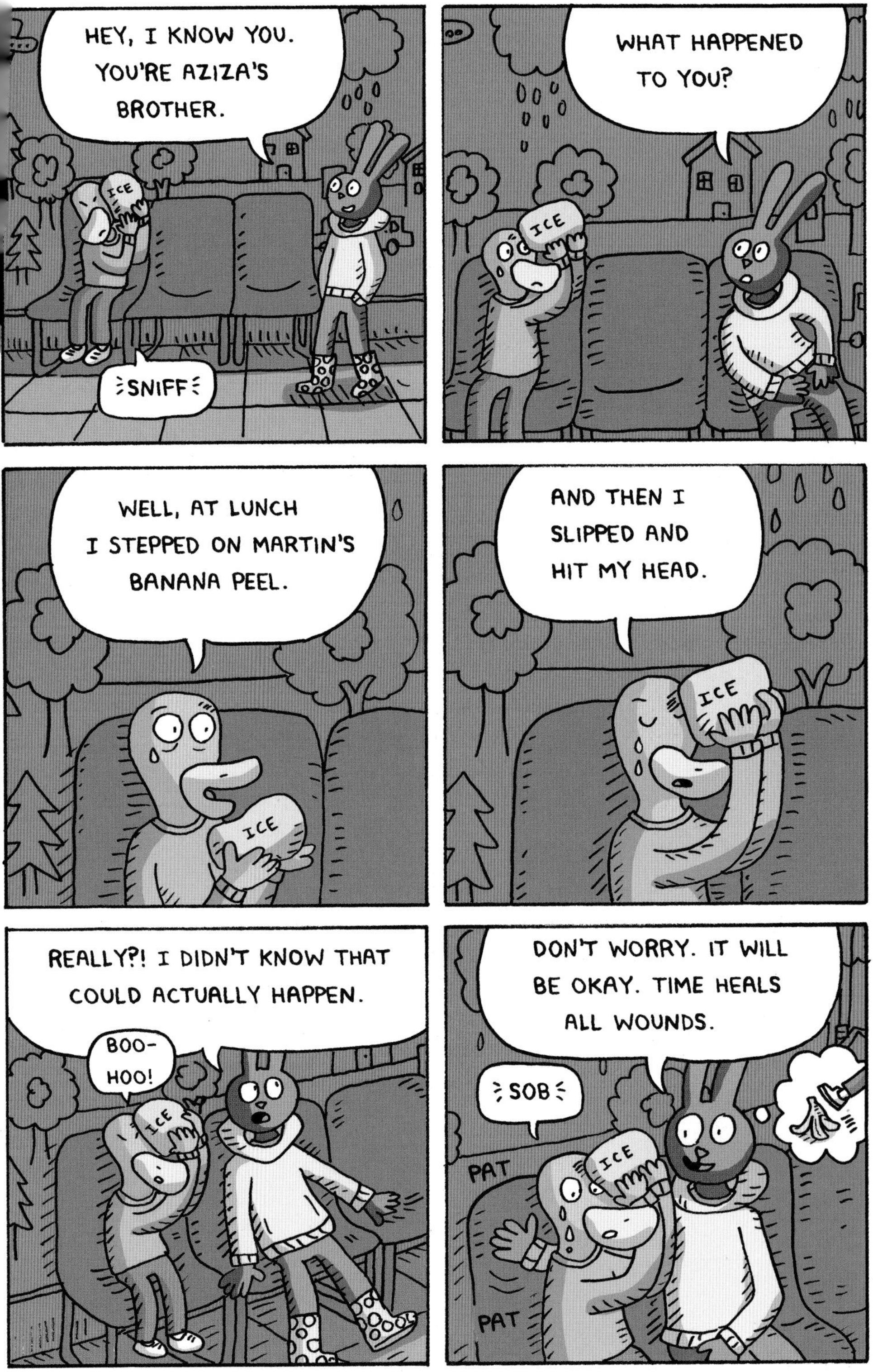
HEY, I KNOW YOU. YOU'RE AZIZA'S BROTHER.
ICE
SNIFF
WHAT HAPPENED TO YOU?
ICE
WELL, AT LUNCH I STEPPED ON MARTIN'S BANANA PEEL.
ICE
AND THEN I SLIPPED AND HIT MY HEAD.
ICE
REALLY?! I DIDN'T KNOW THAT COULD ACTUALLY HAPPEN.
BOO-HOO!
ICE
DON'T WORRY. IT WILL BE OKAY. TIME HEALS ALL WOUNDS.
SOB
ICE
PAT
PAT

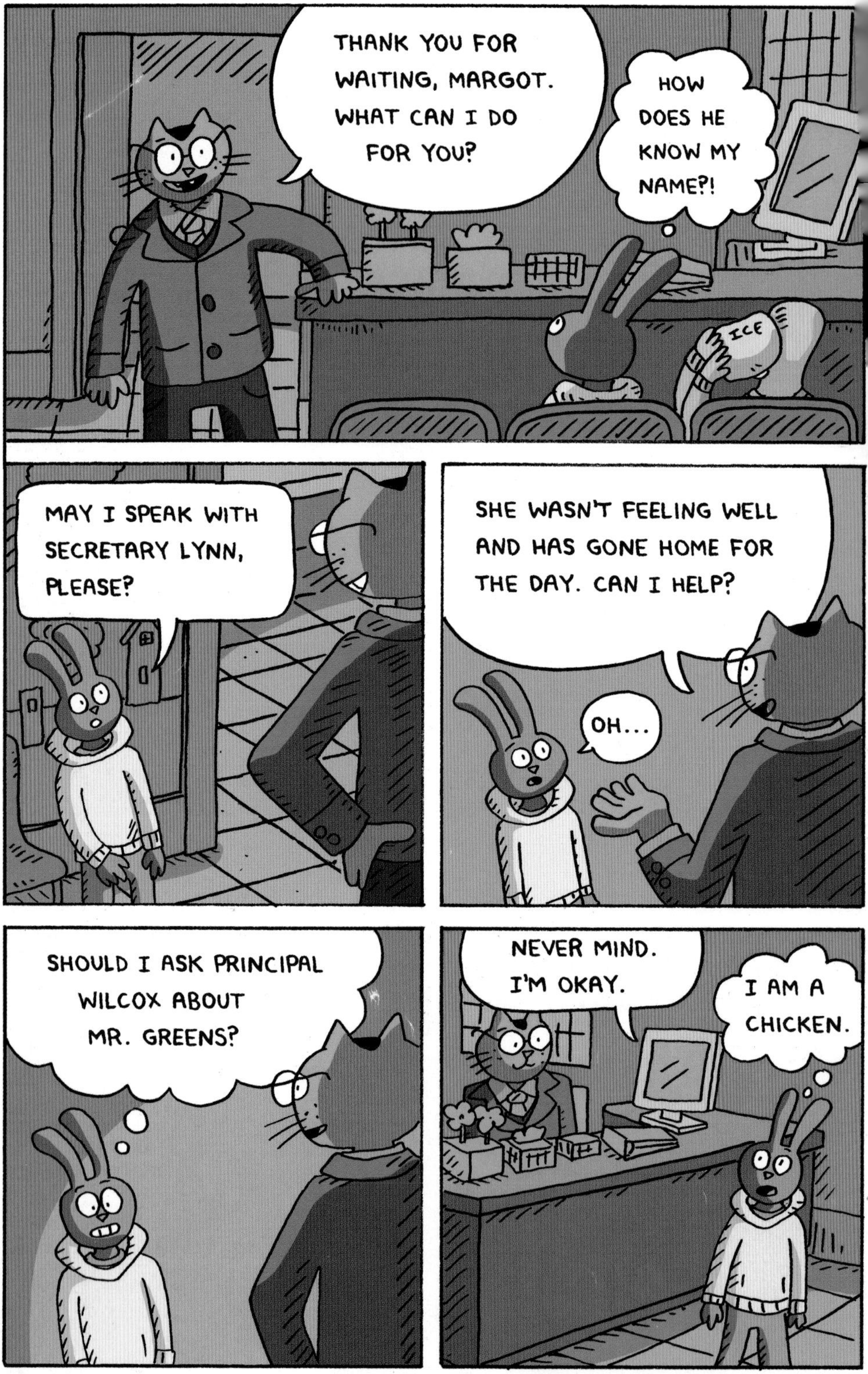
THANK YOU FOR WAITING, MARGOT. WHAT CAN I DO FOR YOU?
HOW DOES HE KNOW MY NAME?!
ICE
MAY I SPEAK WITH SECRETARY LYNN, PLEASE?
SHE WASN'T FEELING WELL AND HAS GONE HOME FOR THE DAY. CAN I HELP?
OH...
SHOULD I ASK PRINCIPAL WILCOX ABOUT MR. GREENS?
NEVER MIND. I'M OKAY.
I AM A CHICKEN.

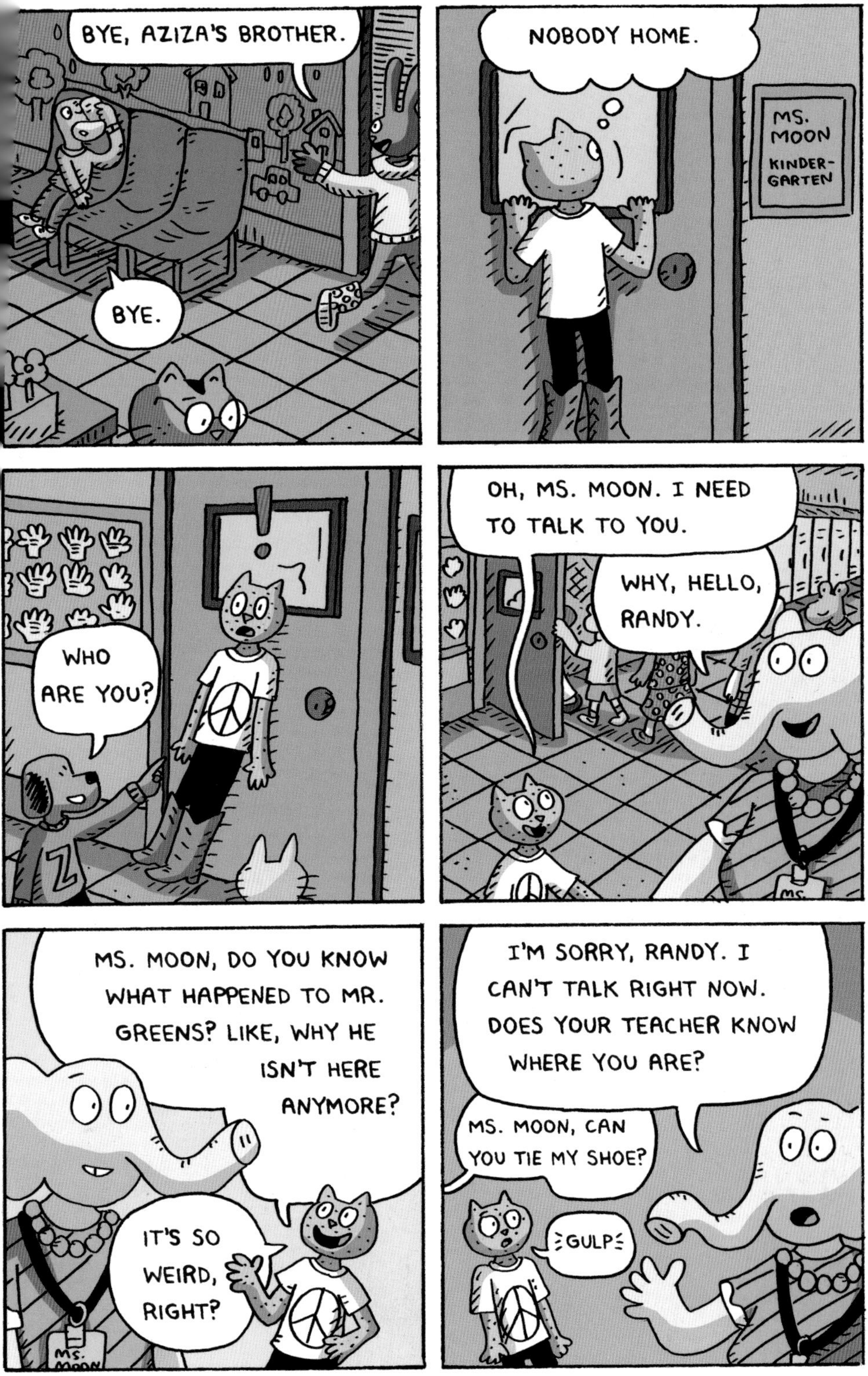
BYE, AZIZA'S BROTHER.
BYE.
NOBODY HOME.
MS. MOON KINDER-GARTEN
WHO ARE YOU?
OH, MS. MOON. I NEED TO TALK TO YOU.
WHY, HELLO, RANDY.
MS. MOON, DO YOU KNOW WHAT HAPPENED TO MR. GREENS? LIKE, WHY HE ISN'T HERE ANYMORE?
IT'S SO WEIRD, RIGHT?
I'M SORRY, RANDY. I CAN'T TALK RIGHT NOW. DOES YOUR TEACHER KNOW WHERE YOU ARE?
MS. MOON, CAN YOU TIE MY SHOE?
GULP

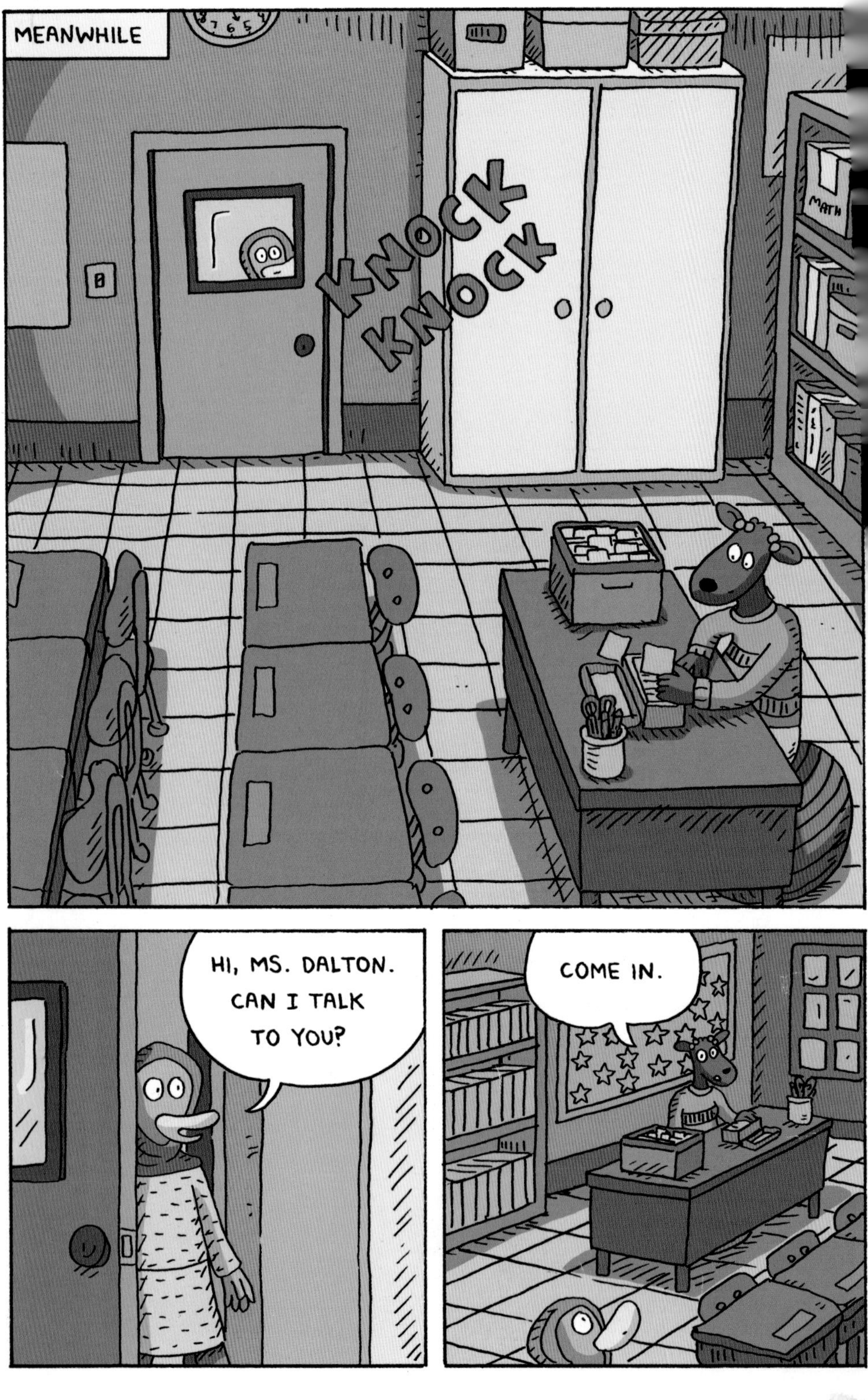
MEANWHILE
KNOCK KNOCK
MATH
HI, MS. DALTON. CAN I TALK TO YOU?
COME IN.

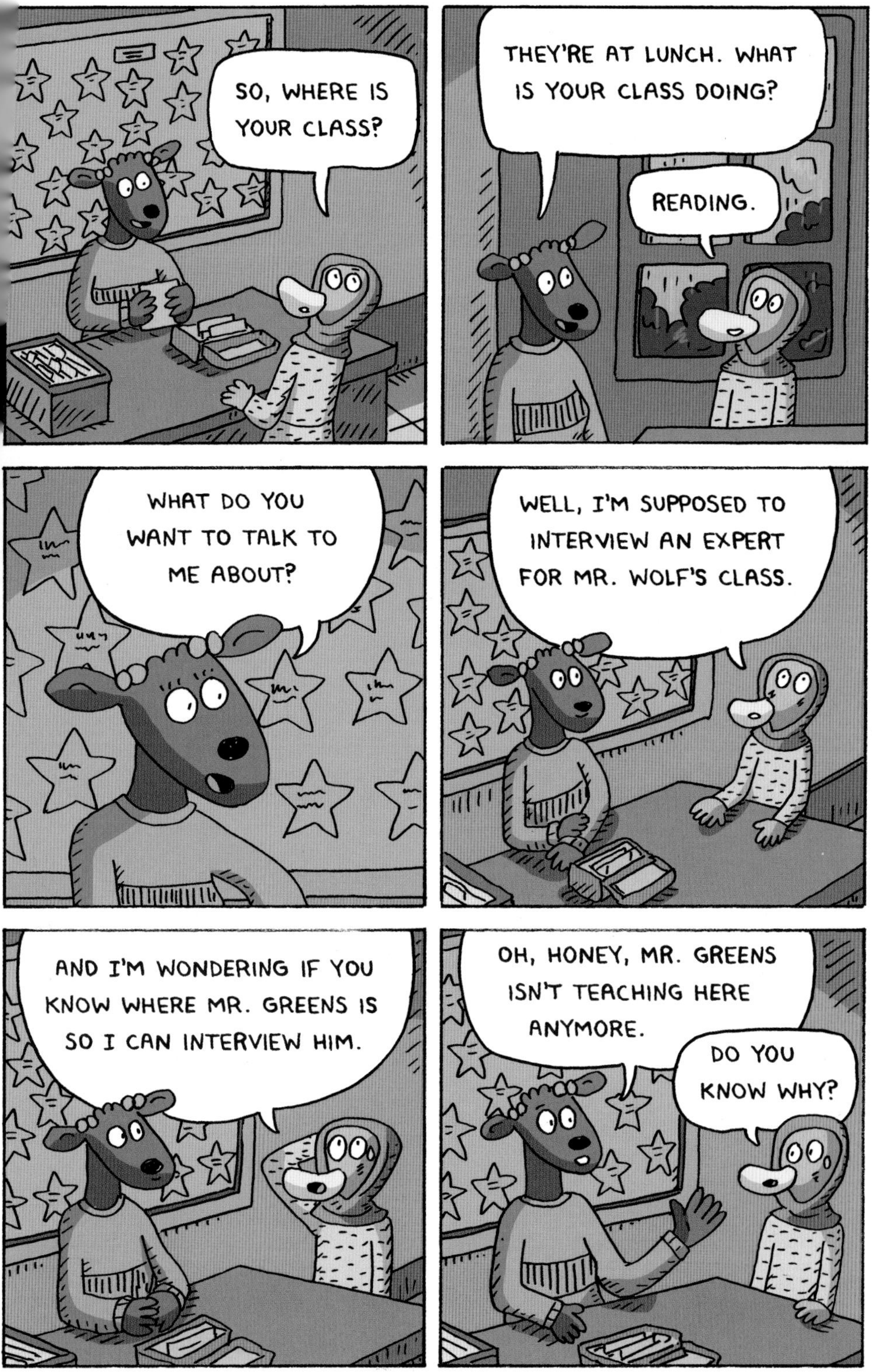
SO, WHERE IS YOUR CLASS?
THEY'RE AT LUNCH. WHAT IS YOUR CLASS DOING?
READING.
WHAT DO YOU WANT TO TALK TO ME ABOUT?
WELL, I'M SUPPOSED TO INTERVIEW AN EXPERT FOR MR. WOLF'S CLASS.
AND I'M WONDERING IF YOU KNOW WHERE MR. GREENS IS SO I CAN INTERVIEW HIM.
OH, HONEY, MR. GREENS ISN'T TEACHING HERE ANYMORE.
DO YOU KNOW WHY?

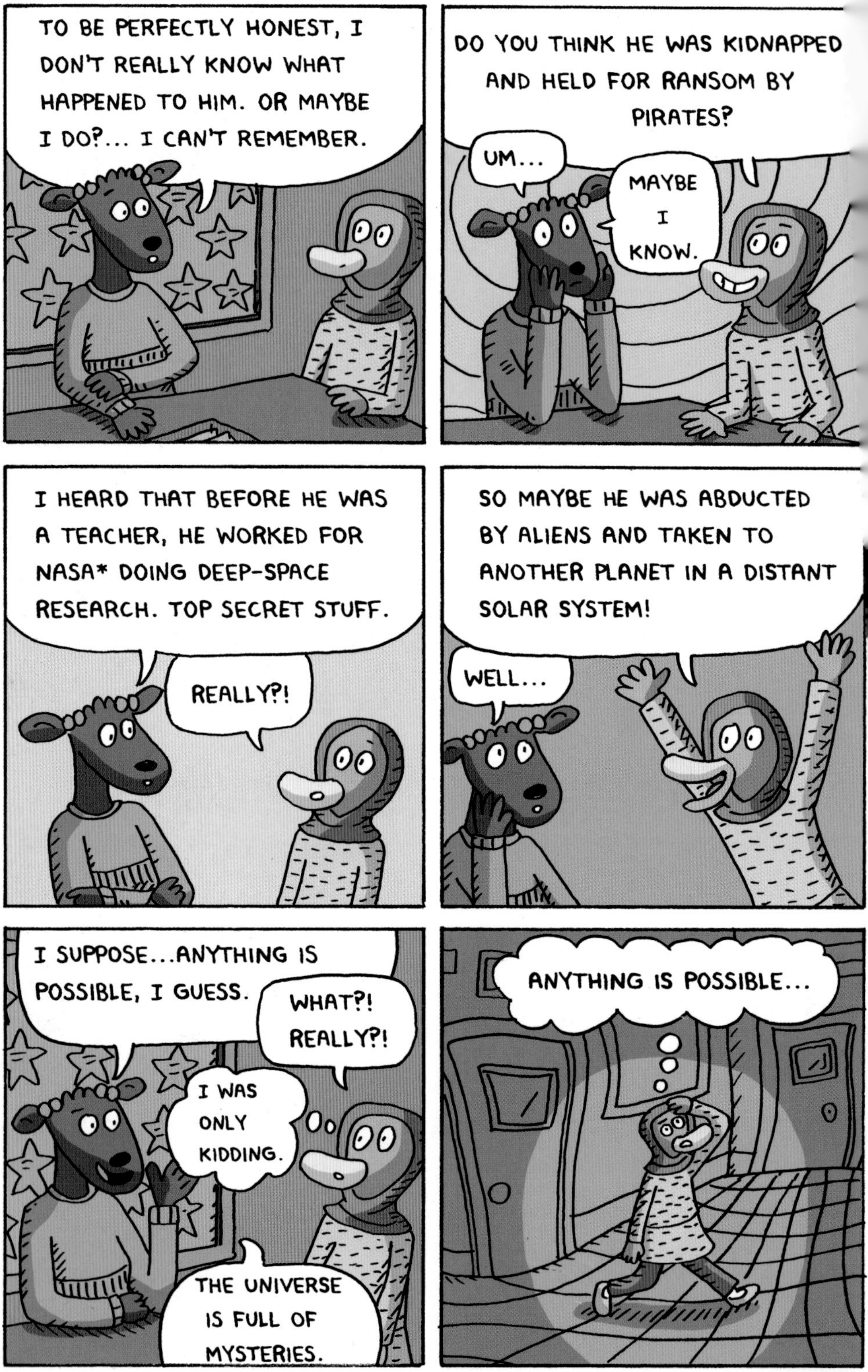
TO BE PERFECTLY HONEST, I DON'T REALLY KNOW WHAT HAPPENED TO HIM. OR MAYBE I DO?... I CAN'T REMEMBER.
DO YOU THINK HE WAS KIDNAPPED AND HELD FOR RANSOM BY PIRATES?
UM...
MAYBE I KNOW.
I HEARD THAT BEFORE HE WAS A TEACHER, HE WORKED FOR NASA* DOING DEEP-SPACE RESEARCH. TOP SECRET STUFF.
REALLY?!
SO MAYBE HE WAS ABDUCTED BY ALIENS AND TAKEN TO ANOTHER PLANET IN A DISTANT SOLAR SYSTEM!
WELL...
I SUPPOSE...ANYTHING IS POSSIBLE, I GUESS.
WHAT?! REALLY?!
I WAS ONLY KIDDING.
THE UNIVERSE IS FULL OF MYSTERIES.
ANYTHING IS POSSIBLE...

*NATIONAL AERONAUTICS AND SPACE ADMINISTRATION

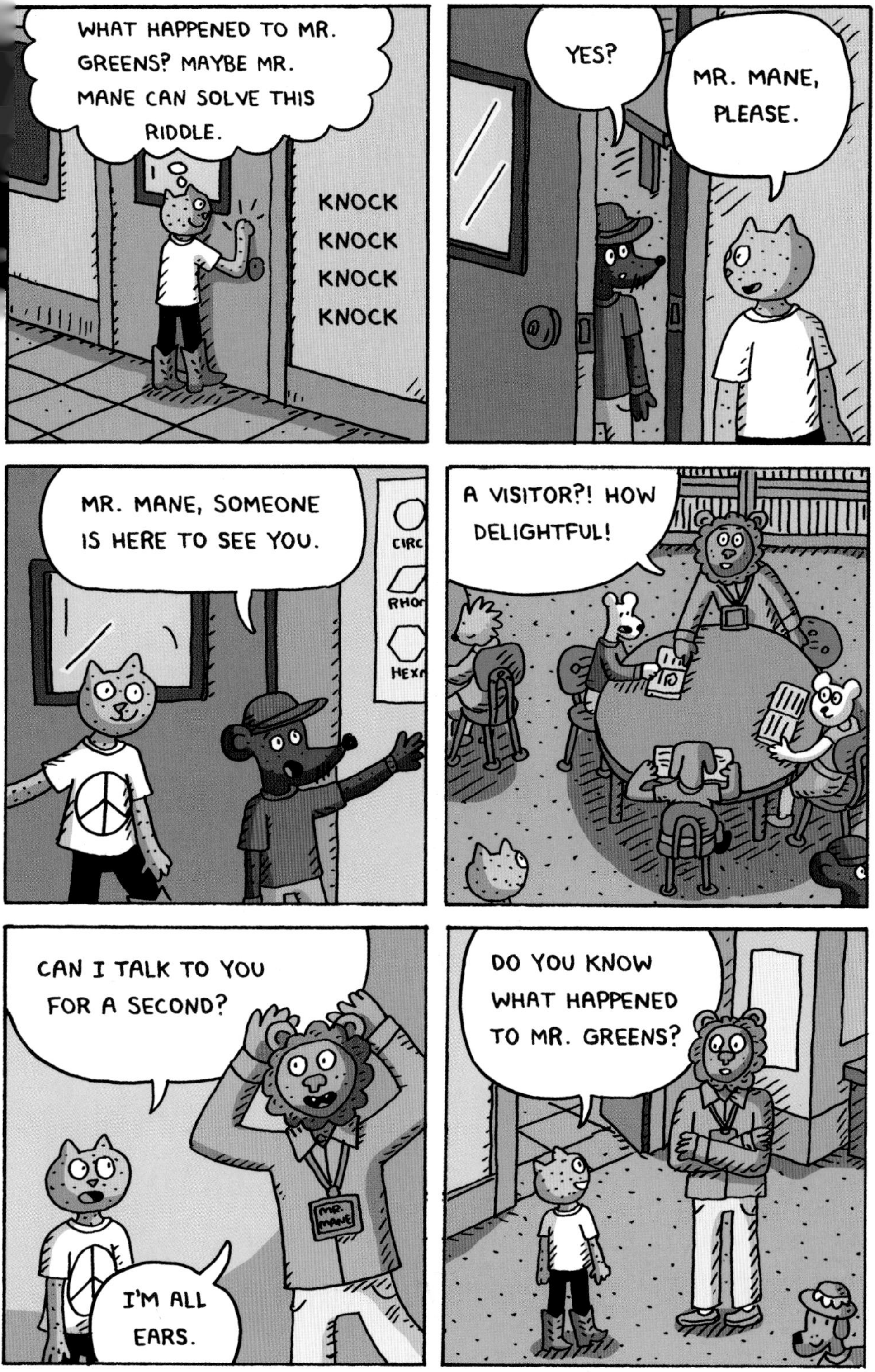
WHAT HAPPENED TO MR. GREENS? MAYBE MR. MANE CAN SOLVE THIS RIDDLE.
KNOCK KNOCK KNOCK KNOCK
YES?
MR. MANE, PLEASE.
MR. MANE, SOMEONE IS HERE TO SEE YOU.
CIRC
RHOM
HEXA
A VISITOR?! HOW DELIGHTFUL!
CAN I TALK TO YOU FOR A SECOND?
I'M ALL EARS.
MR. MANE
DO YOU KNOW WHAT HAPPENED TO MR. GREENS?

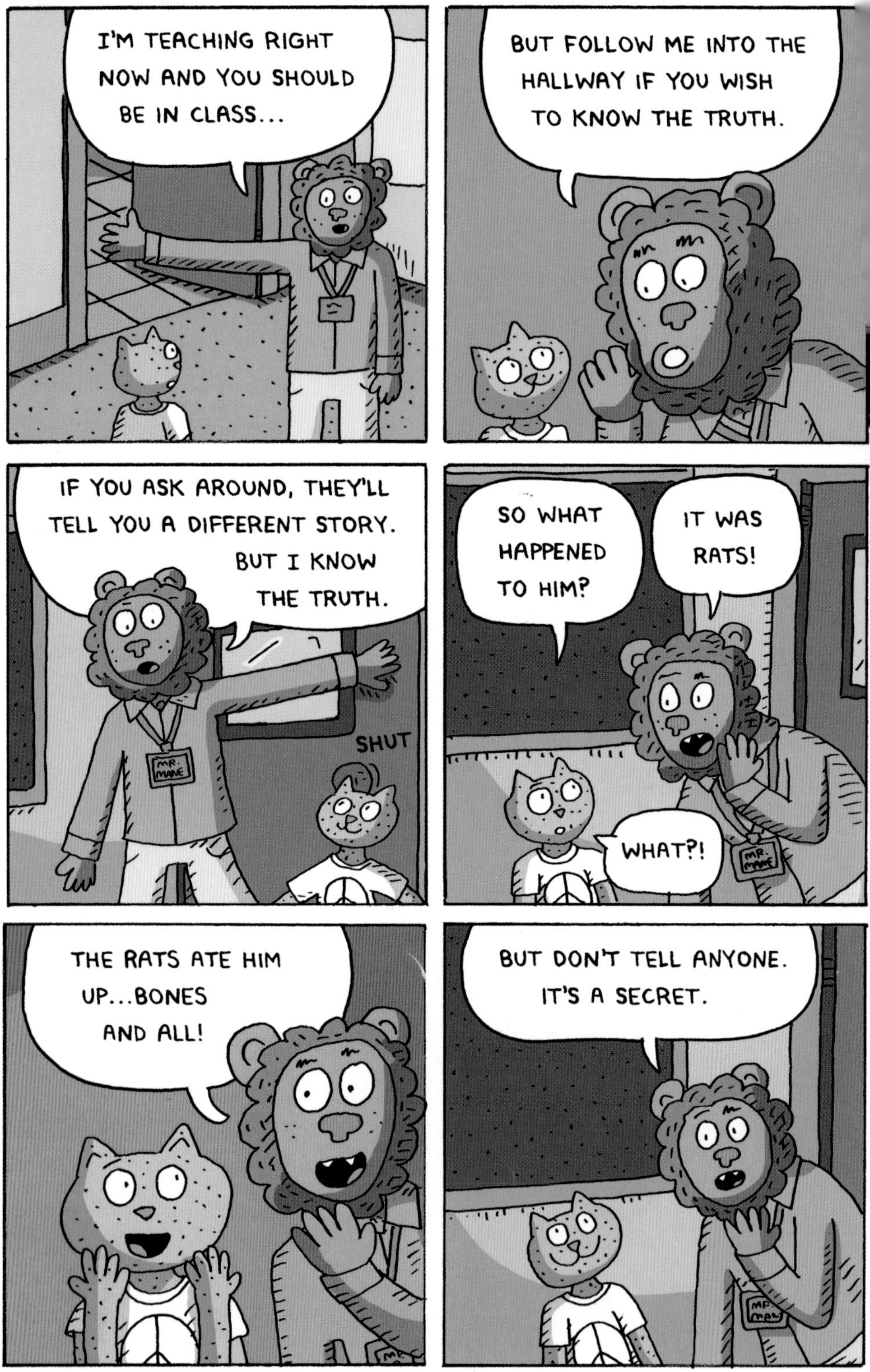
I'M TEACHING RIGHT NOW AND YOU SHOULD BE IN CLASS...
BUT FOLLOW ME INTO THE HALLWAY IF YOU WISH TO KNOW THE TRUTH.
IF YOU ASK AROUND, THEY'LL TELL YOU A DIFFERENT STORY. BUT I KNOW THE TRUTH.
MR. MANE
SHUT
SO WHAT HAPPENED TO HIM?
IT WAS RATS!
WHAT?!
MR. MANE
THE RATS ATE HIM UP...BONES AND ALL!
BUT DON'T TELL ANYONE. IT'S A SECRET.

CHAPTER FOUR

The Truth about Mr. Greens

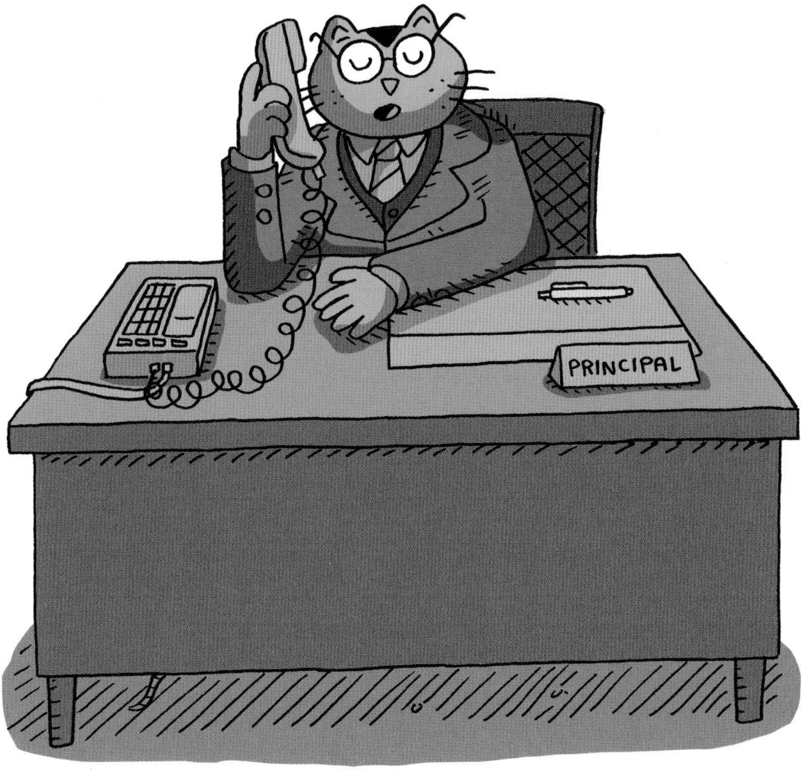
PRINCIPAL

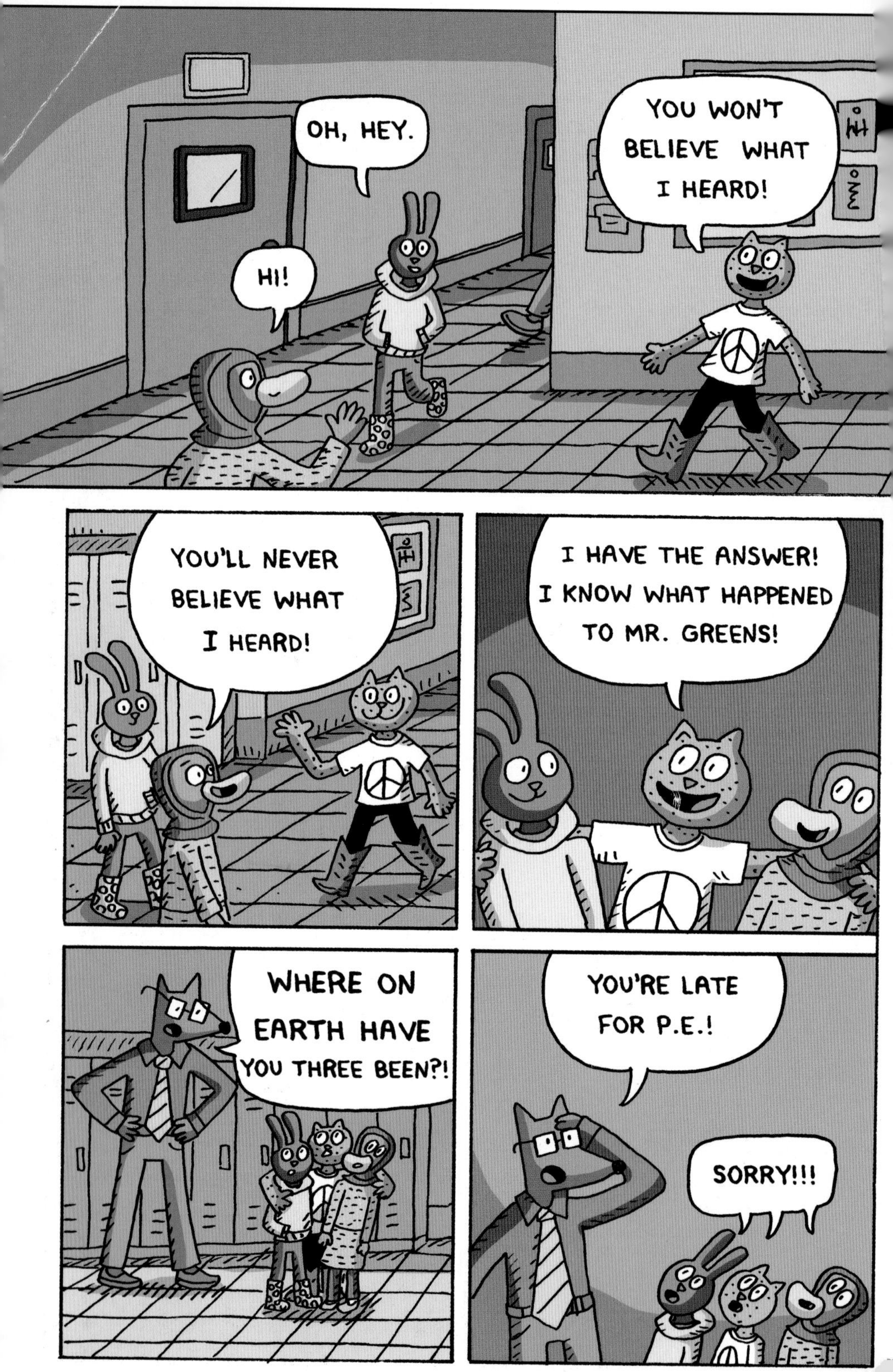
OH, HEY.
HI!
YOU WON'T BELIEVE WHAT I HEARD!
YOU'LL NEVER BELIEVE WHAT I HEARD!
I HAVE THE ANSWER! I KNOW WHAT HAPPENED TO MR. GREENS!
WHERE ON EARTH HAVE YOU THREE BEEN?!
YOU'RE LATE FOR P.E.!
SORRY!!!

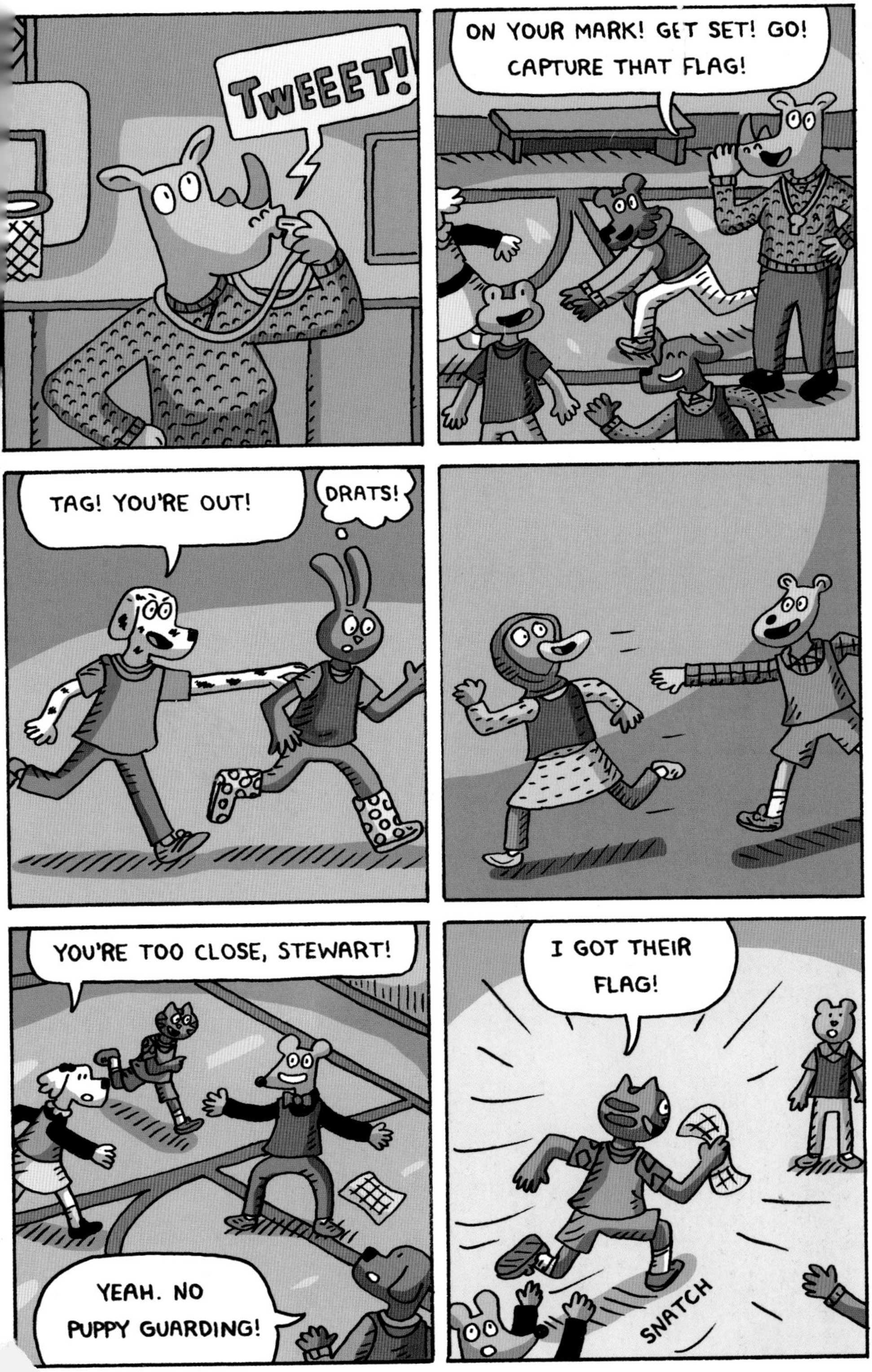
TWEEET!
ON YOUR MARK! GET SET! GO! CAPTURE THAT FLAG!
TAG! YOU'RE OUT!
DRATS!
YOU'RE TOO CLOSE, STEWART!
YEAH. NO PUPPY GUARDING!
I GOT THEIR FLAG!
SNATCH

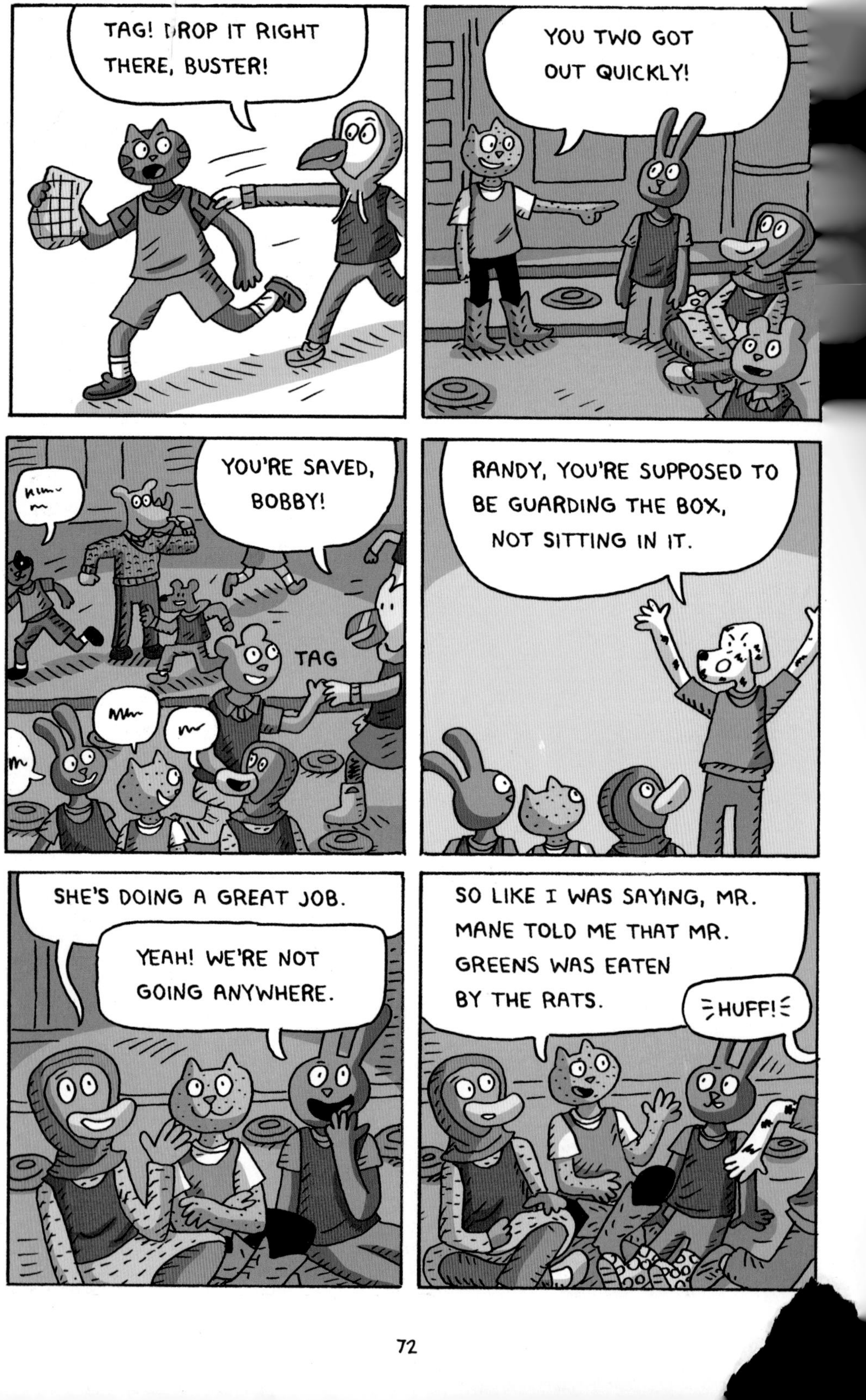
TAG! DROP IT RIGHT THERE, BUSTER!
YOU TWO GOT OUT QUICKLY!
YOU'RE SAVED, BOBBY!
TAG
RANDY, YOU'RE SUPPOSED TO BE GUARDING THE BOX, NOT SITTING IN IT.
SHE'S DOING A GREAT JOB.
YEAH! WE'RE NOT GOING ANYWHERE.
SO LIKE I WAS SAYING, MR. MANE TOLD ME THAT MR. GREENS WAS EATEN BY THE RATS.
HUFF!

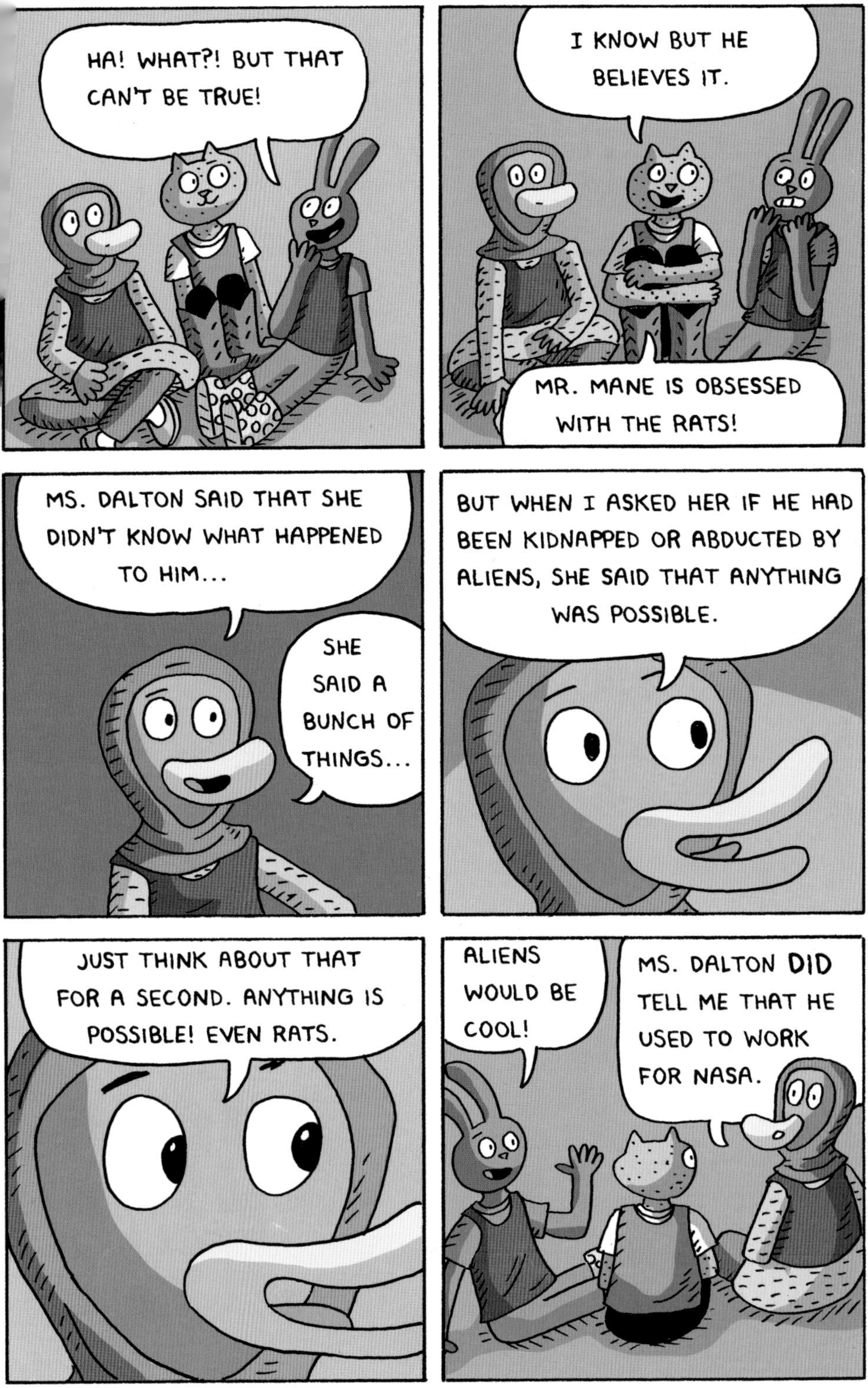
HA! WHAT?! BUT THAT CAN'T BE TRUE!
I KNOW BUT HE BELIEVES IT.
MR. MANE IS OBSESSED WITH THE RATS!
MS. DALTON SAID THAT SHE DIDN'T KNOW WHAT HAPPENED TO HIM...
SHE SAID A BUNCH OF THINGS...
BUT WHEN I ASKED HER IF HE HAD BEEN KIDNAPPED OR ABDUCTED BY ALIENS, SHE SAID THAT ANYTHING WAS POSSIBLE.
JUST THINK ABOUT THAT FOR A SECOND. ANYTHING IS POSSIBLE! EVEN RATS.
ALIENS WOULD BE COOL!
MS. DALTON DID TELL ME THAT HE USED TO WORK FOR NASA.

WHAT ABOUT YOU, MARGOT? WHAT DID SECRETARY LYNN SAY?

I DIDN'T GET THE CHANCE TO ASK HER.

SHE WENT HOME SICK...AND THEN I THOUGHT ABOUT ASKING THE PRINCIPAL BUT I GOT TOO SCARED.

DARN.

I'M SO DISAPPOINTED IN MYSELF! I CHICKENED OUT!

THAT'S OFFENSIVE TO CHICKENS, YOU KNOW.

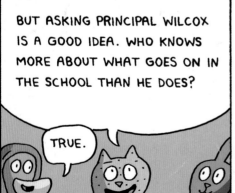

BUT ASKING PRINCIPAL WILCOX IS A GOOD IDEA. WHO KNOWS MORE ABOUT WHAT GOES ON IN THE SCHOOL THAN HE DOES?

TRUE.

ALL WE NEED IS A PLAN TO GET OUT OF P.E.

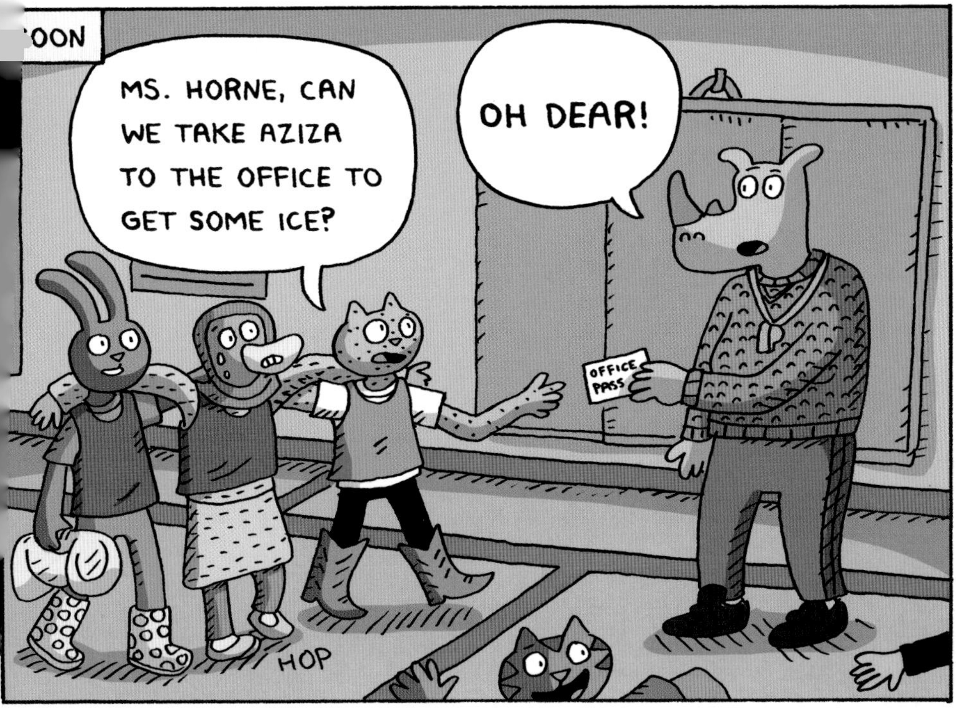
OON
MS. HORNE, CAN WE TAKE AZIZA TO THE OFFICE TO GET SOME ICE?
OH DEAR!
OFFICE PASS
HOP

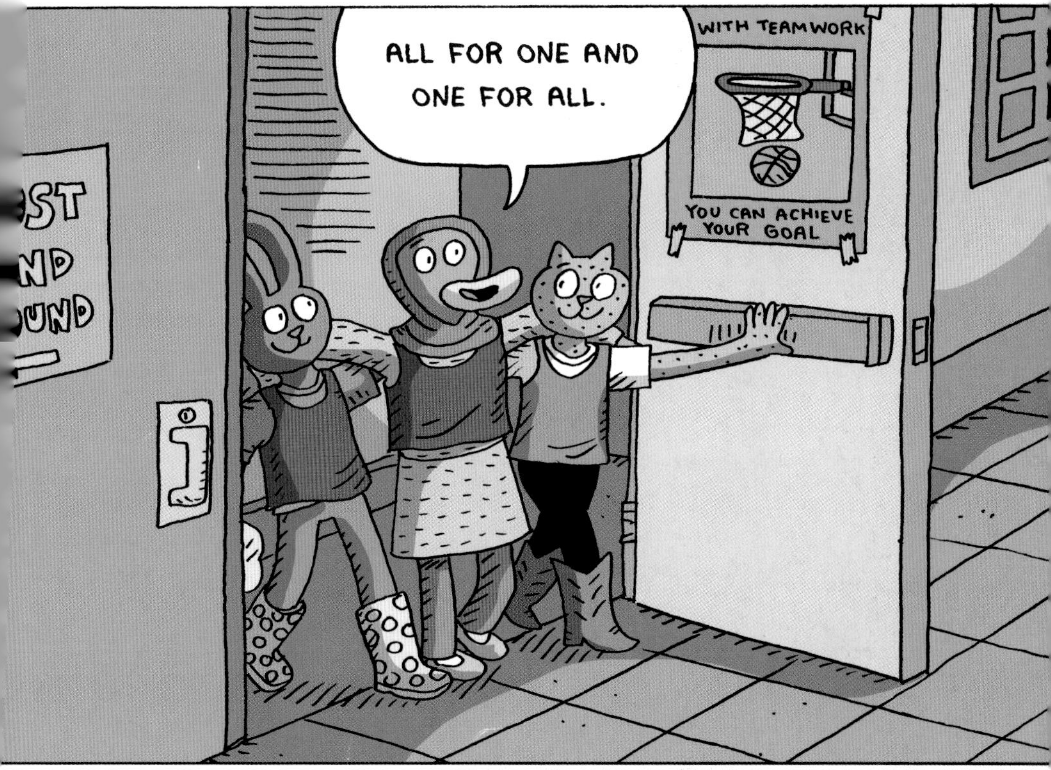
ALL FOR ONE AND ONE FOR ALL.
WITH TEAMWORK
YOU CAN ACHIEVE YOUR GOAL

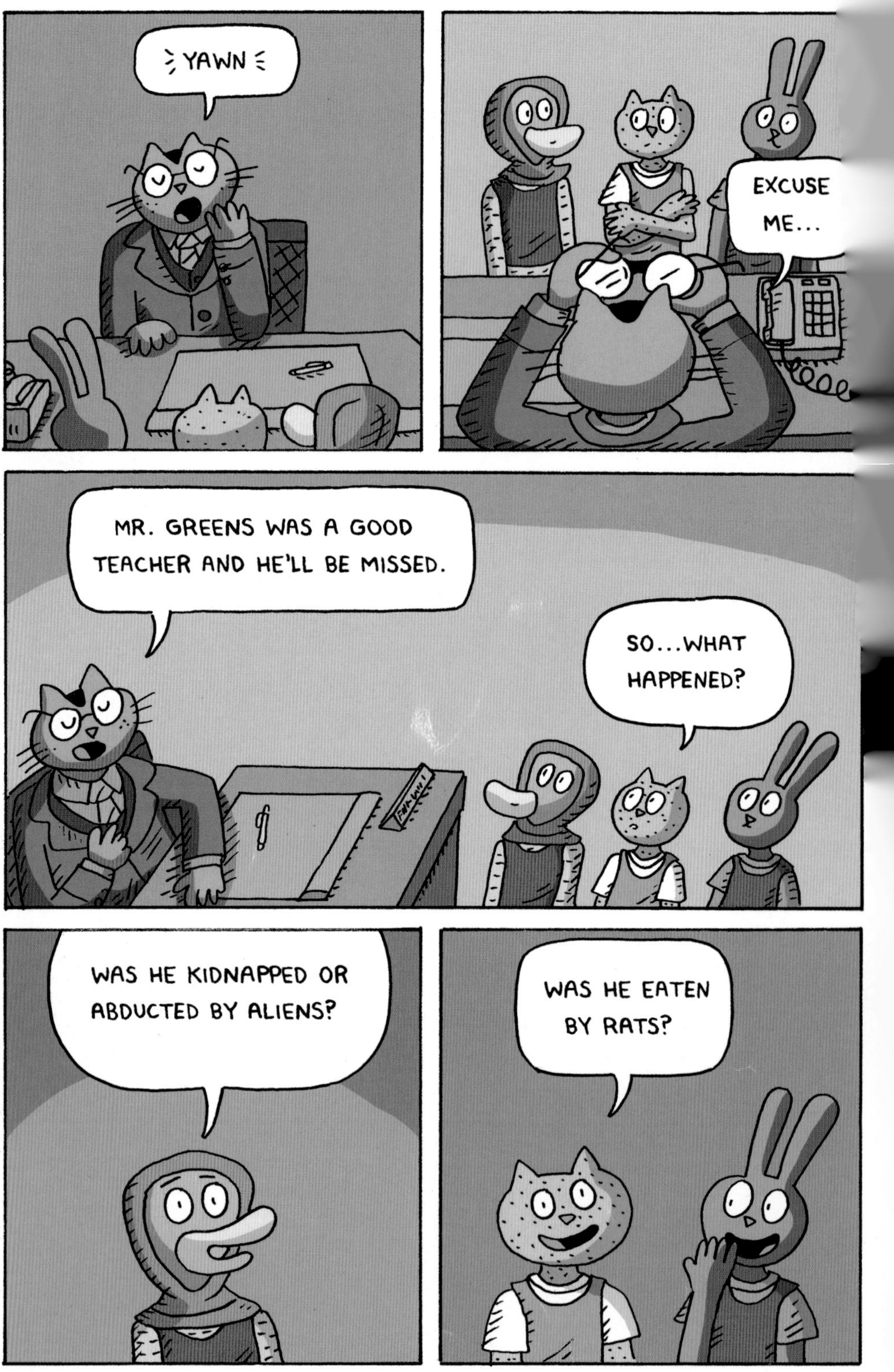
YAWN
EXCUSE ME...
MR. GREENS WAS A GOOD TEACHER AND HE'LL BE MISSED.
SO...WHAT HAPPENED?
WAS HE KIDNAPPED OR ABDUCTED BY ALIENS?
WAS HE EATEN BY RATS?

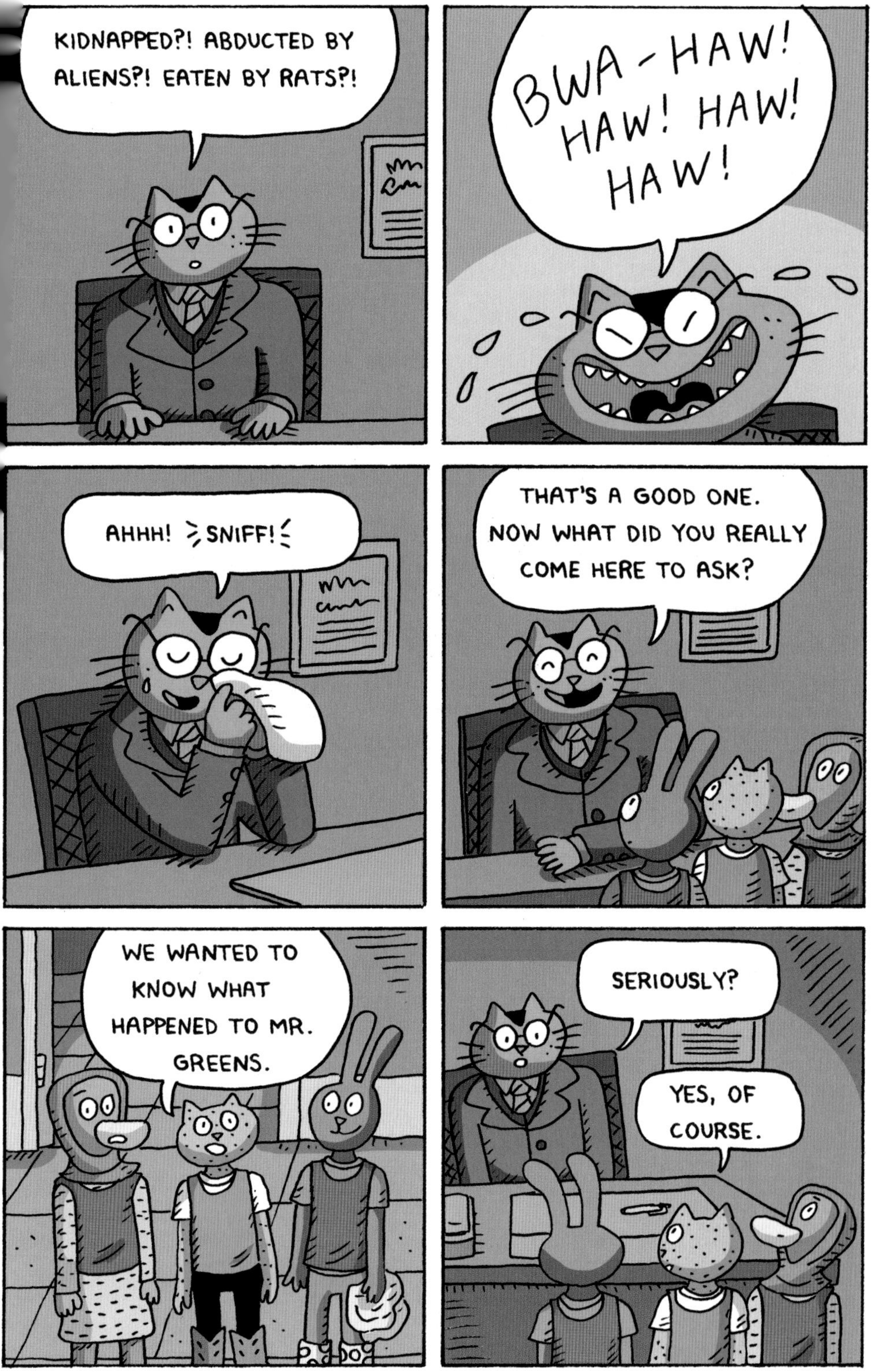
KIDNAPPED?! ABDUCTED BY ALIENS?! EATEN BY RATS?!
BWA-HAW! HAW! HAW! HAW!
AHHH! SNIFF!
THAT'S A GOOD ONE. NOW WHAT DID YOU REALLY COME HERE TO ASK?
WE WANTED TO KNOW WHAT HAPPENED TO MR. GREENS.
SERIOUSLY?
YES, OF COURSE.

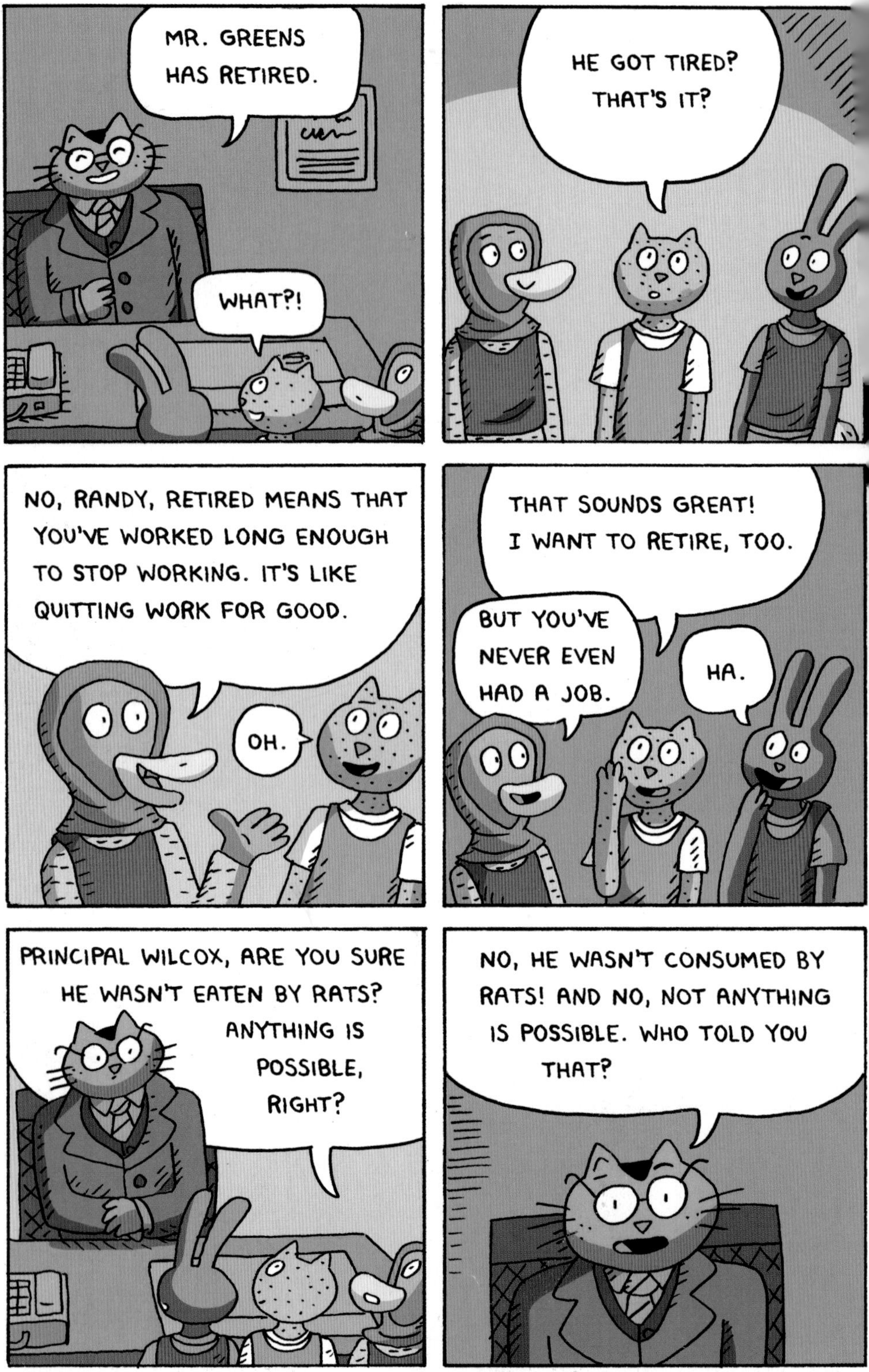
MR. GREENS HAS RETIRED.
WHAT?!
HE GOT TIRED? THAT'S IT?
NO, RANDY, RETIRED MEANS THAT YOU'VE WORKED LONG ENOUGH TO STOP WORKING. IT'S LIKE QUITTING WORK FOR GOOD.
OH.
THAT SOUNDS GREAT! I WANT TO RETIRE, TOO.
BUT YOU'VE NEVER EVEN HAD A JOB.
HA.
PRINCIPAL WILCOX, ARE YOU SURE HE WASN'T EATEN BY RATS? ANYTHING IS POSSIBLE, RIGHT?
NO, HE WASN'T CONSUMED BY RATS! AND NO, NOT ANYTHING IS POSSIBLE. WHO TOLD YOU THAT?

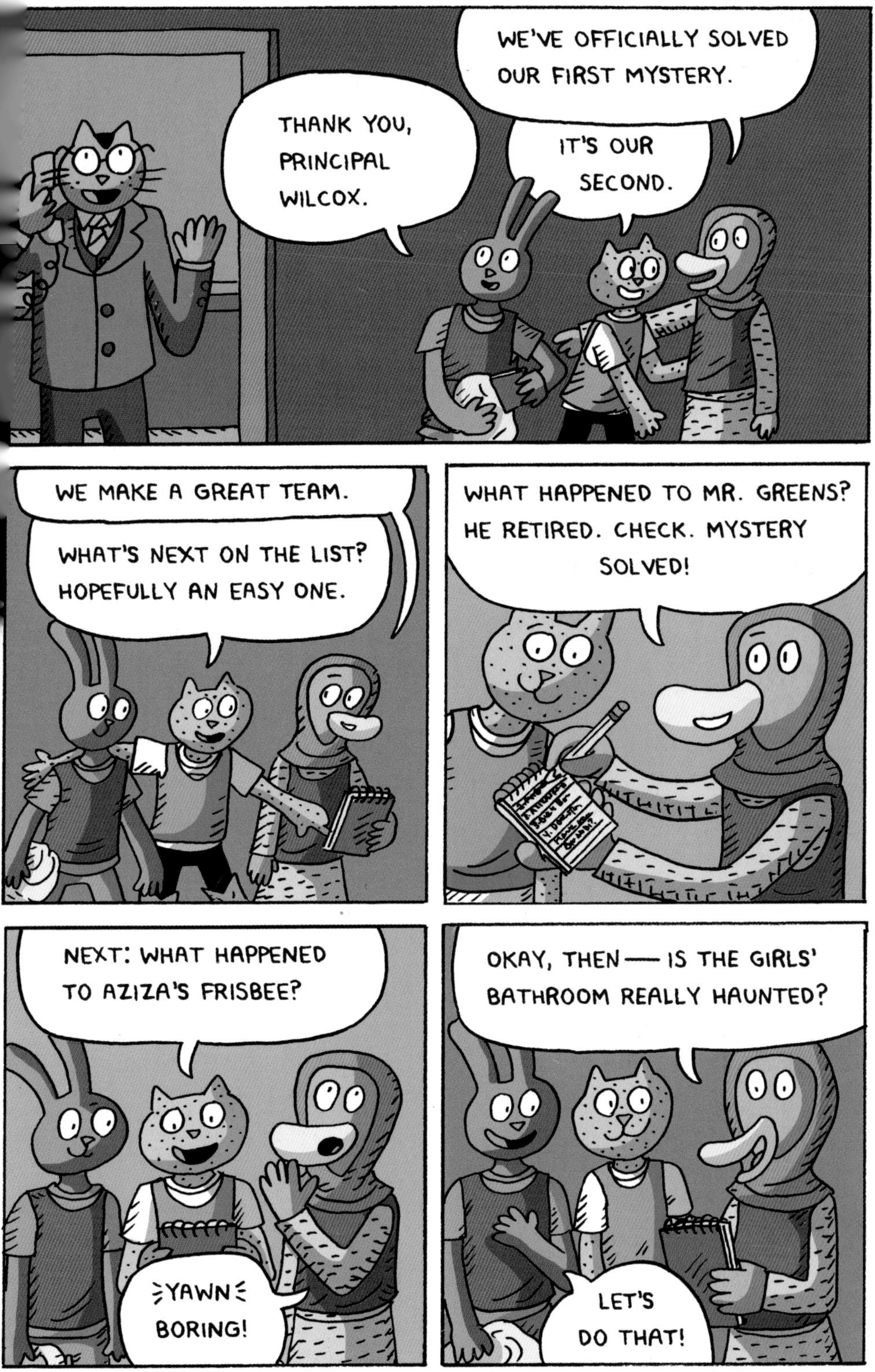
THANK YOU, PRINCIPAL WILCOX.
WE'VE OFFICIALLY SOLVED OUR FIRST MYSTERY.
IT'S OUR SECOND.
WE MAKE A GREAT TEAM.
WHAT'S NEXT ON THE LIST? HOPEFULLY AN EASY ONE.
WHAT HAPPENED TO MR. GREENS? HE RETIRED. CHECK. MYSTERY SOLVED!
NEXT: WHAT HAPPENED TO AZIZA'S FRISBEE?
YAWN BORING!
OKAY, THEN — IS THE GIRLS' BATHROOM REALLY HAUNTED?
LET'S DO THAT!

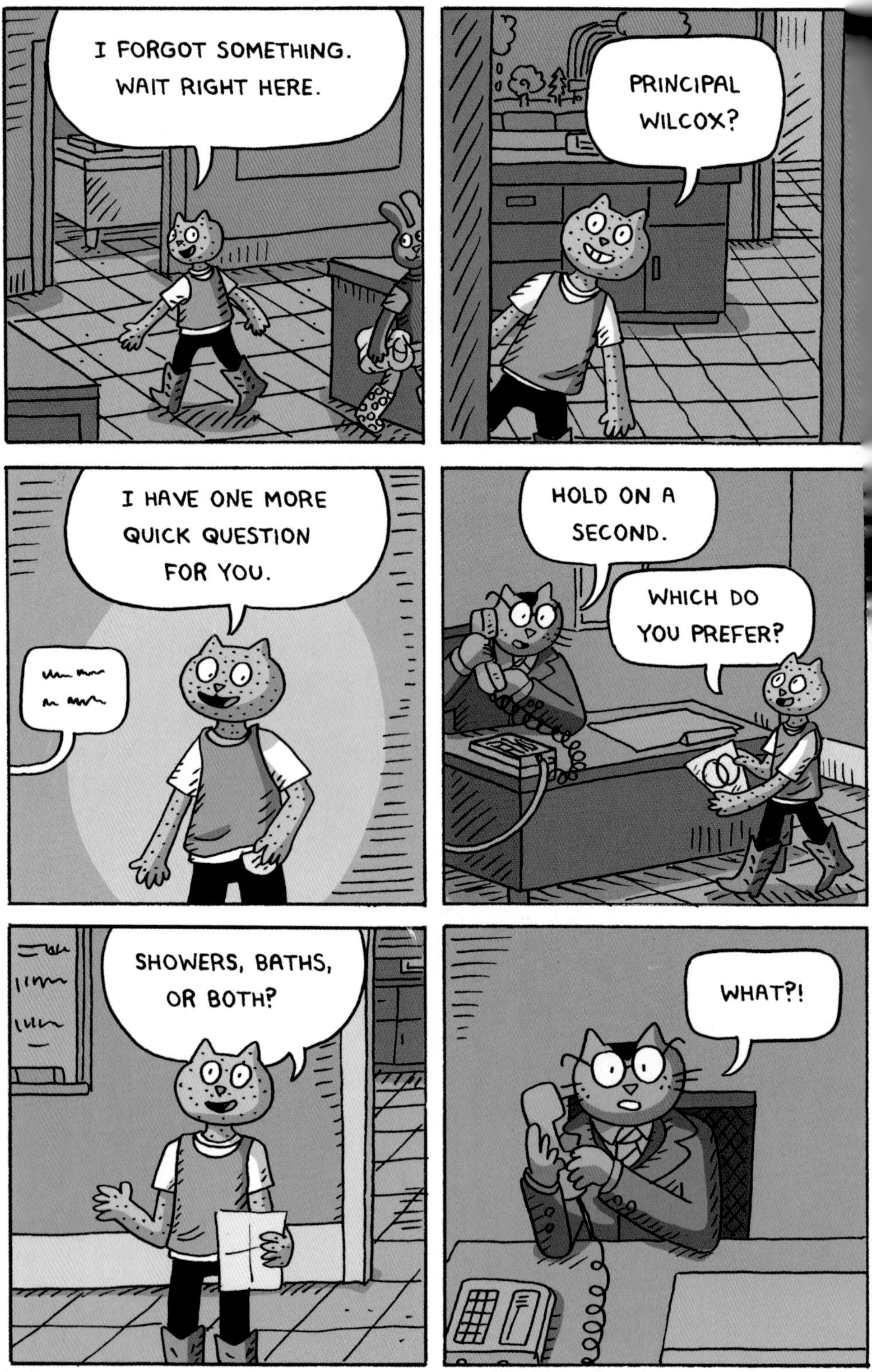
I FORGOT SOMETHING. WAIT RIGHT HERE.
PRINCIPAL WILCOX?
I HAVE ONE MORE QUICK QUESTION FOR YOU.
HOLD ON A SECOND.
WHICH DO YOU PREFER?
SHOWERS, BATHS, OR BOTH?
WHAT?!

CHAPTER FIVE

Locker Surprise

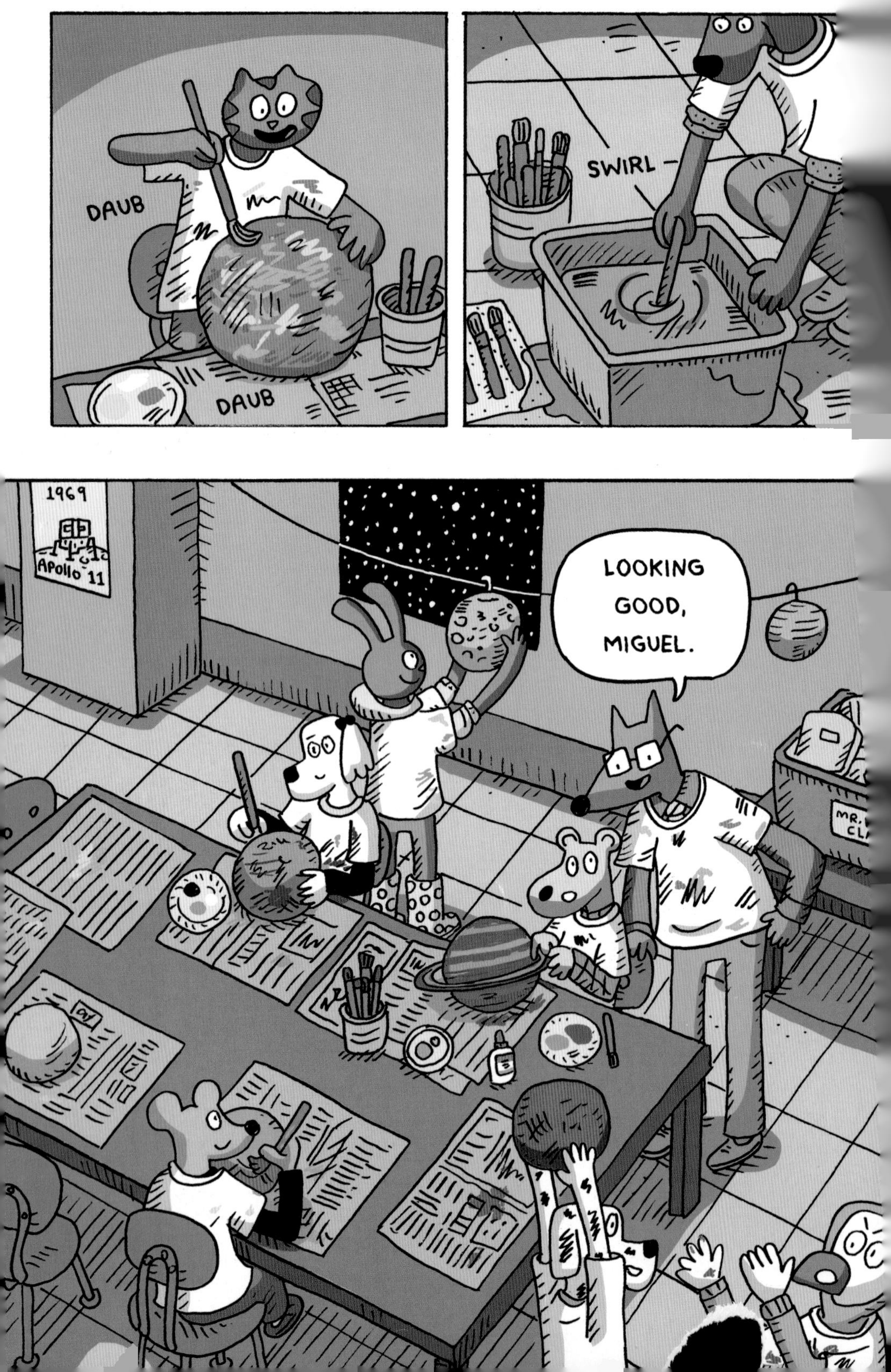
DAUB
DAUB
SWIRL
1969
APOLLO 11
LOOKING GOOD, MIGUEL.

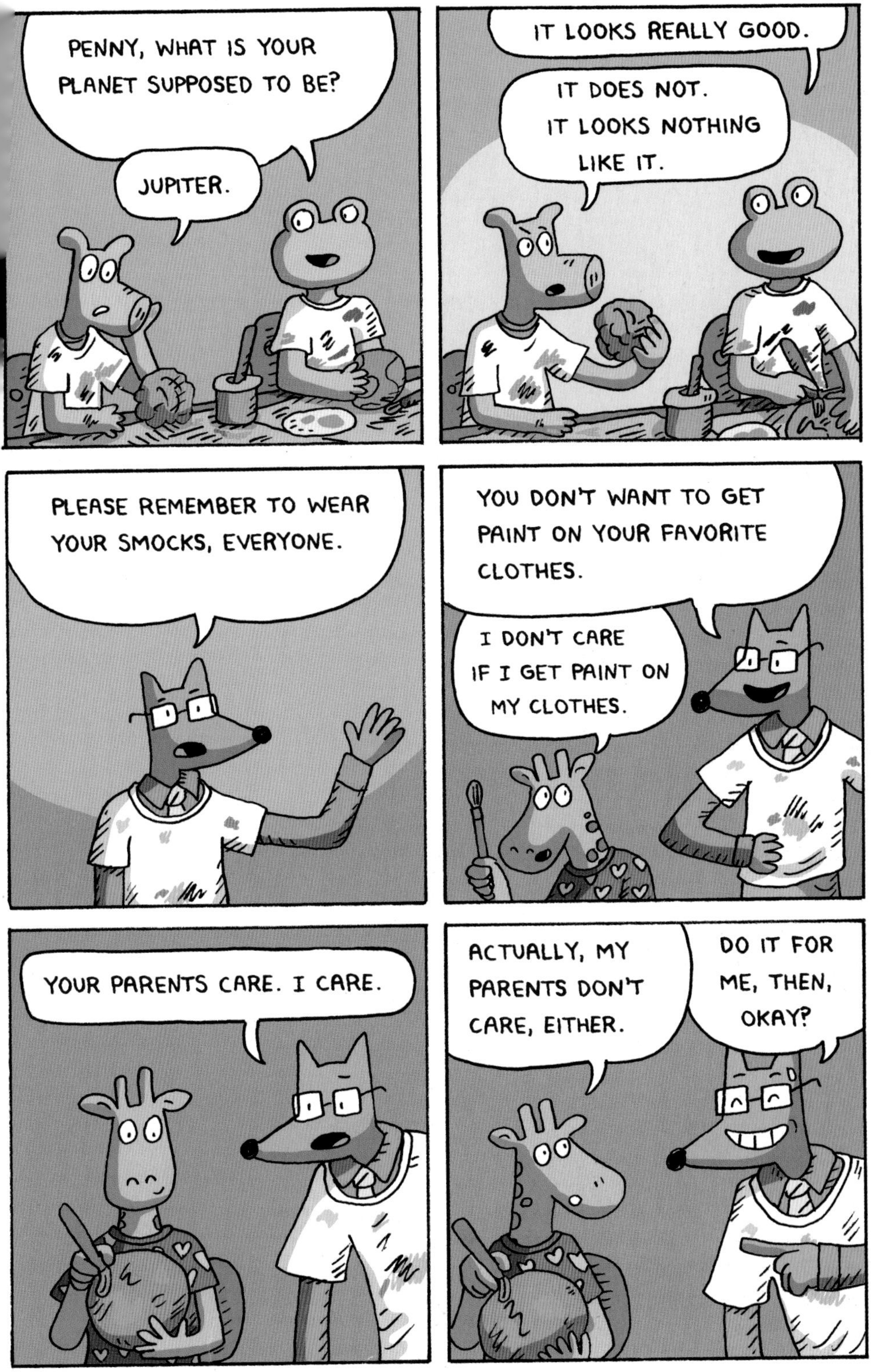
PENNY, WHAT IS YOUR PLANET SUPPOSED TO BE?
JUPITER.
IT LOOKS REALLY GOOD.
IT DOES NOT. IT LOOKS NOTHING LIKE IT.
PLEASE REMEMBER TO WEAR YOUR SMOCKS, EVERYONE.
YOU DON'T WANT TO GET PAINT ON YOUR FAVORITE CLOTHES.
I DON'T CARE IF I GET PAINT ON MY CLOTHES.
YOUR PARENTS CARE. I CARE.
ACTUALLY, MY PARENTS DON'T CARE, EITHER.
DO IT FOR ME, THEN, OKAY?

WHAT DID PRINCIPAL WILCOX SAY?
BATHS.
I ALWAYS FIGURED HE WAS MORE OF A SHOWER KIND OF GUY.
HOW DID YOU GET SATURN'S RINGS TO LOOK LIKE THAT, MIGUEL?
CARDBOARD.
WHAT DID YOU MAKE, STEWART?
DARK MATTER.
COOL!
!
UNBELIEVABLE!
PLANET IN THE TRASH!
WHO THREW AWAY THEIR HARD WORK?

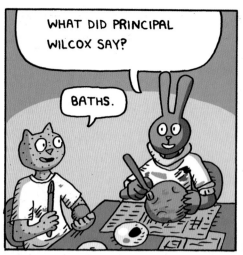

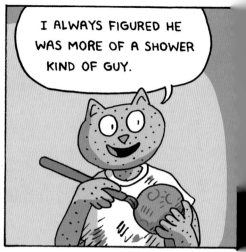

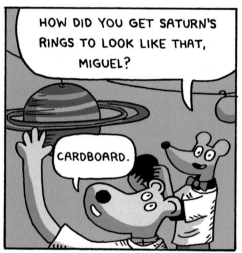

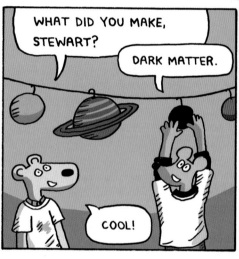

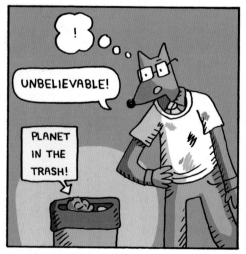

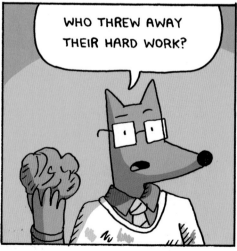

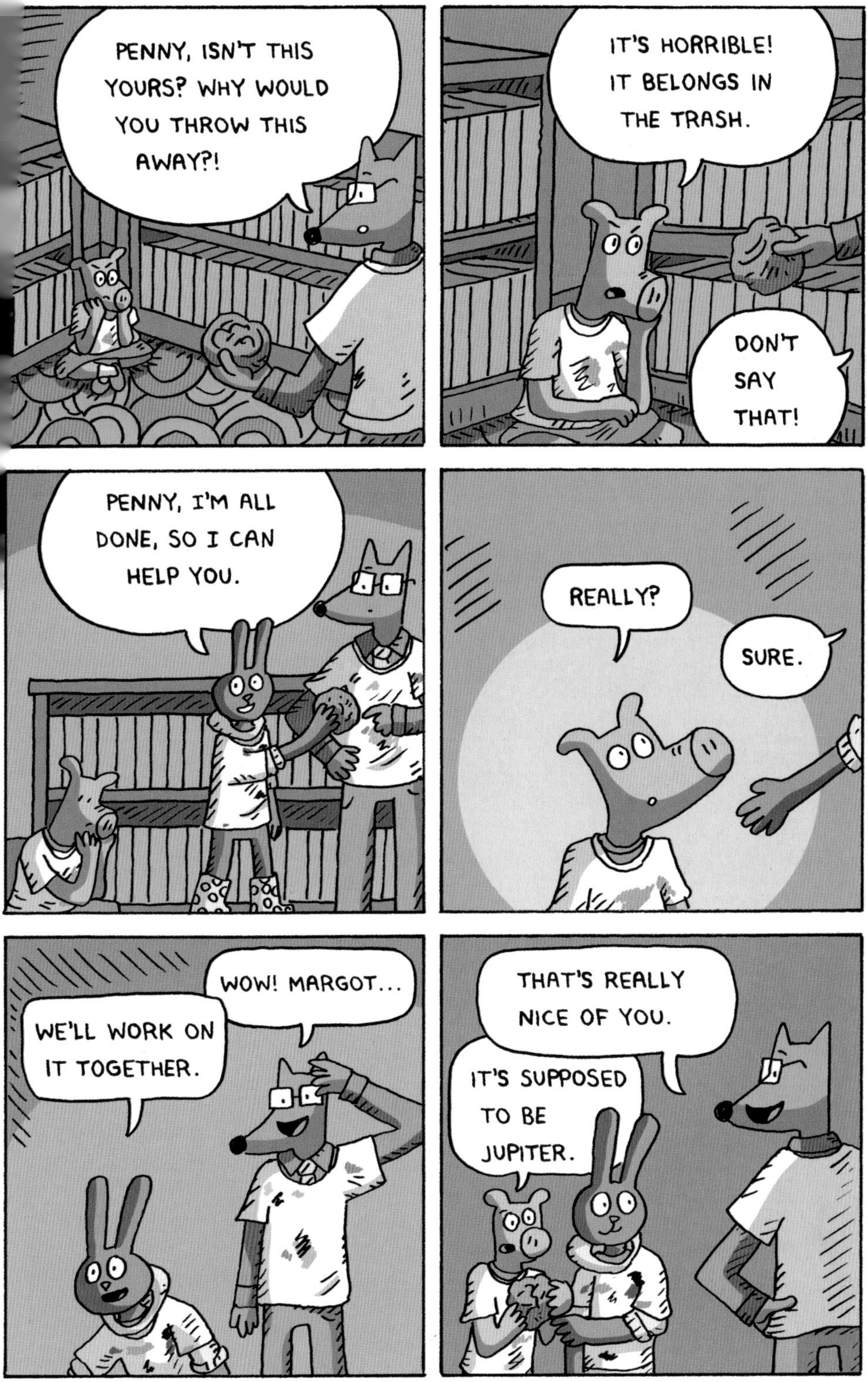
PENNY, ISN'T THIS YOURS? WHY WOULD YOU THROW THIS AWAY?!
IT'S HORRIBLE! IT BELONGS IN THE TRASH.
DON'T SAY THAT!
PENNY, I'M ALL DONE, SO I CAN HELP YOU.
REALLY?
SURE.
WOW! MARGOT...
WE'LL WORK ON IT TOGETHER.
THAT'S REALLY NICE OF YOU.
IT'S SUPPOSED TO BE JUPITER.

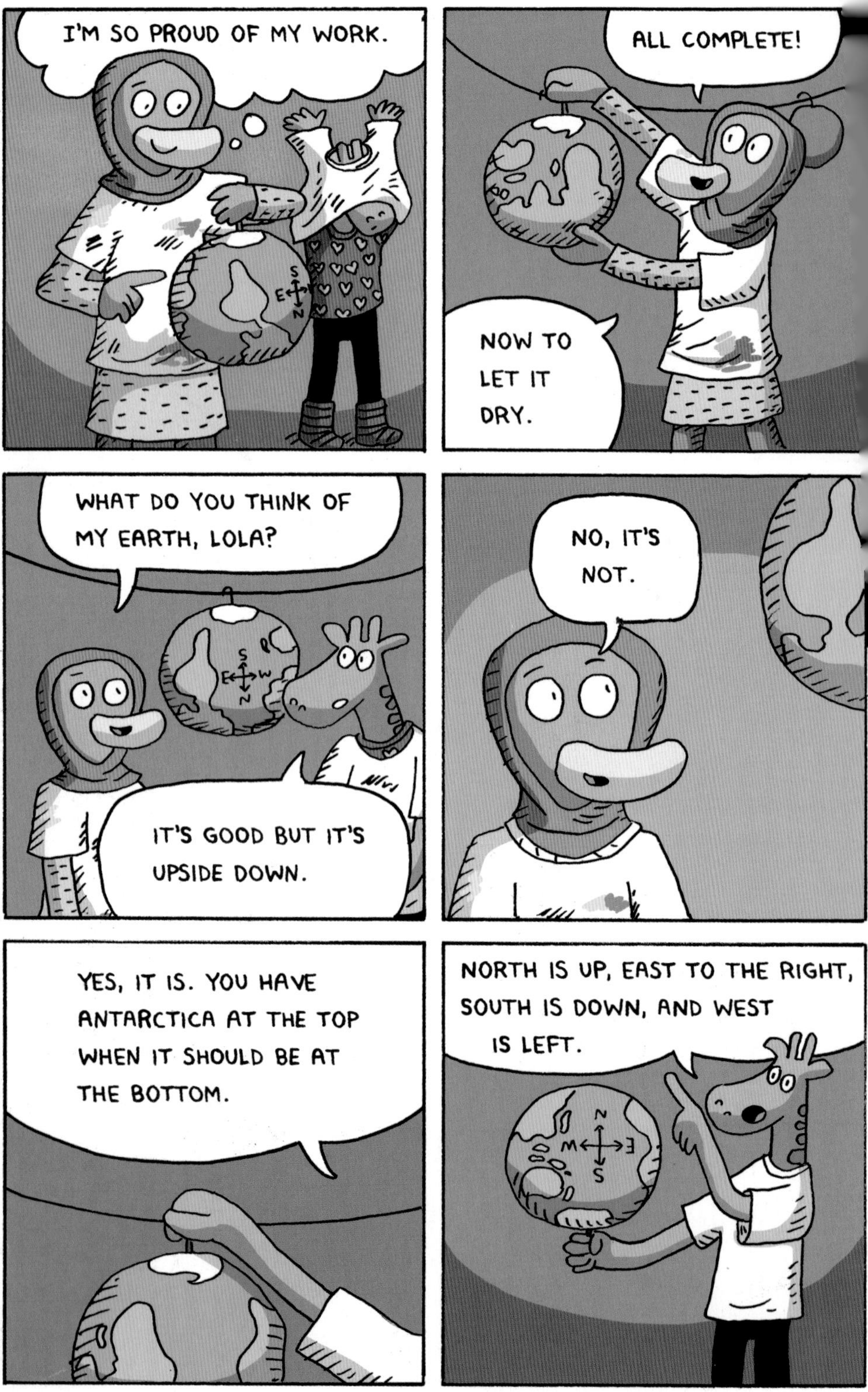
I'M SO PROUD OF MY WORK.
S
E
N
ALL COMPLETE!
NOW TO LET IT DRY.
WHAT DO YOU THINK OF MY EARTH, LOLA?
S
E
W
N
IT'S GOOD BUT IT'S UPSIDE DOWN.
NO, IT'S NOT.
YES, IT IS. YOU HAVE ANTARCTICA AT THE TOP WHEN IT SHOULD BE AT THE BOTTOM.
NORTH IS UP, EAST TO THE RIGHT, SOUTH IS DOWN, AND WEST IS LEFT.
N
W
E
S

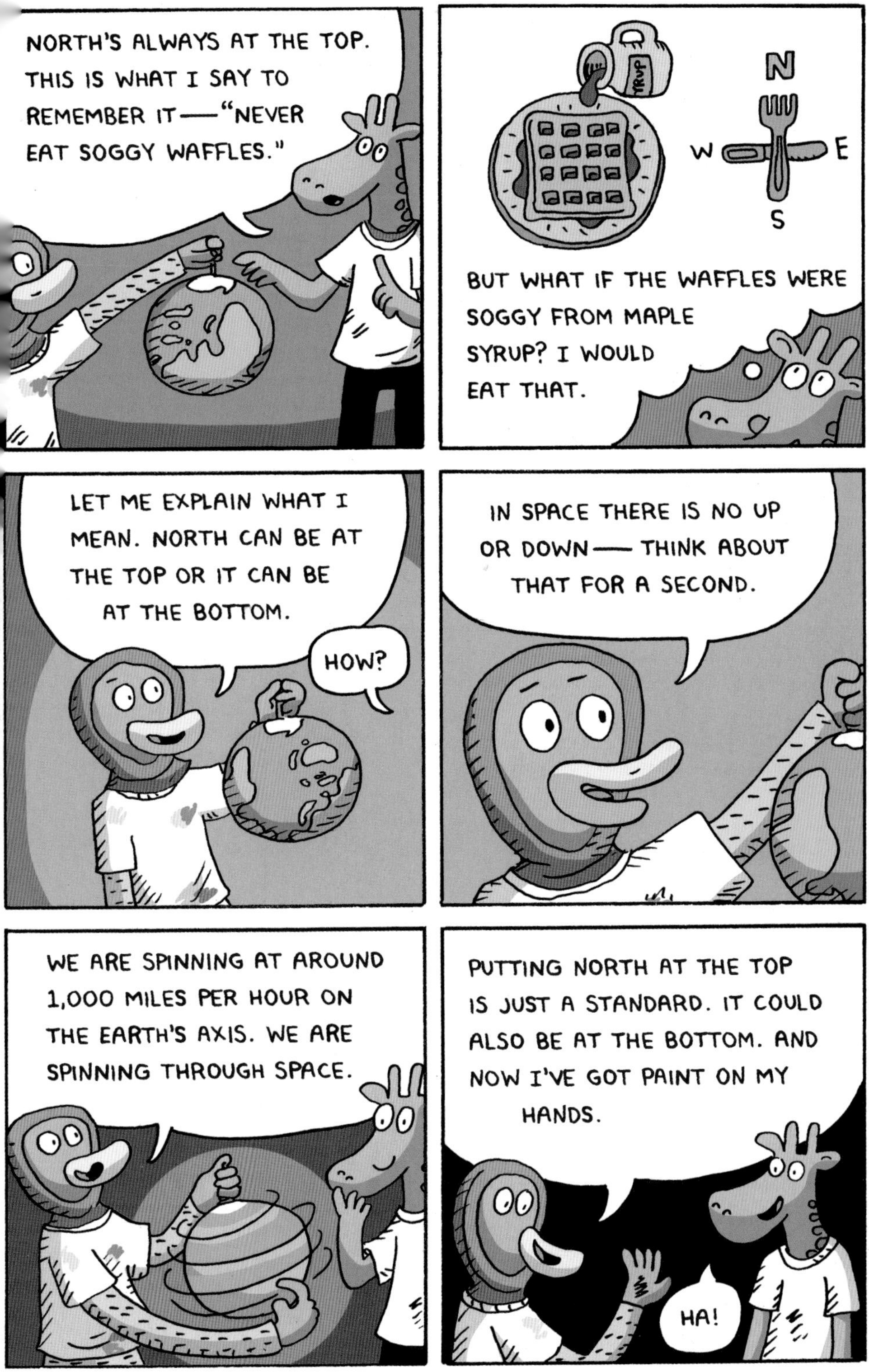
NORTH'S ALWAYS AT THE TOP. THIS IS WHAT I SAY TO REMEMBER IT—"NEVER EAT SOGGY WAFFLES."
SYRUP
N
W
E
S
BUT WHAT IF THE WAFFLES WERE SOGGY FROM MAPLE SYRUP? I WOULD EAT THAT.
LET ME EXPLAIN WHAT I MEAN. NORTH CAN BE AT THE TOP OR IT CAN BE AT THE BOTTOM.
HOW?
IN SPACE THERE IS NO UP OR DOWN—THINK ABOUT THAT FOR A SECOND.
WE ARE SPINNING AT AROUND 1,000 MILES PER HOUR ON THE EARTH'S AXIS. WE ARE SPINNING THROUGH SPACE.
PUTTING NORTH AT THE TOP IS JUST A STANDARD. IT COULD ALSO BE AT THE BOTTOM. AND NOW I'VE GOT PAINT ON MY HANDS.
HA!

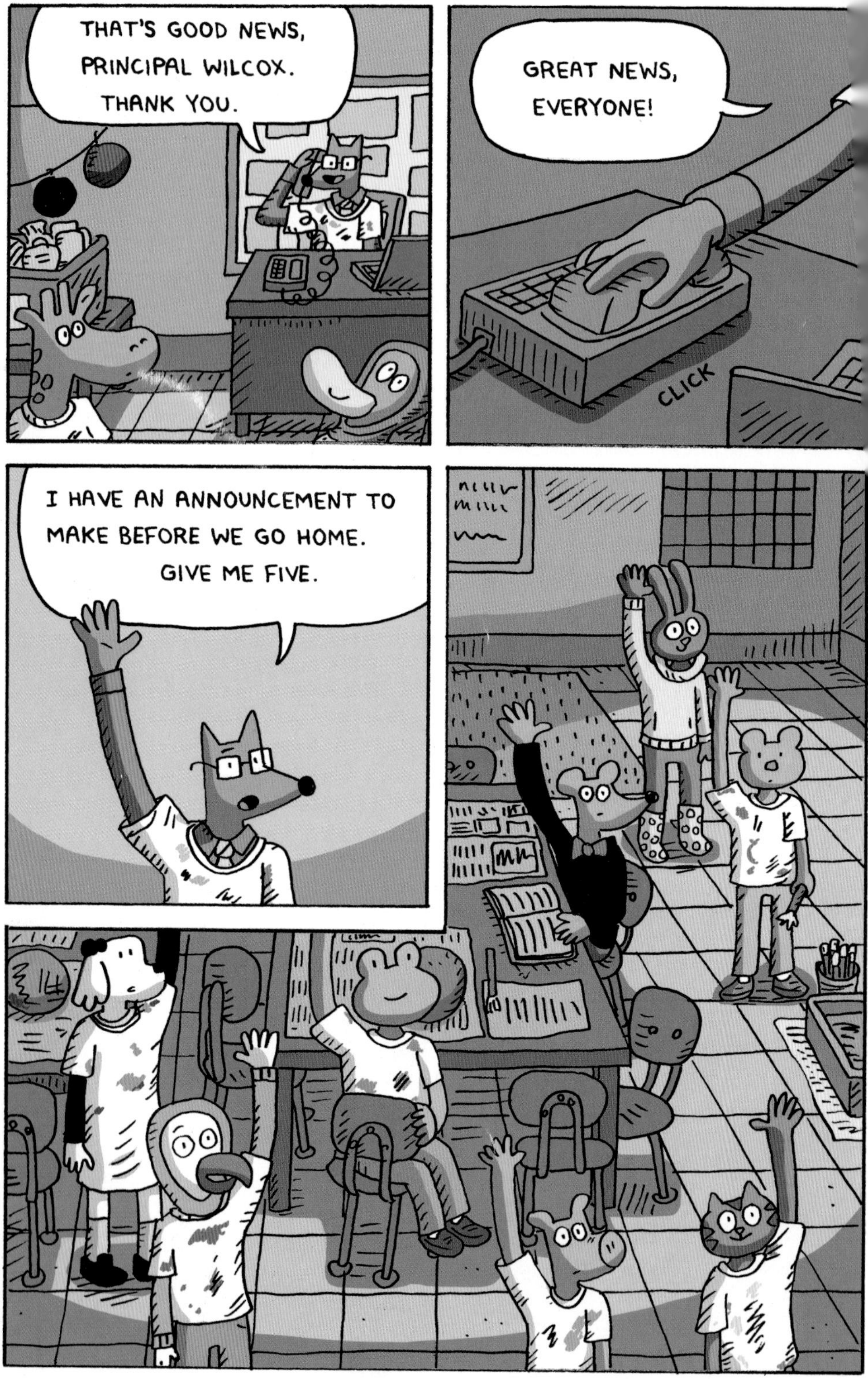
THAT'S GOOD NEWS, PRINCIPAL WILCOX. THANK YOU.
GREAT NEWS, EVERYONE!
CLICK
I HAVE AN ANNOUNCEMENT TO MAKE BEFORE WE GO HOME. GIVE ME FIVE.

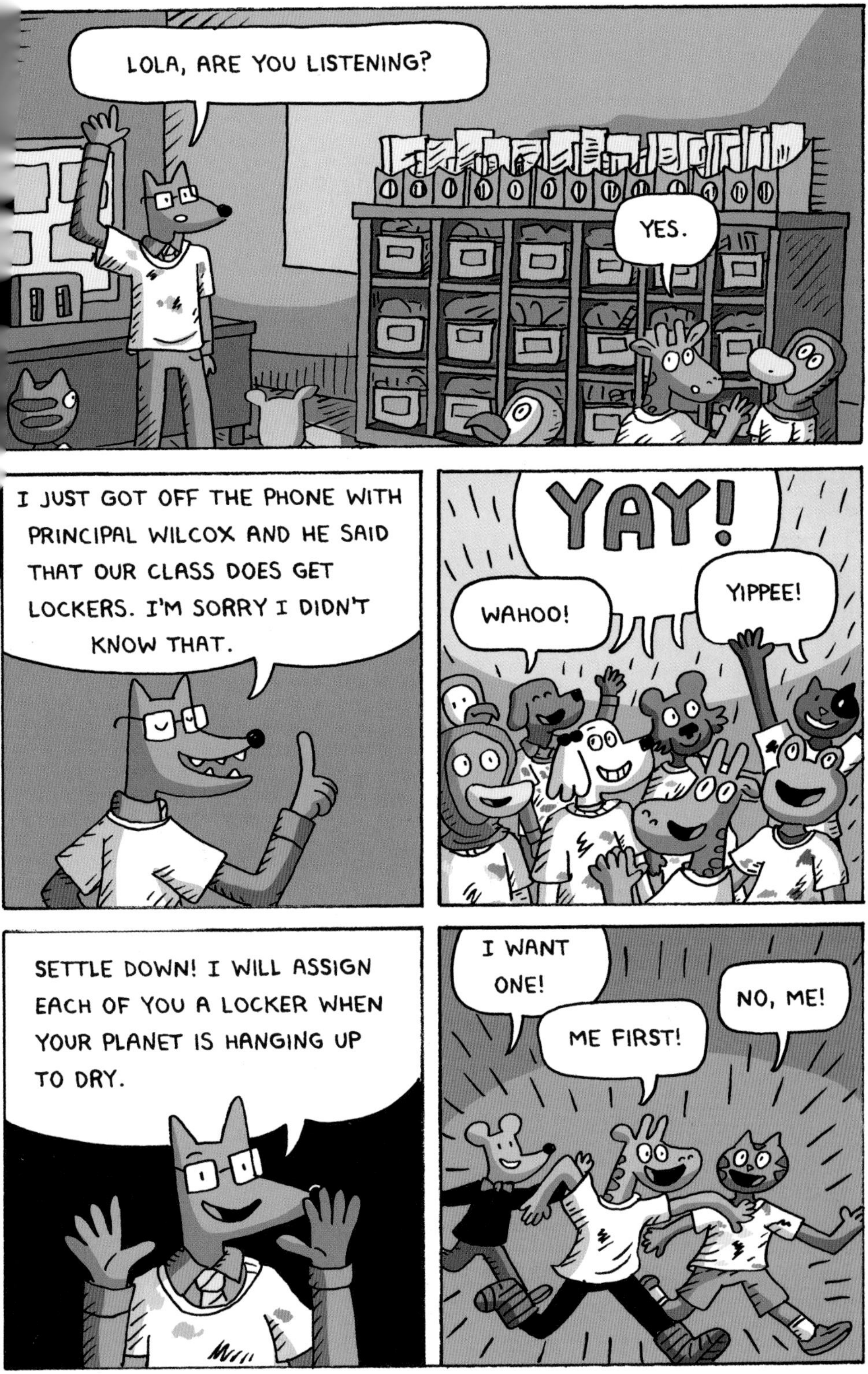
LOLA, ARE YOU LISTENING?
YES.
I JUST GOT OFF THE PHONE WITH PRINCIPAL WILCOX AND HE SAID THAT OUR CLASS DOES GET LOCKERS. I'M SORRY I DIDN'T KNOW THAT.
YAY!
WAHOO!
YIPPEE!
SETTLE DOWN! I WILL ASSIGN EACH OF YOU A LOCKER WHEN YOUR PLANET IS HANGING UP TO DRY.
I WANT ONE!
ME FIRST!
NO, ME!

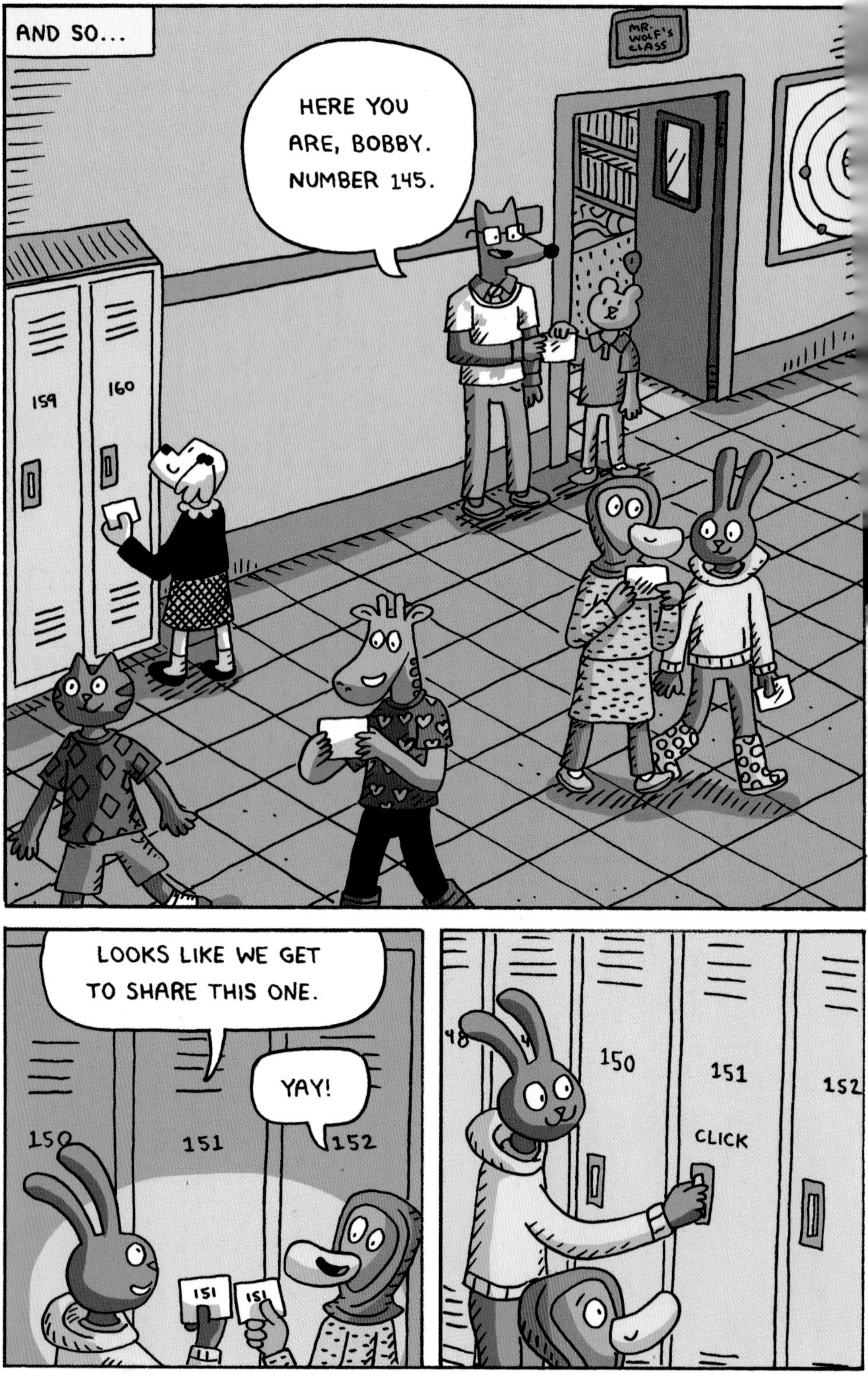
AND SO...
MR. WOLF'S CLASS
HERE YOU ARE, BOBBY. NUMBER 145.
159
160
LOOKS LIKE WE GET TO SHARE THIS ONE.
YAY!
150
151
152
151
151
150
151
152
CLICK

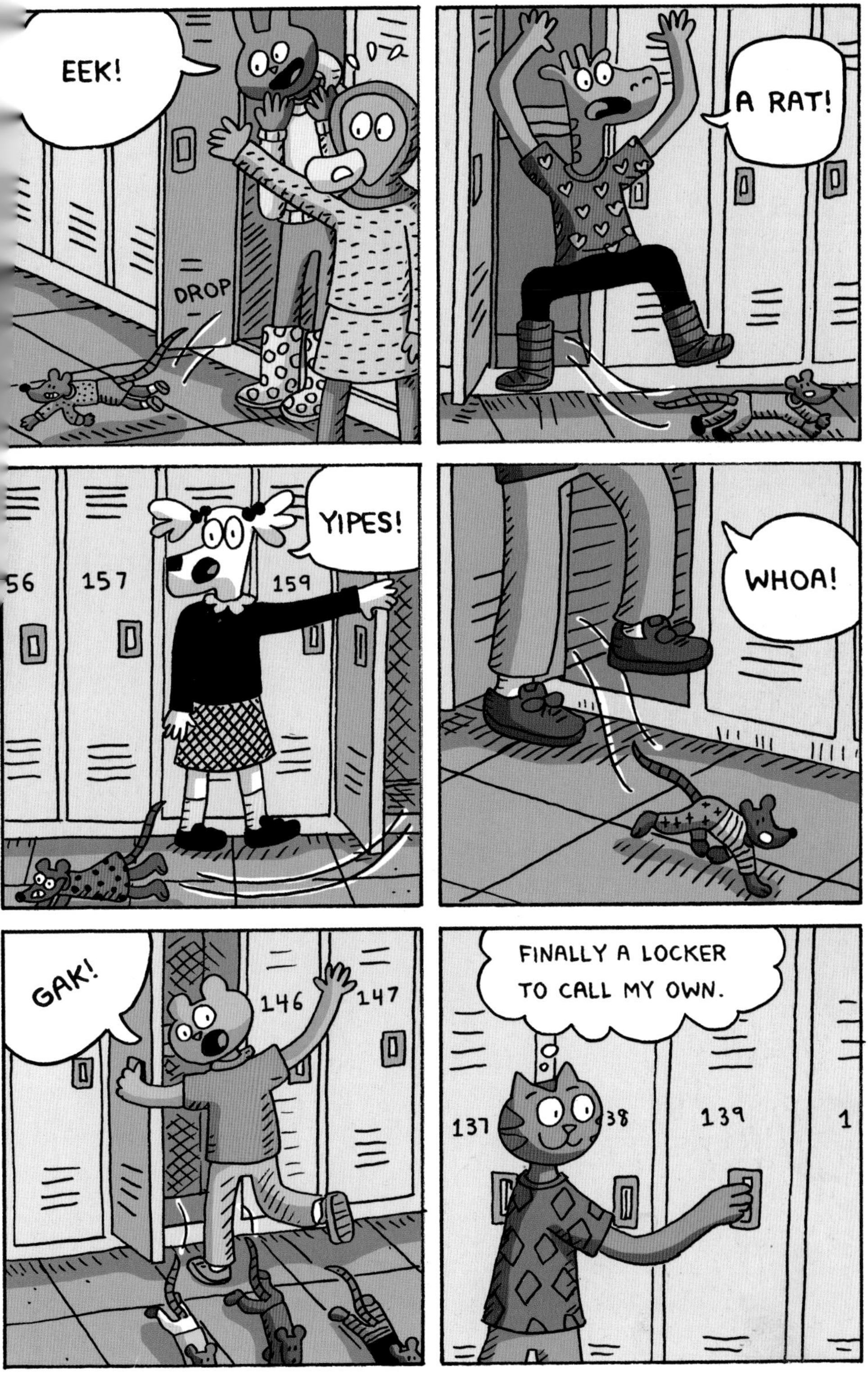
EEK!
DROP
A RAT!
YIPES!
56
157
159
WHOA!
GAK!
146
147
FINALLY A LOCKER TO CALL MY OWN.
137
38
139
1

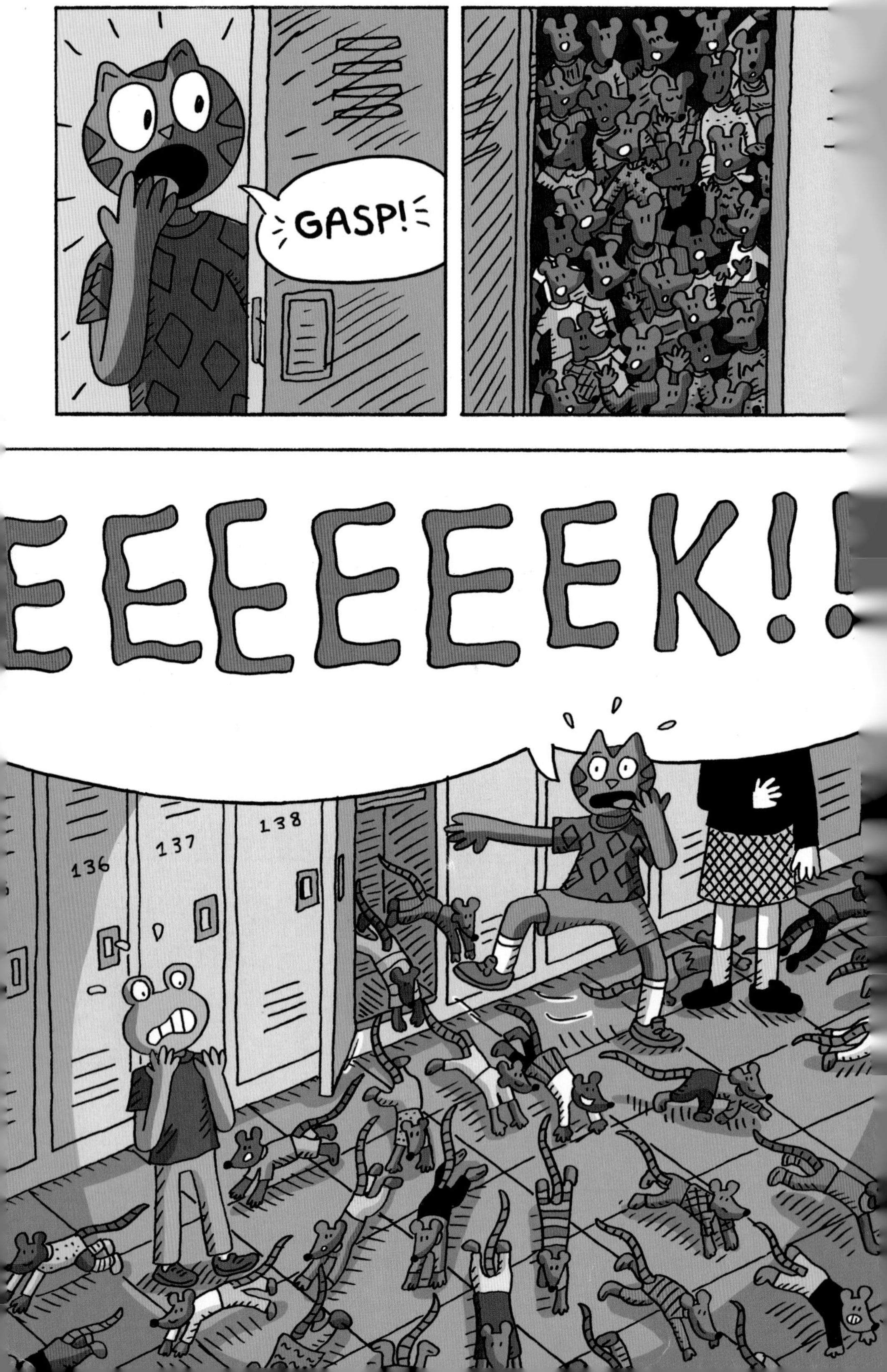
GASP!
EEEEEEK!!
136
137
138

CHAPTER SIX
The Mystery in the Woods

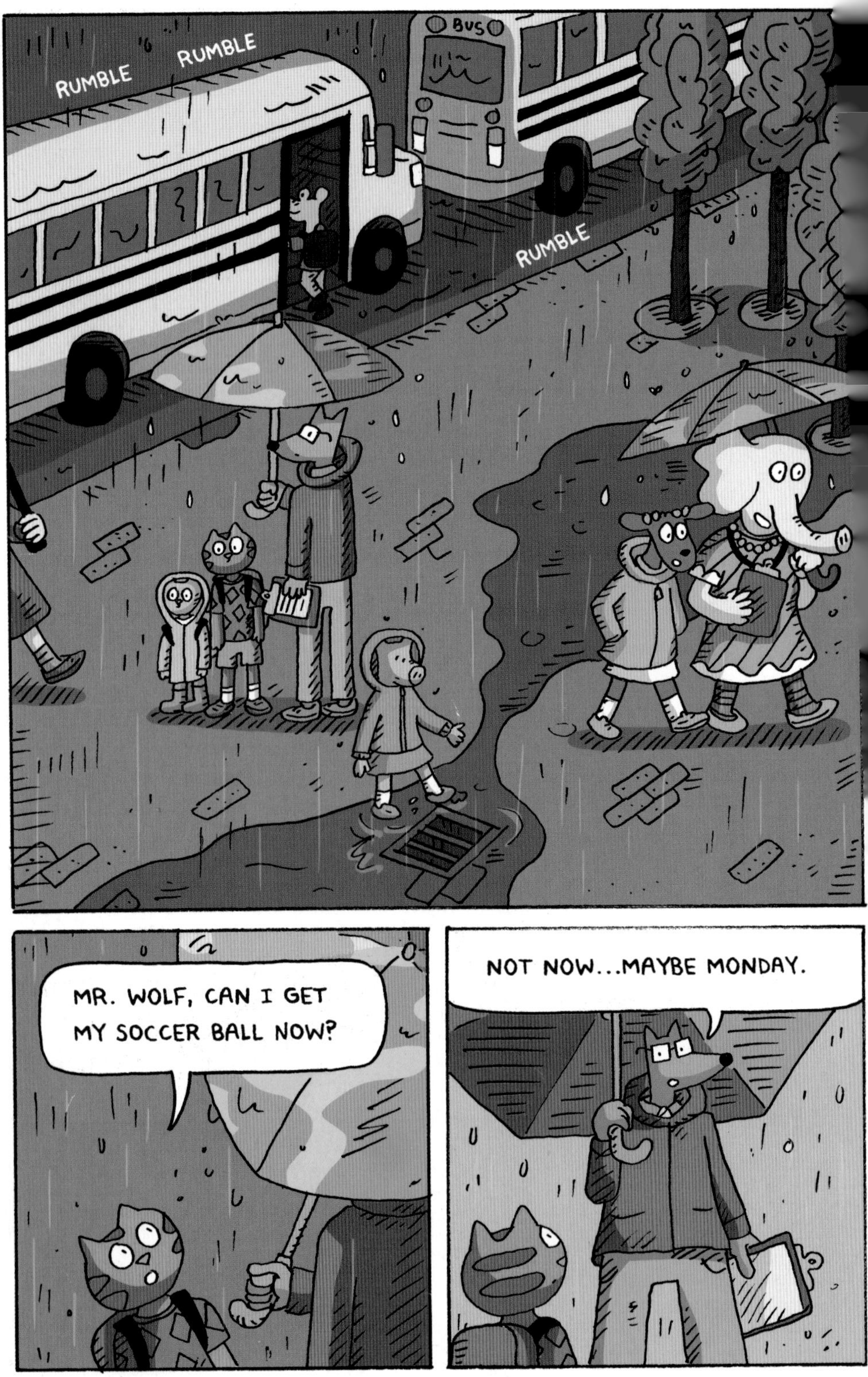
RUMBLE
RUMBLE
BUS
RUMBLE
MR. WOLF, CAN I GET MY SOCCER BALL NOW?
NOT NOW...MAYBE MONDAY.

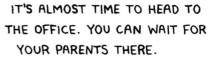

IT'S ALMOST TIME TO HEAD TO THE OFFICE. YOU CAN WAIT FOR YOUR PARENTS THERE.

MOM'S HERE.

BOYS!

PLIP

PLOP

WE SEE OUR MOM.

OKAY.

BYE! HAVE A GREAT WEEKEND!

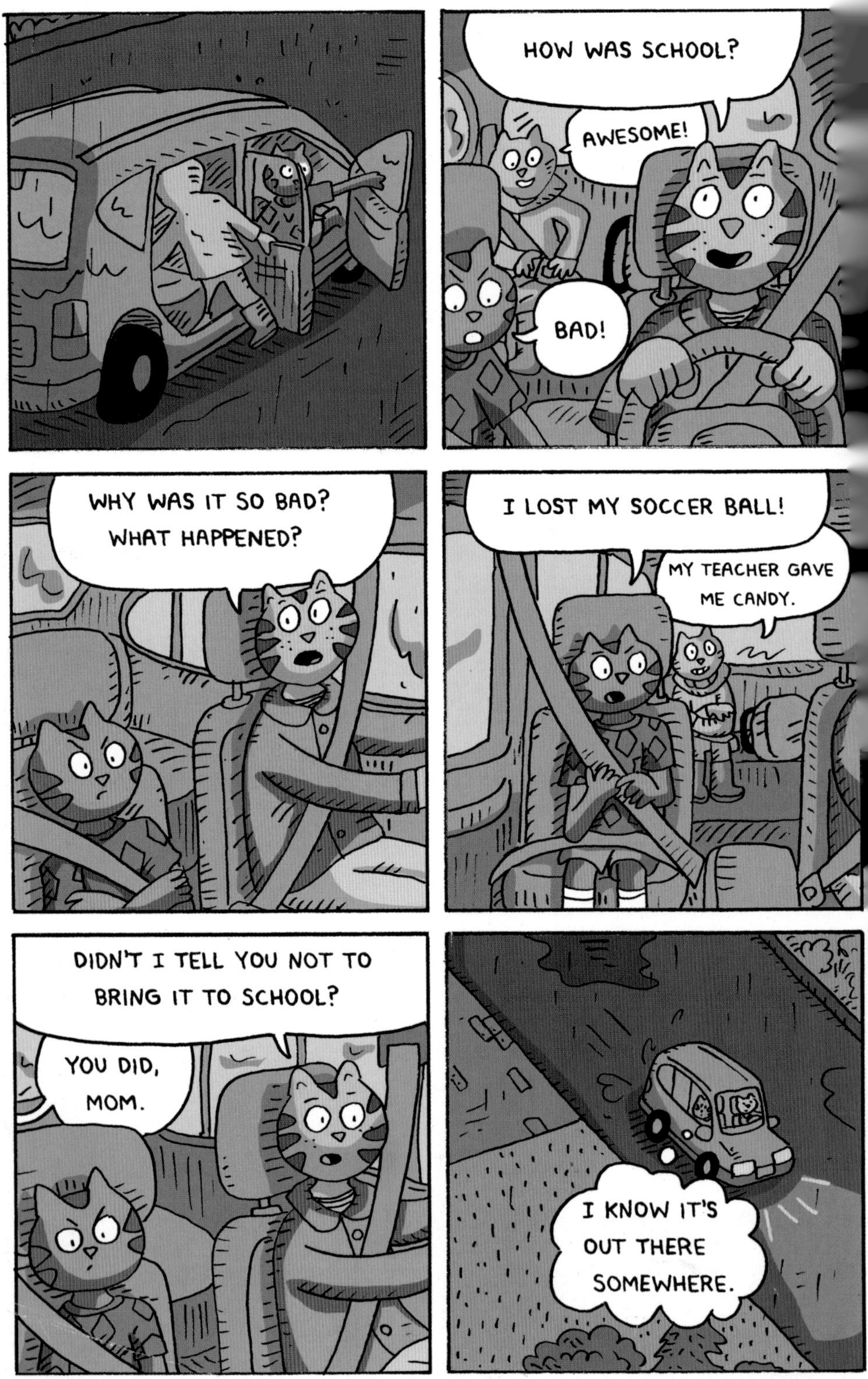
HOW WAS SCHOOL?
AWESOME!
BAD!
WHY WAS IT SO BAD? WHAT HAPPENED?
I LOST MY SOCCER BALL!
MY TEACHER GAVE ME CANDY.
DIDN'T I TELL YOU NOT TO BRING IT TO SCHOOL?
YOU DID, MOM.
I KNOW IT'S OUT THERE SOMEWHERE.

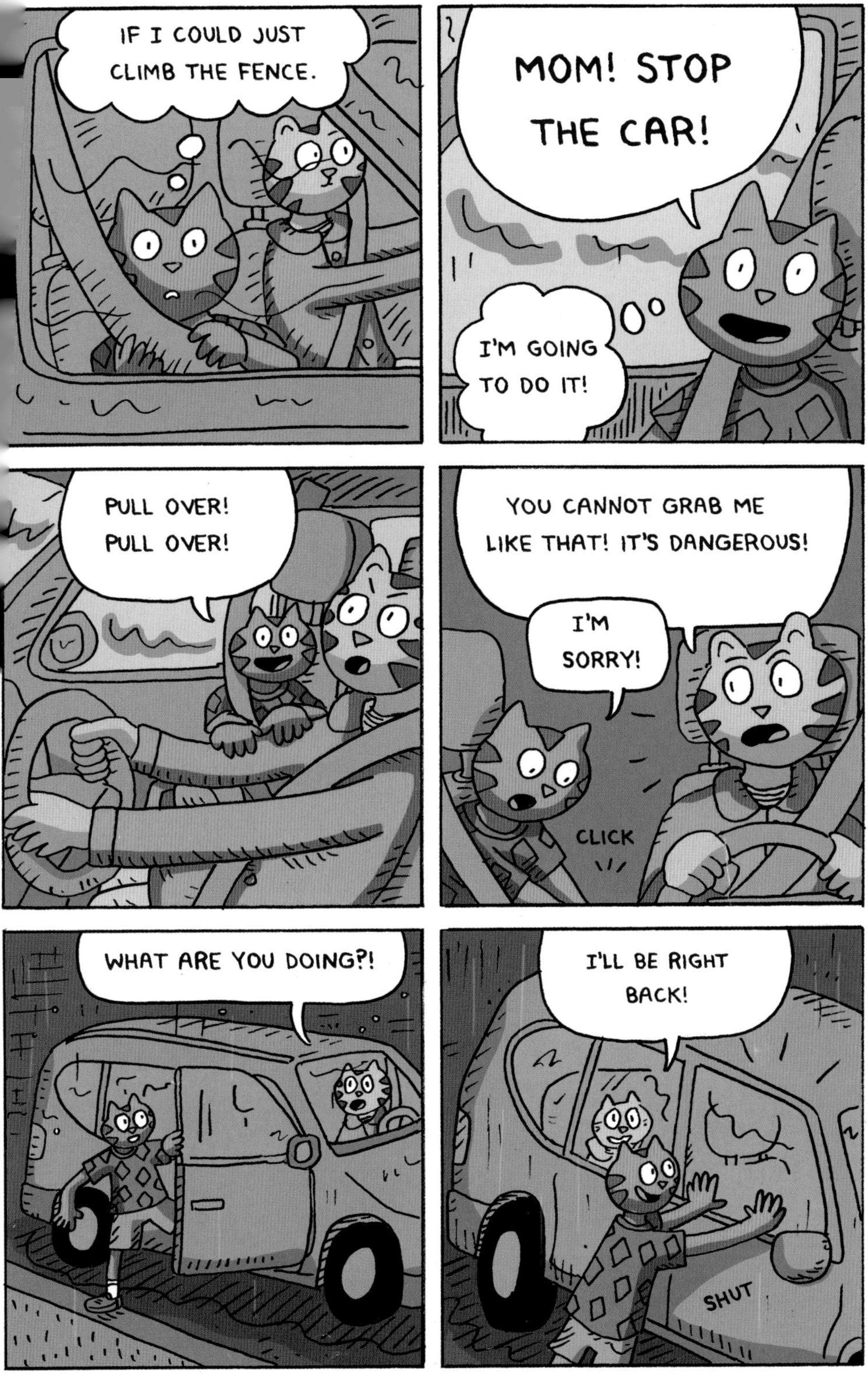
IF I COULD JUST CLIMB THE FENCE.
MOM! STOP THE CAR!
I'M GOING TO DO IT!
PULL OVER! PULL OVER!
YOU CANNOT GRAB ME LIKE THAT! IT'S DANGEROUS!
I'M SORRY!
CLICK
WHAT ARE YOU DOING?!
I'LL BE RIGHT BACK!
SHUT

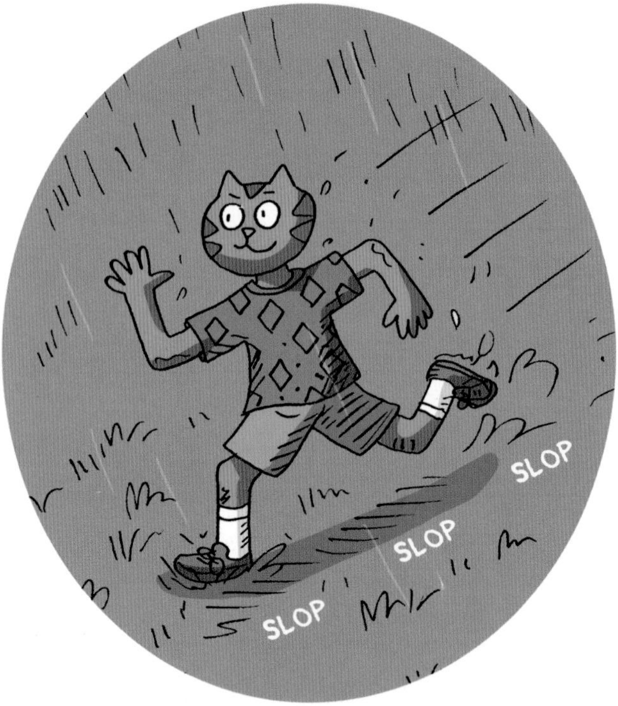
SLOP
SLOP
SLOP

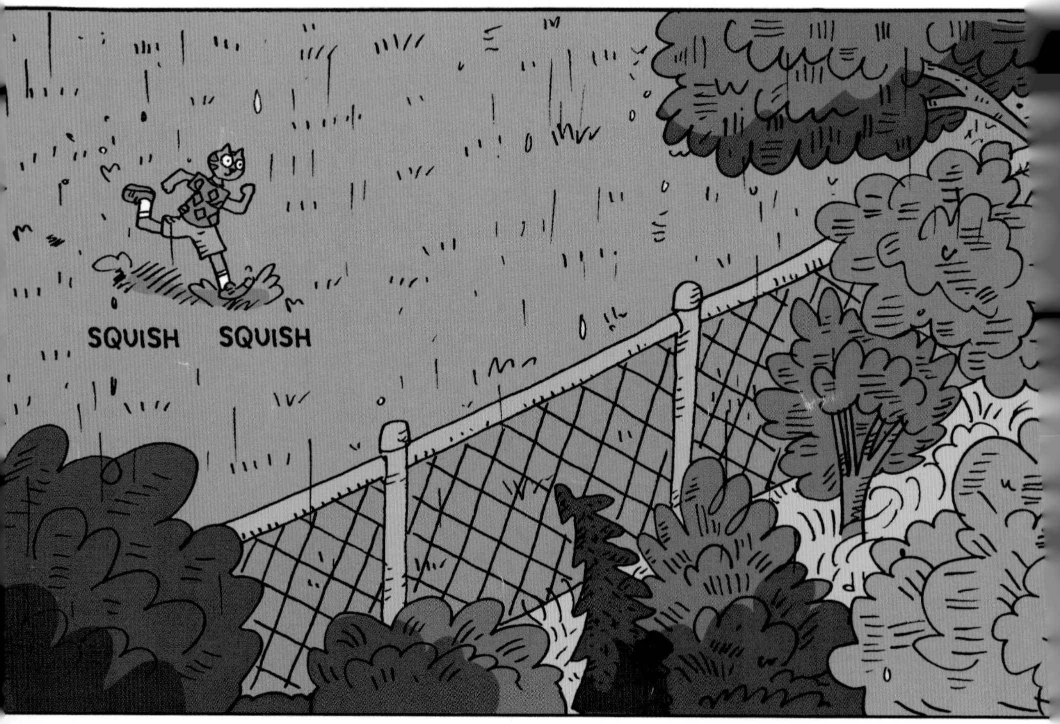
SQUISH SQUISH

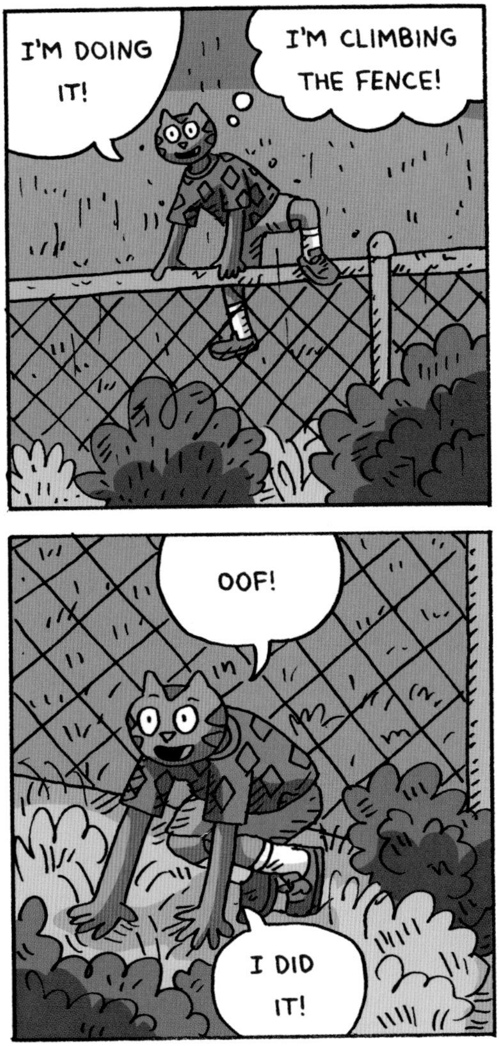
I'M DOING IT!
I'M CLIMBING THE FENCE!
OOF!
I DID IT!

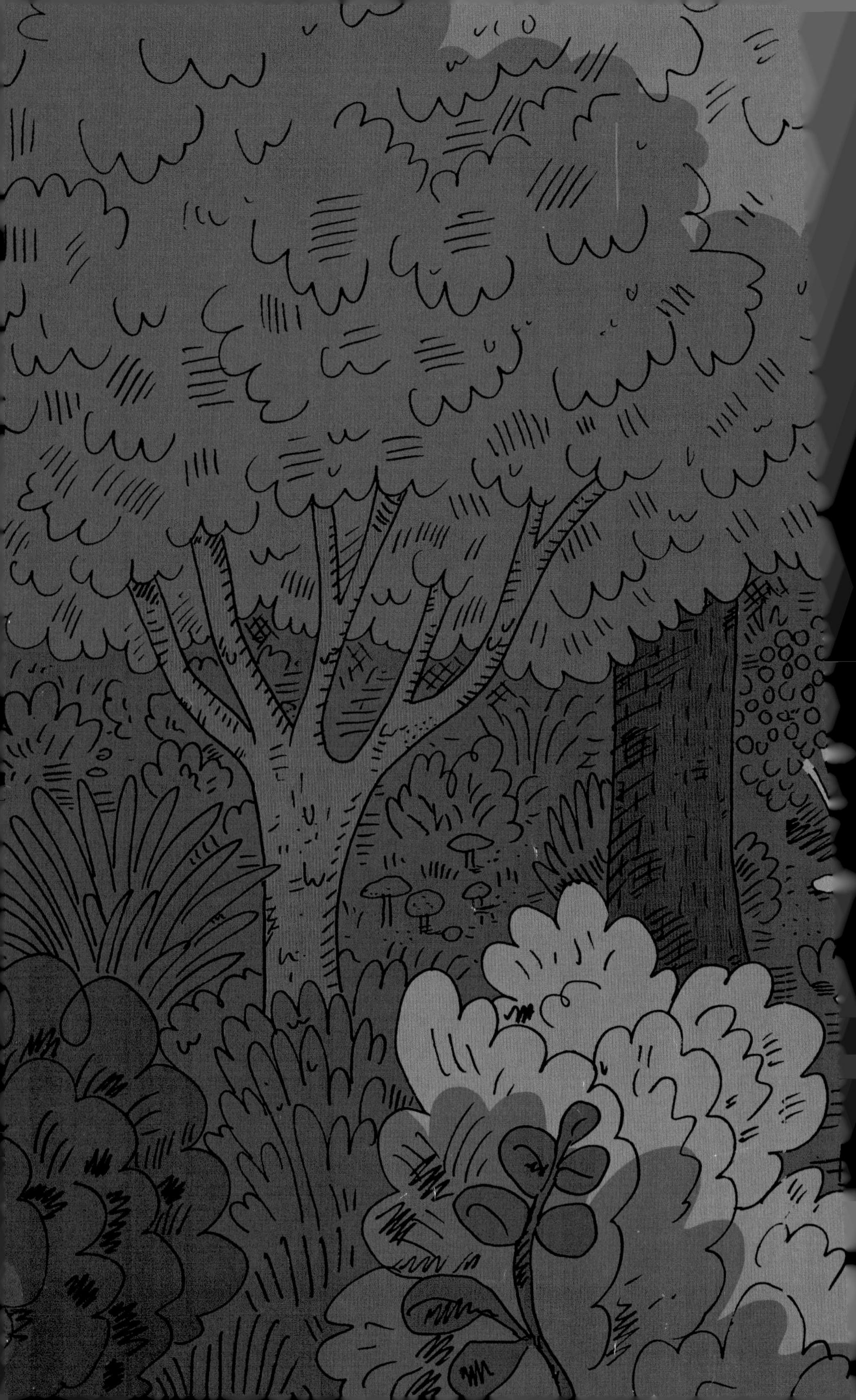

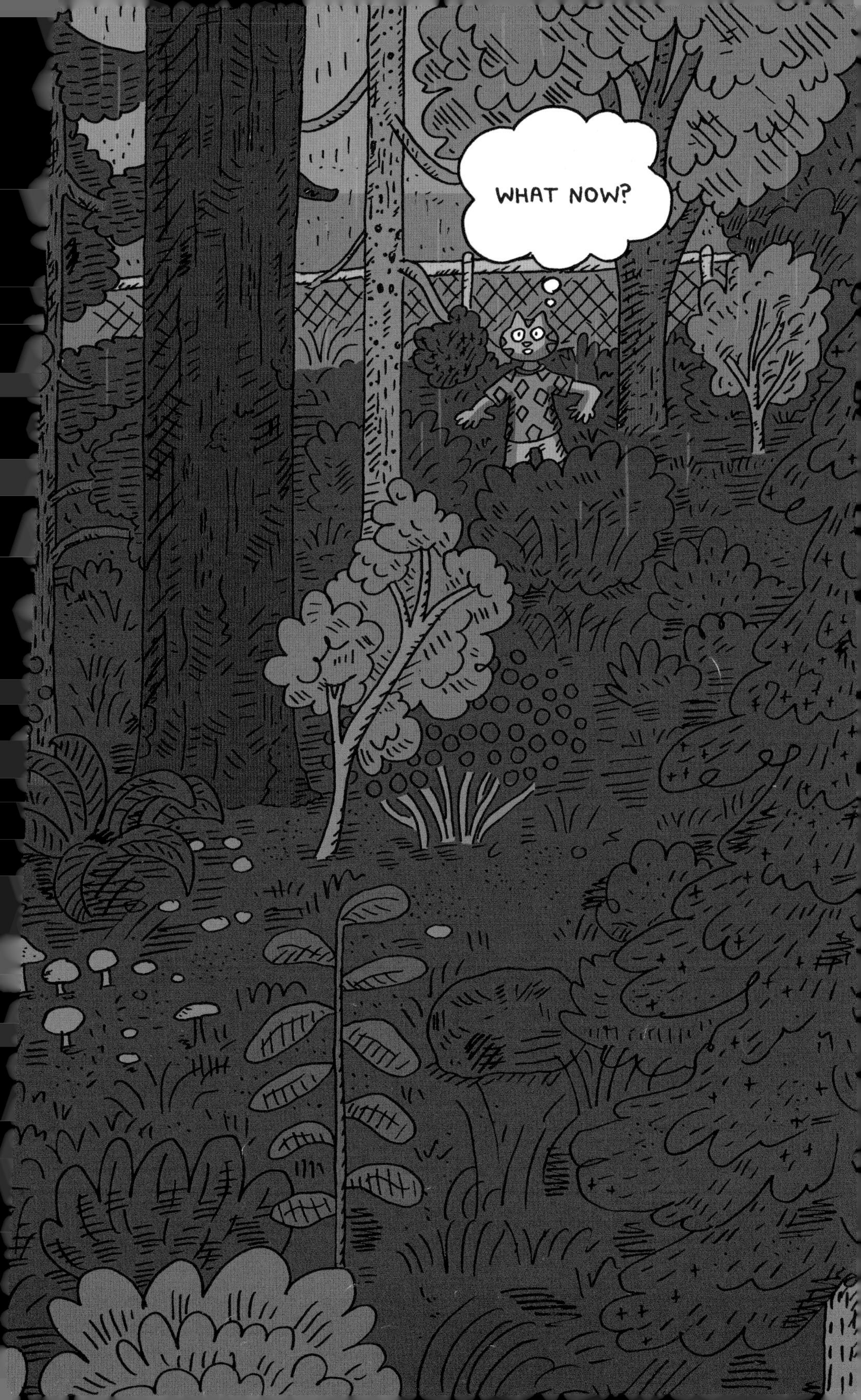
WHAT NOW?

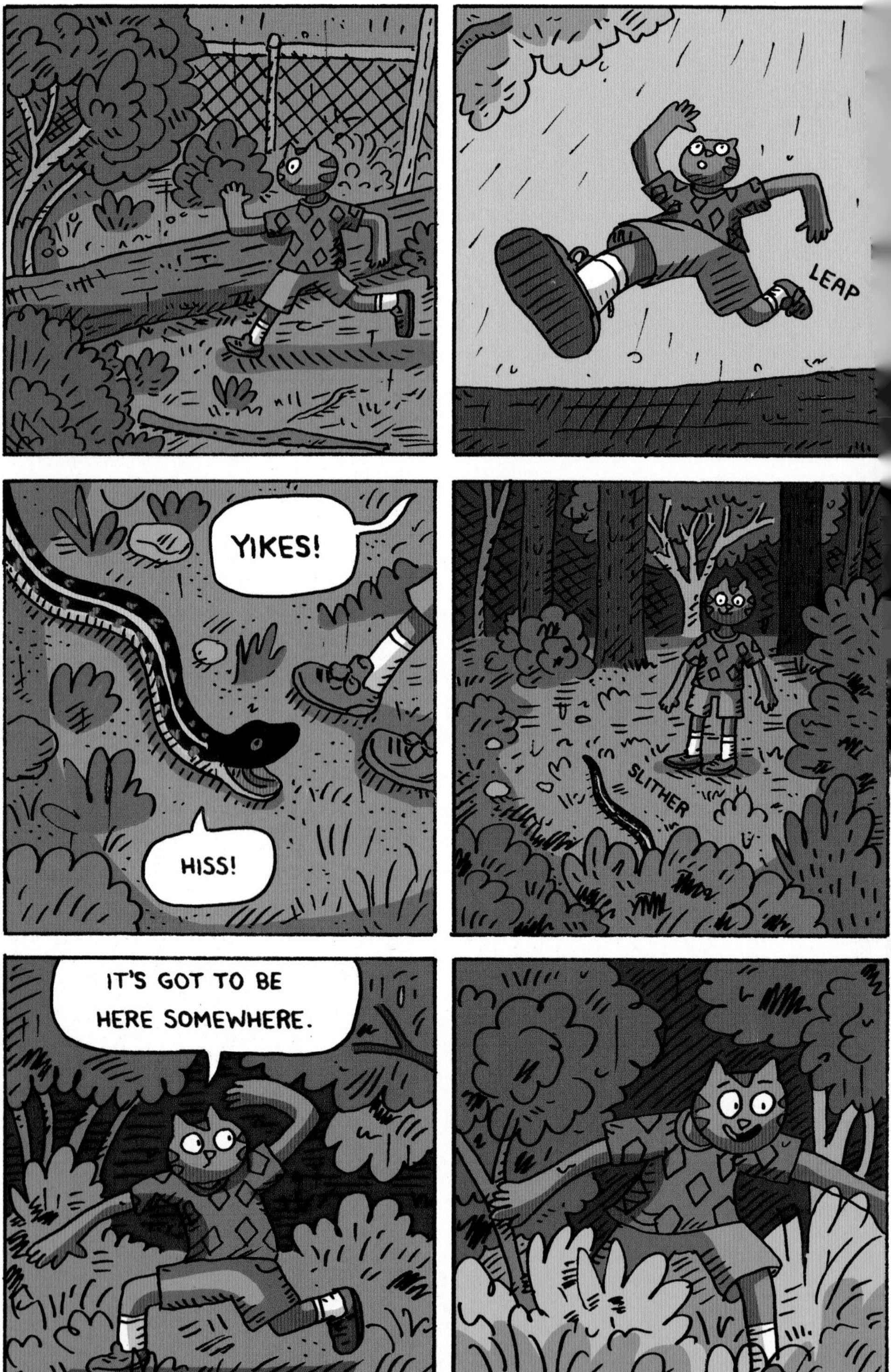
LEAP
YIKES!
HISS!
SLITHER
IT'S GOT TO BE HERE SOMEWHERE.

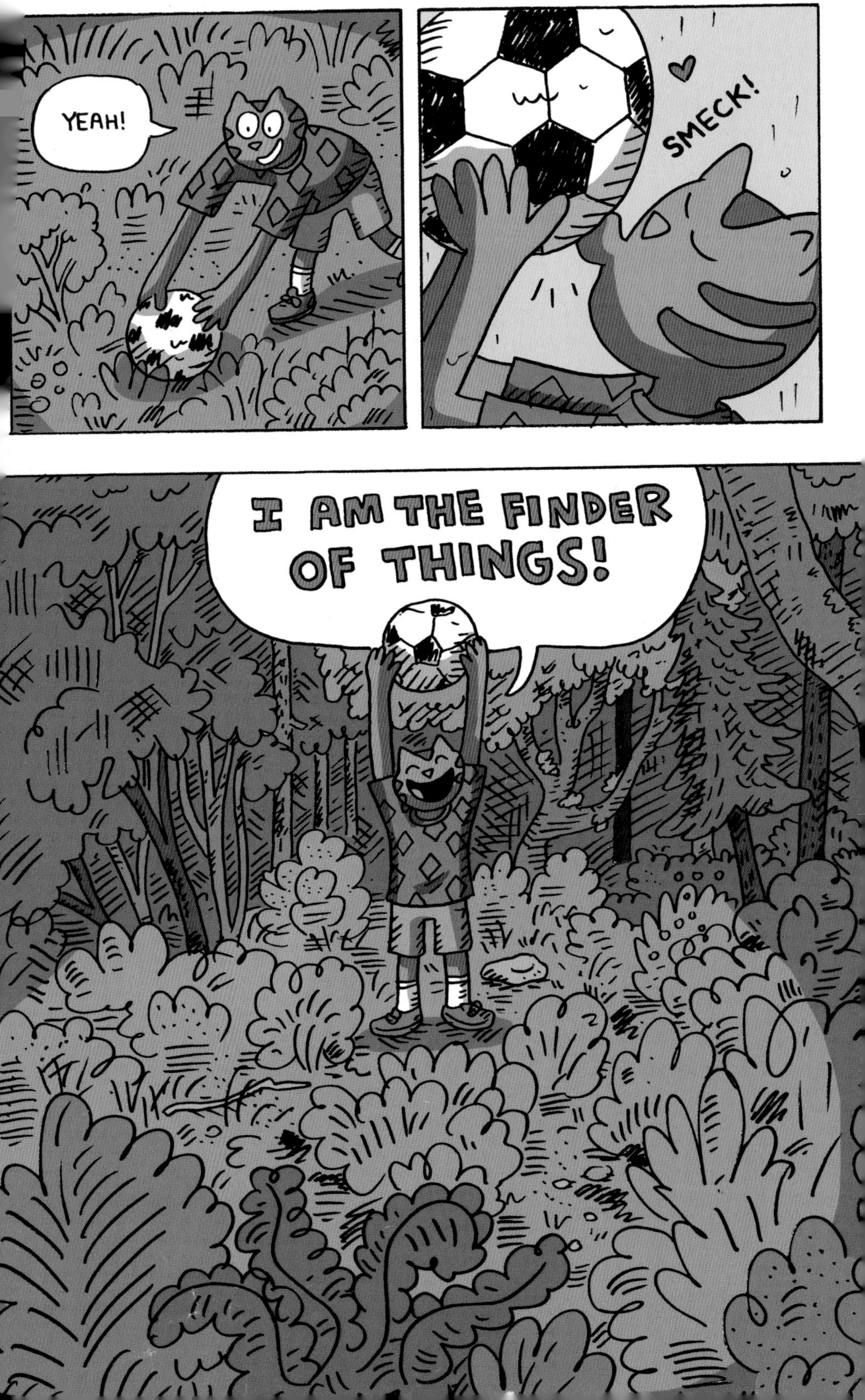
YEAH!
SMECK!
I AM THE FINDER OF THINGS!

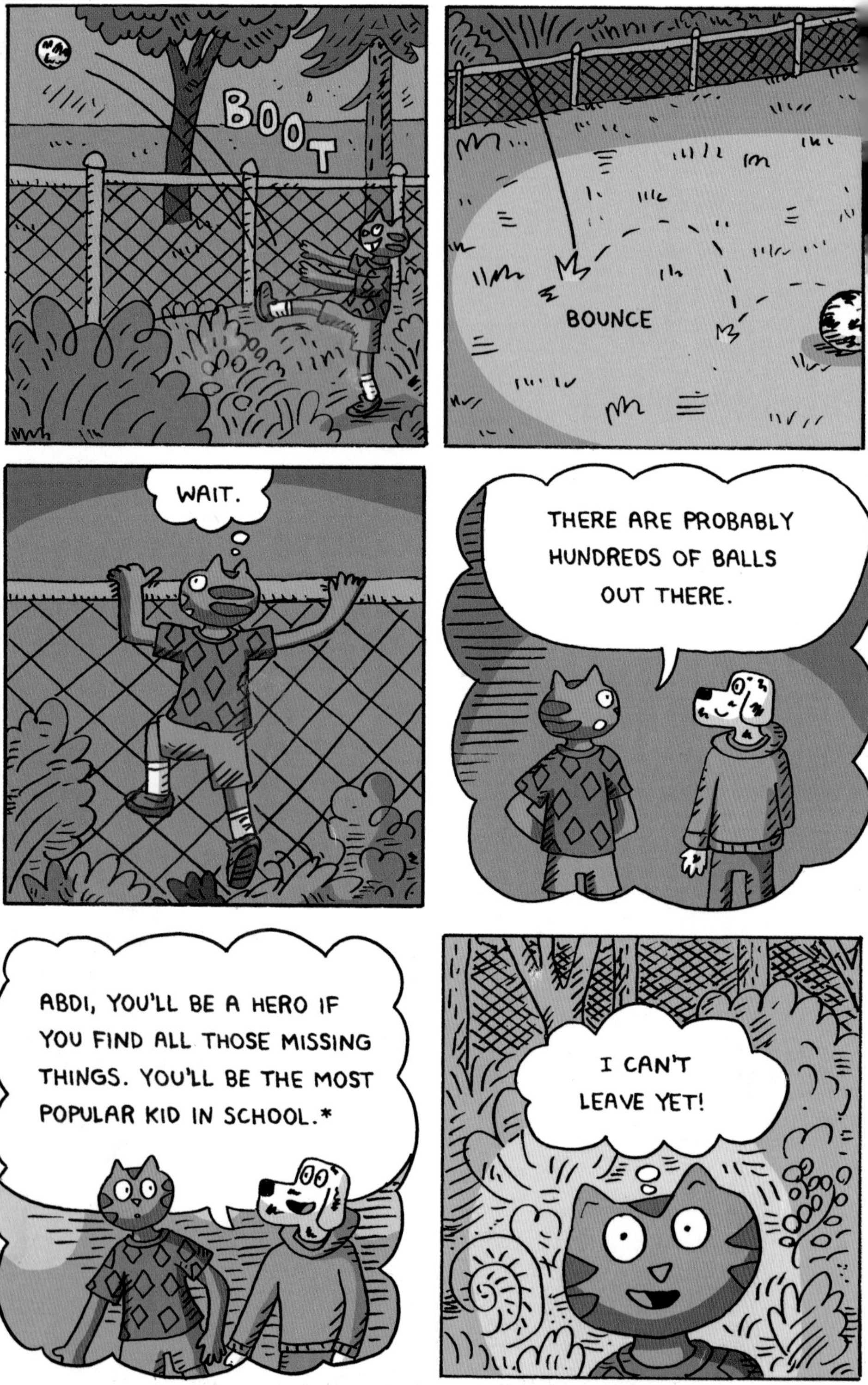
BOOT
BOUNCE
WAIT.
THERE ARE PROBABLY HUNDREDS OF BALLS OUT THERE.
ABDI, YOU'LL BE A HERO IF YOU FIND ALL THOSE MISSING THINGS. YOU'LL BE THE MOST POPULAR KID IN SCHOOL.*
I CAN'T LEAVE YET!

*ABDI'S MEMORY MAY OR MAY NOT BE 100% ACCURATE.

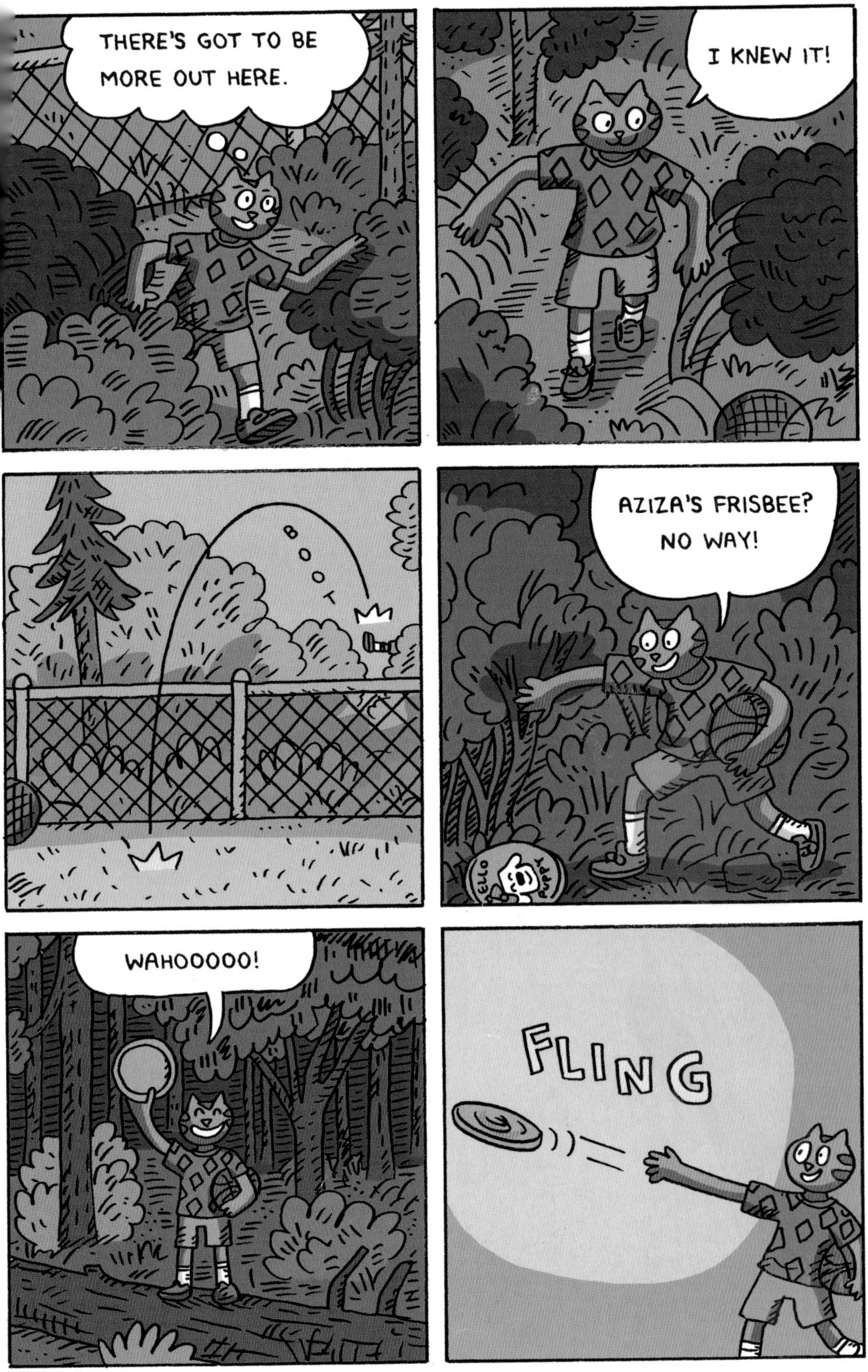
THERE'S GOT TO BE MORE OUT HERE.
I KNEW IT!
BOOT
AZIZA'S FRISBEE? NO WAY!
WAHOOOOO!
FLING

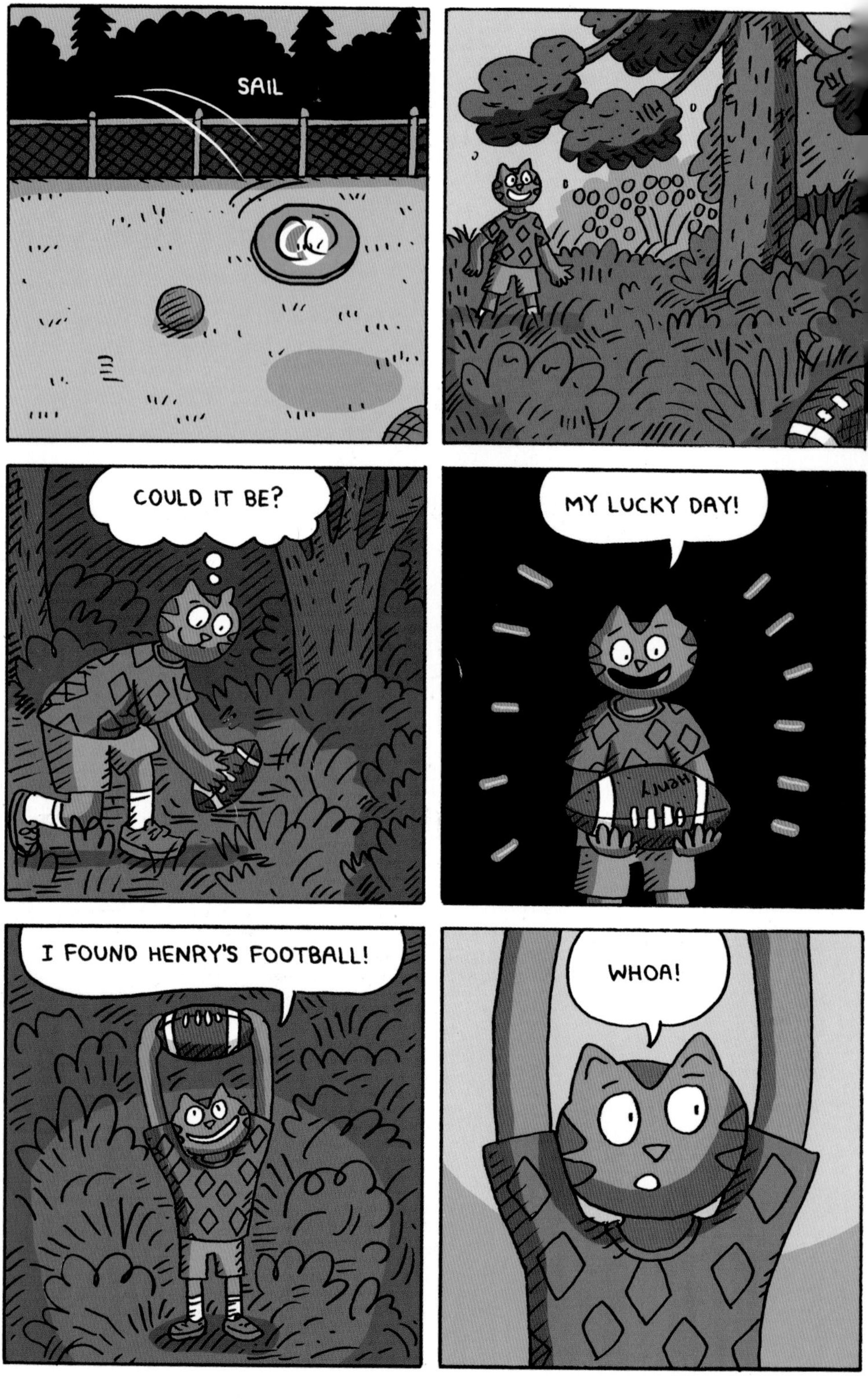
SAIL
COULD IT BE?
MY LUCKY DAY!
HENRY
I FOUND HENRY'S FOOTBALL!
WHOA!

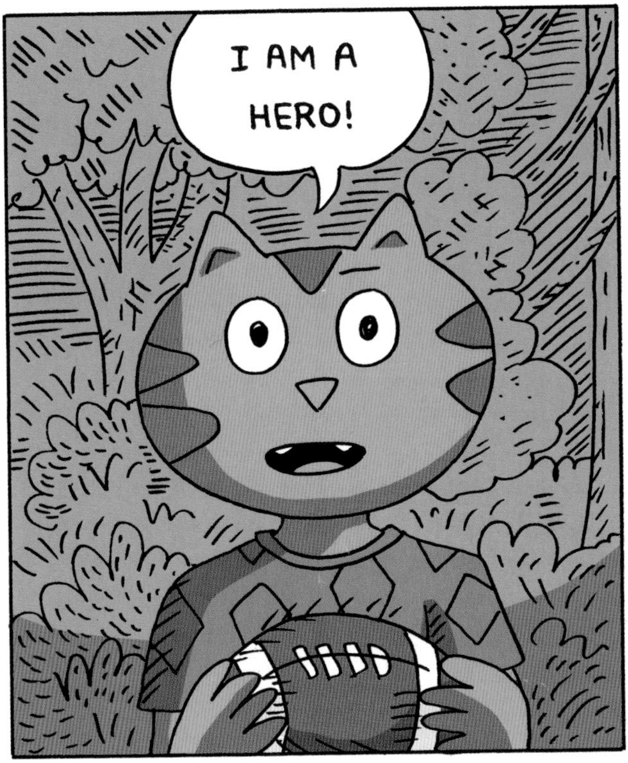
I AM A HERO!

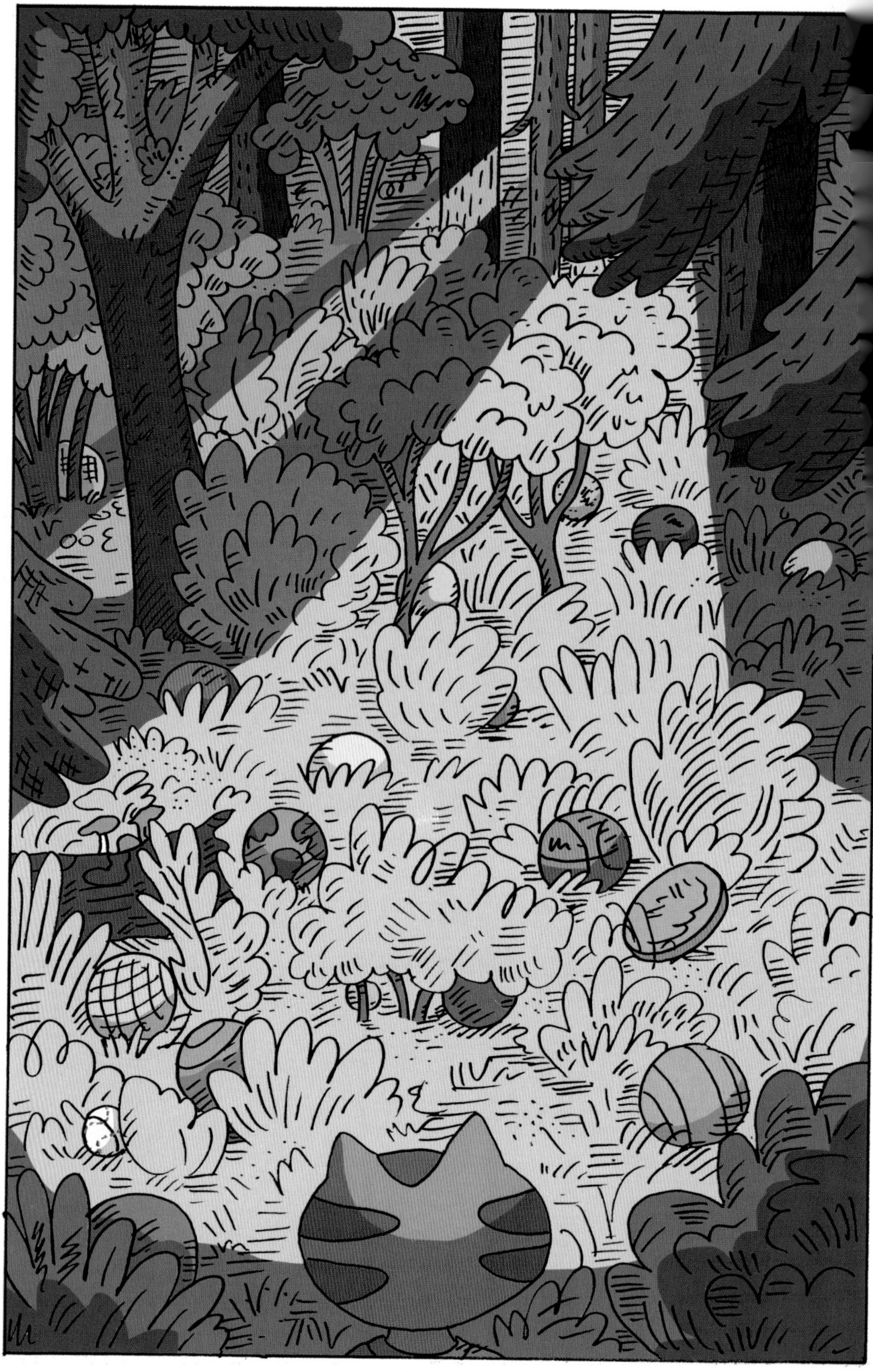

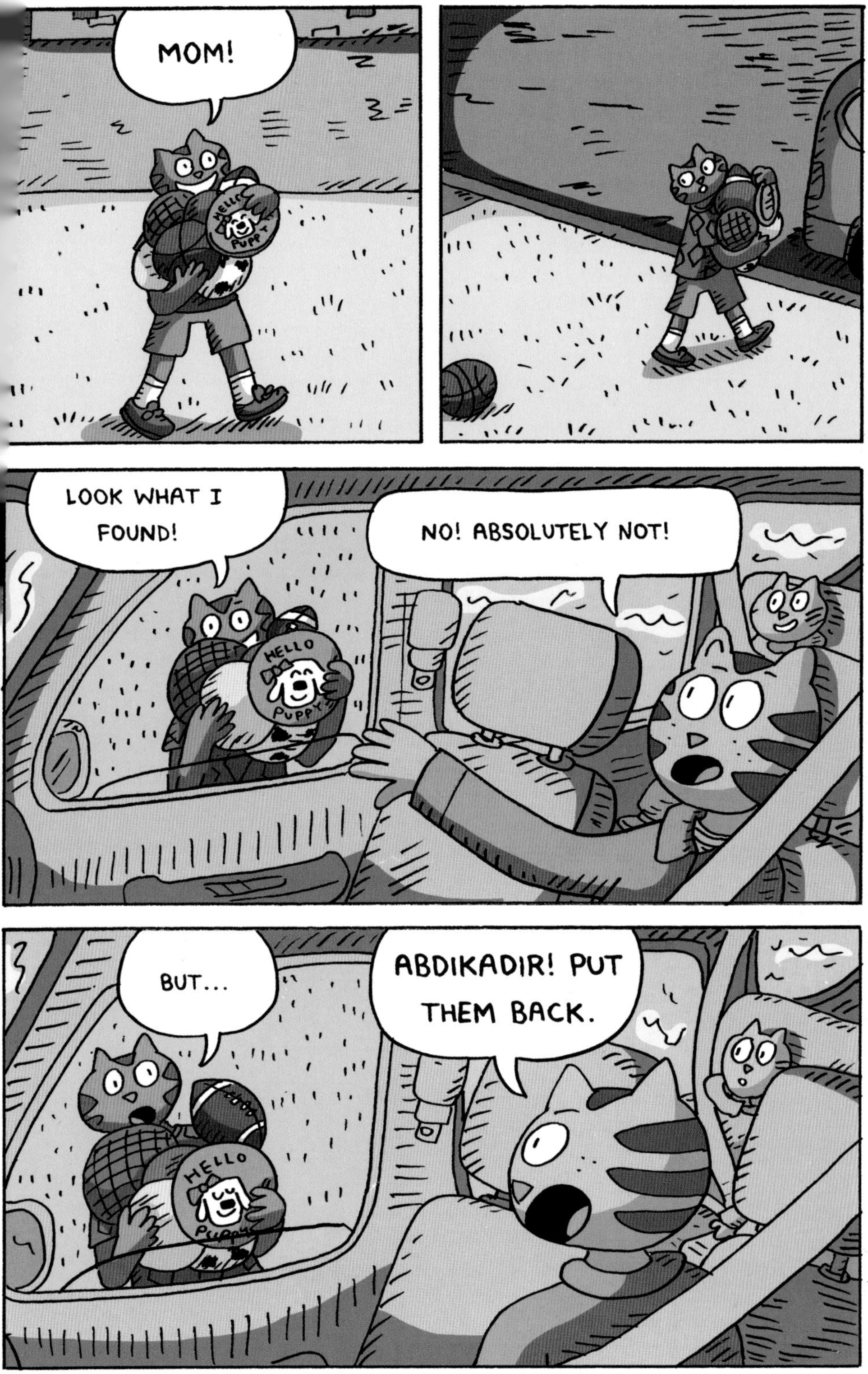
MOM!
LOOK WHAT I FOUND!
NO! ABSOLUTELY NOT!
HELLO PUPPY
BUT...
ABDIKADIR! PUT THEM BACK.
HELLO PUPPY

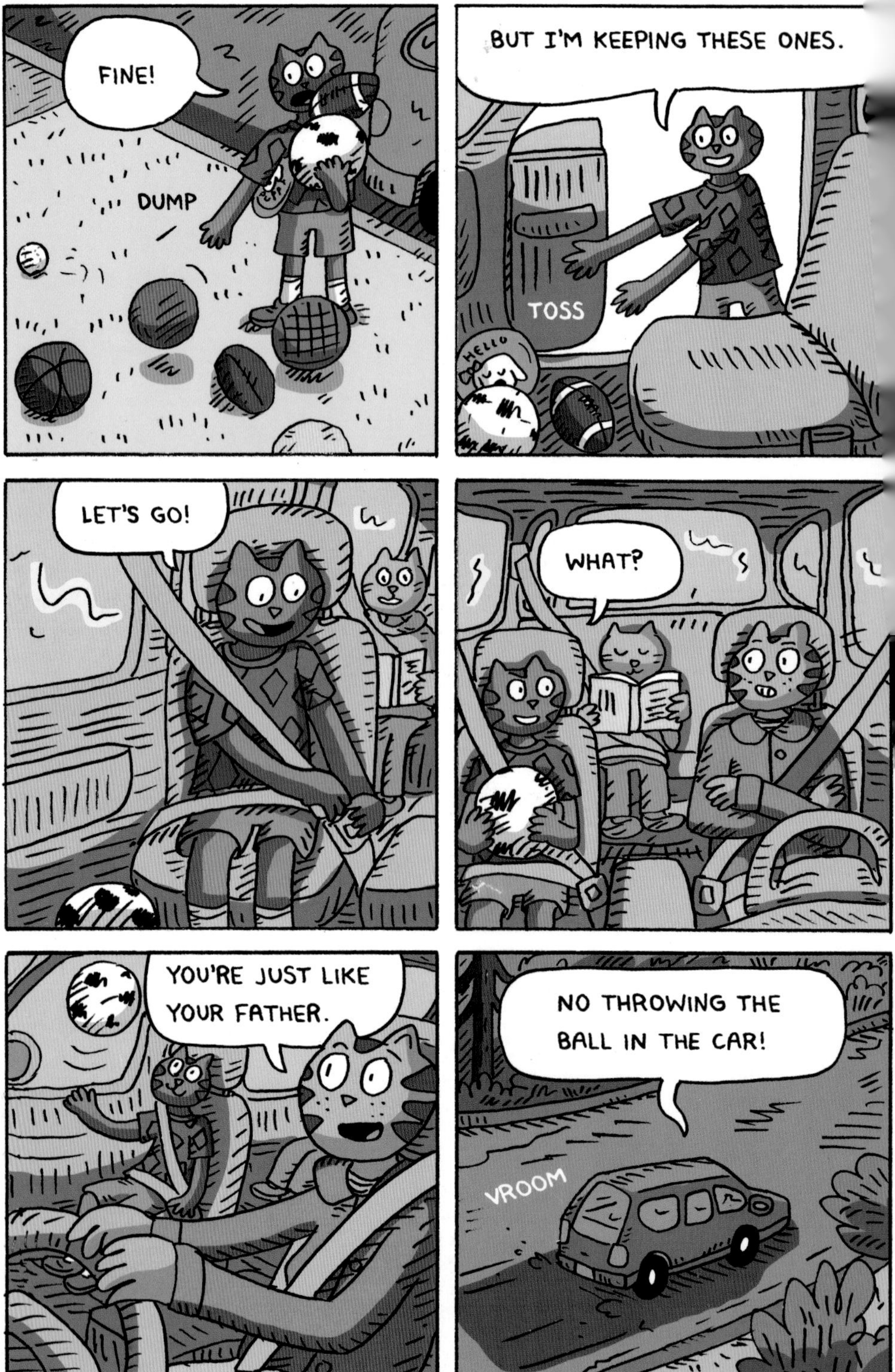
FINE!
DUMP
BUT I'M KEEPING THESE ONES.
TOSS
HELLO
LET'S GO!
WHAT?
YOU'RE JUST LIKE YOUR FATHER.
NO THROWING THE BALL IN THE CAR!
VROOM

CHAPTER SEVEN
Party Time

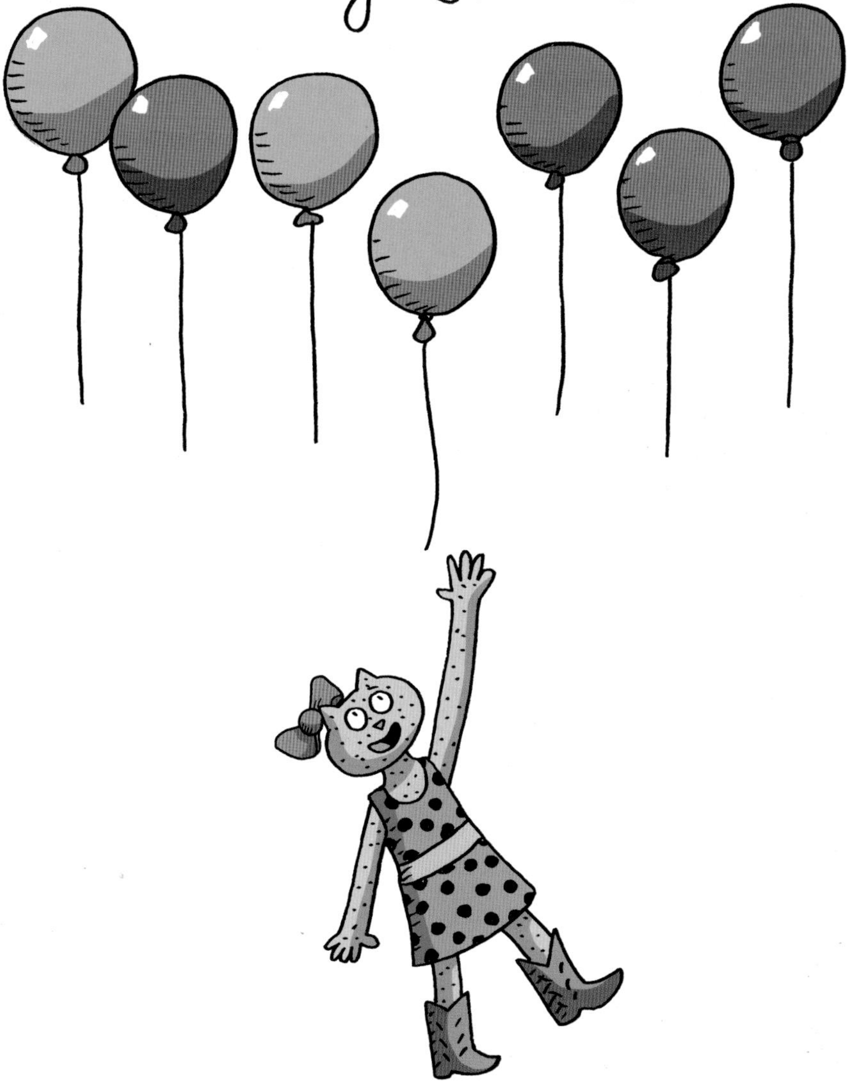

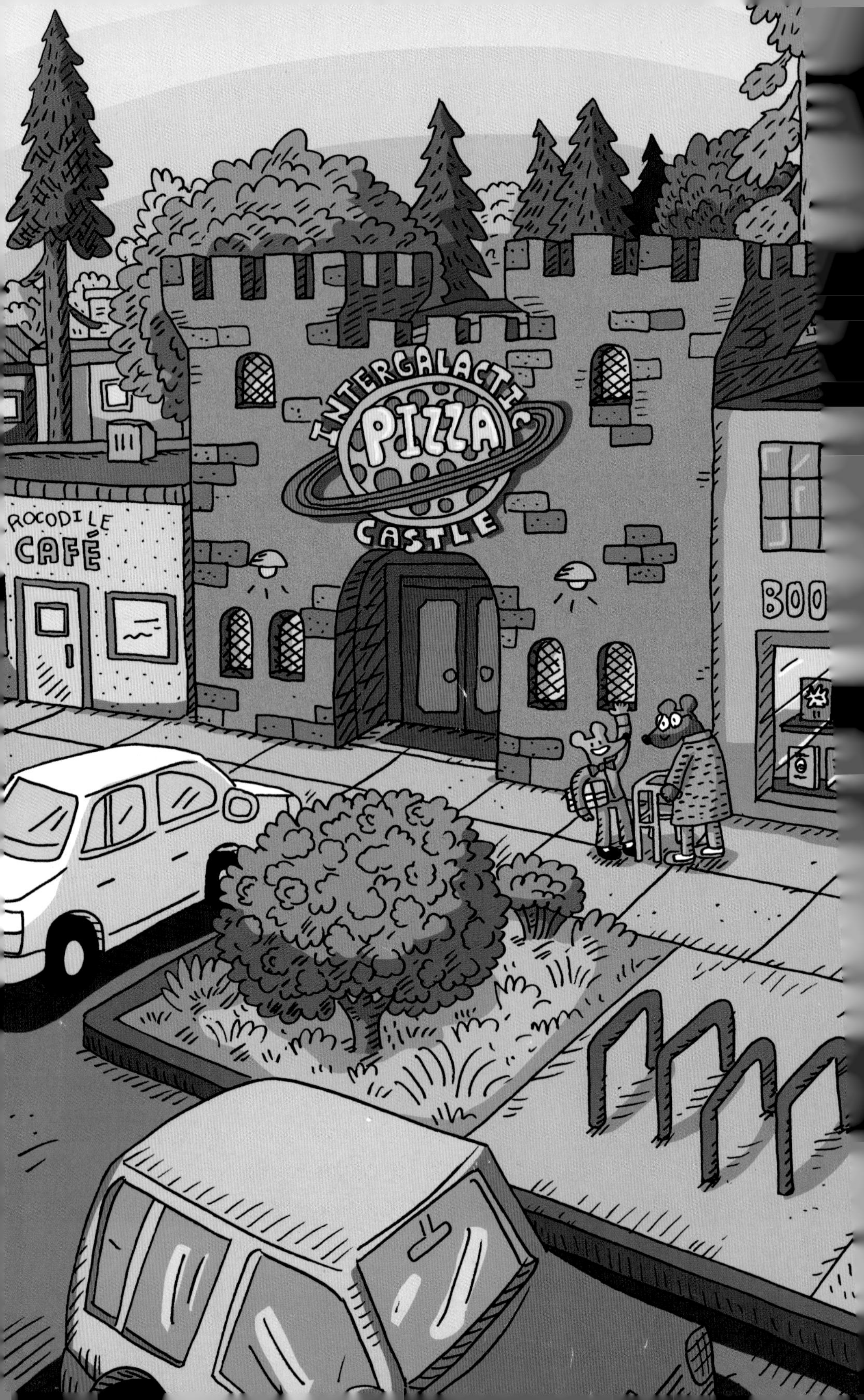
INTERGALACTIC PIZZA CASTLE
ROCODILE CAFÉ
BOO

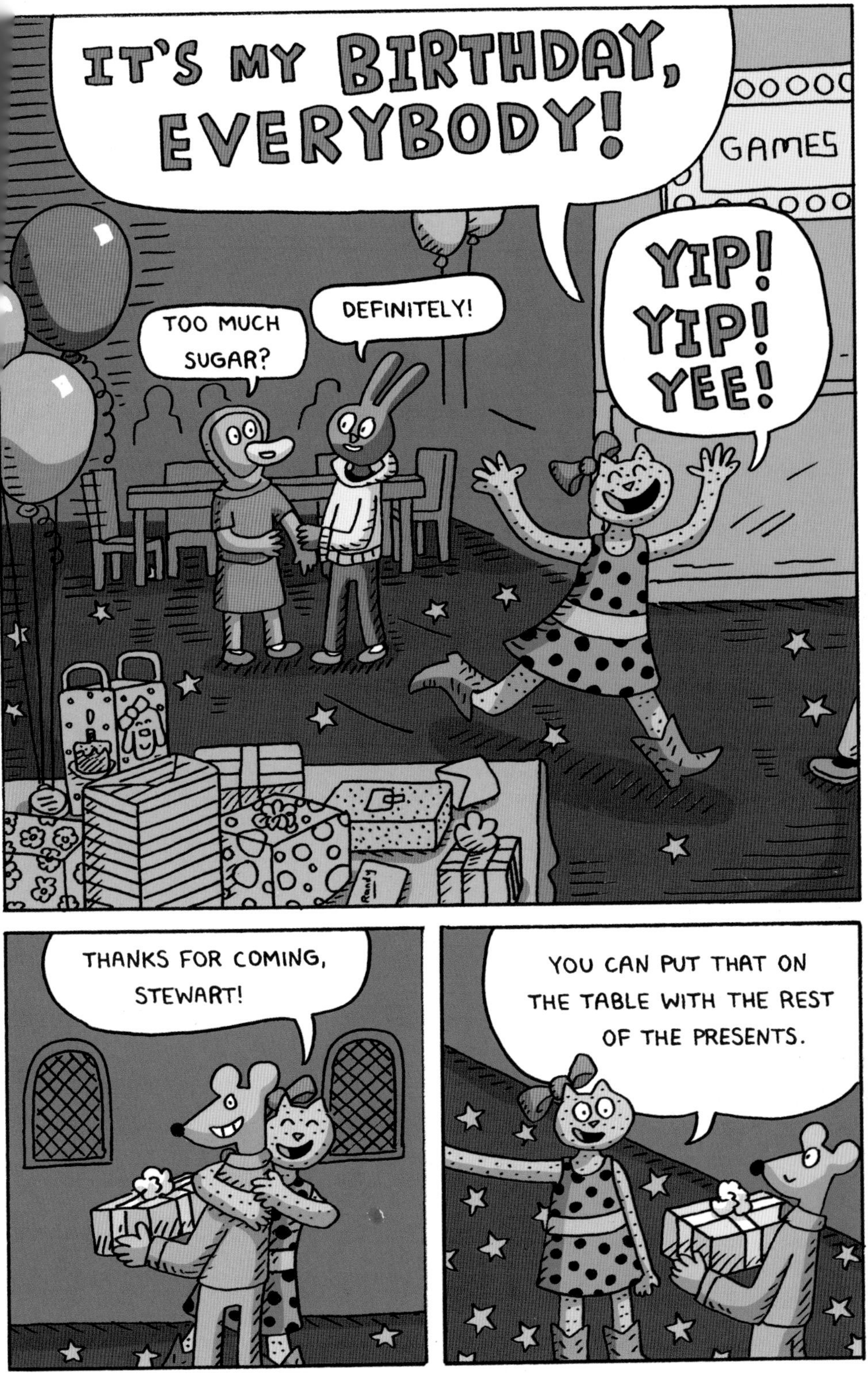
IT'S MY BIRTHDAY, EVERYBODY!
GAMES
TOO MUCH SUGAR?
DEFINITELY!
YIP! YIP! YEE!
Randy
THANKS FOR COMING, STEWART!
YOU CAN PUT THAT ON THE TABLE WITH THE REST OF THE PRESENTS.

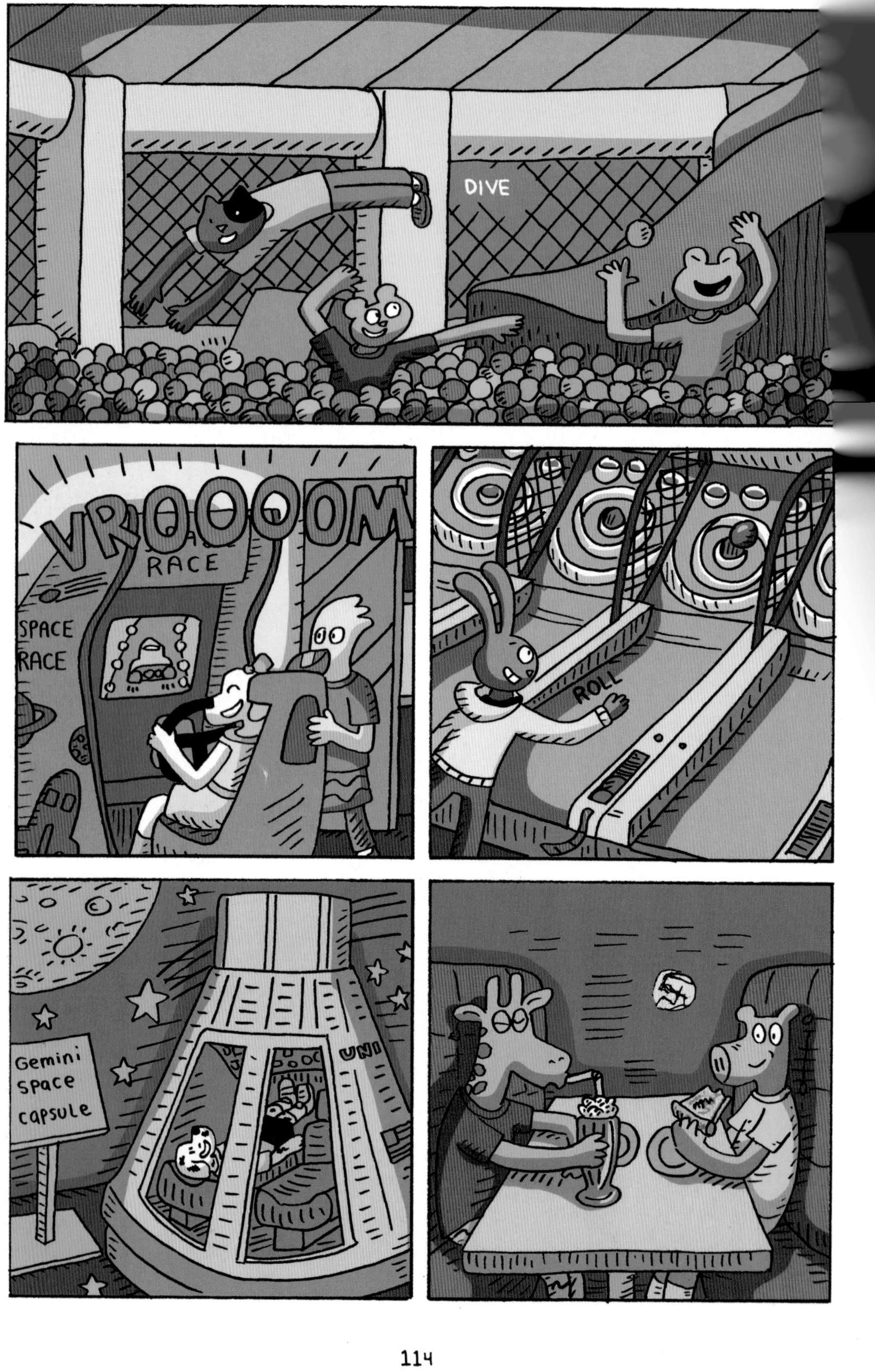
DIVE
VROOOOM
RACE
SPACE RACE
ROLL
Gemini Space capsule
UNI

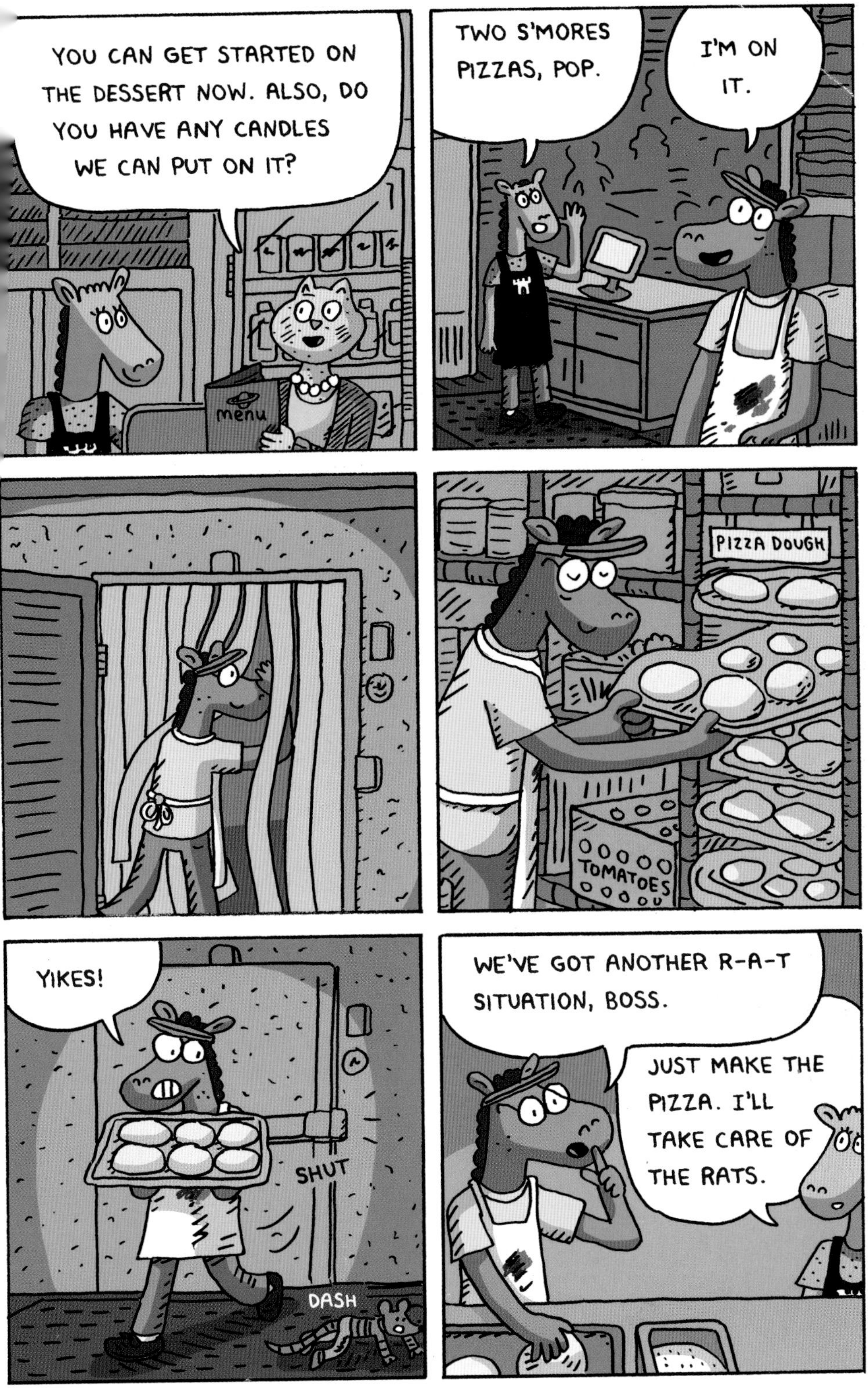
YOU CAN GET STARTED ON THE DESSERT NOW. ALSO, DO YOU HAVE ANY CANDLES WE CAN PUT ON IT?
menu
TWO S'MORES PIZZAS, POP.
I'M ON IT.
PIZZA DOUGH
TOMATOES
YIKES!
SHUT
DASH
WE'VE GOT ANOTHER R-A-T SITUATION, BOSS.
JUST MAKE THE PIZZA. I'LL TAKE CARE OF THE RATS.

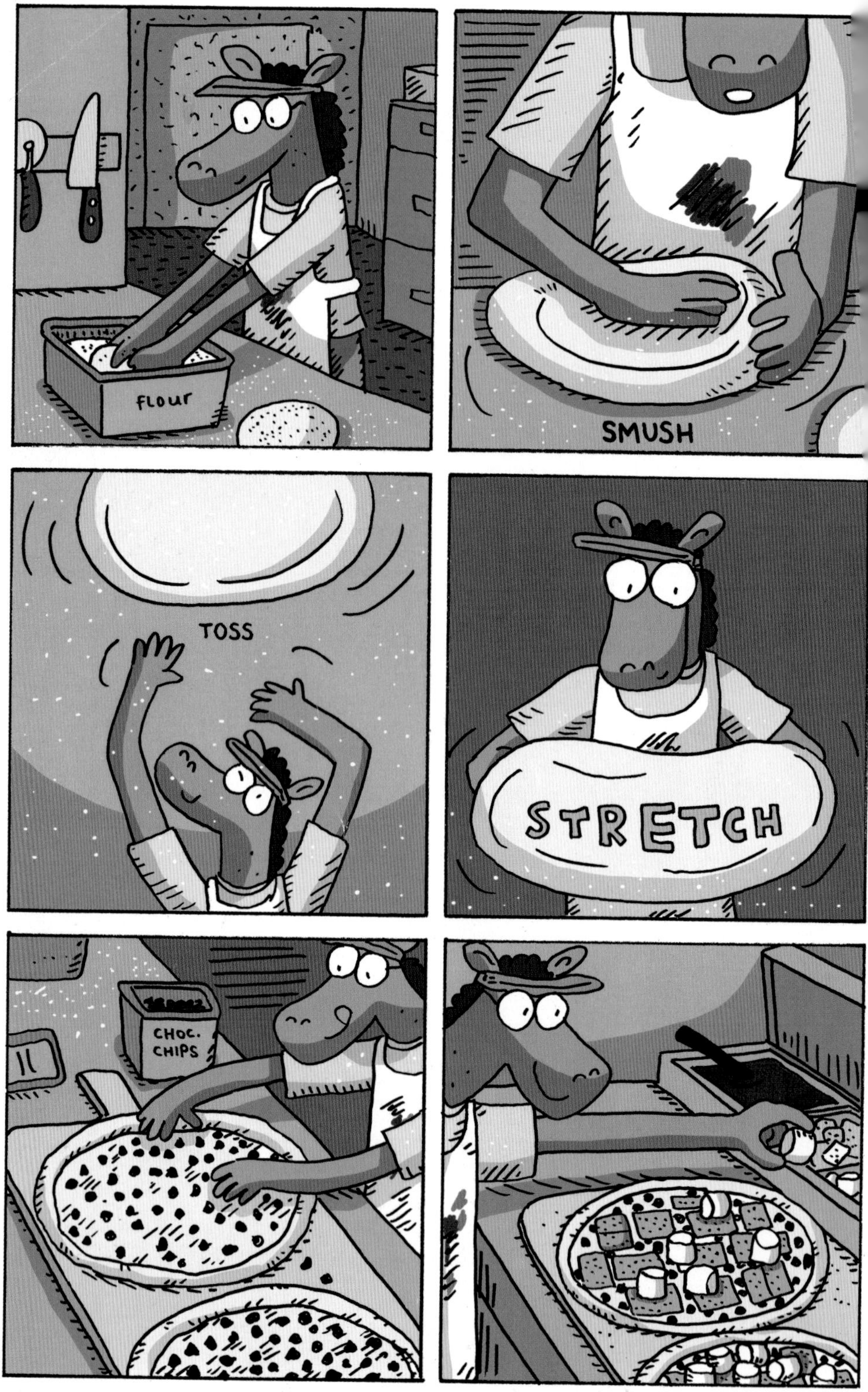
FLOUR
SMUSH
TOSS
STRETCH
CHOC. CHIPS

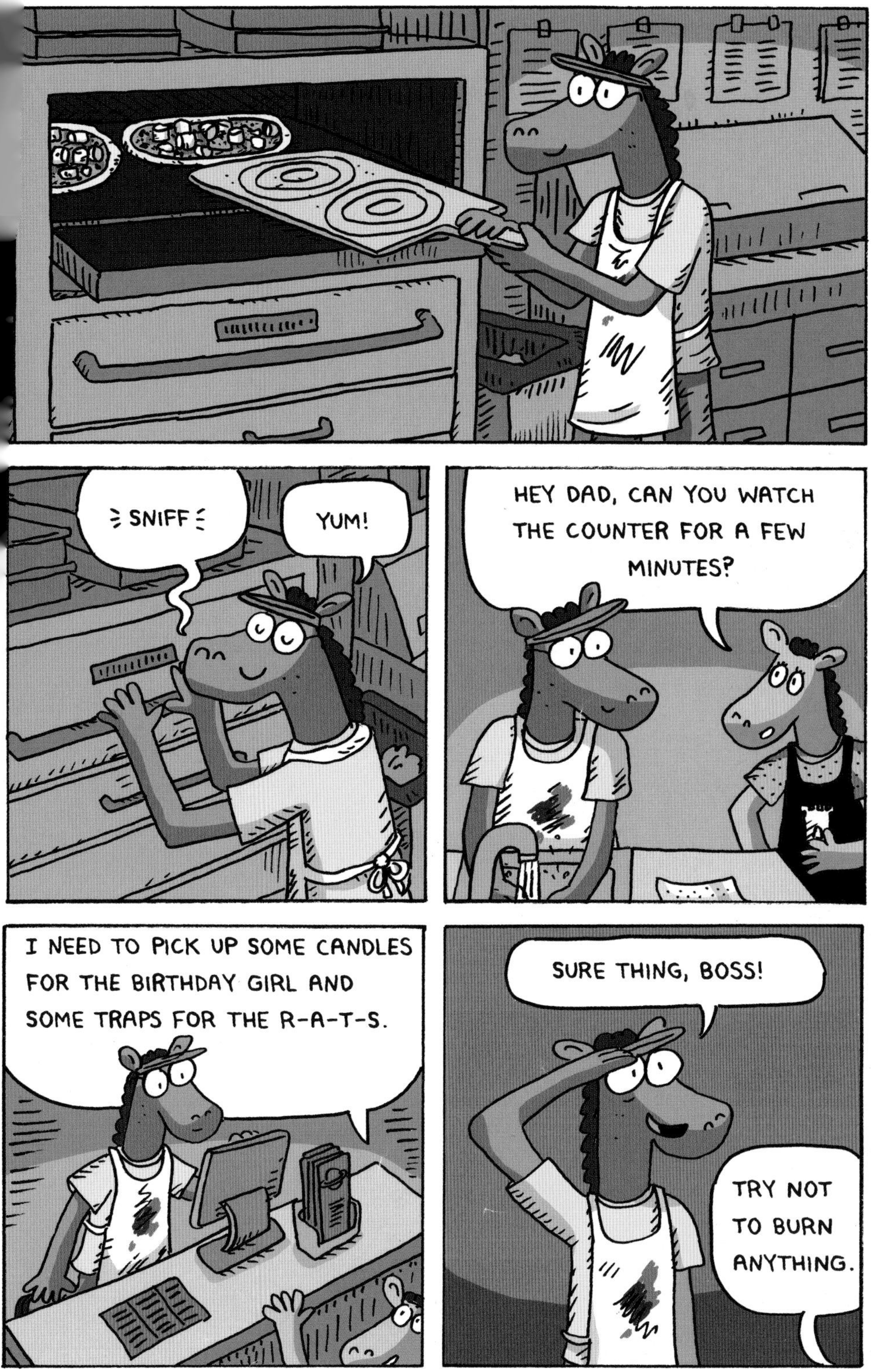

SNIFF
YUM!
HEY DAD, CAN YOU WATCH THE COUNTER FOR A FEW MINUTES?
I NEED TO PICK UP SOME CANDLES FOR THE BIRTHDAY GIRL AND SOME TRAPS FOR THE R-A-T-S.
SURE THING, BOSS!
TRY NOT TO BURN ANYTHING.

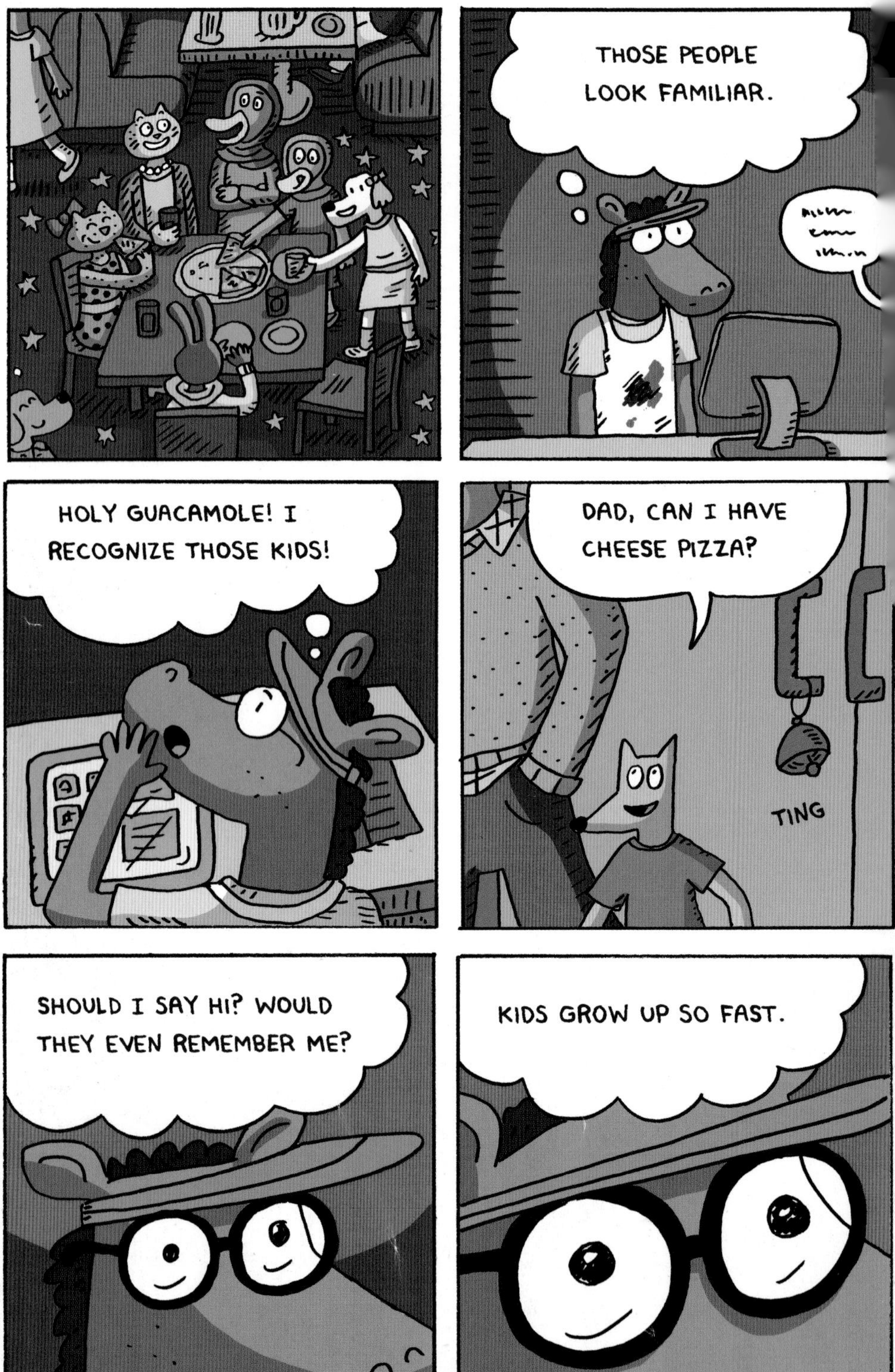
THOSE PEOPLE LOOK FAMILIAR.
HOLY GUACAMOLE! I RECOGNIZE THOSE KIDS!
DAD, CAN I HAVE CHEESE PIZZA?
TING
SHOULD I SAY HI? WOULD THEY EVEN REMEMBER ME?
KIDS GROW UP SO FAST.

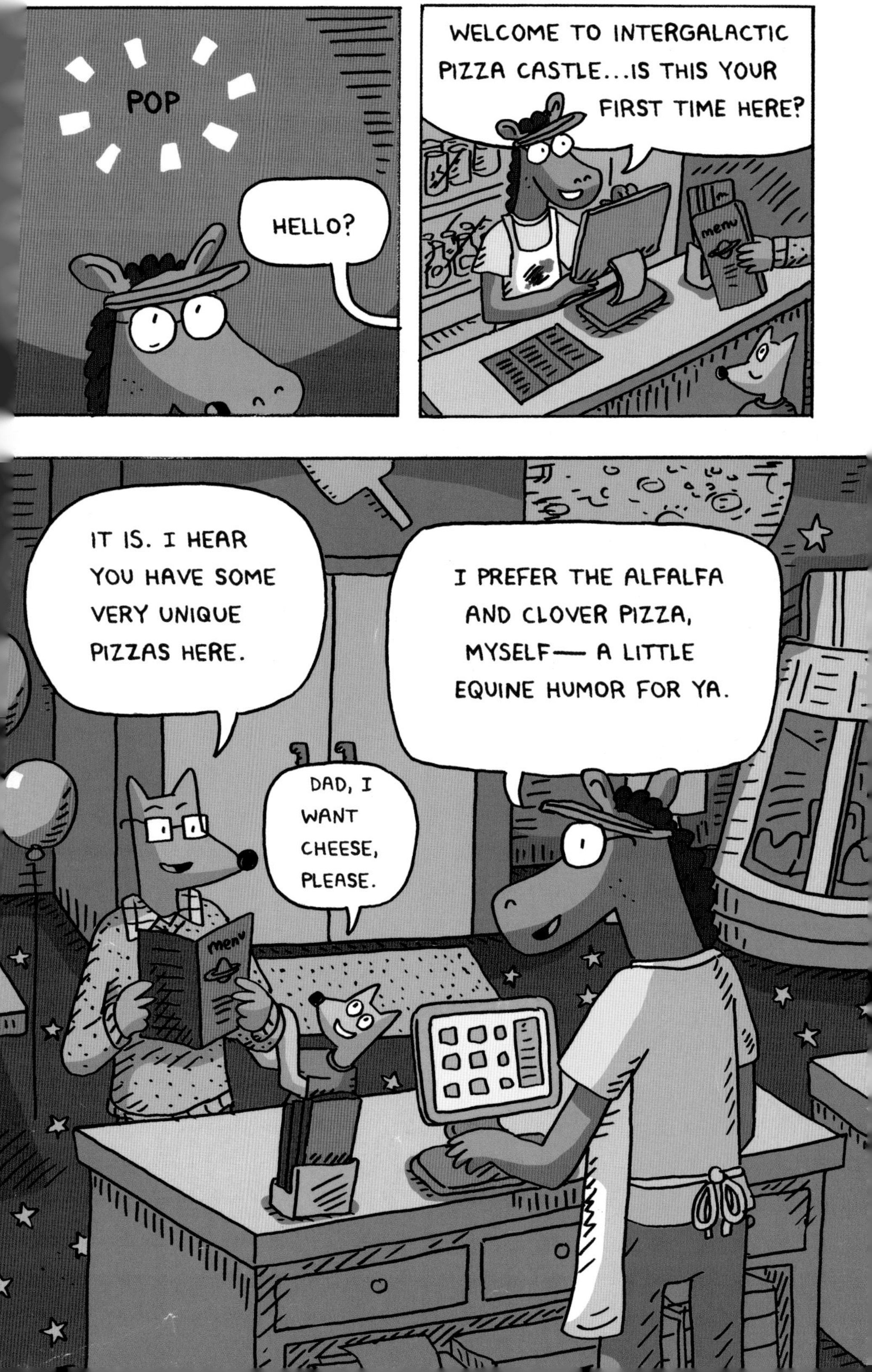
POP
HELLO?
WELCOME TO INTERGALACTIC PIZZA CASTLE...IS THIS YOUR FIRST TIME HERE?
menu
IT IS. I HEAR YOU HAVE SOME VERY UNIQUE PIZZAS HERE.
I PREFER THE ALFALFA AND CLOVER PIZZA, MYSELF— A LITTLE EQUINE HUMOR FOR YA.
DAD, I WANT CHEESE, PLEASE.
menu

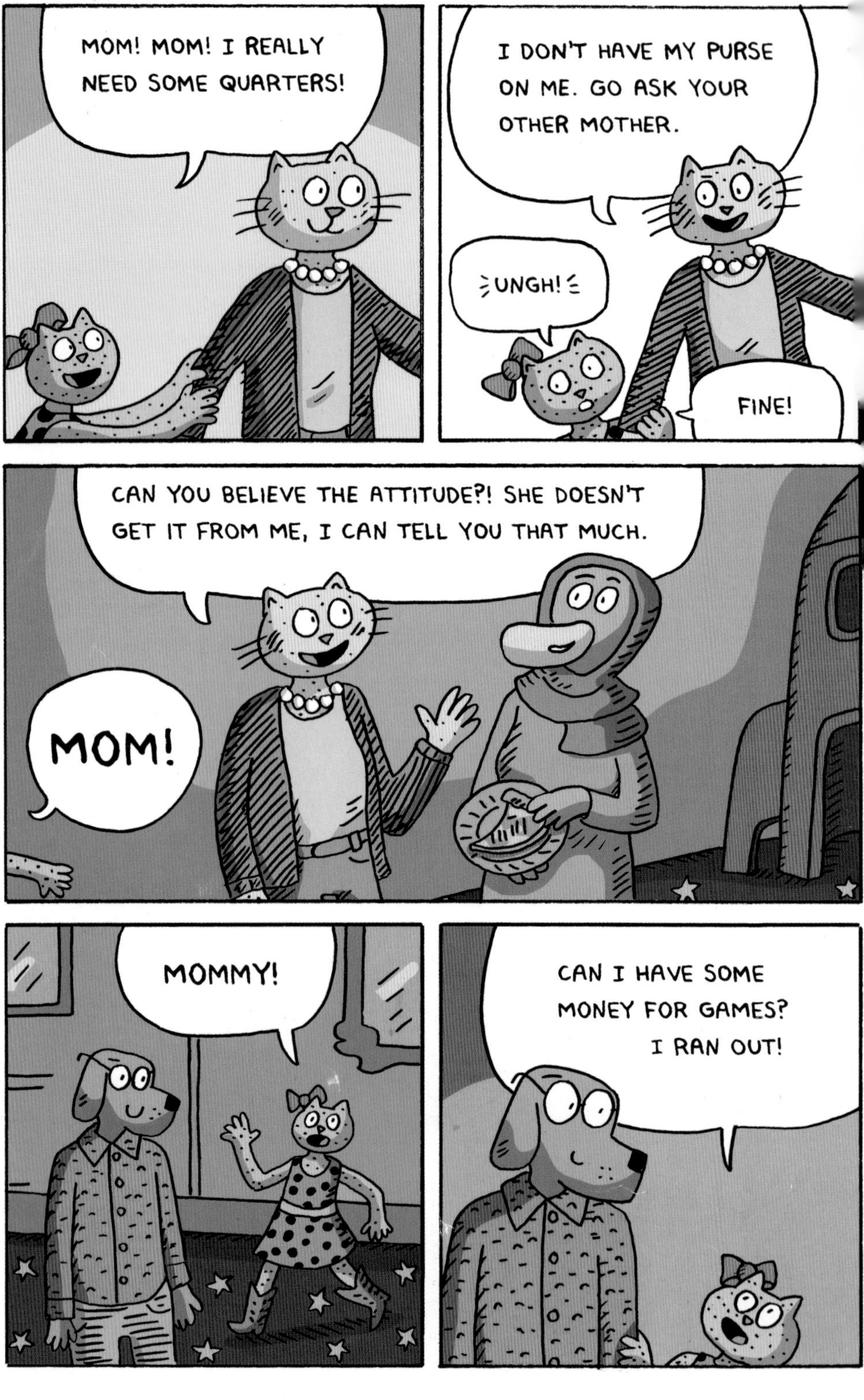
MOM! MOM! I REALLY NEED SOME QUARTERS!
I DON'T HAVE MY PURSE ON ME. GO ASK YOUR OTHER MOTHER.
UNGH!
FINE!
CAN YOU BELIEVE THE ATTITUDE?! SHE DOESN'T GET IT FROM ME, I CAN TELL YOU THAT MUCH.
MOM!
MOMMY!
CAN I HAVE SOME MONEY FOR GAMES? I RAN OUT!

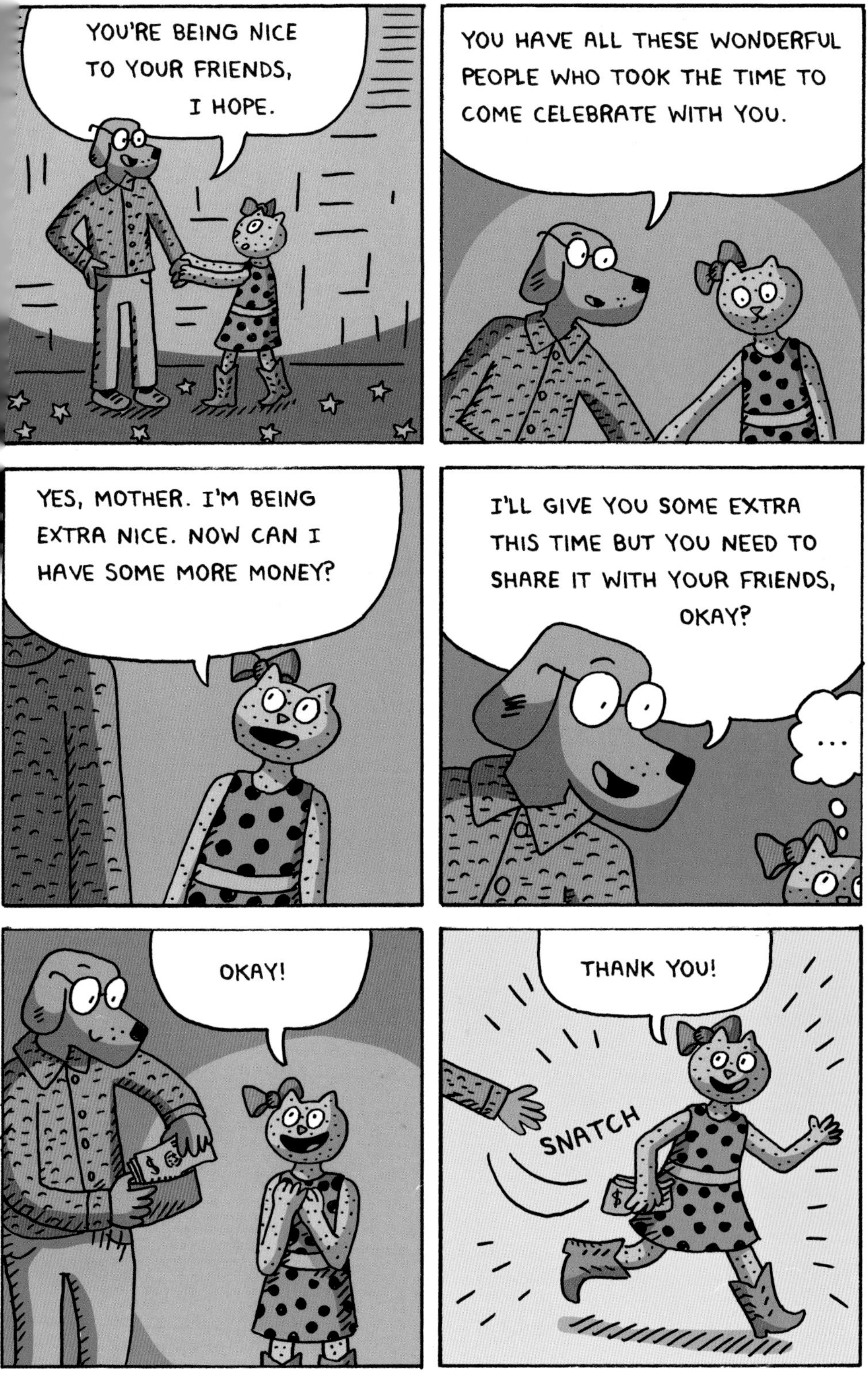
YOU'RE BEING NICE TO YOUR FRIENDS, I HOPE.
YOU HAVE ALL THESE WONDERFUL PEOPLE WHO TOOK THE TIME TO COME CELEBRATE WITH YOU.
YES, MOTHER. I'M BEING EXTRA NICE. NOW CAN I HAVE SOME MORE MONEY?
I'LL GIVE YOU SOME EXTRA THIS TIME BUT YOU NEED TO SHARE IT WITH YOUR FRIENDS, OKAY?
...
OKAY!
THANK YOU!
SNATCH

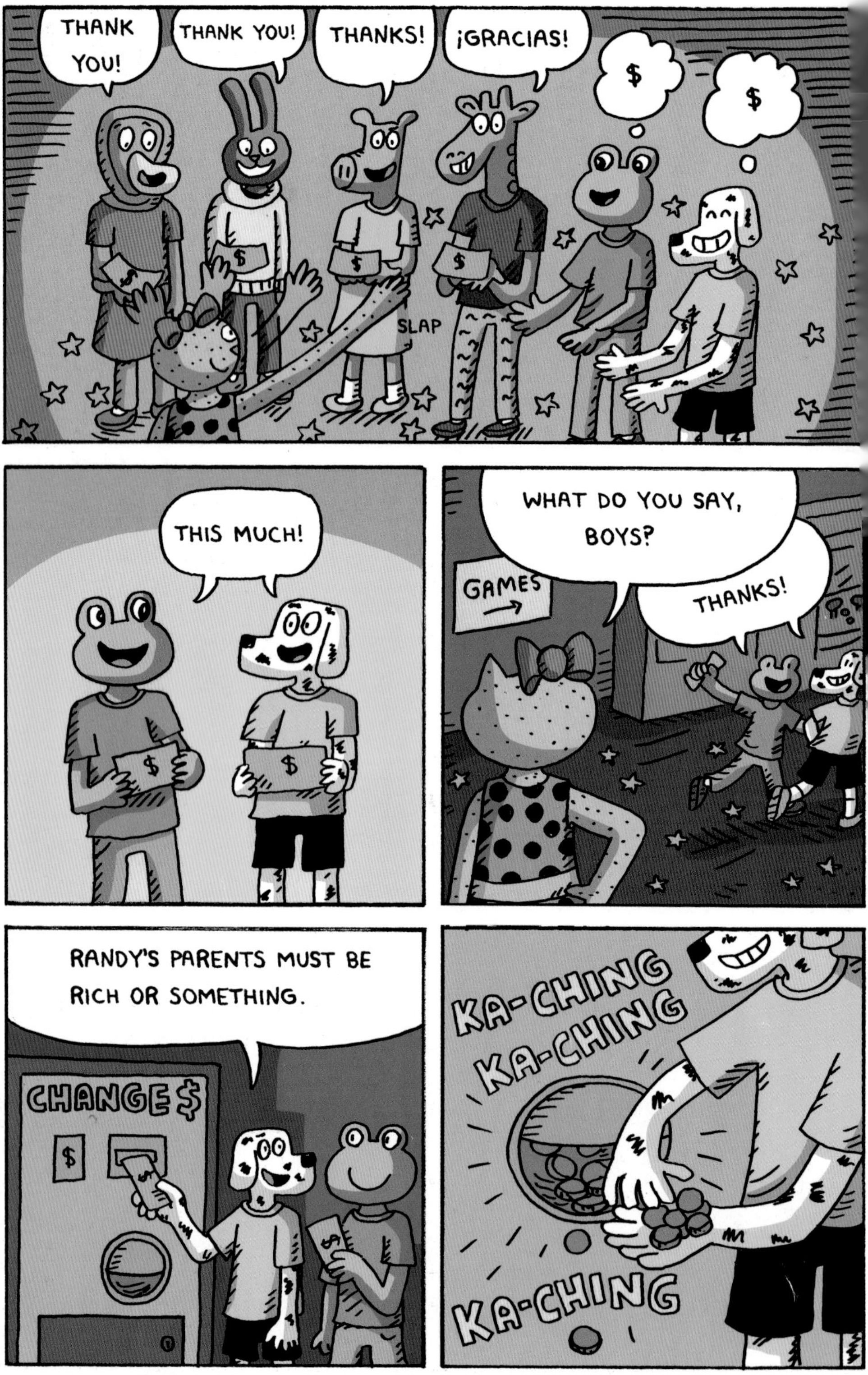

THANK YOU!
THANK YOU!
THANKS!
¡GRACIAS!
$
$
SLAP
THIS MUCH!
WHAT DO YOU SAY, BOYS?
GAMES
THANKS!
RANDY'S PARENTS MUST BE RICH OR SOMETHING.
CHANGE$
$
KA-CHING
KA-CHING
KA-CHING

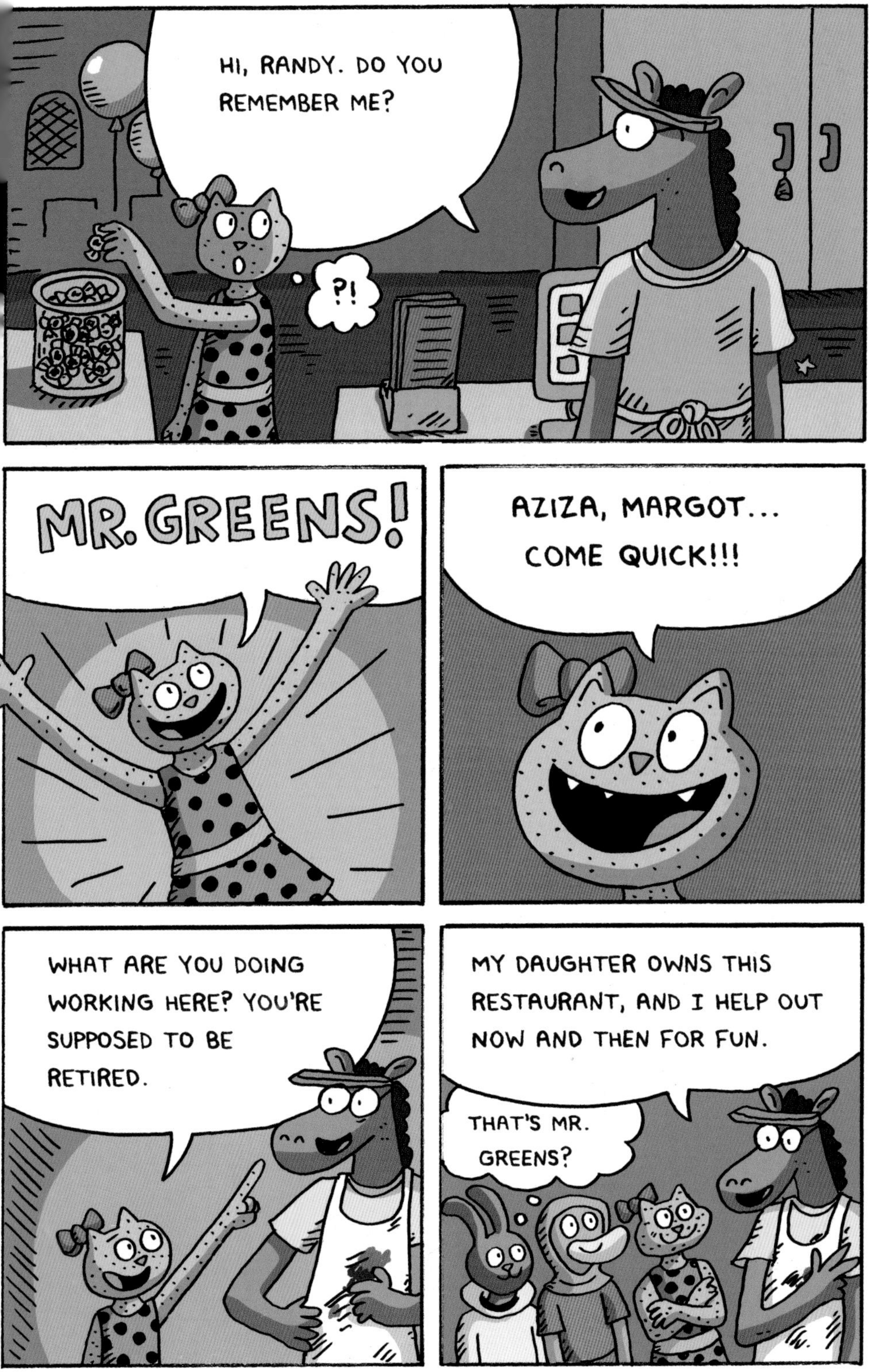
HI, RANDY. DO YOU REMEMBER ME?
?!
MR. GREENS!
AZIZA, MARGOT... COME QUICK!!!
WHAT ARE YOU DOING WORKING HERE? YOU'RE SUPPOSED TO BE RETIRED.
MY DAUGHTER OWNS THIS RESTAURANT, AND I HELP OUT NOW AND THEN FOR FUN.
THAT'S MR. GREENS?

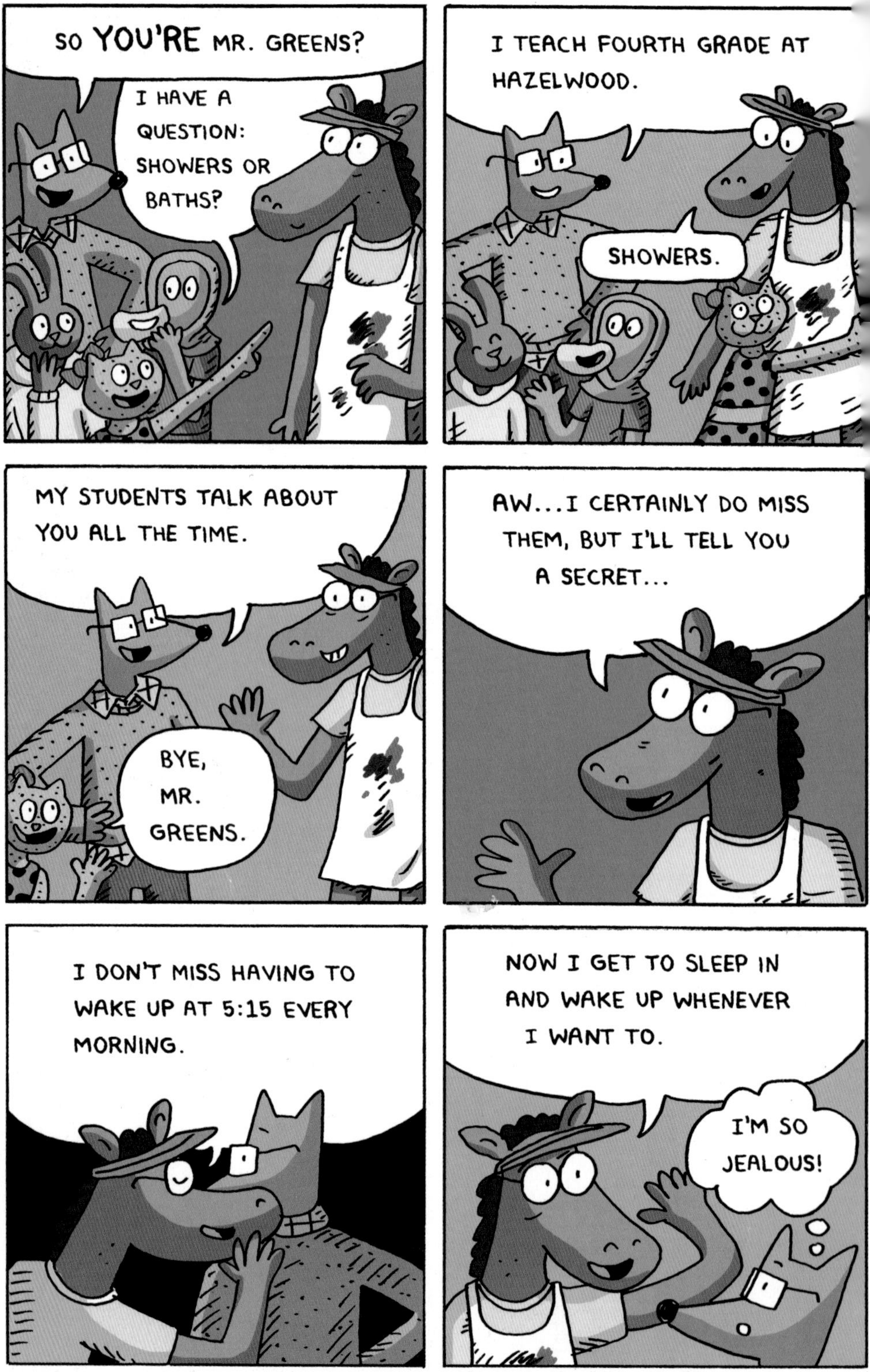
SO YOU'RE MR. GREENS?
I HAVE A QUESTION: SHOWERS OR BATHS?
I TEACH FOURTH GRADE AT HAZELWOOD.
SHOWERS.
MY STUDENTS TALK ABOUT YOU ALL THE TIME.
BYE, MR. GREENS.
AW...I CERTAINLY DO MISS THEM, BUT I'LL TELL YOU A SECRET...
I DON'T MISS HAVING TO WAKE UP AT 5:15 EVERY MORNING.
NOW I GET TO SLEEP IN AND WAKE UP WHENEVER I WANT TO.
I'M SO JEALOUS!

WORKING HERE MEANS I GET TO EAT ALL THE FREE PIZZA I COULD EVER WANT!

PLUS, I GET TO MAKE MY OWN PIZZA IDEAS AND THEN PUT THEM ON THE MENU.

JUST TODAY I'VE CREATED A TOASTED PEANUT BUTTER AND STRAWBERRY JELLY PIZZA.

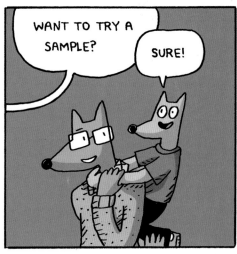

WANT TO TRY A SAMPLE?

SURE!

THANK YOU.

TOSS

CHOMP CHEW

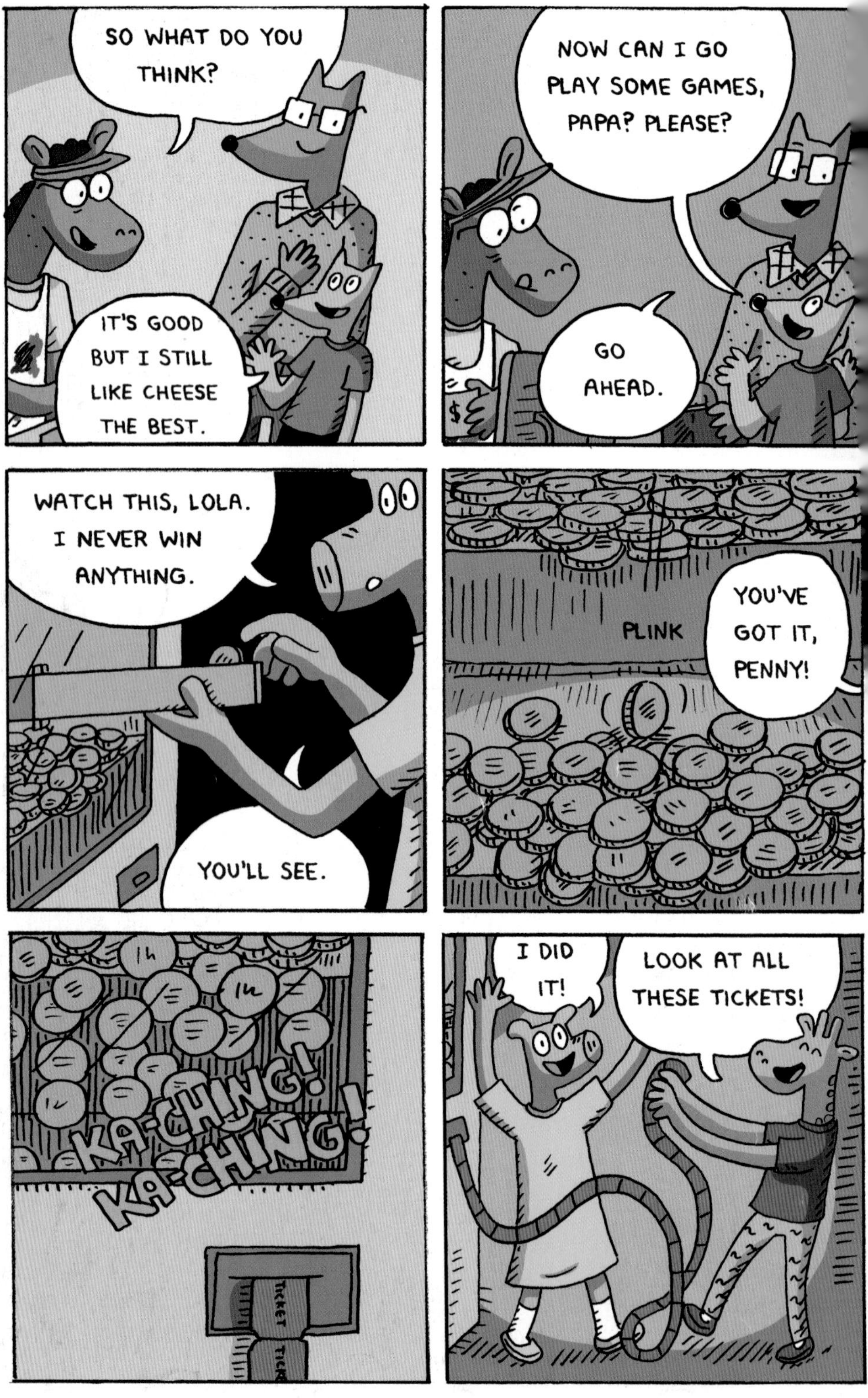
SO WHAT DO YOU THINK?
IT'S GOOD BUT I STILL LIKE CHEESE THE BEST.
NOW CAN I GO PLAY SOME GAMES, PAPA? PLEASE?
GO AHEAD.
WATCH THIS, LOLA. I NEVER WIN ANYTHING.
YOU'LL SEE.
PLINK
YOU'VE GOT IT, PENNY!
KA-CHING!
KA-CHING!
I DID IT!
LOOK AT ALL THESE TICKETS!

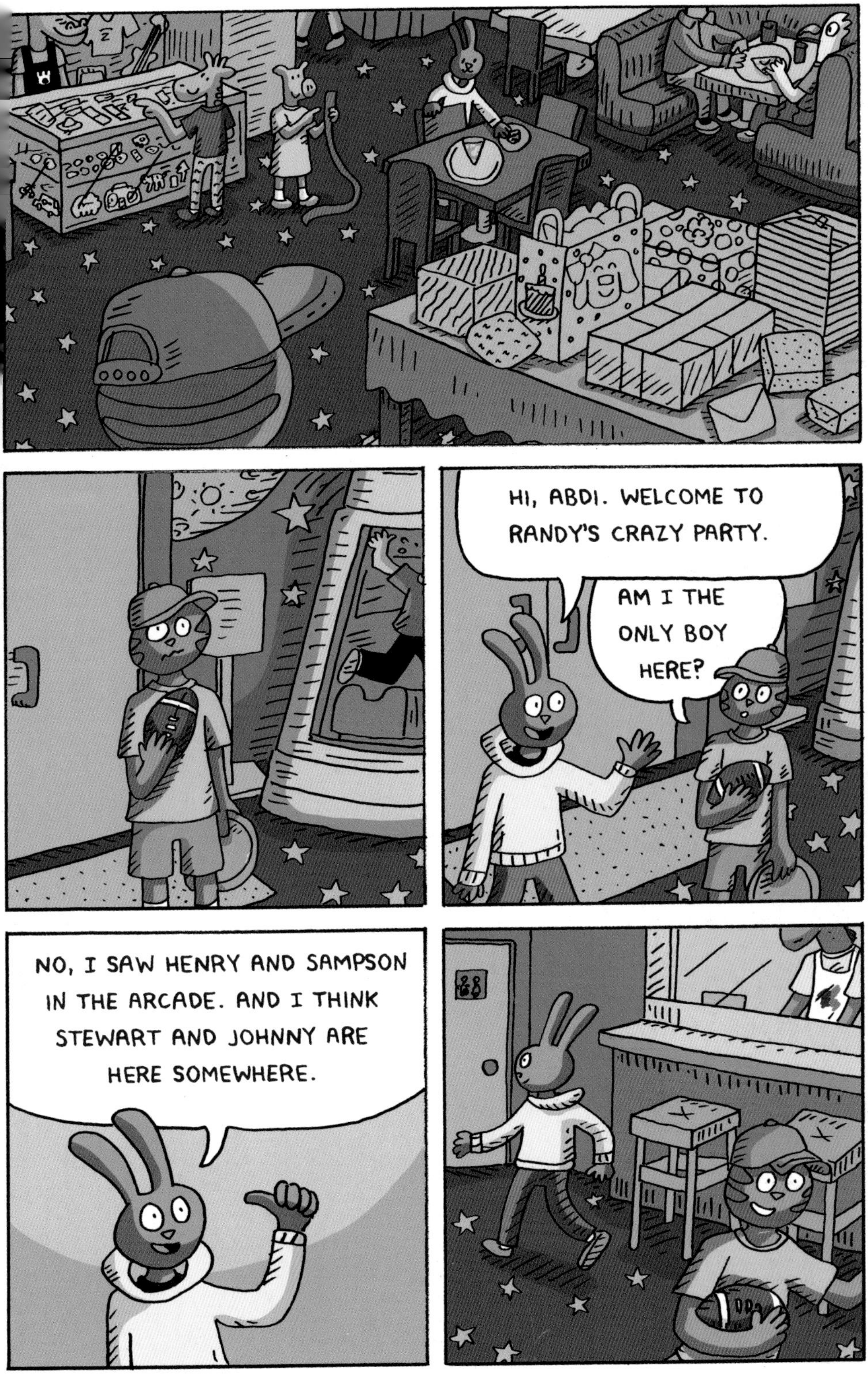
HI, ABDI. WELCOME TO RANDY'S CRAZY PARTY.
AM I THE ONLY BOY HERE?
NO, I SAW HENRY AND SAMPSON IN THE ARCADE. AND I THINK STEWART AND JOHNNY ARE HERE SOMEWHERE.

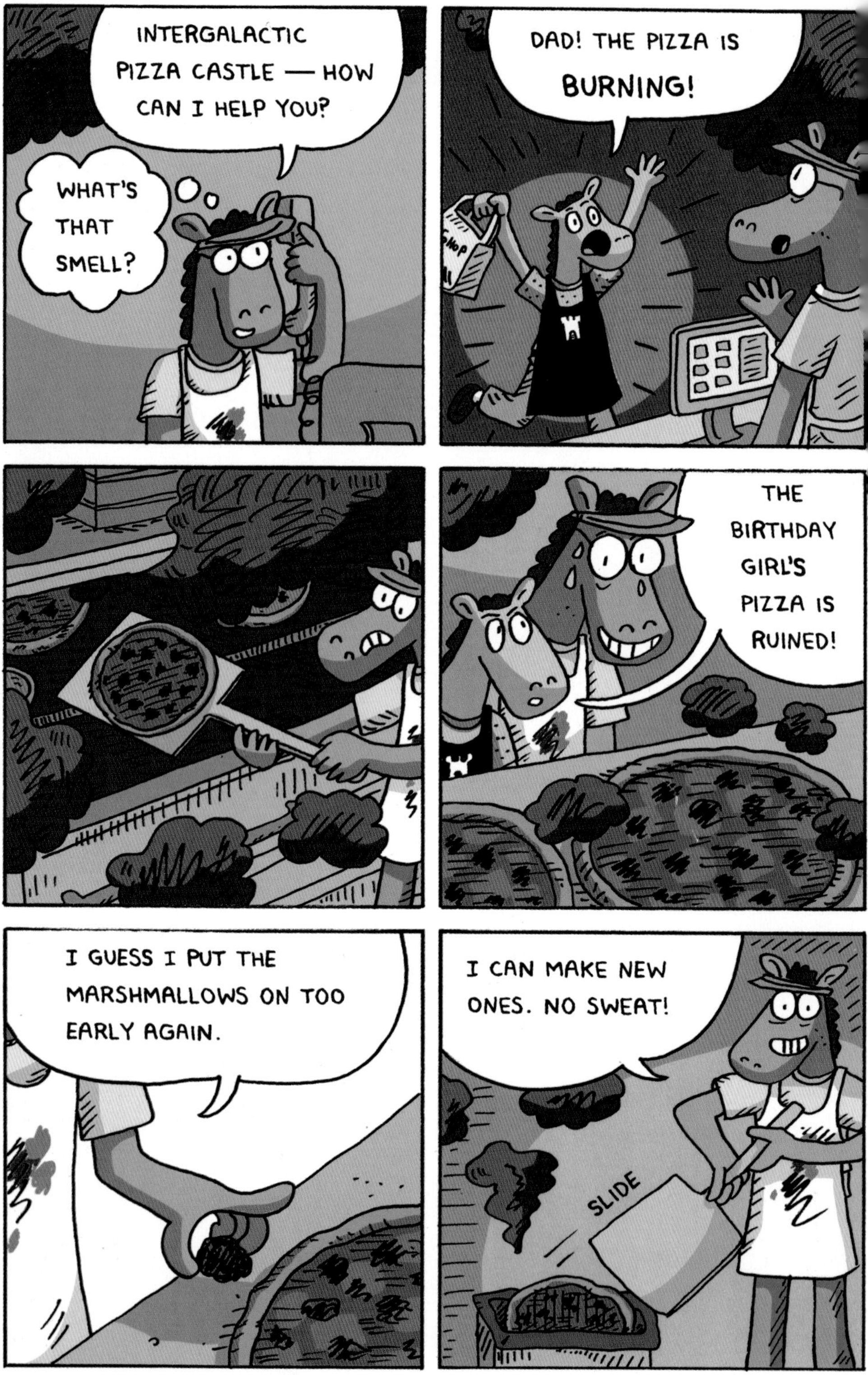

INTERGALACTIC PIZZA CASTLE — HOW CAN I HELP YOU?
WHAT'S THAT SMELL?
DAD! THE PIZZA IS BURNING!
SHOP
THE BIRTHDAY GIRL'S PIZZA IS RUINED!
I GUESS I PUT THE MARSHMALLOWS ON TOO EARLY AGAIN.
I CAN MAKE NEW ONES. NO SWEAT!
SLIDE

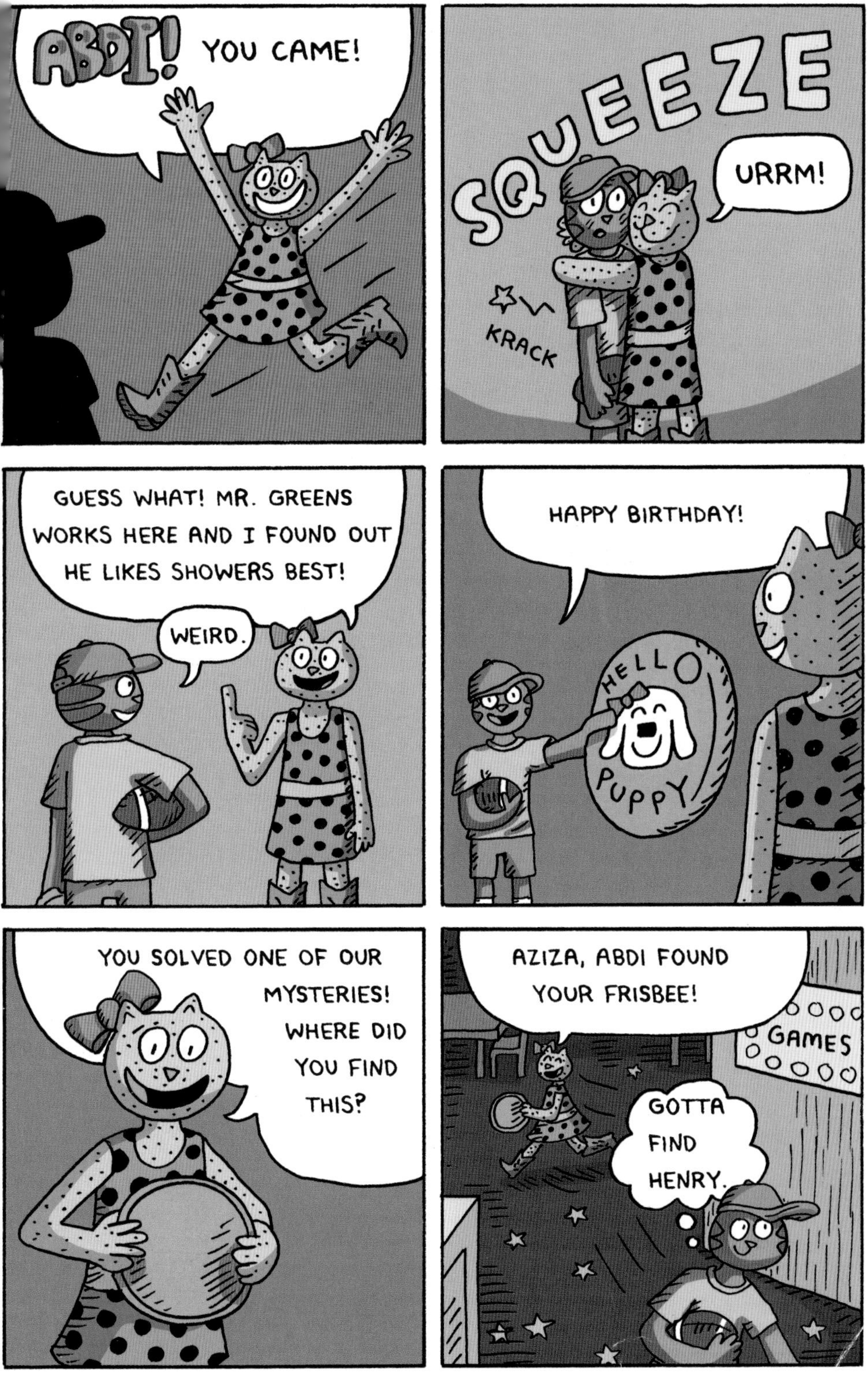
ABDI! YOU CAME!
SQUEEZE
URRM!
KRACK
GUESS WHAT! MR. GREENS WORKS HERE AND I FOUND OUT HE LIKES SHOWERS BEST!
WEIRD.
HAPPY BIRTHDAY!
HELLO PUPPY
YOU SOLVED ONE OF OUR MYSTERIES! WHERE DID YOU FIND THIS?
AZIZA, ABDI FOUND YOUR FRISBEE!
GAMES
GOTTA FIND HENRY.

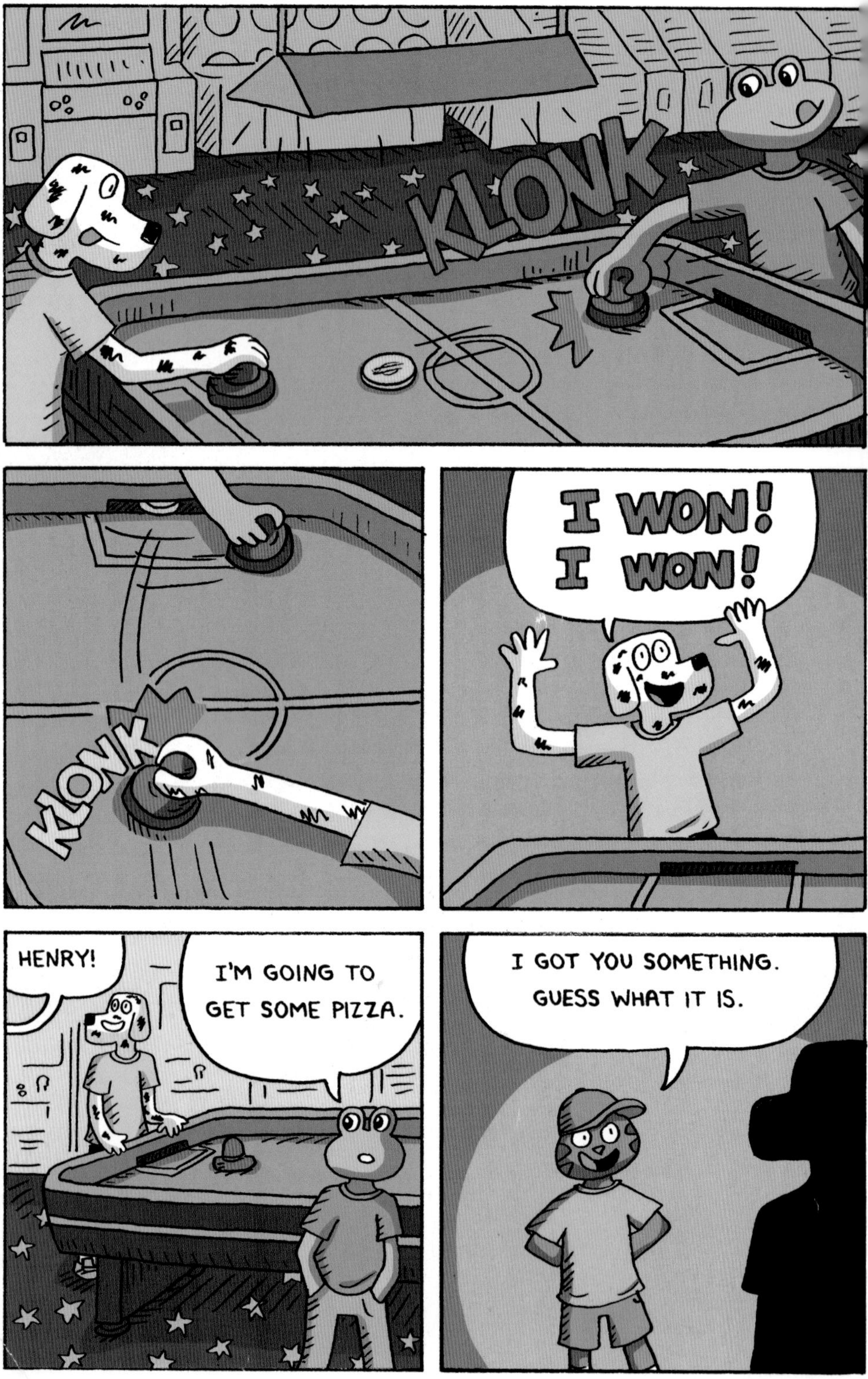
KLONK
KLONK
I WON! I WON!
HENRY!
I'M GOING TO GET SOME PIZZA.
I GOT YOU SOMETHING. GUESS WHAT IT IS.

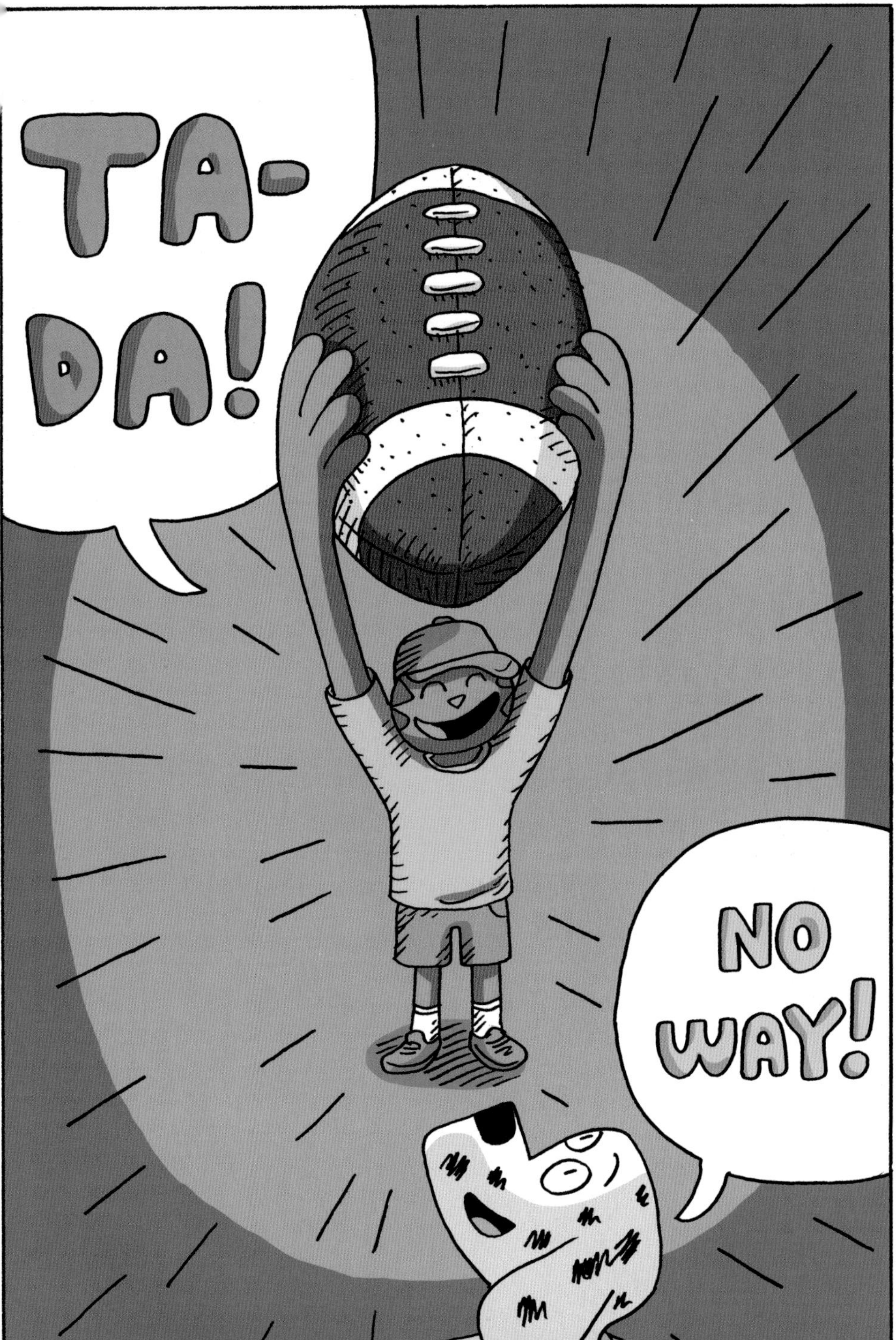
TA-
DA!
NO
WAY!

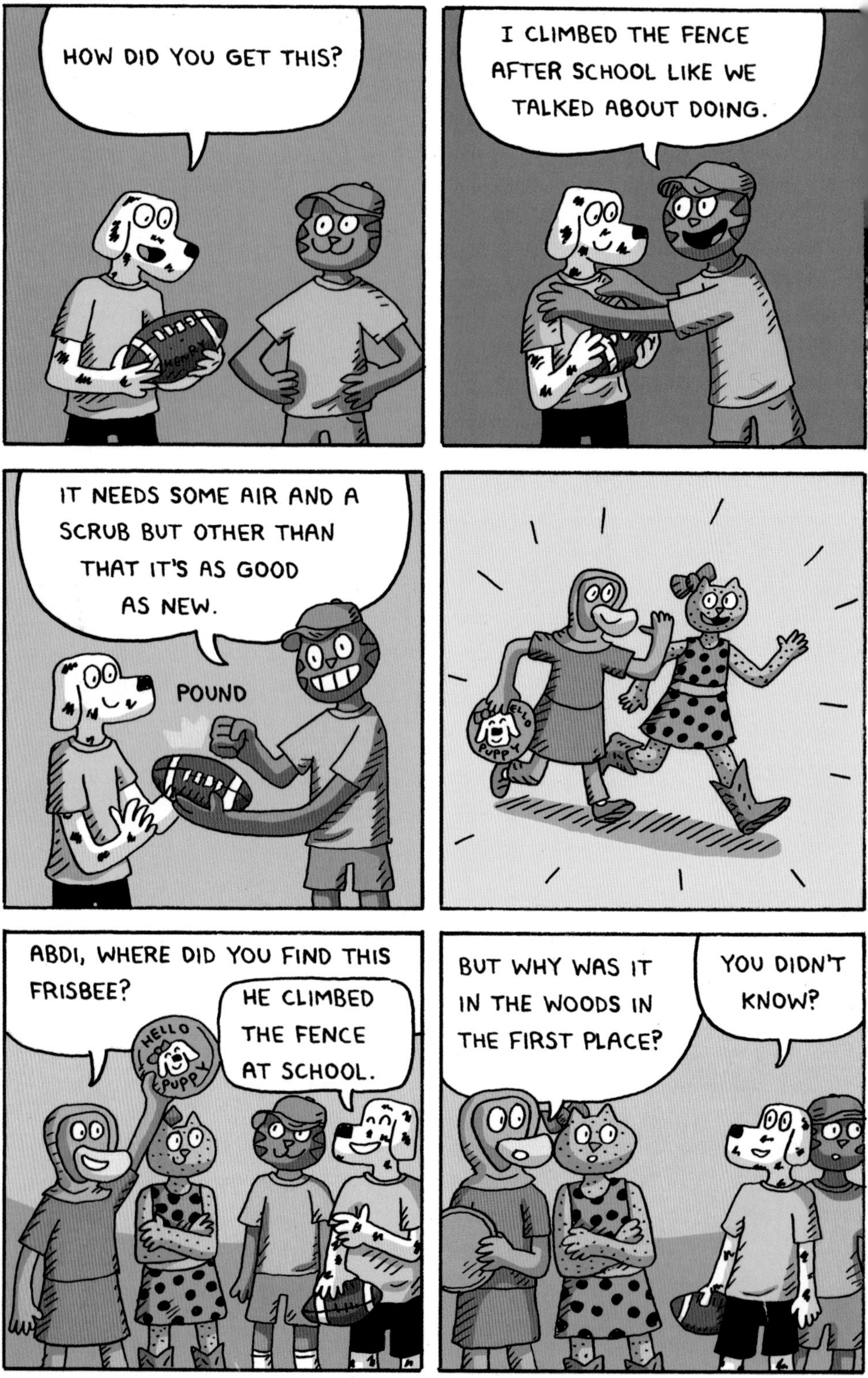
HOW DID YOU GET THIS?
HENRY
I CLIMBED THE FENCE AFTER SCHOOL LIKE WE TALKED ABOUT DOING.
IT NEEDS SOME AIR AND A SCRUB BUT OTHER THAN THAT IT'S AS GOOD AS NEW.
POUND
HELLO PUPPY
ABDI, WHERE DID YOU FIND THIS FRISBEE?
HELLO PUPPY
HE CLIMBED THE FENCE AT SCHOOL.
BUT WHY WAS IT IN THE WOODS IN THE FIRST PLACE?
YOU DIDN'T KNOW?

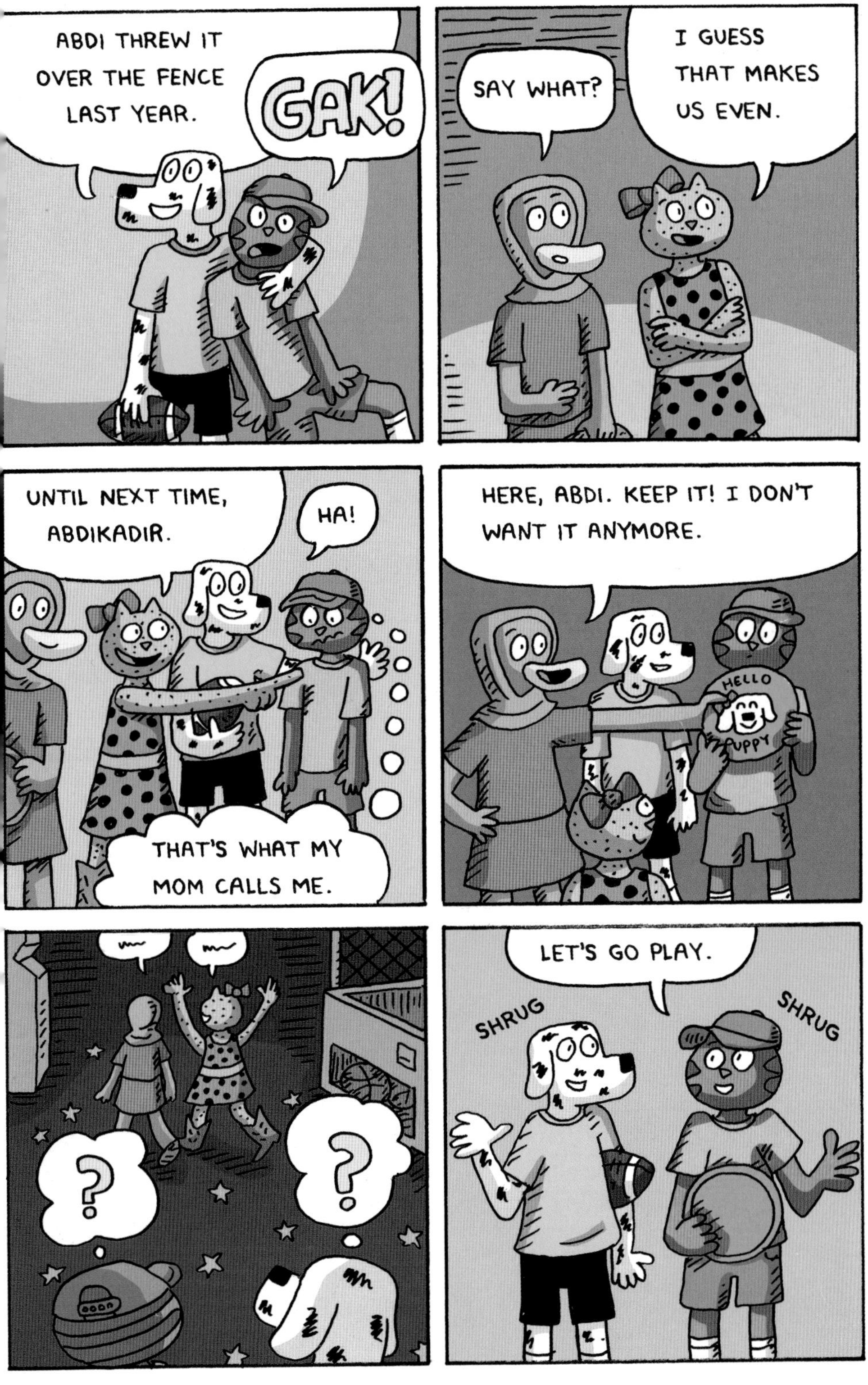
ABDI THREW IT OVER THE FENCE LAST YEAR.
GAK!
SAY WHAT?
I GUESS THAT MAKES US EVEN.
UNTIL NEXT TIME, ABDIKADIR.
HA!
THAT'S WHAT MY MOM CALLS ME.
HERE, ABDI. KEEP IT! I DON'T WANT IT ANYMORE.
HELLO PUPPY
?
?
LET'S GO PLAY.
SHRUG
SHRUG

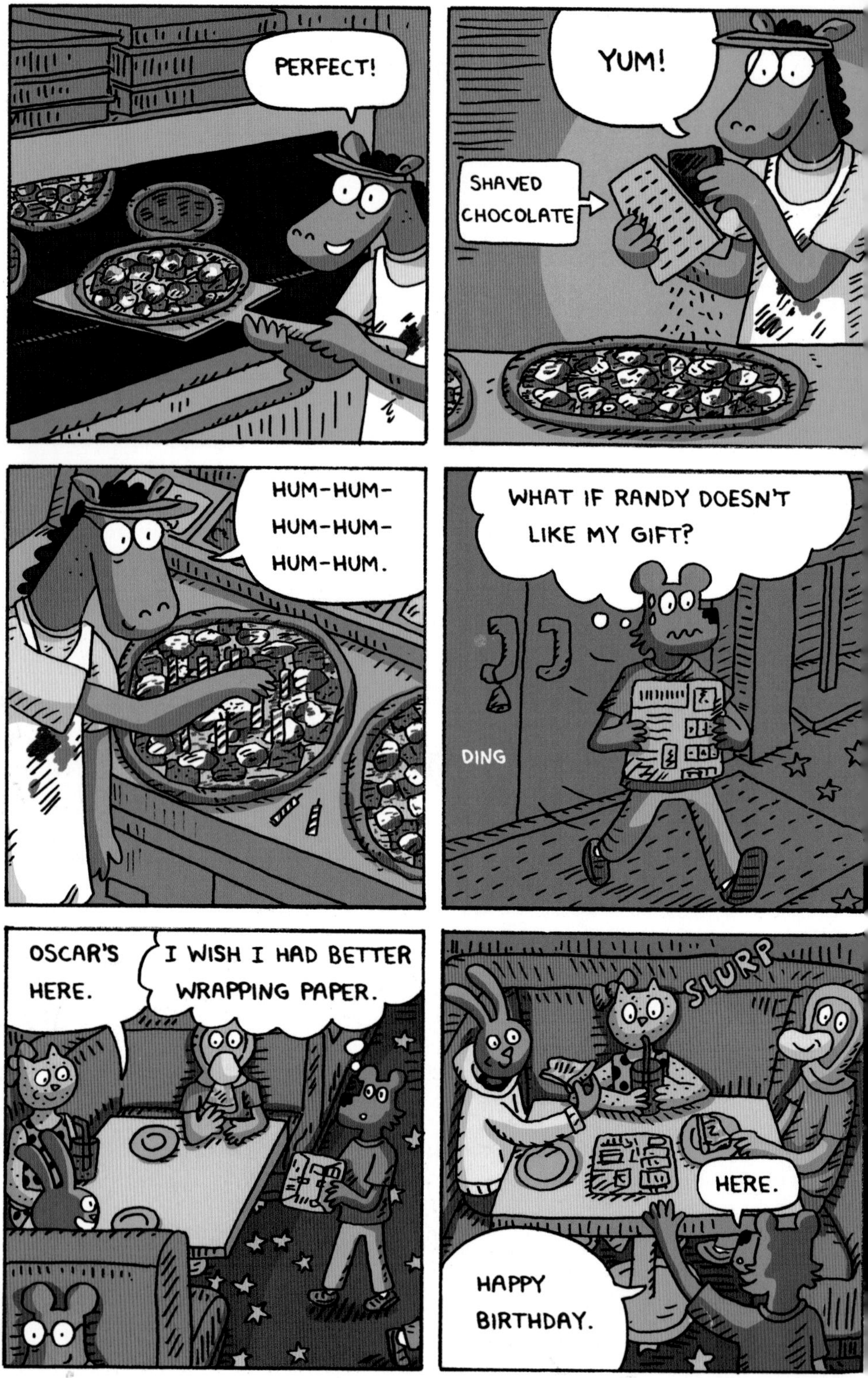
PERFECT!
YUM!
SHAVED CHOCOLATE
HUM-HUM-HUM-HUM-HUM-HUM.
WHAT IF RANDY DOESN'T LIKE MY GIFT?
DING
OSCAR'S HERE.
I WISH I HAD BETTER WRAPPING PAPER.
SLURP
HERE.
HAPPY BIRTHDAY.

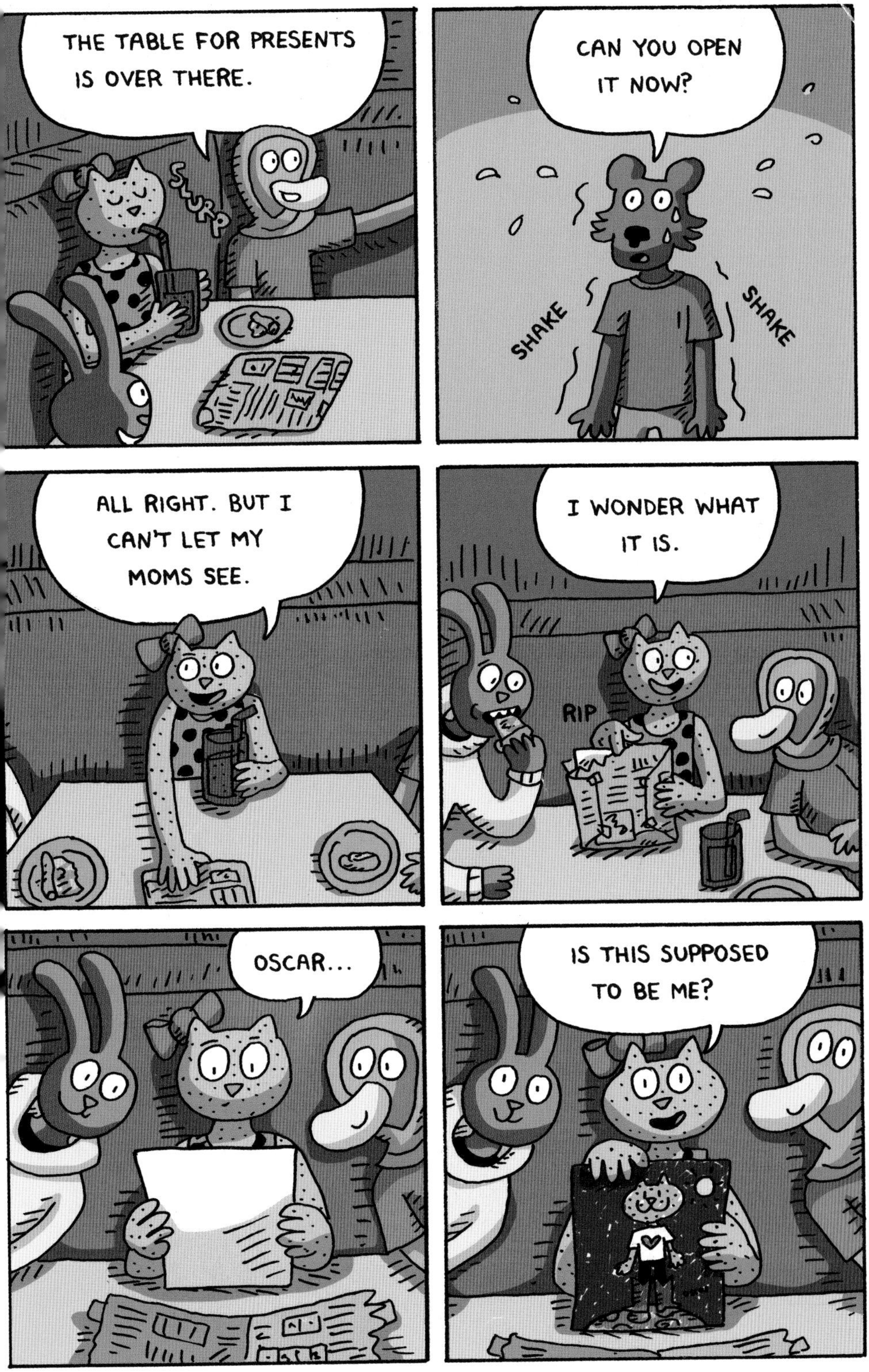
THE TABLE FOR PRESENTS IS OVER THERE.
SLURP
CAN YOU OPEN IT NOW?
SHAKE
SHAKE
ALL RIGHT. BUT I CAN'T LET MY MOMS SEE.
I WONDER WHAT IT IS.
RIP
OSCAR...
IS THIS SUPPOSED TO BE ME?

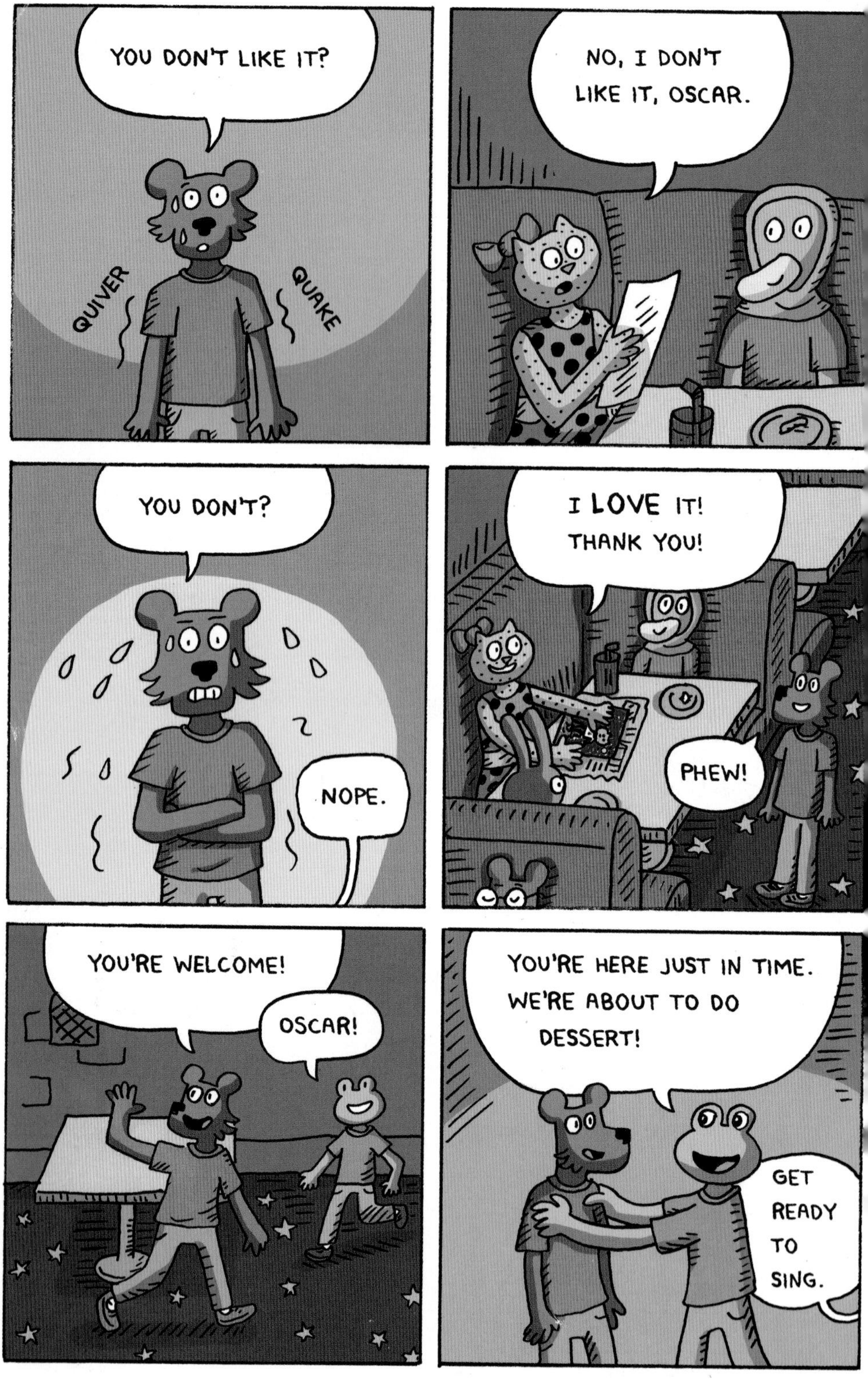
YOU DON'T LIKE IT?
QUIVER
QUAKE
NO, I DON'T LIKE IT, OSCAR.
YOU DON'T?
NOPE.
I LOVE IT! THANK YOU!
PHEW!
YOU'RE WELCOME!
OSCAR!
YOU'RE HERE JUST IN TIME. WE'RE ABOUT TO DO DESSERT!
GET READY TO SING.

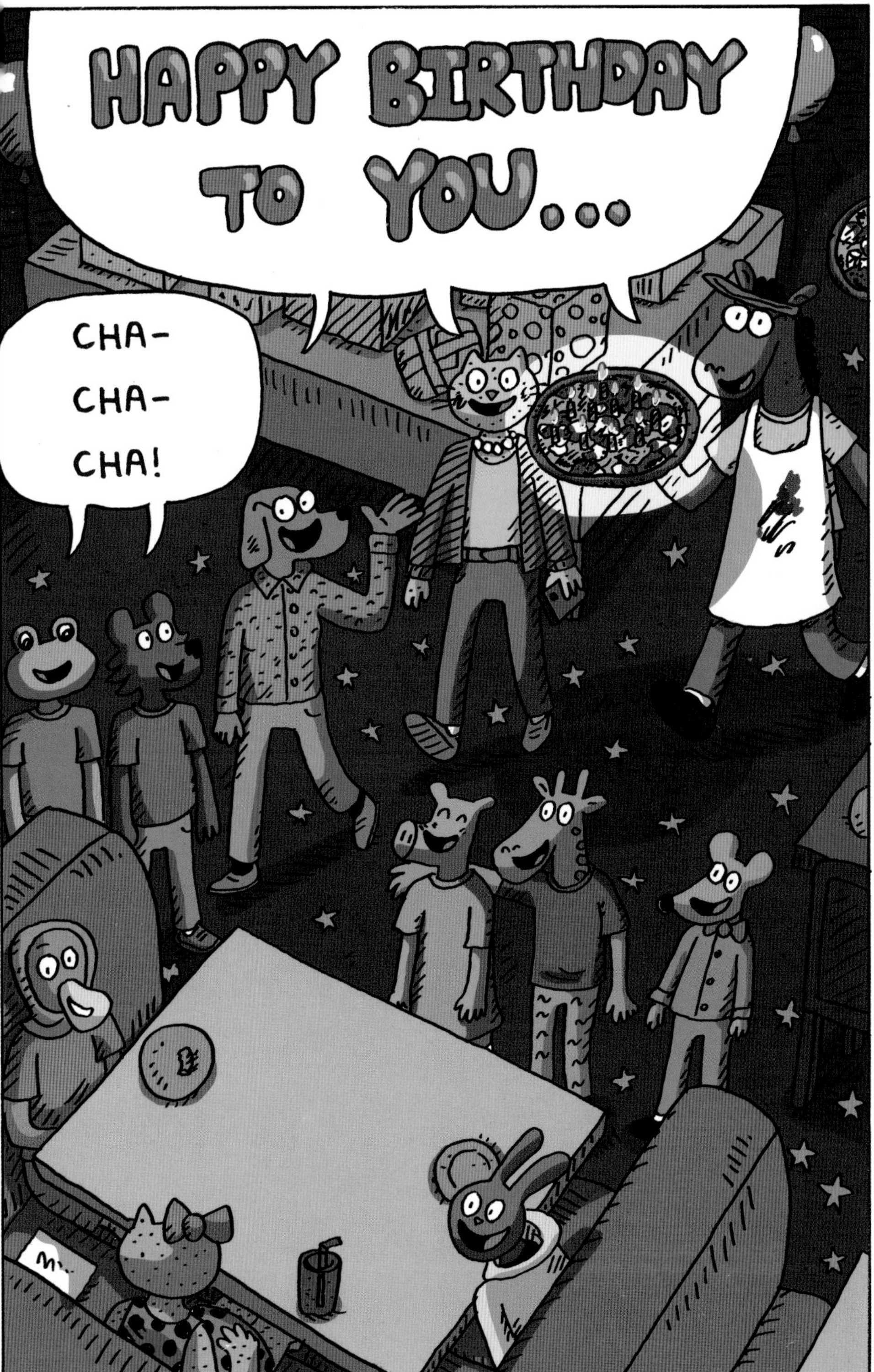
HAPPY BIRTHDAY TO YOU...
CHA- CHA- CHA!

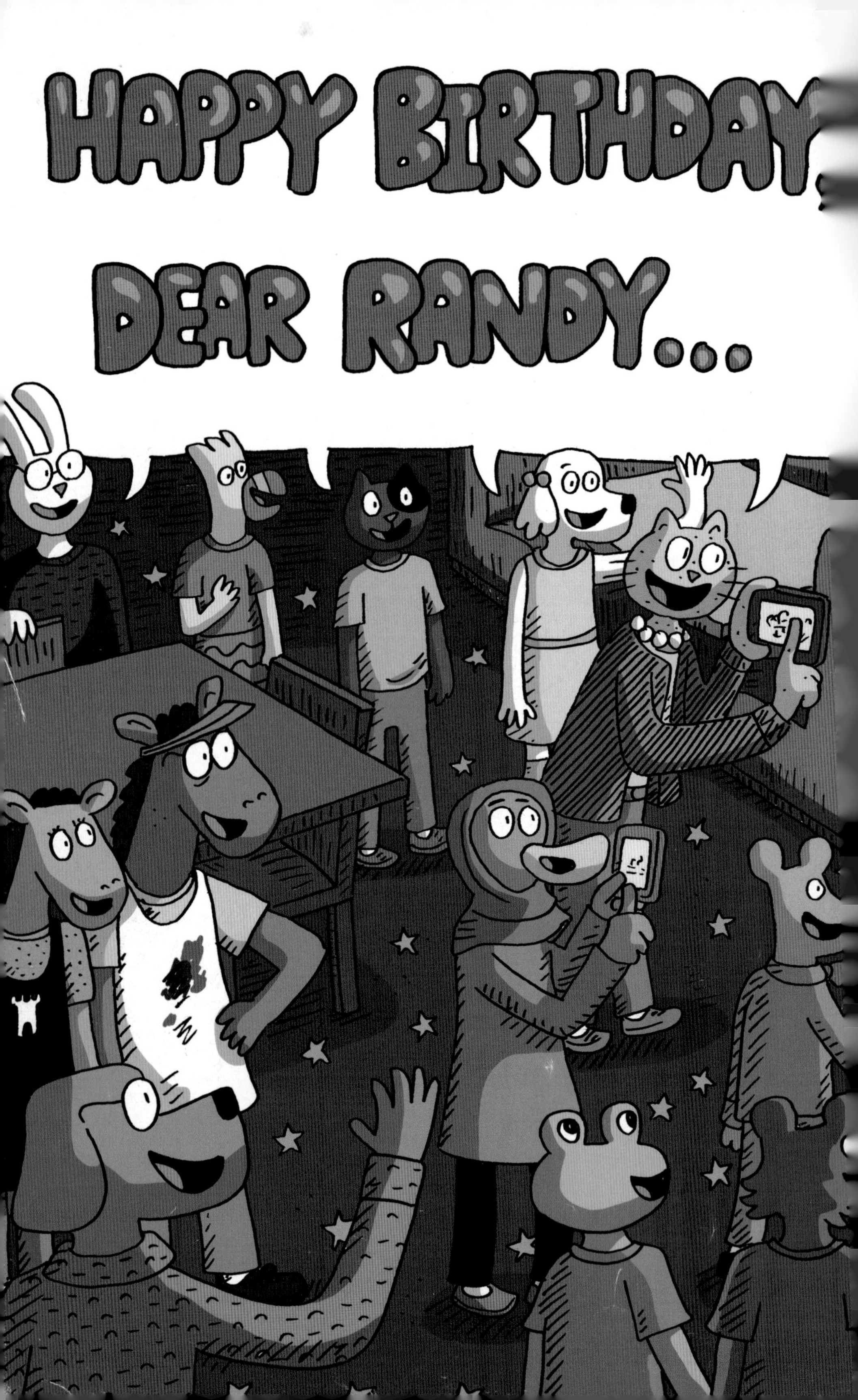
HAPPY BIRTHDAY, DEAR RANDY...

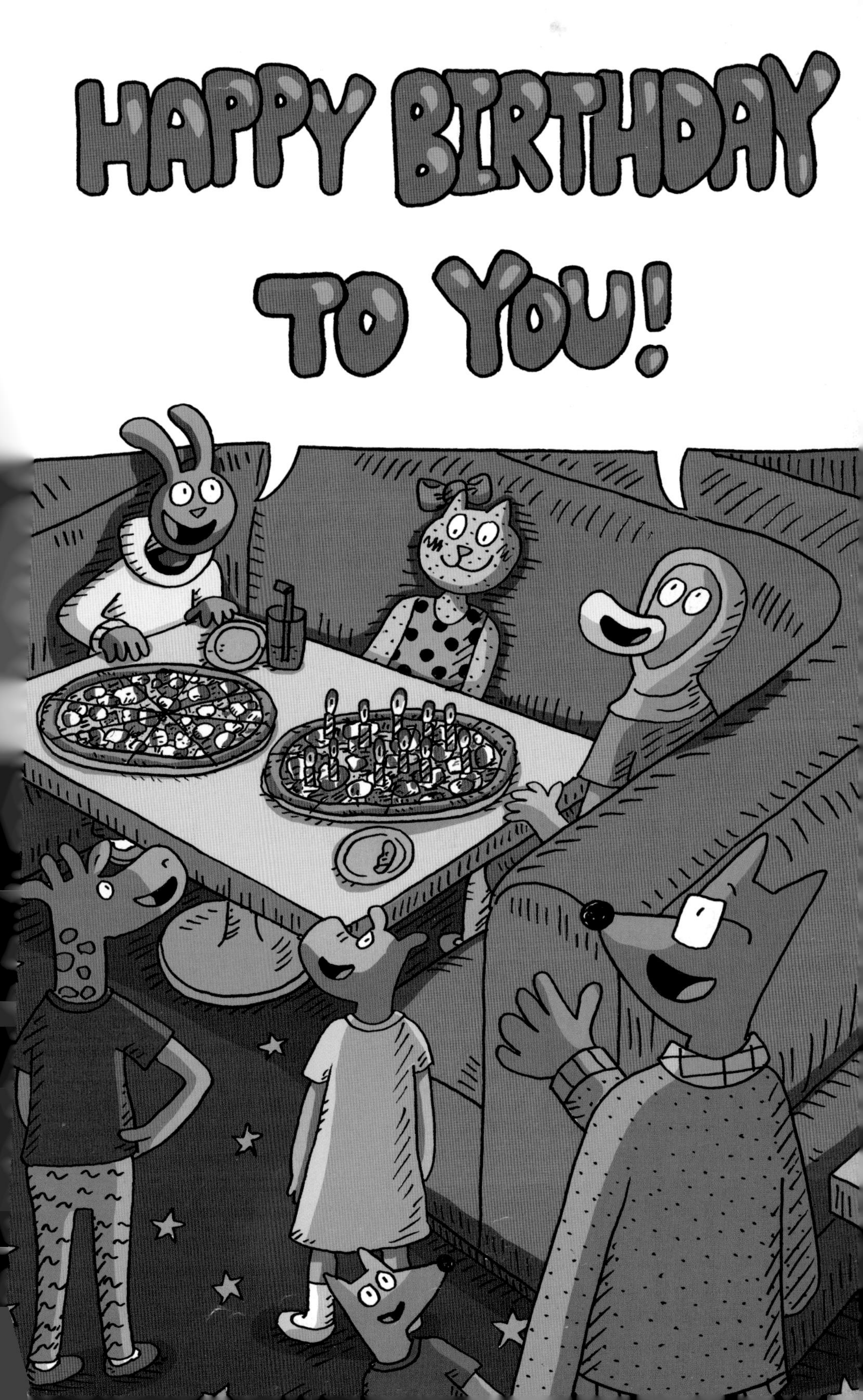
HAPPY BIRTHDAY TO YOU!

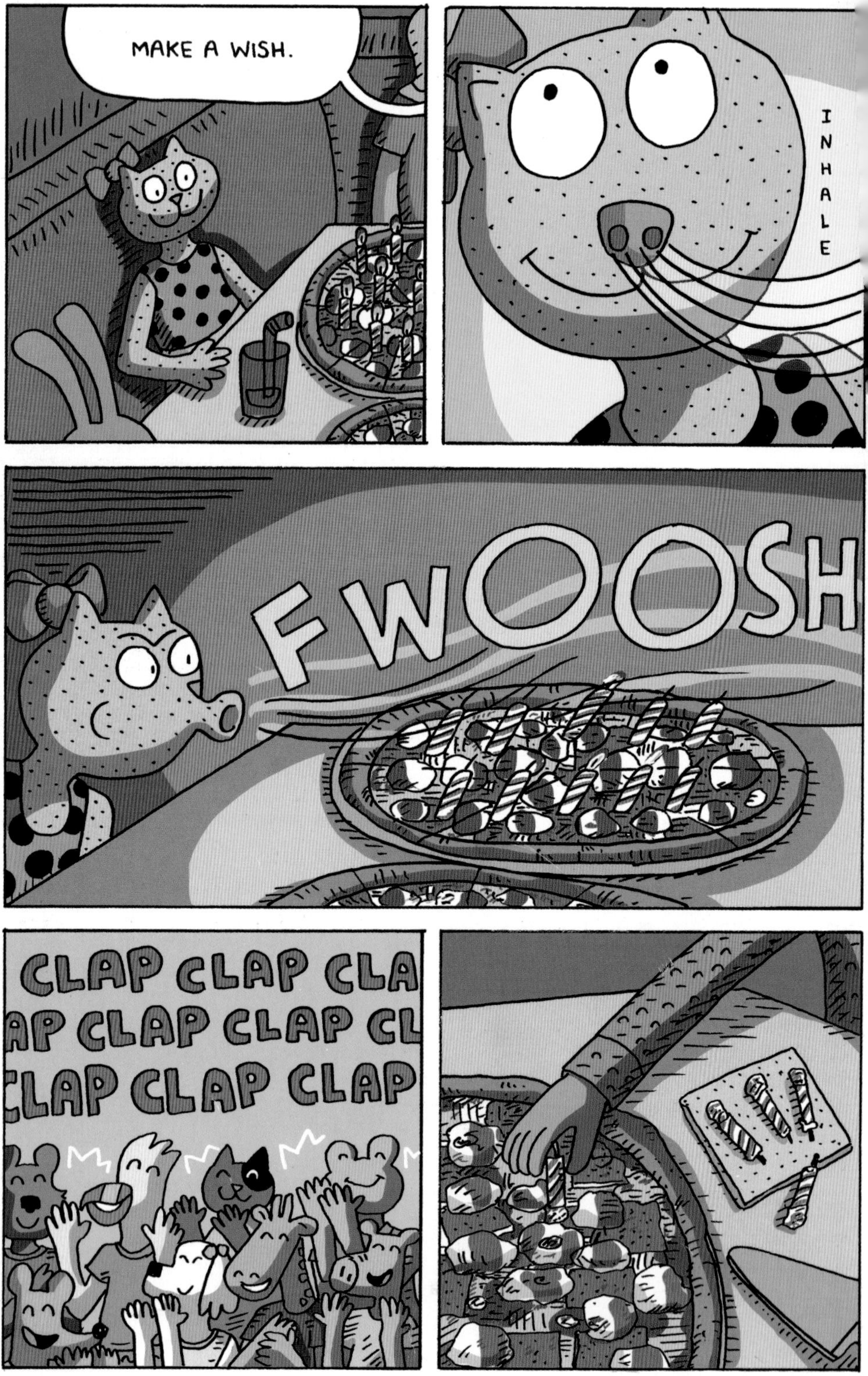
MAKE A WISH.
INHALE
FWOOSH
CLAP CLAP CLA
AP CLAP CLAP CL
CLAP CLAP CLAP

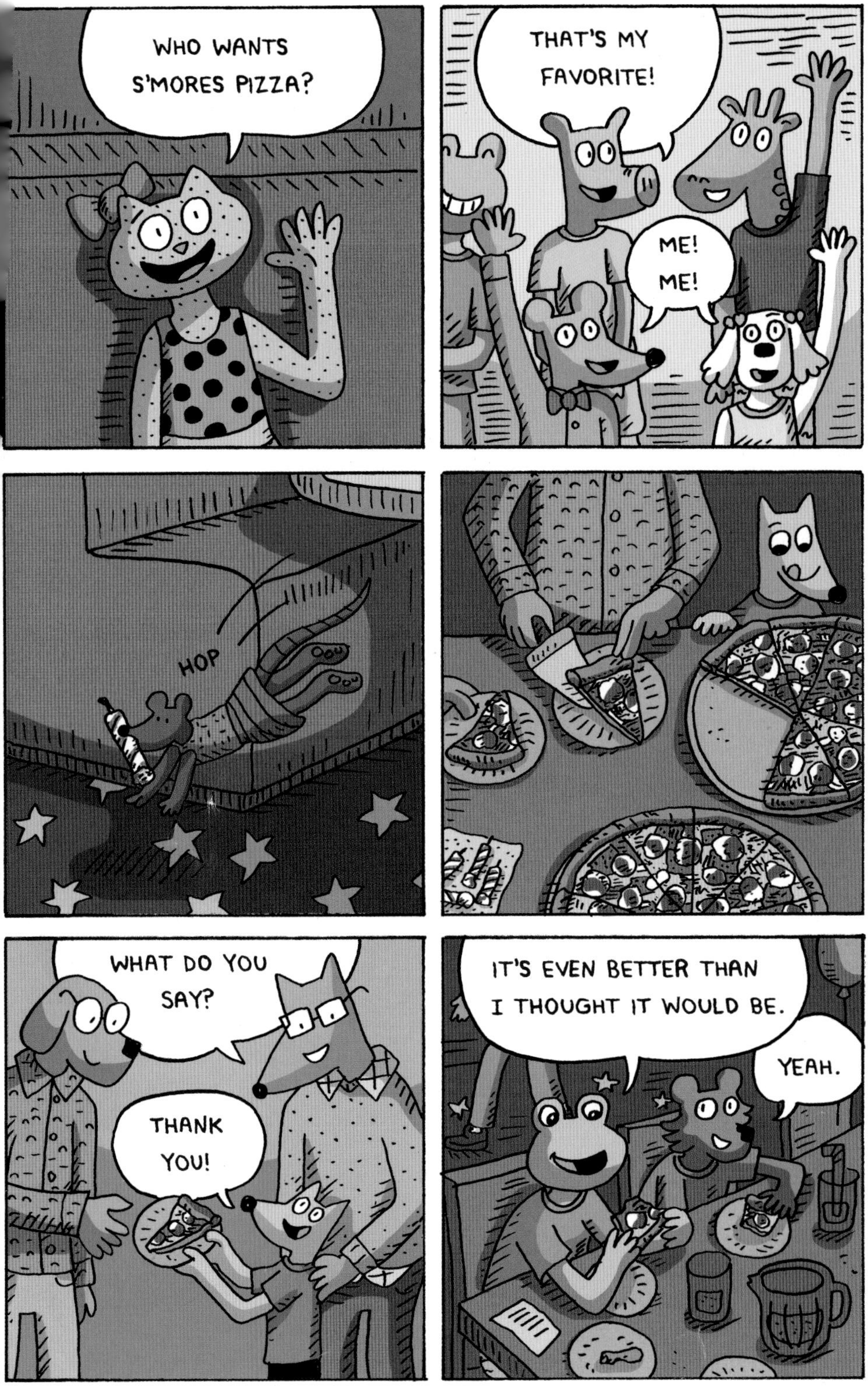
WHO WANTS S'MORES PIZZA?
THAT'S MY FAVORITE!
ME! ME!
HOP
WHAT DO YOU SAY?
THANK YOU!
IT'S EVEN BETTER THAN I THOUGHT IT WOULD BE.
YEAH.

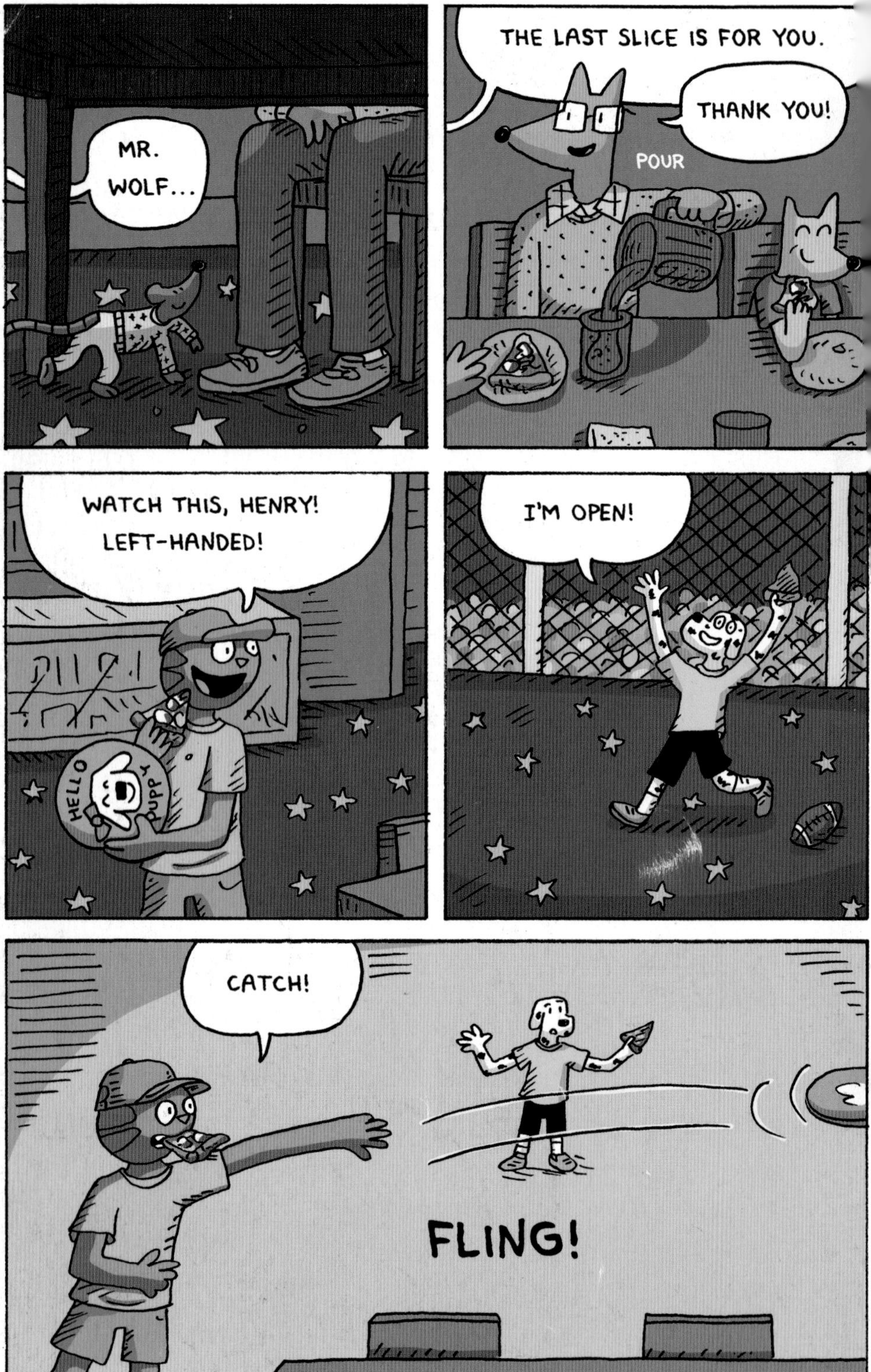
MR. WOLF...
THE LAST SLICE IS FOR YOU.
THANK YOU!
POUR
WATCH THIS, HENRY! LEFT-HANDED!
HELLO PUPPY
I'M OPEN!
CATCH!
FLING!

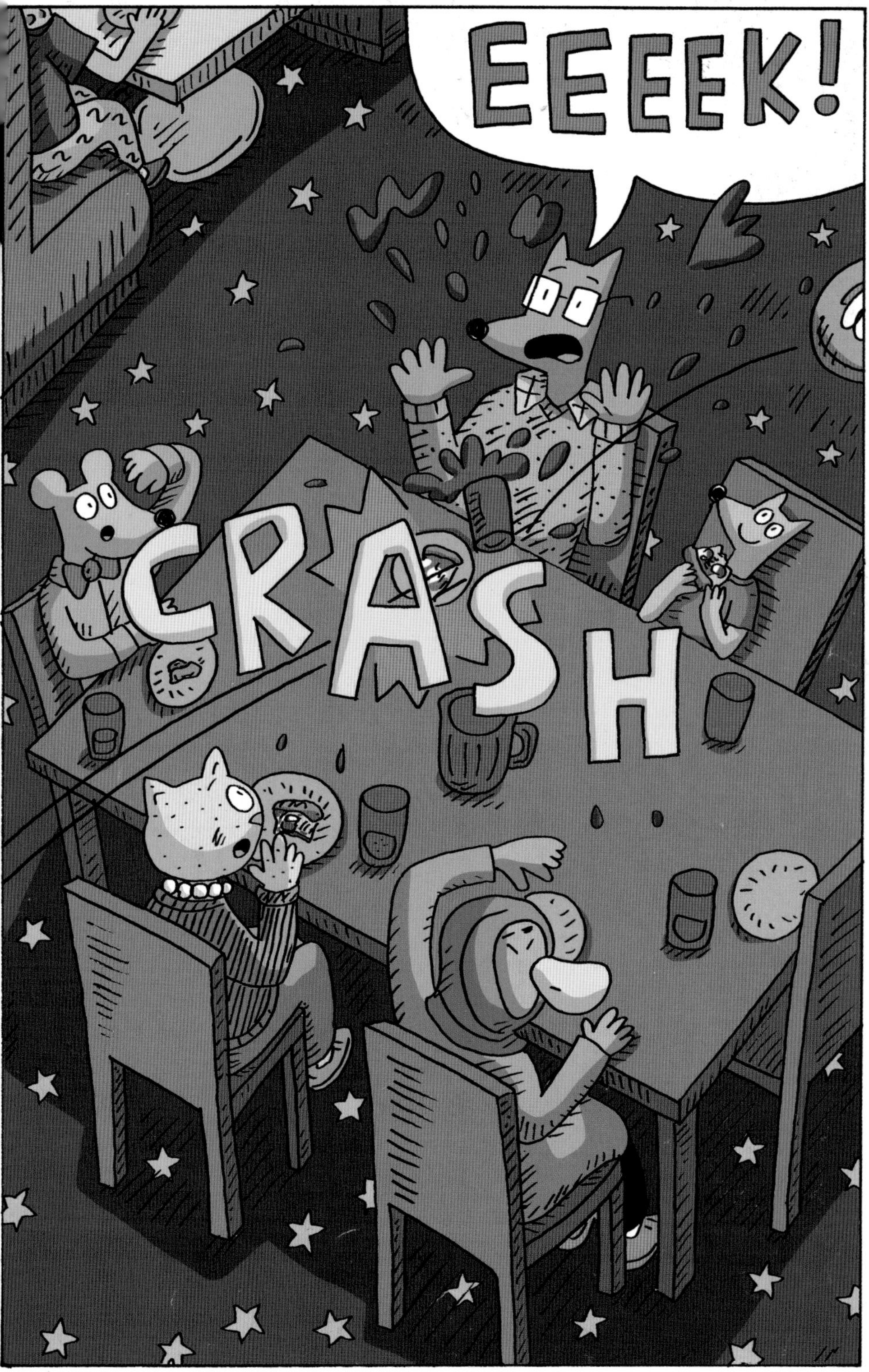
EEEEK!
CRASH

GASP!
OH NO!

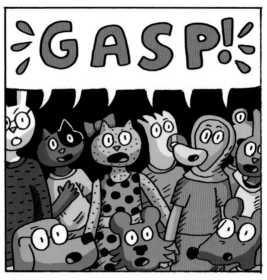

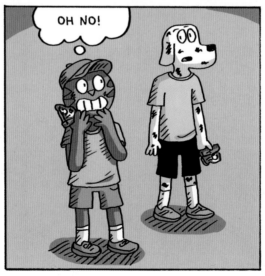

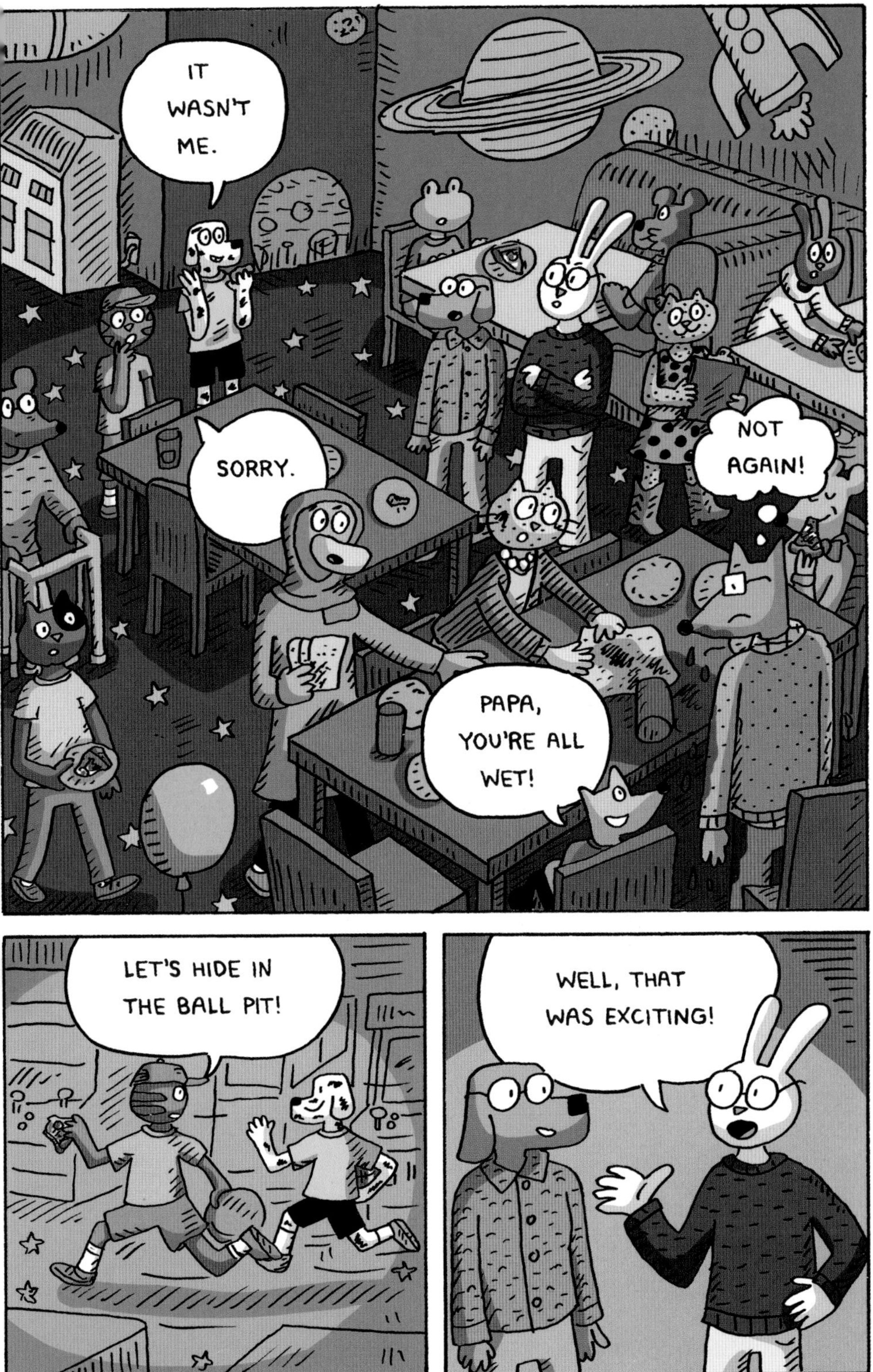
IT WASN'T ME.
SORRY.
NOT AGAIN!
PAPA, YOU'RE ALL WET!
LET'S HIDE IN THE BALL PIT!
WELL, THAT WAS EXCITING!

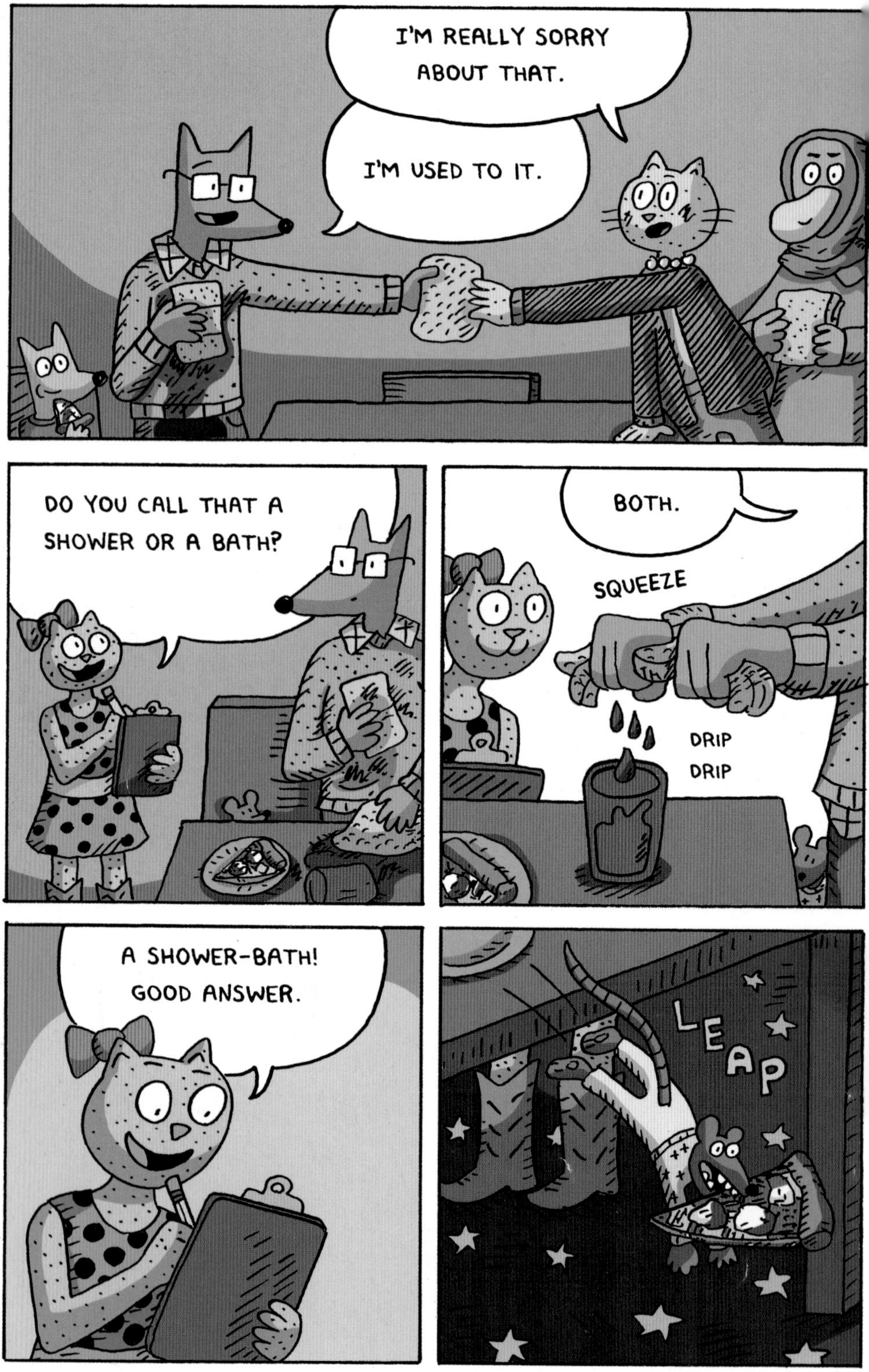
I'M REALLY SORRY ABOUT THAT.
I'M USED TO IT.
DO YOU CALL THAT A SHOWER OR A BATH?
BOTH.
SQUEEZE
DRIP
DRIP
A SHOWER-BATH! GOOD ANSWER.
LEAP

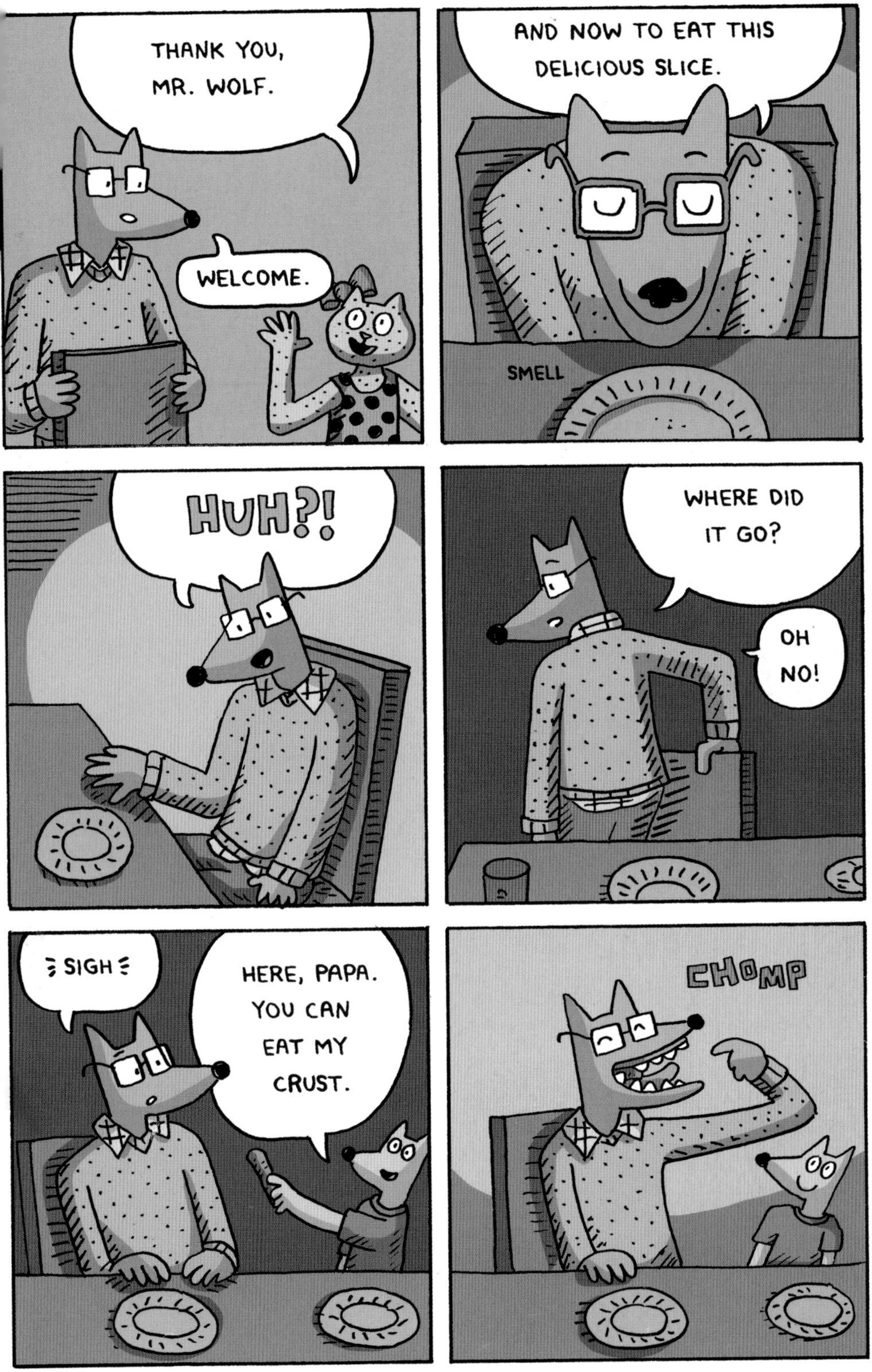
THANK YOU, MR. WOLF.
WELCOME.
AND NOW TO EAT THIS DELICIOUS SLICE.
SMELL
HUH?!
WHERE DID IT GO?
OH NO!
SIGH
HERE, PAPA. YOU CAN EAT MY CRUST.
CHOMP

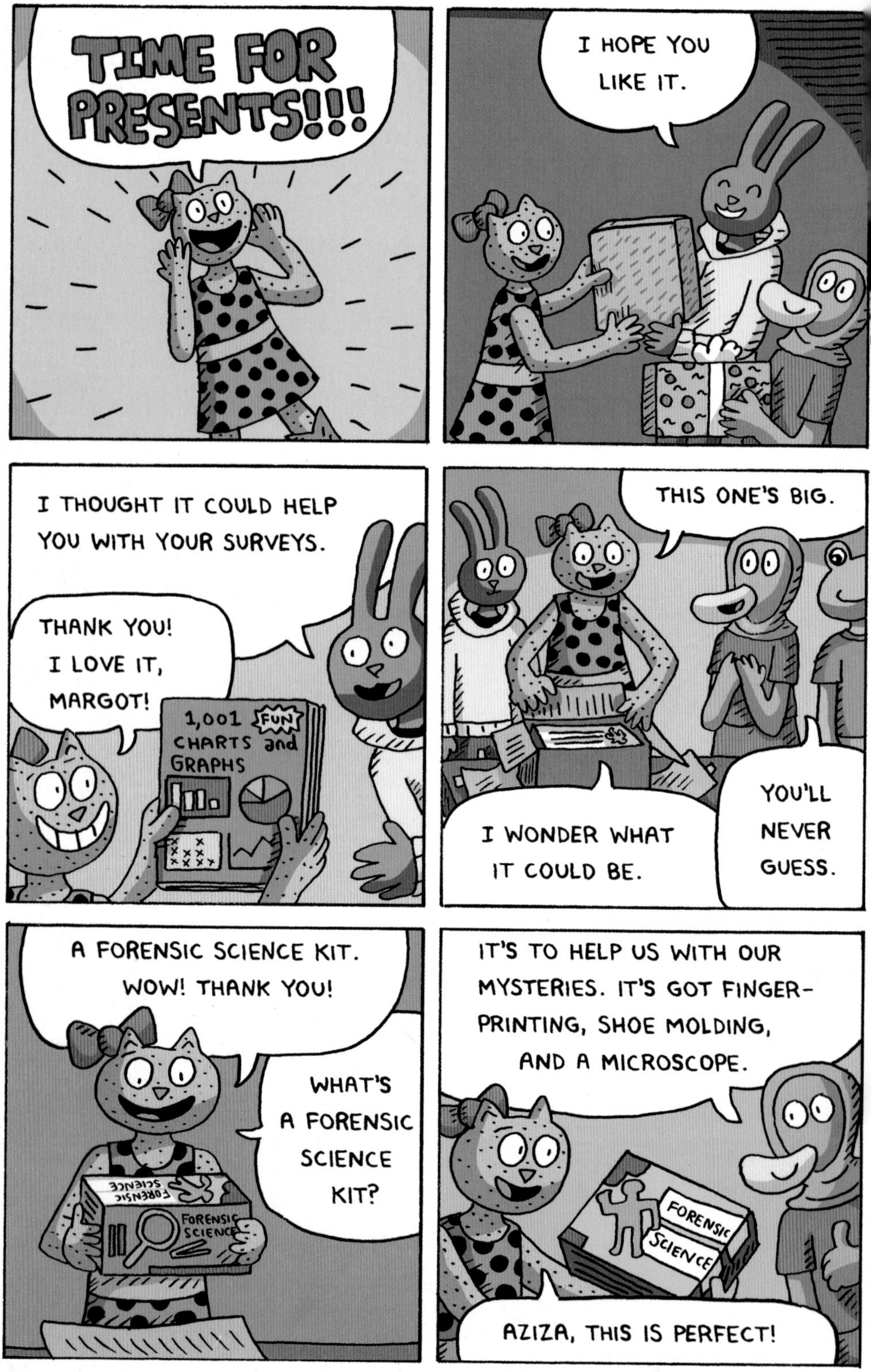
TIME FOR PRESENTS!!!
I HOPE YOU LIKE IT.
I THOUGHT IT COULD HELP YOU WITH YOUR SURVEYS.
THANK YOU! I LOVE IT, MARGOT!
1,001 FUN CHARTS and GRAPHS
THIS ONE'S BIG.
I WONDER WHAT IT COULD BE.
YOU'LL NEVER GUESS.
A FORENSIC SCIENCE KIT. WOW! THANK YOU!
WHAT'S A FORENSIC SCIENCE KIT?
FORENSIC SCIENCE
IT'S TO HELP US WITH OUR MYSTERIES. IT'S GOT FINGER-PRINTING, SHOE MOLDING, AND A MICROSCOPE.
FORENSIC SCIENCE
AZIZA, THIS IS PERFECT!

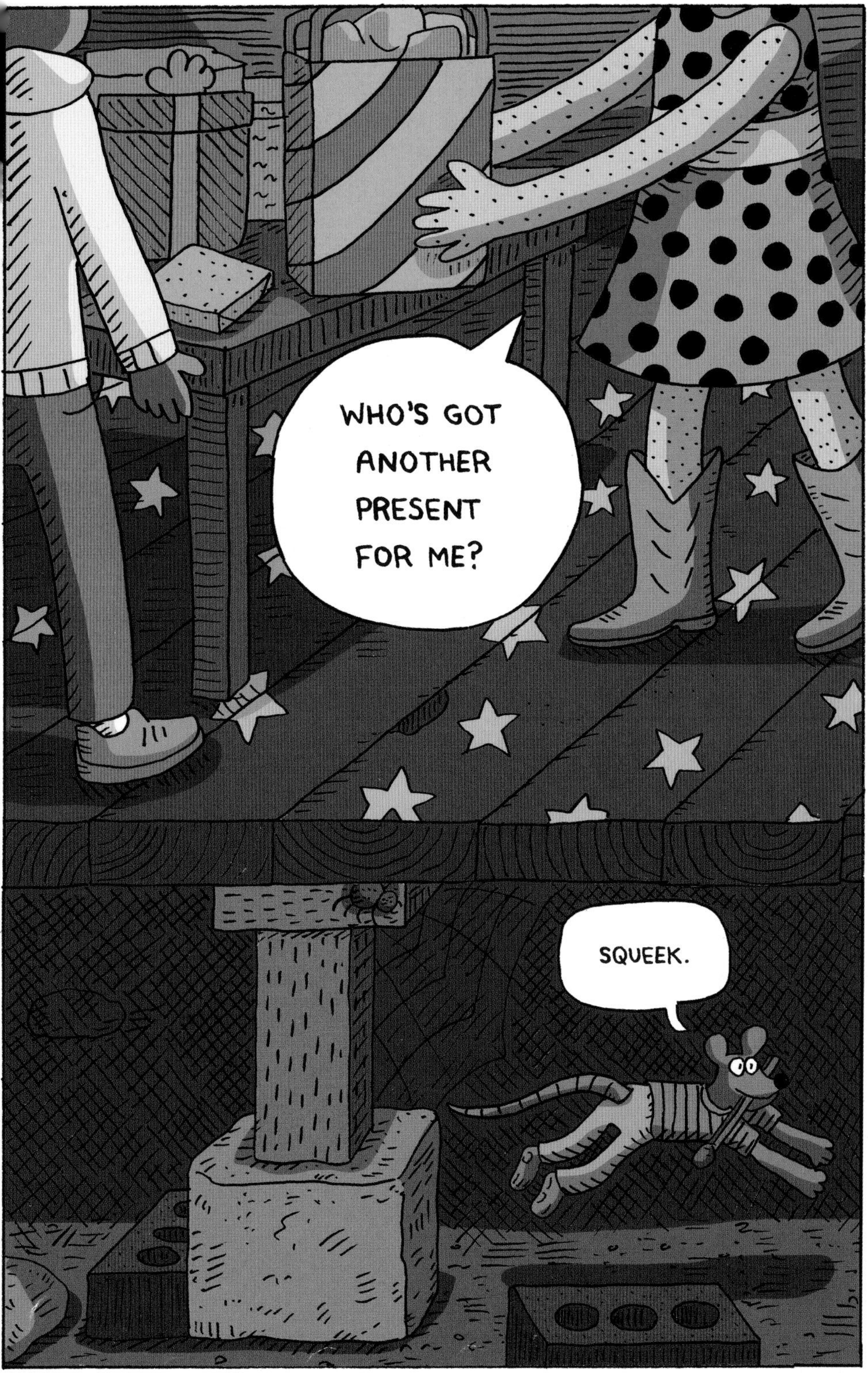
WHO'S GOT ANOTHER PRESENT FOR ME?
SQUEEK.

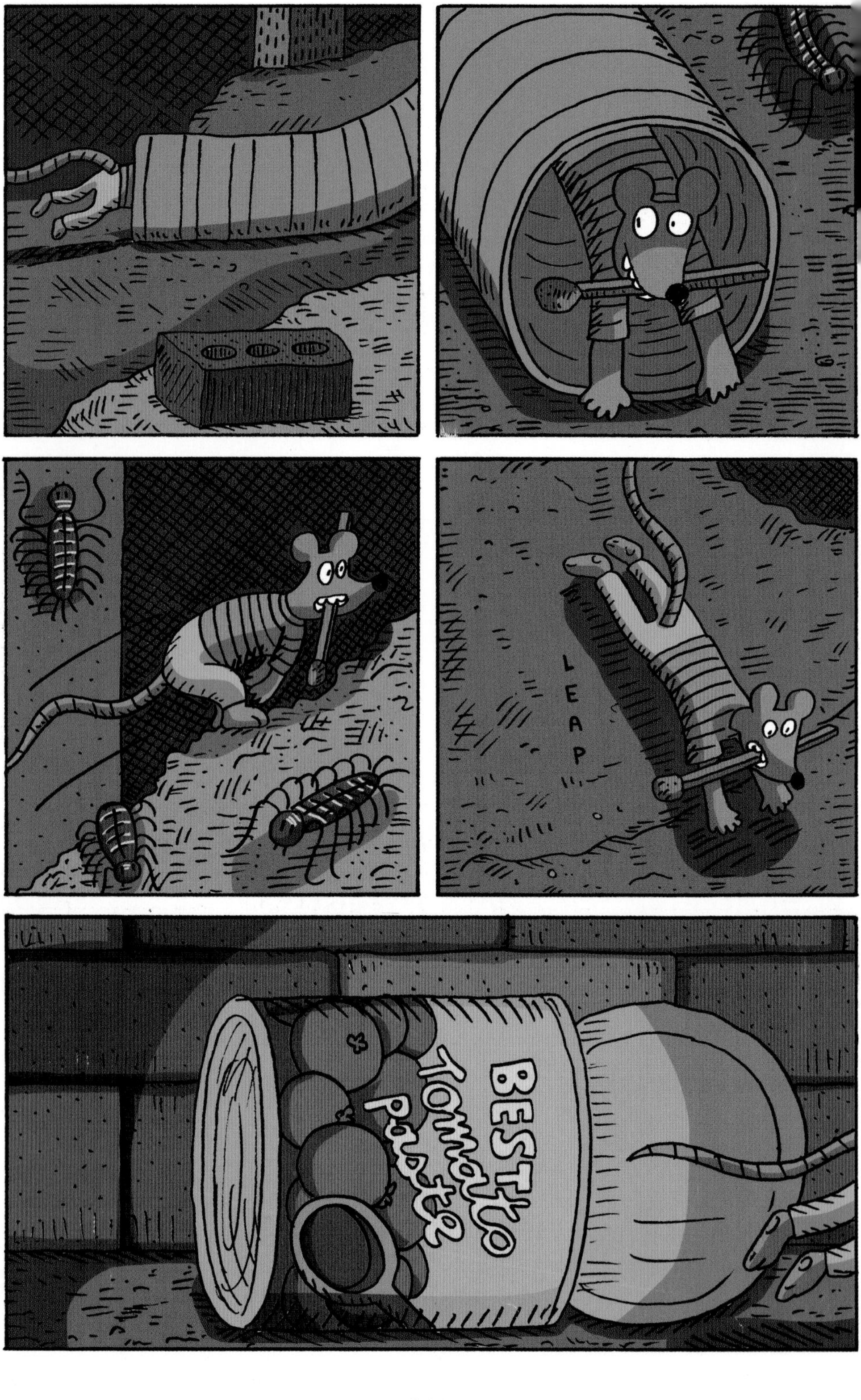
LEAP
BEST
Tomato
Paste

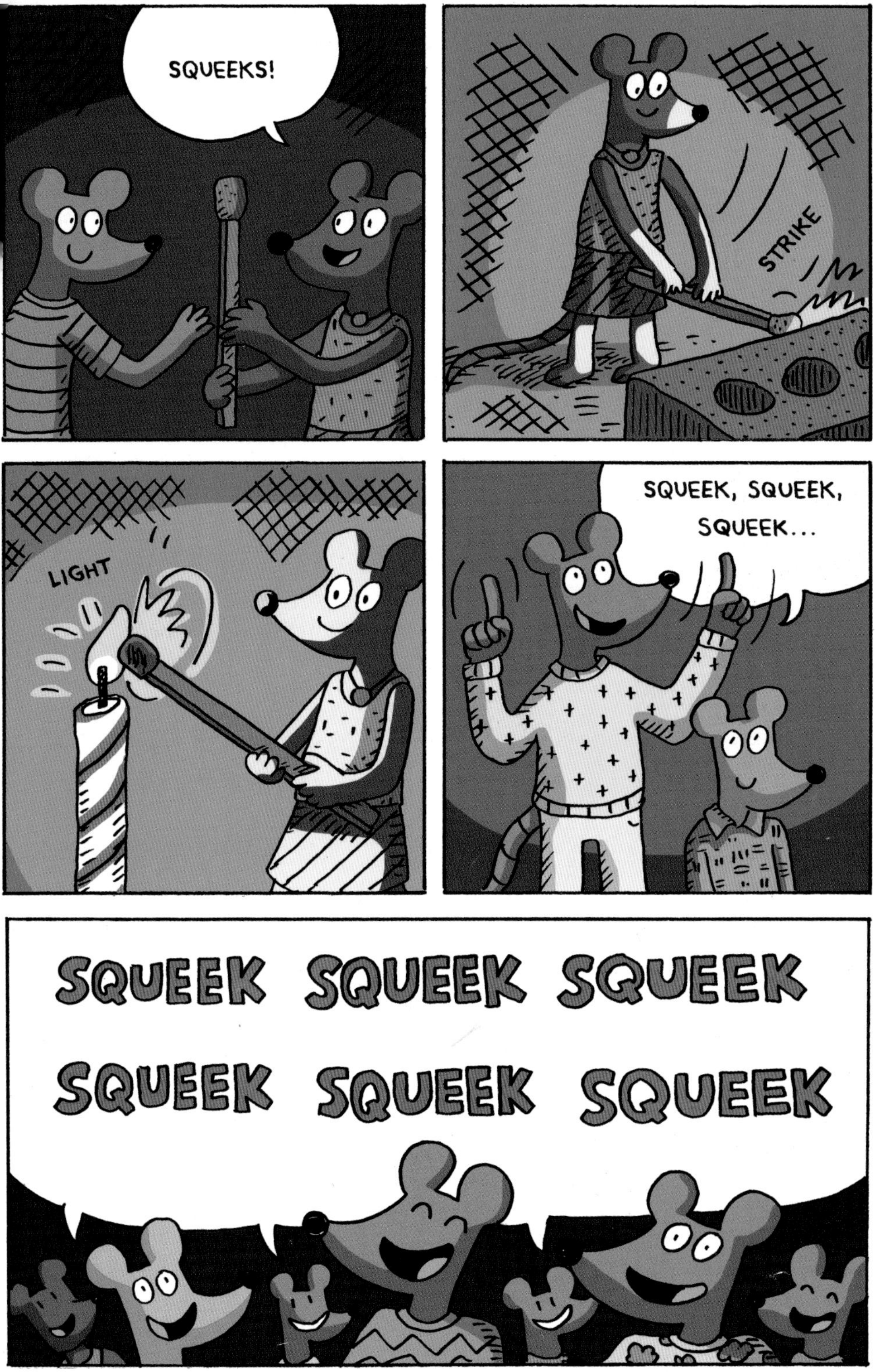
SQUEEKS!
STRIKE
LIGHT
SQUEEK, SQUEEK, SQUEEK...
SQUEEK SQUEEK SQUEEK SQUEEK SQUEEK SQUEEK

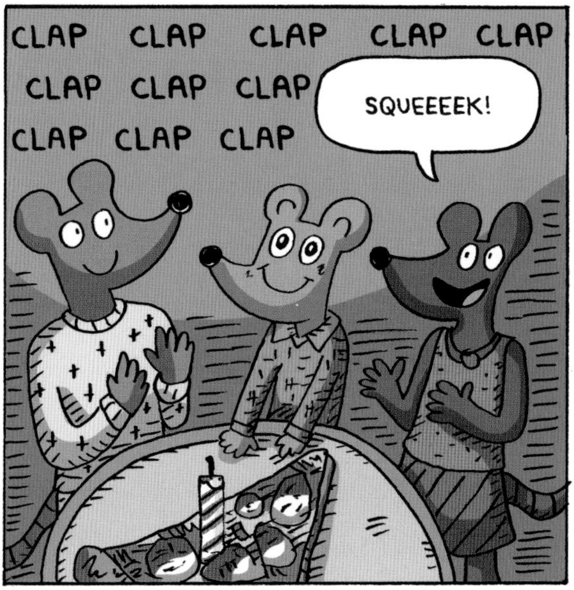
CLAP CLAP CLAP CLAP CLAP
CLAP CLAP CLAP
CLAP CLAP CLAP
SQUEEEEK!

Thank you to . . .

My amazing editor, Cassandra Pelham Fulton; art director, Phil Falco; creative director, David Saylor; and the whole team at Scholastic/Graphix who have helped make Mr. Wolf's Class a reality.

To my agent, Judy Hansen, who has superpowers.

To Tanya, my acupuncturist, who helped my poor arm heal so that I could keep drawing and writing this book.

To my family: As always, Ariel and Marlen, XOXO. And to my mom and dad, who always encouraged and supported my art.

To Calista Brill, who gave me valuable feedback early on. I should have thanked you sooner.

And of course, to all of my students, who give me hope for the future.

This book was made over the course of a year. Thank you, dear reader, for spending your time with these characters and stories, which were once just thoughts in my head.

Author photo by Renée Lopez

Aron Nels Steinke is the Eisner Award-winning illustrator and coauthor, with Ariel Cohn, of *The Zoo Box*. After graduating from Vancouver Film School with a specialization in hand-drawn animation, he discovered the magic of making comics and hasn't looked back since. He teaches fifth graders by day and draws comics by night in Portland, Oregon, where he lives with his wife, Ariel, and their Robin Hood–obsessed son, Marlen. In the summer, when he's not hunched over a drawing board, you might find him swimming the frigid rivers of the Cascade Mountains or possibly hugging a tree.

Don't miss the next adventure in Mr. Wolf's class!

LUCKY STARS

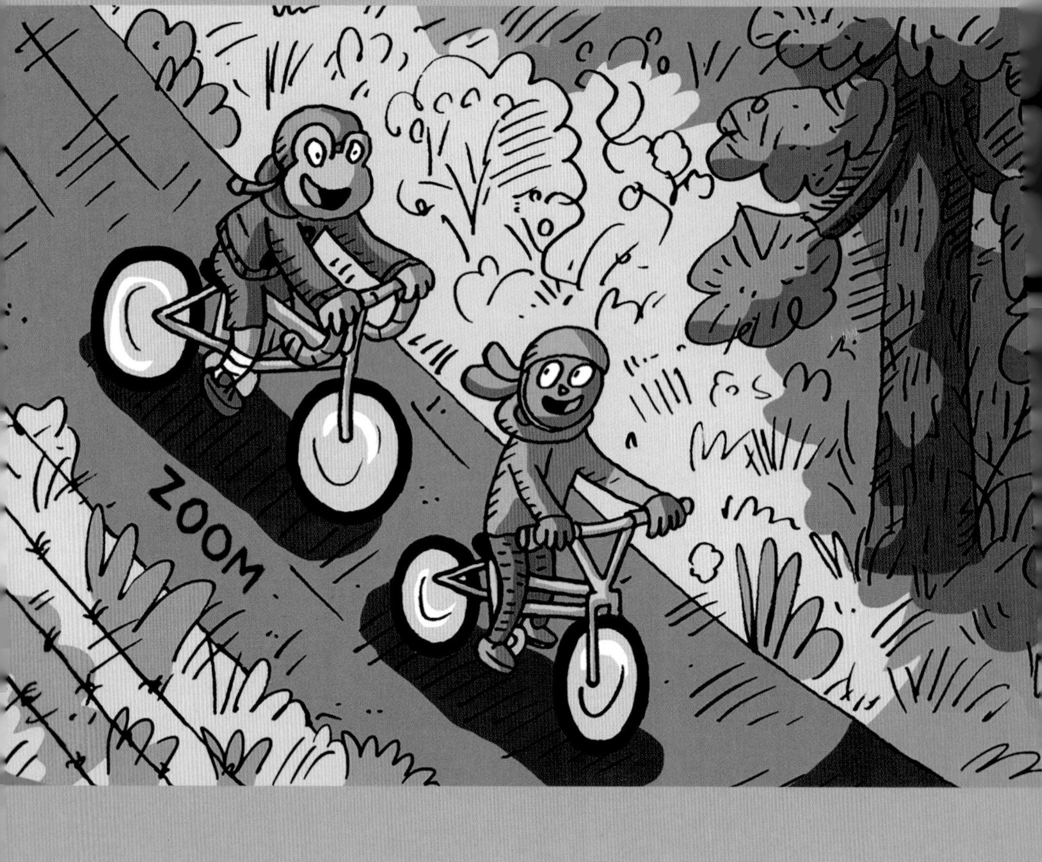
ZOOM